An Embarrassment of

MUNSTERS

Alace Sweets, #3

MariaLisa deMora

Edited by Hot Tree Editing

Proofreading by Whiskey Jack Editing

Copyright © 2020 MariaLisa deMora

All rights reserved. This book or any portion thereof may not be reproduced or used in any manner whatsoever without the express written permission of the publisher except for the use of brief quotations in a book review. This is a work of fiction. Names, characters, places and incidents are either the product of the author's imagination, or are used in a fictitious manner. Any resemblance to actual persons, living or dead, or actual events is entirely coincidental.

First Published 2020

ISBN 13: 978-1-946738-62-2

DEDICATION

*Evil is unspectacular and always human, and
shares our bed and eats at our own table.*
~W.H. Auden

For all those who work to right wrongs, large and small. The world is a better place with you in it.

Contents

Prologue	1
Chapter One	4
Chapter Two	13
Chapter Three	37
Chapter Four	73
Chapter Five	97
Chapter Six	142
Chapter Seven	192
Chapter Eight	220
Chapter Nine	239
Chapter Ten	306
Chapter Eleven	313
Chapter Twelve	361
Chapter Thirteen	406
Chapter Fourteen	416
Chapter Fifteen	423
Epilogue	425

ACKNOWLEDGMENTS

Given what's going on in the world right now, it feels strange to be doing something as normal as writing acknowledgments for a new book. The coronavirus and Covid19 has changed the landscape of our lives forever, in ways we still have not identified. I kinda want the book world to be my place away from the madness, but I also kinda wanna acknowledge the challenges.

This book didn't pour out of me, as some do. Owen, who you'll find occupies as vocal a role in this book as he did the previous one, was persnickity about when he'd be available to talk. Alace was all about the changes in her life, and I filled in the bones of her scenes fairly easily. But, Owen was looking for his inspiration in outside sources, I guess, while Alace had hers within herself.

We got all the words down in the end, and I'm proud of the way both characters chose to express the driving need they share to protect those who are vulnerable. Owen drove me to do more research into a greater variety of things than in the past, and as so many authors are, I'm sure that I've hit watchlist status. I should apologize to whoever is assigned to track me. I promise it's research!

Many thanks to Becky and her crew at Hot Tree Editing. As always they treated my work with the utmost respect, helping me move the story forward in many ways. Thanks, too, for the assistance from Mel with Whiskey Jack Editing. You never fail to inspire me to dig a little deeper to find the true emotions behind the actions. Mega thanks to the techies who listened to my multitude of questions out on the Reddit subboards, and my investigative sources who provided guideance regarding technology referenced in the book. Any errors are all on me.

A special shoutout to my early reader Kori, whose feedback and enthusiam for the story gave me the courage to continue. Without that encouragement, you might not be holding this story now. #FansToFriends is the truth between us.

And now, I give you more Alace. As Owen says, "She's scary as fuck, and it's entirely earned. Don't show fear, don't give her your back, and believe everything she tells you." He's just the same, and they are gonna trip all your triggers.

Woofully yours,
~ML

Prologue

Kelly stumbled to his feet, head swinging wildly back and forth as he took in the scenery around him.

Where am I?

He didn't have an answer to that question. He knew it was important, but nothing he could see was even vaguely familiar. The darkness surrounding him was quiet, shot through here and there by moonbeams that failed to illuminate much more than the pine boughs through which they filtered.

He was naked, but nudity had become such a natural state it wasn't worth the brain cells needed to truly catalog it. He was also aching all over, and one of his eyes wouldn't work right. The tissue was sore to the touch, enough to make his eyes water when he pressed a fingertip against the damaged flesh. A rigid stiffness in his muscles informed him that he'd likely been lying on the forest floor for a while. An image flashed through his head of a white trash bag caught on a bush or fence. Shaking his head, he pushed past the fear and pain, trying to stay focused on what was most critical.

Gotta save Shiloh.

He could hear no noises, not even a hoot from an owl to break the stillness. The stark lack of sound raised the hairs on his arms.

He turned in a slow circle, unsure of what direction to go but struck with the knowledge that he couldn't stay here. Wherever "here" was.

There.

Something flickered in the distance, small and close to the ground, hidden now and again as the wind gusted. It was a tiny blue flame that drew him in. As he got closer, he saw it was a camp stove, similar to one he'd seen used on a long-ago camping trip.

He was closer yet when he saw how light reflected on the face of the man seated on the other side. Even without speaking or calling out, he knew the man was watching him, had seen him, probably since he'd taken the first step.

"Please." Kelly stumbled, toes tangling on a root that threatened to take his legs out from under him.

He stayed on his feet with effort, groaning aloud at how the pain in his head swelled with the movement.

"Hey. What's going on?" The voice was quiet and low, probably meant to be calming. But threaded through the sound, Kelly heard the tension of alarm, not out of place from a man startled by the sudden appearance of a stranger at his campsite.

Unconcerned with his own nakedness or injuries, uncaring that the man towered over him when he stood, unflinching as the man's gaze cataloged each of Kelly's many injuries, Kelly stood and trembled with fear for Shiloh.

"Mister." His voice wavered, and that was another thing Kelly couldn't muster any unease for—he had to push through. *Shiloh is the only thing that matters now.* "You gotta help me." Kelly stumbled again, and the man reached out for him, fingers wrapping around Kelly's arm to guide him past the tiny flame that had stood as a beacon in the night. Warmth surrounded him, a softer comfort than he could ever remember experiencing. "You gotta save my sister."

Chapter One

Alace

"I don't like this." She tipped her head backwards, hanging it over the top edge of the chair as she stretched out her muscles. "It feels alien."

"It's natural as life, beloved." Eric's tone was amused, and Alace lifted a hand to flip him off. He chuckled, and then the heat of his hands settled on her stomach, the baby beachball protruding from her body cradled between his palms. "Braxton-Hicks contractions are the body's way of getting ready for the main event."

"I'm not doing anything, just working away, and then suddenly my body decides to take over. I don't like this." She raised her head and glared down at Eric as he pressed a kiss to her belly. He wasn't even attempting to stifle his chuckles. "You're breathing funny. Stop it."

"Alace, it's going to be okay."

"You don't know that. You can't know how it's going to be. I've read that the alien contractions can go on for months." The authority websites she'd looked up had been scary when they got into the topic. She'd found that militant mommies posting their stories online didn't make for the most restful reading material. "I don't want that."

"Then it's a good thing you only have weeks, not months to go." He kissed her belly again, fingers stroking along either side, traveling down, then up, leaving calmness and relaxed muscles in their wake. "Let me get my coat off and I'll rub your feet and legs."

"My ankles are swollen again, aren't they?" Alace threatened to lift her feet into Eric's crotch as he crouched in front of her, but he grinned and intercepted them in mid-swing. "I can't even see them unless I contort like a…like a…contortionist. My brain stopped working today too, apparently. I can't think of a better word than that."

"Pregnancy brain. Hormones are a real thing." He nodded and stood, shrugging out of his suitcoat to reveal the width of his shoulders. Her mouth grew dry as his hands deftly rolled up his sleeves to show off sinewy forearms. The juxtaposition of bare skin against fabric and a span of chest and stomach she suddenly wanted access to were a combination she couldn't resist. *Won't even try.*

"Take off the shirt, too."

He laughed and complied with her demand, turned towards the dresser in their bedroom, and draped the shirt there while he hung the coat over the doorknob. This uncovered the spread of skin and toned muscles that made up his broad back.

"I wanna make love."

He'd gotten used to her abrupt and blunt requests over the past few months, but the darkening hunger in his eyes when he turned back to her left Alace breathless. "My baby need me?"

"Yes." She scooted her butt to the front of the chair, then used the arms to lever herself into a sitting position. Feet flat on the floor, she pushed with legs and arms until she was upright. Standing on the toes of her socks, she removed them one at a time, then shoved her stretchy maternity pants down her legs, taking panties along with them. "Yes, I do."

An hour later, they were lounging together in bed, Alace wrapped around Eric as much as she could manage with the beachball belly in the way. He'd rucked up her shirt and had a hand on her hip, fingers drawing mindless figures against her skin. In the past week, her breasts had begun leaking during sex, and she didn't like how it felt, so she'd kept on the shirt and nursing bra, complete with pads. No matter how she came to their bed, Eric simply rolled with it, never asking for more than she was willing to give.

"Do you ever wonder what your life would be like if you had a normal wife?"

Shit.

She stilled, hoping he'd ignore her question. *Wrong thing to say, idiot.* When he shifted and placed a folded knuckle underneath her chin to lift her face, she knew she was out of luck.

"Define normal. I can't make an assessment unless I know we're speaking about the same traits and behaviors."

Alace rolled her eyes. *There he goes, gettin' all lawyerly on me.*

"No, Alace. You can't make a statement like that and then expect I won't want to dig into it at least a little."

"Just, you know. Normal. Like, in the head and stuff." His lips made a tiny moue she wanted to kiss, but she closed her eyes instead. "Someone you can be proud of and stuff. You know what?" She shook her head but was careful not to dislodge the pressure he held against her chin. "Never mind. Pregnancy brain, like you said."

"My wife is perfect for me." The hand that had been teasing the skin of her hip flattened and slipped down the curve of her ass, gripping and pulling her tight against his side. "She's randy in bed, which I like a lot. She fits against me as if she were made for me. She's intelligent with a healthy dose of common sense, so we are able to have active dialogues about things that interest us. She praises my culinary skills, even if we both know my cooking is mediocre. She's invested in her career, but not to the detriment of my own. She loves my mother. And she does so much good in the world that people will never know. Frankly, that's because she doesn't look for fame or praise. She merely does what's right." He brushed his nose against hers, and Alace opened her eyes to see him staring at her. "She's a little bit like a superhero, but without the cape. So in my mind, while she may not be normal by some of society's standards, she's perfect for me. She's also pregnant with our child, which means she gets a pass on some self-doubt things she normally wouldn't be dealing with." After pressing a soft kiss to her lips, he pulled back and grinned. "I rest my case."

"I love you." As happened every time she uttered those words in his presence, the effect on Eric was immediate. His arm tightened around her, his hand gripped more firmly, the skin and muscles of his face softened, and the desire for her burned in his eyes once again. "So, so much. I can't even say."

"Beloved," he said, as if that single word—that fucking, *fucking* word—meant everything. *It does.*

Her phone chimed, the three-note ascending tone designed to get her attention. Eric didn't say anything as he pulled her closer, his arm extending across to retrieve the phone from the nightstand. Without looking at the screen, he handed the device to her then reached the other direction, picking up the TV remote and pointing it at the screen mounted on the wall. Something she'd given in to when she'd wanted another monitor for her computer, acknowledging to Eric it did provide the best of both worlds. Since her office was in their bedroom for the duration of the pregnancy, they'd spent an inordinate amount of time in this room. He kept the volume low, and she pressed her lips to his chest in silent thanks.

One glance at her phone's screen had her struggling to sit, a feat only successfully accomplished with Eric's assistance. Then she was stuck leaning backwards on both arms, unable to sit fully upright as she normally would, all efforts foiled by the bulge of the baby.

Legs splayed wide in front of her for balance, Alace groaned when she fruitlessly tried to shift one. "I gotta…" She panted, shortness of breath caused by the—*I guessed it*—huge beachball bulge of the baby. "Feet…floor…chair." Eric sat up, and she hated him in that instant. Not the man, but his ability to move around as he desired without issue. He moved to stand in front of her. "You're a weird-breathing asshole who put this baby in me."

"I love you, too," he shot back as he helped her maneuver to the edge of the bed. Then he lifted, and she marveled at how—by dint of his strength—her ass rose smoothly from the mattress until she was finally upright. At which point, Eric had to take a step backwards and bend from the waist, because her—*there's a theme here, really*—belly was in the way. "You steady, baby?"

"Fuck you. Yes. I'm good." Then she stumbled over something on the floor, and he gripped her upper arms a moment longer, ensuring she remained on her feet. "Dammit. I can't see the floor. Was that my shoe? Move it, whatever it was."

He smiled. "I'm confident you'll find all of this humorous in about a month." Then he crouched, and she silently fumed because he could still conduct that maneuver at all, much less without being out of breath. "Floor is clear." He stood and leaned in to brush a kiss against her lips. "I love you."

She bit her lip, holding the return sentiment inside until she couldn't anymore, and burst out laughing as she reassured him, "I luv you moar."

"Still love drunk." He kissed her temple as he turned her, walking next to her on the way to the chair in front of the desk. "Will you be long, beloved?"

"Not sure." All joking set aside, real and pretend, she remembered the message she'd seen on the phone. "Owen texted."

"He's on hiatus, I thought." Eric pushed her chair towards the desk, keeping her from the exertion.

"Was. Not sure what this means, but he invoked a high alert phrase." *Which was what had me scrambling at the speed of pregnant lady.* She unlocked the drawer to the left of where she sat and waited for Eric to retrieve the laptop and battery from inside. As he reassembled the computer, she smiled. "You're a super sweet guy, Eric Ward. You're gonna be a great daddy."

"I hope so." He finished and set the device on the desktop. "Want the monitors connected?"

"Not yet. I'll see what's shakin' first." Face angled up, she scarcely had to wait before Eric complied and swooped in for a firm, closed-mouth kiss. "Thank you."

"Always my pleasure, baby." He pressed his lips to hers again. "I'll be right here if you need anything."

True to his word, he put a knee to the mattress and crawled back up the bed, shoving a pillow behind his shoulders as he settled himself against the headboard. He flashed her a smile, then focused his attention on the TV screen. Alace watched him a moment longer, then turned to the computer in front of her.

Powered up, it took her three screens of credentials to insert herself into the closed network she shared with Owen. Over the past four months, they'd worked several gigs together, each more rigorous than the last. After the final one had been put to its bloody bed, he'd told Alace he was going off-grid for a couple of weeks. That was two weeks ago, so she'd expected to hear from him soon. What she hadn't expected was an out-of-the-blue SOS signal.

The icon representing him was active, limned in green, showing he was online now.

Before Alace could type in a greeting, a request for a video connection appeared on the screen. She grabbed her headset as she accepted, plugging it into the computer before slipping the earpieces into place.

The image resolved into a bedraggled Owen staring at her, piney woods the backdrop to his exhausted-looking, unshaven face. Where he'd chosen to go hiking and camping was a notorious stretch of East Coast geography, often rumored to be the setting for literally dozens of body dumps.

Wonder if he stumbled onto something unexpected.

His first words tore that thought away.

Chapter Two

Owen

When Alace appeared on the tablet, he jumped straight to business without even a greeting. "Two weeks before we shut down the pedos selling sibs, they had a successful event. You said you were able to dump everything from their systems. If it included the previous auctions, I need to know the names of the buyers."

Alace stared at him briefly through the camera, then dipped her chin. Over her shoulder, she added to what apparently was an ongoing discussion, "Eric, I need the extra monitors plugged in." Then, with her gaze turned back to Owen, she promised him, "We've got it all. Everything we need."

He took in a deep breath, his eyes going beyond the tablet to where the child sat. Twenty minutes ago, the boy had stumbled into his early morning campsite, naked and unaware, bruising blooming over his torso.

The rustling first heard in the distance intensified, and Owen held his hand low to block the fuel cube flame as best he could, cursing even that tiny bit of light to blind him. The sun wasn't yet tinting the skyline, but whatever had been sleeping in the nearby scrub was apparently awake and headed his way. Mostly small varmints in this area, but black bears had been known to wander down from the nearby mountains to dig for grubs in the fertile ground. With a hand on the gun strapped to his thigh, he waited.

The dim light didn't reach far between the trees, but the sounds indicated whatever was coming, it was arrowing straight towards him and the flame. Then the light glimmered off a shape about four feet high, bipedal, and thin. A child? He had only a moment to consider before a naked boy about twelve years old stood across the small clearing.

"Hey." The boy didn't react to the sound, just stared at him. Owen's gut twisted as he took in the purple splotches along the boy's upper arms and legs, mixed in and overlapping more bruises in green and yellow, all indicating long-term abuse. "What's going on?" He stood, wanting to be on his feet for this encounter.

"Mister." The high-pitched and wavering voice backed up Owen's gut feeling the child hadn't hit puberty yet. He was immature physically, too, which could be racked up against long-term starvation, Owen guessed. The boy wove back and forth, clearly exhausted and virtually out on his feet.

When he stumbled, Owen smoothly moved in time to save him a tumble. He kept the boy from going to his knees and pulled him to one side of the camp stove. Owen swept the sleeping bag from the still-hanging hammock and wrapped it around the boy as he guided him to sit.

"You gotta save my sister."

"What?" Preoccupied with cataloging the injuries the boy had suffered, because Owen had seen more bruises on his back and flanks, he hadn't quite heard anything past the echoing "mister," which had drawn the protective instincts to the surface. The boy in the warehouse had called him mister, and been worried about his sister, too. For a moment, Owen thought maybe he'd imagined the boy's words.

"My sister, she's still there. He's got her."

A chill colder than the North Atlantic flowed over Owen. He got the boy situated and then crouched slightly away, next to the camp stove. The boy was so cold he wasn't even shivering, but the flesh of his arms where Owen had gripped was chilled to the bone. Too fuckin' cold. *"Who's got your sister?"* He put the pan *of water on to boil, but instead of the oatmeal he'd been planning to prepare, he dug into his food bag and pulled out a freeze-dried dinner.* Food will help warm him. This kid needs to eat. *He brought out his flashlight, too, and wound the handle a few times before setting it aside, pointing the stream of light off to the side to keep from blinding either of them. "Were you there, too? Did you escape somehow? Is it family or what? Foster care?" No way would he gloss over the boy's questions or story, making nice for polite society. At this point, anything the kid said was truth, simply based on his physical condition and the fact he'd been dumped in this place, out of all the land along the East Coast. "Tell me what's going on."*

"Not fosters. That was before. Now, our owner still has her."

Owen's hands stilled, and he turned his head to see the boy staring at him, an anguished expression on his face.

Owner.

His gorge rose, bitter bile flooding his mouth. "What can you tell me about that?"

"He bought us a few weeks ago and I made him mad. Everything's been..." His voice trailed off, and from the twist his features adopted, Owen thought if he'd had any spare fluid in his body, he'd be weeping. "It was hard, mister. Real hard. I made him mad, but it

was just to keep Shiloh safe. I promised her I'd keep her safe."

"We're going to get her out of wherever she is." Owen didn't hesitate to make the promise, because he'd turn over every mountain even if Alace wouldn't help. She will, though. *He had faith in her, and the realization surprised him, because faith and trust were different beasts, both earned, but through different processes. The fact Alace had impressed him enough for him to hold her up to that kind of standard was shocking but good.* "I need you to tell me everything you know. Drink this." *He handed the kid his water bottle.* "Pull the top up to open it." *At the boy's troubled stare at the bottle, Owen reassured him,* "It's only water. I promise. I'll take a drink if that puts your mind at ease."

"It's just..." *The kid made a face, nose scrunching in a way that had Owen lowering his estimation of the boy's age by a couple of years.* "I can't let anything happen to her. I'm all she's got."

Dumping the meal into the now-boiling water, Owen stirred it with a spork and set it aside. He used a stick to knock the still-burning fuel cube onto the sandy ground inside the fire ring. "You're dehydrated and dangerously chilled. I want to get some water into you, and then you'll eat that." *He was breaking small sticks into kindling as he talked, tilting the tip of his chin towards the pan of food.* "And we'll talk. I need to get the story, but know this—what's your name?"

The boy's chin lifted, and Owen saw the muscles of his throat work as he swallowed hard. "Kelly."

"Kelly, my name's Owen. I'm a kind of specialist. I specialize in helping people who are in exactly the kind of situation your sister is in. To do that, I'm going to need to have all the information I can to make sure when I help her, I don't inadvertently hurt any good guys." Kelly's gaze didn't waver, boring deep into Owen. "I'm not going to hurt you or her. I promise you. Swear to you the water's safe, and so is the food. Your job is to give me the info I need. Can you do your job to help Shiloh?"

Kelly nodded slowly and lifted the bottle. He had a fleeting wrestling match with the top, then got it open and took a deep swallow, his gaze still not leaving Owen's face. "You're going to hurt the bad guys?" Owen lifted one shoulder, giving Kelly the only response he'd allow himself. "Good." Kelly swallowed again, this time seeming easier, and took another deep drink from the bottle. Owen tipped his head towards the pan of food. Kelly reached out and gripped the handle, dragging it close enough to lift, even that small weight stretching his limits. With the pan propped against his legs under the sleeping bag, he held the spork awkwardly in his fist and shoved the first bite into his mouth, spitting it out immediately and hissing. "Hot." The next sporkful he put in his mouth was cooled first by blowing on it.

Satisfied the boy would continue eating, Owen set his teeth and moved from adding kindling over the sputtering fuel cube to stacking more wood in place. He hated fire. Fortunately this would have to be a small one because they wouldn't be here long, but while they were, Kelly needed the extra warmth. And Owen needed the light to see the boy's face more clearly. The flashlight was nice, but if he aimed the beam at the boy's face, any conversation would feel more like an interrogation than a debriefing. By the time he sat back on his heels, the flames had caught and were feeding from the kindling to the lower pieces of wood.

Glancing at Kelly, he saw the pan was now empty and set to the side. Spork evidently abandoned, the boy was wiping his fingers against the ground when he caught Owen's gaze and nodded, then lifted the bottle of water—now missing a couple of inches at the top—and drank again. Thinking ahead to walking out of the woods, Owen winced at the idea of the kid setting his bare feet on the trail. He dug through his backpack again and brought out a fresh shirt and set of socks, all he had to offer. Kelly took the clothing with a muttered, "Thank you," and somehow managed to pull everything on under the cover of the sleeping bag.

"Okay, now that we've got you on the way to being warm again, let's hear it. Tell me everything, Kelly. What happened, how did you wind up where you were?" Owen glanced around the clearing and decided he needed some distance to clear his mind, because his instincts were to pull the boy close and reassure him,

let him sleep, keep him safe, and not to stress him even more. Debriefing him would definitely be stressful, so Owen used the fire as a barrier and settled across the small space. Close enough to reassure, far enough away to allow himself to be effective. "Tell me how you came to be with your owner."

"We were in a big building but stuck inside a tiny room. They took us to a bigger room and there were a bunch of men. They...they touched us. Some of them in bad ways. Our owner pinched our muscles and had us get down on all fours. There was this one guy in charge, and he started shouting things, but not like he was mad. The men shouted back, but nothing made sense. Then it was over, and they took us to another tiny room, but there were plates of food waiting, cups of water." *He glanced over at the bottle of water, set aside so he could dress in the poor selections Owen'd provided.* "We were so hungry. It had been days since they'd given us anything. We ate it all."

"It was drugged, wasn't it?" *Owen scowled at the ground, the ease with which he understood the traffickers' methods making him nauseous.* I'm not like them. "You can't feel bad about that. I'm sure they planned everything down to the last detail. It's what they do, Kelly. They've got it down to a science."

"Yeah. I don't remember anything after that for a long time. When I woke up, I was a box in the back of a truck. I could hear the wheels on the highway, and we were going fast. The wind was whistling through *the holes in the top of the box. I freaked out, because I didn't see Shiloh. I...I started crying and screaming, because I'd promised her I'd find a way to save us."* He shook his head, and Owen was humbled at the idea of the loyalty that had driven this boy—a child in fact—to try to keep his sister safe, even in unbelievable conditions. *"She was in a box next to me. It was really hot and the metal sides burned, but then after it got dark, the wind was so cold, I could hear her teeth chattering."*

"What happened next? Did he stop anywhere or drive straight to where he kept you?"

"He didn't stop except for gas. That was when he heard us whispering to each other. I had put my fingers through the holes, trying to reach Shiloh. She was so scared, Owen. I just didn't want her to be scared anymore. He hammered on the top of the box and shouted at me."

The man had probably picked the most remote fueling station, worried about the kids calling for help. Intimidation and isolation would have been effective tools in keeping the kids cowed and quiet. Fucker.

"His house was at the end of a long road, rough because it had a bunch of holes I guess. When we got there, I saw a bunch of other kids, all like us. We weren't supposed to talk, not to each other and not to him, but at night or when he went away, everybody did it anyway. Just whispering, you know?"

The skin of Owen's arms pulled into gooseflesh. "He has a bunch of kids?"

Kelly nodded. "Uh-huh. We were numbers fifteen and sixteen. He didn't let us use our names. We were just the pack. The dogs had names, but we were numbers."

"The dogs?" Owen fed another branch into the fire, gritting his teeth when the flames flared up, throwing sparks into the air. He hated fire with a passion, and here he was making this one bigger.

"Yeah, they were part of the pack, too."

"When you say pack, what does that mean? Did you live with the dogs outside? With the other kids?" Every detail added onto the image Owen had in his head, every nuance of Kelly's story a building block for this unexpected mission.

"Yeah. There was a shed we slept in at night, in piles." The kid gestured around him, as if indicating bodies strewn all around. "It was open on the front, so the more dogs you could talk into sleeping with you, the warmer you were. The older kids were their favorites. They'd been there so long and had slipped them so much food, the dogs loved them."

"How old were they? How old are you, Kelly?"

"I'm…I don't know. I think thirteen? Shiloh is ten. I keep track of her birthday. It's September third. She's always real good, Owen. The other kids were a mix.

Some older and some younger. The oldest probably a couple years older than me, and the youngest was five. He did okay for himself. I think the pack might have been all he knew. He didn't talk at all, ever." Kelly's expression was strained, earnest anxiety dragging furrows in his forehead.

"When you talked at night, did the others tell their stories? How they came to be part of the pack?" It killed him to speak about the kids' living situation in such a way. Echoing the known taxonomy was the quickest way to keep Kelly on track. "Did the man own them, too?"

"Yeah. Everyone who told a story was kinda the same. Some of it was different, but mostly the same. One of the boys, Dominic, he really helped us out the first few days. If it wasn't for him...I didn't know the rules, and the man was always after me about something because I kept messing up. Dom helped a lot. The other boys were more likely to steal our food or push us out of a good sleeping spot than they were to help with anything."

"Was Shiloh the only little girl?" He didn't have a good feeling about this. At ten, if she were as underweight as Kelly she would appear asexual in nature, but if all the children were kept naked, then her physical differences would stand out like a beacon.

Kelly's face twisted with remembered anger. *"Yeah."* That was nearly a growl, rattling up through *the boy's chest and throat, a sound of such rage Owen became empathetically angry for him. "She was the only female. The rest of us were male."*

God bless. *The man had stripped even the more common human terminology from the kids like calling them boys and girls. What could possibly have been the reasoning for forcing the kids to live as dogs?* "Were they mean because of that?"

"Yeah, that's what made the man mad. The others kept picking on her. She was so much smaller than everybody except the youngest kids, and those all had their protectors in the pack. After a while, all Shiloh had was me. The older boys kept picking on her, especially if I wasn't right there. They'd force her to fight. Made me sick. I hate them. I hate the man, too." Kelly's bottom chin bumped a couple of times, and Owen watched the struggle as he fought for control. The boy dragged his bottom lip into his mouth and bit down hard to force the emotion away.

Owen waited for Kelly to take a drink from the bottle and then asked, "What happened to make the man mad? Why did he bring you out here and leave you? I'm assuming that was him that did it, right? Or were you able to run away?"

"I'd never leave Shiloh like that." At the suggestion he'd abandon his sister, it looked like the boy was on the verge of exploding upward from where he sat. The sleeping bag fell to the ground as he flung his arms

wide as if to keep even the idea at bay. His breathing spiked, and white showed all around the irises of his eyes. Panting, Kelly semi-repeated himself, "I would never leave her."

"Okay. Okay. I believe you, Kelly. I do. She's your sister, and you'd do anything for her."

"I would. I did. I had a chance to run away so many times, but I couldn't take her with me. So I stayed because I couldn't just leave her behind."

"The man brought you out here? How far was the drive? Do you know his name?" *Brow scrunched into a frown, Kelly shook his head, and Owen groaned at himself.* One question at a time. He needed to focus on what had led to the man dumping his bought and paid for property, something Owen knew was expensive. Participating in those auctions took a next level of affluence and influence, no matter if the income was gained legally or not. If he'd purchased sixteen children, he'd be rich enough to consider himself untouchable, no doubt. "Sorry, Kelly. What happened so you wound up here?"

"One of the boys was being a jerk to Shiloh and I got into it with him. I took my licks, but he was hurting too. I wasn't going to let him think he could do what he wanted. I knew the man didn't like it when we fought like that. But Five had hurt Shiloh. She was all scraped up. Then the man put his hands on her and I just...I couldn't stand it. Not one more time. I didn't think, *though. We all knew not to try and fight him. He had the remote. He could do what he wanted."*

Owen's thoughts swirled at the information Kelly had divulged. Owen set his concerns aside for now. Regardless of the source of her injuries, this part of the story was about Kelly. I can't help her until I find her. "Remote? What was that for?"

Kelly angled his chin to the side, and Owen saw two marks on his neck. "For the collars. It's how he kept us at the cabin."

"Jesus." *He jerked his gaze from the boy and stared at the flames dancing in front of him, forcing himself to stay seated. So many kids kept as part of a pack mixed with dogs, forced to sleep outside, fighting each other for survival, dehumanized in every way, and controlled by painful shock collars.* "I have a friend who can help. I'm going to call her now. I don't want to tell her about you yet, so I'll need you to be very quiet while I'm on the call with her. Then we'll get out of these woods and head to my house. I'll keep you safe, Kelly. I promise you. And I'm going to find Shiloh."

He looked up, staring at the boy. Kelly's expression was open and pleading, the anguish he was enduring at being separated from his sister there for anyone to see.

"I promise."

Keeping his breathing steady on the call was no small feat, but Owen managed it. Hearing Alace say they had everything they needed to find out who'd bought Kelly and his sister firmed his resolve. *We can do this.*

"What's your source?" Alace's question was expected, standard even, and Owen found it difficult to not simply tell Alace about Kelly. Something had him holding back, though, and he tried not to question his gut reaction.

"A contact reached out. I'm not too far from the trailhead"—more like under an hour, which she would know if she mapped the Wi-Fi hot spot—"and wanted to get things rolling before I hit the road." Alace's expression sharpened, her gaze flicking to the camera and then away to whatever files she was manipulating. "I'm going to have to go home and take care of something before I can be the boots on the ground, but the more data we have and can dig through, the better it'll be."

"Urgency? Other than wanting to get these kids out of these bastards' hands?" Alace's gaze flicked back to the camera. "What's up with the earbuds?"

"Habit to have you in my head." Owen let his brief smile fade, knowing it appeared strained. "Pretty fuckin' urgent, boss lady. I know of one sibling pair sold, a brother and sister. I want their buyer first, but then I'm going to want to deal with the rest of the buyers. I have to get these kids back to their families." Kelly shifted uncomfortably, drawing the sleeping bag back up over his shoulders, head ducking down to rest his forehead on his bent knees. *Shit.* His posture said it all. *The kid doesn't have a family to go home to.* Even when Owen rescued Shiloh, the two of them would be back in foster care, something that had obviously failed them miserably. "This pair, the info indicates they may have been surrendered to the ring via CPS, boss lady. If we have source info for the kids, that would be a secondary priority."

"I saw data about the origin of most kids, so we likely have what we need." Alace sat back in her chair, and Owen watched as her eyes moved rapidly side to side. She was reading whatever she'd surfaced on her screens. "Want me to share this on the tablet or wait until you're home and at your regular setup?"

"Wait until I'm home. I'll bug out of here soon as we finish talking and then let you know when I walk in the door."

"I'll know when you walk in the door." Alace's head tipped to the side, and one corner of her lips quirked upwards. "You know I've got security feeds from your place."

Maybe I should tell her now. He inclined his head, acknowledging what she'd said. "That you do. Has there been any blowback or chatter about the organic material the fire left behind?" She shook her head deliberately, hair moving slowly as her eyes stayed fixed on his through the video. *Shit. She knows something.* He tried to pass off the fact he'd low-keyed the dead bodies he'd torched after the last mission. "Good news then. It could be that the next one will go as fast and easy."

"Did you find what you wanted when you went to the woods, Owen?" She knew how much he'd needed the quiet of the empty forest to clear his head. The noise from the last mission had not subsided quickly, but over the hours and days of solitude, it had at least diminished in volume. Owen had taken his time, waiting until he'd found a better balance in his head to turn back towards the trailhead and civilization. That peace let him look past the anguish and terror the rescued kids had lived through and finally rest in the knowledge that he and Alace had been able to save so many.

"I did." He didn't look at Kelly but was relentlessly aware of the boy sitting there. Throughout the conversation, he'd felt the weight of Kelly's gaze on him from across the fire, and Owen had scarcely flinched as he spoke aloud things that could have him sent to jail for a long stretch if shared to the wrong people. The boy was wilting, slumping as the hot food and warm fire conspired to ease the tension in his muscles, and knowing he'd be out soon spurred Owen to finish up this conversation. Getting on the road was critical. But he wanted to at least acknowledge to

Alace that he might be leaving the woods with more than he expected. "And then some. You'll see soon."

"Be safe, Owen." Chin lifted, Alace stared at the camera. "I'll keep digging. Sibling pair, sold to a single owner, source in the foster care system. We've got this, frand."

He grinned at her, appreciating more than ever the fates that had thrown them together. "I like your style, boss lady. Frands for life." Without letting her respond, he disconnected and set the tablet in his lap.

"Is your friend going to help us? She gonna help me and Shiloh?" Kelly looked skeptical, and Owen didn't blame him. Even being cautiously optimistic right now would feel weird to a boy who'd been without hope for so long.

"She is, and I am, and we're going to get Shiloh out."

As he turned off the tablet and satellite Wi-Fi hot spot and stowed them into his backpack, Owen put off addressing the boy further. Sunrise was breaking the horizon, painting the skyline and clouds with pastel shades of pink and blue, looking like cotton candy as they increased in intensity with every breath.

The kid was exhausted. He was seriously malnourished and had been beaten within an inch of his life, then dumped into the woods to die. In a more perfect world, Owen would have used the Wi-Fi to connect to the authorities, calling them in to pick up the kid, and happily waltzed off up the trail, leaving Kelly to be taken care of by the people trained to do so.

This isn't a perfect world.

Owen wasn't going to question why the same fate that had brought him and Alace together had apparently dropped this kid directly into his path. After all, Owen might have access to the only source of information that would not only save the boy but also give him something back that had been taken from him—his sister.

It was only weeks ago that Owen and Alace had taken down the sex trafficking ring he now suspected had also sold Kelly and Shiloh. Such a short time since he'd crouched between two cages, each holding a sibling pair, and with Alace's voice in his ear, had promised them he was one of the good guys. Then he'd killed seventeen men in cold blood, never balking an inch at what was needed. Finally, when all was said and done, he'd unlocked those cages and dozens more, and walked the survivors out into the dank night air and freedom.

During the operation, Alace had found an opportunity to hack into the traffickers' computer systems, and at the time, had promised Owen she had everything needed to ensure none of the buyers would escape. Time would tell, but he believed her. Believed in her. Believed in her commitment to righting wrongs. The same ideology that drove Owen, too.

Now, call completed, it was time to again talk to Kelly and see what else he could offer.

Keeping his gaze steadily trained on Owen, the boy sat and waited. His fingers trembled where they clutched the fabric swaddled around him. Even with a sunburn layered over his tan, the bruises on his arms stood out in stark contrast to the skin stretched tight over his bones. Dirt ground into his hands matched that decorating the skin of his knees, testifying to how he'd been forced to live for weeks, hunched over on all fours like a dog. Stumbling out of the dark, Kelly's first thought, his first words, had been worry about his sister, and that had continued through the tale Owen had pulled out of him so far.

Owen thought again about how he'd retreated to the woods in an effort to quiet his mind, feeling overcome by the misery he'd witnessed. Things no child should ever be forced to endure, and each tiny face turned up to look at him had reminded him of Emma. So he'd been searching for serenity, a way to forget, even for a while—and had been somewhat successful. Time flowed differently in the woods. Less constrained by clocks, more driven by immediate need. Was he tired? Then rest. Hungry? Eat. He'd been on his way back out to civilization because it was time. He'd recharged enough to take on the next challenge.

And here was one specially made for his knowledge and talents. That bitch fate had put the perfect mission in his path, which meant Owen had a target, the means to execute, and a reason to take it on.

First would be identifying the buyers from that auction.

He glanced across the fire.

No, first is getting this kid out of the woods. That would mean making him as comfortable as possible since Owen would have to carry him much of the way.

"You said you were in foster care at one point. Is that who took you to the place where the men were?" Sickening, but it was not unheard of for evil to work its way into the foster care system. If that was the case, the knowledge could give them a clue regarding any new organization beyond the ring they'd busted.

Kelly shook his head, lips pressed tight together. His shaggy hair fell over his forehead and into his eyes, swiped to the side with the back of one hand.

"Did you know the person who took you there?" Another shake, but this one turned into a slow nod, as if Kelly remembered something. "Do you know a name?"

"No." The boy's voice was high-pitched like a broken bell, rasping and painful to hear. Owen held up a second bottle of water until Kelly nodded, then tossed it over. Fumbling the catch, Kelly snatched up the bottle as it landed in the dirt next to him, tossing an apprehensive glance at Owen as if he might take back the offer. "But I saw him at the rec league. He volunteered." Another glance fraught with fear and trepidation. "He's a cop."

Owen didn't try to hide the way his lip curled at the news. Not because he was afraid to go up against law enforcement. He'd done that often enough, never giving a shit who a mark was or what position they held in society. All that mattered was what he could keep them from doing again.

"That don't matter. Bad men hide in all kinds of places. Blue uniforms are merely another way to disguise their sickness." Owen paused, thinking. "You think your foster home folks are looking for you?" Kelly shook his head again, hair falling into his eyes once more. "Why not? If they weren't the ones who sold you, then wouldn't they be worried about you?"

"He came to the house and said he had to take us. They assumed we were bad." Kelly sniffed and coughed, and Owen's back went straight when he saw him shiver even though he was wrapped up in the sleeping bag. "Our folks died. They weren't bad people, but they OD'd." He sniffed again. "Didn't matter. I'd been taking care of us for a long time before that happened."

"All right. Do you know your full name?"

"Kelly Gilson." Kelly's head tottered sideways, and he caught himself as he began to slump over. "I don't feel so great."

"Okay. Continued conversation can wait until we're back at my place." Kelly blinked at him, a long, slow sweep of his eyelids, confusion clear in his expression. "I'm going to take care of you, and I'm going to get your sister. Kelly, I promise you that it's going to be okay."

"No, it's not. Don't lie." The flat statement took him aback, and Owen paused in place, staring at the boy. "That's the last thing my dad said to me, and it wasn't true."

"I keep my promises." Owen set to work gathering up the few things left to pack, scrubbing the dish and spork Kelly had eaten from with a handful of sand before wrapping them in a rag and shoving them into his bag.

It didn't take long, but by the time he finished and was ready to douse the small fire, Kelly lay curled on the ground, eyes closed. Burying the few embers with dirt, he stomped and kicked at the contents of the fire ring until comfortable it had no fuel to flare back up. Shouldering the pack, he bent over and lifted the boy, who was dangerously featherlight in his hold.

"I keep my promises," he repeated for the benefit of the trees surrounding them. Adjusting his grip on the boy, Owen settled Kelly against his chest. The touch of the boy's forehead was like a furnace through his shirt, and he realized exhaustion might not be the only reason Kelly was sleeping so deeply.

"Always."

Chapter Three

Owen

He'd placed a still-sleeping Kelly on the back seat, torso and legs stretched sideways across the length of the bench in as comfortable a position as Owen could make for him. He'd tucked the sleeping bag around the boy after buckling him in loosely. In the brief time it had taken Owen to maneuver him into the car the sleeping bag had fallen to the ground and, muttering under his breath, Kelly had begun shivering violently but never fully roused.

It was clear that weeks of poor living conditions, and at least one overnight stay in the woods at the mercy of the elements, had not been kind to the boy. Kelly's steadily rising fever was concerning, as was the cough that had cropped up during the walk to the car.

It took an anxious hour to make his way home, and Owen triggered the garage door opener from halfway up the drive, ready to be inside. Kelly's coughing had gotten worse, and Owen was antsy to get the boy where he could properly tend to his needs.

Leaving the backpack for now, he kept the sleeping bag around the boy as he scooped Kelly up and walked to the interior door. Standing patiently for the facial recognition software, he blew out a relieved breath when he heard the soft click of the lock disengaging. The light changed from the steady green that told him his house had remained undisturbed during his absence to a light amber, indicating an authorized entry. He'd called it peace of mind insurance when Alace asked about the system, wondering if it might be a bit of overkill. *Worth every penny*.

Once inside, he carried Kelly into what had been a large walk-in pantry at one point. Owen had converted the space into a fully stocked medical room, complete with a waist-high, free-standing counter that doubled as a treatment table. With what he had on hand, he could provide significant support for Kelly without requiring the involvement of official medical professionals.

It'd be better if I can manage to take care of things.

In the past, he'd occasionally been forced to use an EMT one town over who was willing to bend his ethics for things Owen had needed beyond what he could do himself. But he suspected it would take exactly one nanosecond for the man to get on the horn reporting him if Owen showed up with a young boy who'd been so clearly abused. *Not that I'd blame him, normally.* But Owen absolutely did not have time for the hassle of explanations right now.

With the sleeping bag still bundled around the boy, Owen checked Kelly's temperature and then listened to his lungs. *Clear, thank God.* The higher than normal temp could be a problem, but acetaminophen would take care of most of it. If the illness was a cold, it would have to run its course. He was anxious to commence solving the puzzle of where Shiloh was, but the boy held priority. So Owen would clean him, clothe him, feed him again, and then let him get some real rest.

Then he'd call Alace, and they'd get to work.

The screen mounted on the wall behind him buzzed, and Owen turned. He huffed a laugh at the message displayed.

What the actual fuck, Owen?

He gave the camera in the corner of the room an exaggerated smile, then indicated the boy on the table and held up five fingers.

I can call. The text showing on the screen changed before the buzz sounded. **Plus you're wired for sound. Just talk to me.** The plea in that statement surprised him, and Owen pulled in a deep breath.

"Hey, so yeah. This is why I called earlier. This is Kelly Gilson, and he stumbled into my campsite not long before dawn. He's the brother part of that sibling pair I told you about." He pinched the skin on the back of the boy's hand, pleased with how quickly it flattened. "He was dehydrated and hypothermic when he found me. I fed and watered him, got him warm, and now I've got him here. He's running a fever, but maybe the elevated temp is nothing more than being dumped unconscious in the woods like he was. I suspect he was out there for hours."

The screen buzzed.

Sister's name?

Owen offered her a true smile this time. Without a single comment about his judgment in bringing the boy home, Alace swung into action. She didn't need anything else from him, because for her, the why didn't matter. *She trusts me.* That struck like a gentle blow each time he thought about it. Looking back down at Kelly, he started the process of cleaning the scrapes and wounds covering too much of the boy's skin.

"Shiloh. She's Kelly's little sister. Guy who bought them has a unique fetish. He's keeping a bunch of kids and dogs as a big pack. Look at his hands and knees." He lifted one of Kelly's hands, turning it palm up so the camera could capture the depth of the soiling ground into the skin. "I've never heard of anything like that, so there's a chance the guy's alone. But you know how the true freaks are."

Buzz.

Those assholes flock together.

"Yes, they do. So I'm going to get him cleaned up and then feed him again and then see how much more info I can get. The guy's got fourteen or fifteen kids, calls them by their acquisition number. Fifteen here"—he shook his head at the idea of calling the kid by that ridiculous name—"fought with Five over the sister. The owner asshole got tired of the disagreements and tried to kill him. Obviously, he didn't succeed, and I expect he thought exposure would finish the job for him." Another wave of shivers washed over the boy, skin lifting in gooseflesh. "He was nearly right."

Buzz.

What do you need?

"Time. Time and info. You dig out what we've got on the previous buyers and put your gigantic brain to work on the puzzle of which one is the mega dick who bought Kelly. We've got to find the sister. She's the only girl in the group. That could go downhill real fast without Kelly there to protect her." He threw away another handful of antiseptic wipes and stepped back, studying the boy. "This isn't working. I need to get him into the bathtub." He blew out a long breath, turning ideas over in his head. "What do I need? I need clothing for him. Something comfortable and easy to put on. He wasn't wearing a stitch when he showed up. I made do while getting him out of there, but everything I have is too big. A delivery of hot soup or something else to eat would be good. I've been gone long enough anything I left in the fridge is going to be bad, so maybe some regular groceries, too?" Slipping his arms underneath Kelly's back and knees, he lifted the boy and sleeping bag, turning to face the camera. "And anything else you think I need. You're the brooding hen here. I'm the clueless-but-fun uncle type."

Got you covered.

He was reading the message as the buzz sounded, already nodding at the camera. "I know you do, Alace. You've got my back, always."

The tablet was silent, but he knew Alace was still watching. She took compliments about as well as Owen himself did, which was to say not well at all.

Hefting the boy a little higher, he tipped his head to the door. "Bathroom next. There's no screen in there, but you can alarm the one in here and I'll hear it." Turning, he gave the camera his back in an honorary gesture of trust he knew Alace would pick up and understand. "Thank you, Alace."

***

Alace

She remained seated in her chair after disconnecting with Owen. Staring blankly at the screen, she didn't see the reams of information scattered across the display in a variety of documents. Her mind's eye was stuck on the image of Owen holding the unconscious young boy to his chest, as if he had transformed into a father about to put an exhausted child to bed after a day full of wholesome and character-building activities. The way he'd handled the boy laid out on the table had told the same story, Owen keeping at least one protective hand on the child's form in case he moved. He'd been still and quiet, this boy named Kelly, this ghost who'd simply happened to stumble on the campsite of a man uniquely positioned to help him.

Alace had never believed in coincidences.

Even when it meant the alternative placed the boy as a pawn in a game she didn't yet see, poised to target her friend in a way that had the potential to erase his whole world. And if Owen lost the chance to do the missions, as he called them? It wouldn't be pretty. *Might as well take him out myself if that happens.*

There was no way Alace could have stated her concerns at the time, not using text as she was, and not with Owen halfway across the country from where she sat in her bedroom. He'd have gotten pissed and shut her out. She knew, because it was how she would have reacted if someone had done the same. His self-assigned mission right now was entirely about that boy. Owen was hyper-focused on Kelly's health and safety, and part of his fixation was going to include finding the sister and bringing her home. Anything that got in the way of that would be kicked to the curb. Fast.

Since communication was the most critical element for what they did, distance didn't normally matter. Given the methods they'd chosen—talking their way through a job still meant instantaneous communication as long as there was connectivity, no matter if it was text, voice, or video.

For a conversation of this magnitude, Alace wanted to have at least voice. Better would be a vid call, where miniscule variances, including simple nuance of tone, could be mapped and categorized. Even as measured and controlled as the two of them were, Owen had his tells. *As do I.*

Better yet? A surprise visit to Owen's edge-of-town home in northern New Jersey.

Alace glanced over her shoulder at Eric, unsurprised to find him studying her with a steady gaze.

"Nope. You are exceedingly pregnant and can't even tie your own shoes. No way. You are not flying off to wherever it was Owen is."

It was annoying sometimes how well he knew her.

Straightening to face the computer again, she mentally ran through the list of things Owen had asked for. Some would be a simple online order to a grocery store for delivery. One or two would require more personal handling to get what was necessary in the timeframe within which they needed to work. Huh. *Now it's both of us in this.* She shook her head and clicked on an anonymous browser within a remote session window.

"I know I can't go." At her words, Eric stirred behind her, the covers rustling as he shifted closer. Fingers flying over the keys, she gathered items into her cart, adding in a variety of additional options. She set up a concierge delivery, which would be handled expeditiously, then waited for the confirmation message. Heat bloomed across her skin as Eric's hands landed on her shoulders, strong fingers wrapping around and holding loosely. "But something's not right. There are things I can't tell you, but trust me when I say I'm fairly confident this isn't what it looks like."

Another remote window gave her the option of logging into another network, which she did, and then she accessed a drive on a different cloud-based system. The display had a half a dozen coded names, and she studied the ones that glowed a light green. Of the three available assets, she selected the one she knew would be positioned closest to where Owen lived and initiated contact.

As she waited for the response, she looked up at Eric, finding his gaze fixed on her, not the computer screen. As always, he only saw her, and she smiled, lifting her chin with a demand he quickly gave in to, bending deep and brushing his mouth across hers.

"I love you," she whispered as he pulled back, warmed inside when his gorgeous eyes softened with pleasure. "I'm worried about him. I wouldn't do anything to hurt her."

Alace was unable to avoid a tiny flinch when that last sentence escaped. The guilt she continued to feel over a near-miss with the pregnancy early on didn't seem to be fading. Eric was bothered every time the remorse surfaced, so she tried to keep the feeling in check as much as possible. He and the doctor had both assured Alace her miscalculation around how much activity was okay was normal, but the idea she could have hurt Eric by what she still saw as her selfishness wouldn't go away.

"Beloved." His voice rumbled against her skin, his lips skating along the edge of her jaw until he nibbled and plucked at the lobe of her ear. "Of course you wouldn't. You love her."

"I do." It was truth, and something that still surprised Alace sometimes. Not that she could have feelings for this baby, an extension of Eric who she loved with all her heart—but the depth of those emotions. "So much."

"I wish he were closer so we could do more to help him." Eric pulled back, his gaze pensive. "It feels wrong to simply sit here and do nothing." His eyes closed, and he danced the tip of his nose alongside hers. "But I trust you to take care of our friend. And I'll take care of you. Sometimes that taking care is reminding you of the changes in our lives. That's all, Alace. It wasn't a dig or anything. You know I was never angry or upset. Innocence in intent."

"I like when you take care of me." The idea of innocence being credited to her was humorous, so Alace offered Eric a quirked grin when his eyes flashed open, his expression hooded in response to her sultry and teasing tone. "All the time, mister."

"My baby always needs me." Soft lips touched hers and moved gently, placing tiny kisses at each corner of her mouth. "Love you so much, Alace."

He straightened and glanced at the computer screen, then back at her. "I'll go get you some snacks. Put your feet up until I get back." She nodded, and he lifted a hand from her shoulder, traveling across her skin to caress the nape of her neck. The touch left a trail of heat behind that in different circumstances would have turned to arousal. Eric's words reminded her of the needs at hand. "Do your thing, get Owen what he needs, then start digging and figure out why this kid just happened to stumble into his path. That doesn't add up."

"Right?" Alace shook her head, her single-word exclamation admitting her concern on that point. Eric was still laughing as he walked from the room, and she settled back at the keyboard. When she could no longer hear his footsteps, she muttered to the screen, "Even Eric the lawyerly says so."

Three hours later, she'd messaged with Owen a dozen times, following his progress with the boy into the rooms where there were cameras and screens. Kelly had woken enough to eat some of the pho she'd had delivered, Owen having to handle the utensils needed for the chicken and noodles. The boy's fever had gone down, but his coughing was still worrisome to hear. Alace had gone back and forth between the desk and the bed, and back again a couple of times, switching from the computer to a tablet as needed. Kelly was sleeping now, in what appeared to be a true, restorative sleep, and it was time for the difficult conversation she and Owen needed to have.

She typed in a message to that effect, sending it along with a silent pulse of the alarm to bring Owen's attention to the screen. He nodded without speaking, and she watched as he brushed Kelly's hair back from his forehead, his palm pausing briefly to check the boy's temperature. *How does he know to be such a—* Dad felt wrong, even as a thought, but she couldn't think of anything else that was as appropriate.

He stalked from the room, and she saw from the camera he must have left the door ajar, light seeping in from the hallway. She tracked his progress through the house, not surprised when he wound up in the kitchen, standing in front of the refrigerator with the door open. At least he had food in it now.

Speaking to the air, which meant to her, he said, "Give me a couple of minutes, Alace. I'll call you on vid when I'm ready."

She tipped her head slightly. His tone was tolerant, pleasant, but the words were dismissive. Why would he want her out of his security system?

She keyed into the screen mounted on the cabinet beside the refrigerator. **What are you going to do?**

His face was hidden from the camera positions she had available, and that restriction was uncomfortable. Effectively blinded, she couldn't sort out what he was thinking just from the side of his head.

He didn't respond, so she pulsed the alarm on the screen.

Owen's laugh was sharp and bitter sounding. "Oh, I hear and see you." He didn't move, still posed in the refrigerator opening, one hand resting on the corner of the upper freezer, the other gripping the door handle, knuckles standing out white and strained. "But you aren't hearing me."

I hear you. You want privacy. But this impacts us both, Owen. She stared at what she'd typed out and slowly backspaced over everything except the first sentence. She sent the message and then closed the program override allowing her the level of control she'd been using. She then closed the terminal window within a remote session, and finally shut down the computer, leaving the battery in place for now, since she wouldn't be leaving the room.

Tablet in hand, she levered herself out of the chair, shuffling towards the bed. Eric flipped back the covers and slipped from her side back to his. She smiled at him and gratefully crawled into the heat his body left behind.

"All done for now?" He helped with the pillows, propping them behind her back so she could rest comfortably in a semi-upright position. The pregnancy-induced reflux had been bad over the past couple of months, and they'd quickly learned that lying flat was a sure way to guarantee she'd be woken up in unpleasant ways.

"Until Owen calls. We need to talk through some stuff, then I can be done for a while. I've already uploaded everything pertinent, most of which he already knows." She glanced at Eric. "How much do you want to know about this one?"

Eric sat silently, lips pressed tightly together. Her husband worked for the county as a prosecutor, and there had already been so many times when his ethics had him begging off from deeper knowledge about the gigs. Intellectually, he understood every effort she and Owen put forth was for the greater good, and he could and did always support her. But in an abstract way. The actual implementation of the plans was where he typically waved off more information. She trusted him implicitly, and for her it was never about whether he'd have to testify against her someday. There would be no true plausible deniability for him, not with his moral standards. Her private fears had more than once surrounded the possibility he was afraid he'd see the truth of the person she was inside. Dark, vengeance-driven Alace was a different beast from the tamed-down version curled up in his bed.

Trying to rein in those doubts wasn't easy, and at times like these, it was harder than others. When she was in the midst of a job, the unwavering conviction of rightness was palpable. It was what drove her forwards and enabled her to make the decisions she did without flinching. It would only be later, after the adrenaline rush was past, after things had been solved to her satisfaction, after the decisions had been made and accepted—when she'd stare at herself in the mirror and wonder what Eric saw when he looked at her.

"Tell me everything you're comfortable with, Alace. There are kids involved, and it's bad, right?" She nodded, holding his gaze. "Tell me everything then. We can't let kids be hurt."

Her eyes slipped closed, that word—that single, fucking, fucking word—standing out in the darkness behind her lids like a neon sign. *We.*

Without questioning his sincerity, she launched into the story. "Owen and I took down a trafficking ring a few weeks ago. That was the last gig we worked." Eric's eyes narrowed, and she nodded. "Yeah, the one on the news. The base of operations was outside Philly, and after everything was said and done, Owen wanted to take off for a few days. It was…" She swallowed and wrinkled her nose at the bitter taste climbing the back of her throat. "Intense. But Owen saved dozens of kids. Those were only the ones they'd been holding, too. He saved countless others from the same kind of fate by not letting the bad guys walk away."

"You saved them, too. Don't sell yourself short, Alace."

Affection for him welled up in her, and Alace blinked away sudden tears. "Don't be nice to me right now. I can't take it. Too many feels." The brilliance of Eric's grin made her laugh, which caused the baby to do a tight somersault inside her. "Oh, don't make me laugh, either. I don't think she likes it." Eric caressed the swell of her belly with his palm, his touch slipping up over the curve and back again, coming to rest on top. "So, yeah, it was intense from either side of the equation. But worth everything." She traced a fingertip along one edge of the tablet, wedging her nail into the space where the case came together. "I got into their systems before we razed the place, leaving ample information for the authorities to put things together, but I downloaded their client list, including all past auctions. I didn't leave any information about clients, nothing but the bastards who'd been kidnapping and selling. They were all handled, so no worries about them escaping the system, you know?" She cut a glance to Eric. His gaze was fixed on her belly, but from the troubled expression he wore, she knew he wasn't seeing her. The media had been all over the story since it broke, and broadcast images of the burned-out building included shots of the rows of cages where the kids had been kept. There'd been dozens of videos showing family reunions, complete with tears and wailing, as well as a multitude of angry questions for the various departments in charge of the investigation. Alace didn't feel badly about how hobbled those investigators were. Not having faith in the system freed her from sharing any of the relatives' expectations.

"Casey Marquette is working the case." Eric angled his face so he could look at her. "We went to school together. He reached out a few days ago asking for any pro bono hours the county or state would allow. A couple of the kids that were rescued are from here, Alace. I'm going to be working their cases locally, taking statements, and coordinating with Casey's office."

"Well, shit. I didn't know that." She rested the tablet on her chest and stretched out her arm. He clasped her hand, threading their fingers together. "Do you want me to stop here, then?"

"No. If I know more, it will help me do a better job for them. I can't use anything I learn here, but it will make me work harder."

"Hero complex. I love it."

Eric snorted. "Takes one to know one."

"Whatever." She squeezed her eyes shut and focused on their connections, his hand cradling their child in her womb, fingers woven together in a tight grip. "We make a good team, Ward. I'm glad I kept you around."

"As if I'd have let you go." When she glanced at him, she was pleased to see the easy expression was back on his face. "Never let you go, beloved. You're mine. Both my babies are stuck with me." He gave her hand a squeeze. "Back on topic. You left the info on the kidnappers and folks running the ring, but not the buyers? Why?"

"We…" She hoped the nanosecond of hesitation wasn't apparent to Eric. It wasn't a lack of trust in him but an ingrained sense of self-preservation that made her brain balk before admitting what she was. "Disappeared all the buyers who were on site. There were five men, and they belong to me now. Their identities, their lives, everything they had is mine. Each of them provided us with connected and well-developed personas online in the spaces where reputation is even more important than in high society. I'm going to use those to hunt for more bad guys." His head moved up and down in a slow nod, but she could tell she hadn't answered all his questions yet. "Their wealth funds the search. I've been judicious with management, and most of them had faceless agreements with financial firms, so as long as I adopt their tone and style of communication, there are no red flags. By the time anyone actually misses the sick bastards, I'll have drained everything."

"What will you do with it all?"

Alace grinned, because that was the easiest of all the questions he could have asked. "A number of charities and programs have already found themselves the recipients of large anonymous gifts, a process which will continue. Owen and I agreed neither of us wanted to profit from this gig, so what's not used in the pursuit will be donated." She snorted indelicately. "It's surprisingly difficult to give away that much money, but where there's a will—"

"There's a way." The tip of his finger trailed along her cheek, tucking a strand of wayward hair behind her ear. "You and Owen, you both amaze me. I'm humbled by your dedication, Alace. Humbled and proud."

"It's what's right. The things that happened to those kids aren't acceptable. The money is also funding accounts for their ongoing care. Some of them were hurt, Eric. Badly. Those without physical scars will still live with the memories all their lives. The least that can be done is to take care of everyone as well as we can. To ease their way in the world, financially. We can't take back what was done to them. The terror and pain. But we can walk ahead of them and smooth the path. There's plenty of money for that." His head jerked back in surprise. "Oh, yeah. I know what you're thinking. There were more than a hundred kids rescued from the single location. Trust me when I say there's enough money recovered from the organization and the buyers."

She winced and stared down at her belly, watching as a foot crossed from the side and up to press against where Eric's hand rested. He laughed softly and tunneled his hand under the covers and her clothing until he was skin to skin, and then he rubbed the heel of their daughter's foot. "She's proud of Mommy, too."

"Pray God she'll never need to know about what Mommy does." Alace grimaced when the baby shifted again, applying pressure against her bladder. "I gotta pee." She swung her legs off the bed and swore when Eric shoved his hands underneath her ass, helping lift her upright. "I hate this part of it all."

"Not long to go now." He took the tablet when she held it out to him. "If Owen calls before you get back, want me to answer it?"

"Yeah, I've got no secrets from you except the ones you want me to keep." She paused and stared at him thoughtfully. His open and loving expression astonished her all over again. "Which are less and less these days. Maybe that's something we should discuss, too."

"Mmhmm. Right now, you should go pee."

"On it." She had scarcely rounded the corner into the bathroom when a cramp hit, strong enough to steal her breath. Lips pursed tightly, she leaned a shoulder against the linen closet, hands running up both sides of her rigid belly. Forcing herself to breathe slowly, she pulled in measured amounts of air with each inhale and blew it out in a disciplined exhale as she waited it out.

"Alace?" Eric's voice held a note of concern, and she clamped her lips together. "All okay, baby?"

"Uh-huh. Yep. Braxton Hicks is not my friend." The cramp eased, and she made it to the toilet, taking care of her business quickly. Pulling herself back upright using the edge of the sink, she leaned against the porcelain and stared at her reflection, focusing on her eyes. "I've got this," she whispered. Another cramp took hold, cinching down on her stomach forcefully, the pain a solid band around her back. She dropped her head low, letting it dangle between her shoulders, attention focused on the pain and on breathing through it.

"Beloved?" A warm hand settled on her low back, Eric's thumb stroking a soothing path across the tense muscles. "More contractions?" Alace nodded, eyes remaining closed. "Are they regular?"

She stopped herself in mid-headshake and shrugged. "Not." She blew out a breath. "Really."

"I'll keep track of them for a little bit, see if there's a pattern." He sounded so calm she pried one eyelid open and rolled her neck until she could see his face. His expression matched the tone. "We'll wait to call the doctor until you think it's time."

As rapidly as it came on, the cramp eased, and she stood upright and washed her hands. "Okay." Drying them on the hand towel draped over the side of the sink, she turned to face him. "Did Owen call yet?" Eric held up the tablet in the hand not curled around her hip and shook his head. "Okay." Heaving a sigh, she deliberately relaxed the muscles in her shoulders. "I'm gonna waddle back to bed."

He grinned and ducked his head, his hand moving to her elbow as he paced beside her through the room. Covered to her waist with blankets, she waited for Eric to get settled next to her and then leaned against his shoulder. "You remember the trip back from New Mexico?"

He stiffened, and she turned her head to press a reassuring kiss against his skin. "Yes. Of course, Alace. Why?"

"I tried to tell you I wasn't a good person. Not a monster-slayer, I think, were my exact words. I was trying to scare you off by pulling back the curtain a little. That was before I knew you didn't scare easily." She trailed a finger along the back of his hand, hiding her smile when he turned the hand over invitingly, clasping tightly when she pushed her fingers between his. "I've changed my mind."

"Oh? In what way?" His casual tone was a lie that she decided to let him keep.

"I do kill the monsters. Even if it's not my hands doing the work, it's my decision to pursue people who are monsters." She cradled her belly with her other hand. "If at some point my daughter learns what I do, I have to believe she'll have enough of her daddy's goodness inside her to see my work for what it is."

"Vengeance," he whispered, scarcely loud enough to be heard.

Pleasure flashed through her at how well Eric—fucking, *fucking* Eric—understood her. Had always seemed to understand her. "Vengeance for those who cannot take it on their own. I fight for those who've been abandoned by society's rules. I don't see myself changing."

"I wouldn't want you to." When Eric's head turned, it was to pin her with his gaze, blazing and ferocious. "Because the work you do, the cases you take—they matter. It's pro bono work of the highest caliber."

"Oh." The contraction had come out of nowhere, startling the sound out of her. "Another one," she hissed out between clenched teeth. "If you're—oh, man—keeping track."

"I am," he assured her, lifting their joined hands to rest against her stomach, sliding them up and down in a slow caress. "You do what you need to, Alace. I'm here. I'm not going anywhere."

"That's good." She rocked her head back and immediately decided that wasn't a good position, dropping her chin to her chest instead. "I'd hunt you down if you tried to leave." The sentence was broken into phrases by her breathing, but it got the reaction she'd aimed for as Eric chuckled at her.

The tablet buzzed and Alace shook her head, silently telling Eric not to answer it.

He did anyway, and his first words to Owen showed how he'd chosen to interpret her actions. "Give Alace a minute, Owen. She might be in the early stages of labor and is having a contraction."

"Oh, wow." Owen's voice held a tone of awe. "Holy cow. Is she okay?"

"Yeah, the doctor said the baby's ready any time, so we're waiting things out to see if these will keep going or peter out." Calm and reasonable, Eric structured his response in a way that also reassured Alace, reminding her that this was all normal and expected. Just like the doctor had said. "How's young Kelly?"

"You saw that, huh?"

Alace breathed through the tail end of the contraction as she listened to their conversation.

"He's better already. Fever's coming down, and the food stabilized him more than I expected. The last time he woke, he was back to asking about his—how much did you hear, Eric?"

"Everything. It's all good, Owen. I understand the kind of case you guys are facing with this one. He asked about his sister?" Alace lifted her head in time to see Owen's nod. "Who do you have to care for him while you look for her?"

"I don't know. That's part of what I wanted to talk to Alace about."

"If you lived closer, you could bring him here to me." Alace's tightened grip on Eric's hand had him looking at her. "Is it over?"

"Yeah." She reached out to take the tablet as she blew out what the books had called a cleansing breath. "Not as intense as the last one, so possibly they're tapering off. False alarm."

"Natural order of things is all. Our time will come when they don't fade." Eric bumped her shoulder. "I'll go get a cold bottle of water while you chat with Owen." He slipped out of bed, careful movements barely jostling her as she sat propped against the headboard. "Back in a few minutes. Text me if you have another contraction and I'm not back yet."

She watched Eric walk from the room before giving Owen her attention. "Hi."

"He's good for you. I wasn't sure about it at first, but damn, woman, he's a truly good guy." Owen gave her his crooked smile, the one she always sensed cut closest to the core of who he was. "Keep him."

"I intend to." She shook her head. "Tell me about the hike, and how everything happened, and what we need to do now."

"Damn, Alace. Bask in the moment a little, why doncha?" His smile changed, evening out, muscles around his eyes relaxing and flattening his expression. This was "work" Owen, and she appreciated his willingness to drop into their productive mode so easily. "I was on my way back out. I hadn't told anyone other than you where I was headed, and the timeframe I gave you was longer by a few days than what I wound up taking. There's no way anyone could have known when or where I'd be at any given time. I know what you're thinking, and it's nothing I haven't already gone over in my head a thousand times. Why me, why there, why this kid? Am I right?"

"Yeah." She breathed out the word. "Something doesn't add up, Owen. It's like you were targeted for this. A baited trap."

"Maybe fate targeted me." He lifted his chin. "We've seen it happen in bad ways before. Innocents who were in the wrong place at the wrong time, and we've never questioned that scenario. It only makes sense that the opposite would be true sometimes." Alace was shaking her head before he finished speaking, and he held up a hand to stave off her ready argument. "No one knew I was there. Have I hiked the Barrens before? Yes, but never from that trail. It's a big geographic feature, and I've covered about a tenth of it, always coming from a different angle. That trail isn't the closest to my house. It's unremarkable in any way, other than it leads to a lake I wanted to see. Only if they'd tracked my car would they know, and I've got a sweeper mat I park on in the garage. My car was clean when I got home, exactly as it was when I'd left. If I'd decided to eat breakfast on the road home instead of in the forest, Kelly wouldn't have found me. He found *me*, Alace. If it were a setup, if I were doing this as a setup, I'd have the target do the finding. There's an innate trust in one's own actions, so having the target discover the bait provides greater chances of simple acceptance. He wandered up to me. He had to have been lying there when I made camp, and I just didn't go that direction to dig my cathole, you know? I went the other way. These are not manufactured accidents. These are true coincidences. I'm not going off gut here but off my years of training and human study." He made a face as he pulled in a hard breath. "Fuckin' fate, really? That's all I kept thinking. That and 'don't be an idiot, don't let yourself be duped, be real, Owen.' I am being real, Alace. This kid, Kelly, he needs us in a way I haven't seen since—" Owen interrupted himself and angled his gaze away from the camera for a second before looking back, resolve sitting heavily on his features. "In a long, long time. He needs us, me. If there's no us on this mission, then I get it. You've got shit goin' on. But you should understand that I'm not backing off."

A contraction picked that moment to take hold, and Alace stared at him with narrowed eyes. "Gimme a minute."

His eyes widened comically. "Are you having another labor pain thing? Already? That doesn't look like it's going away. What's the time? Eric said to text him. I can do that. You—" He fluttered his fingers at the camera. "—do whatever it is you're doing." Eric's phone dinged, and she glanced over to see it resting on the nightstand on his side of the bed. It dinged again. "Should I call your landline? His phone's there in the room, right?" She shook her head, unable to answer him. "Okay. I'll just wait here with you. You doin' okay? Want me to count or something?"

Alace blocked out his voice, letting it drone on in the background, focused on the intensity of the contraction. The progression was relentless, determined, as if her body was going to do this whether she was ready or not. Between her legs was wet, her ass heating from the outside, and Alace lifted the covers, looking underneath to see the bottom of the T-shirt she'd stolen from Eric soaked all along the hem. "My water broke."

"What?" Owen's voice was so comically high-pitched she glanced at the tablet in her hand, thankfully still on the right side of the covers. "That's it, I'm calling your landline." Eric's phone dinged and then buzzed against the wooden surface, vibrating sideways. "He's not answering."

The contraction intensified suddenly, clamping around her with force, and Alace bit off the groan that wanted to slip free. "You're calling his cell."

"Eric!" Owen was shouting at the camera, and Alace spared a moment of thought to highlight how hilarious Owen's expression was. *I'll remember this for later.* "I can't do anything from here."

She leaned her head back against the headboard as the contraction eased. "It's okay. He'll be back in here in a minute. Owen, I uploaded all the buyer information to your folder. I went through and analyzed them, and there are four that jumped out at me. All four were repeat buyers, which lines up with what Kelly told you about the other kids. All four also own remote property within a three-hundred-mile radius of the park. All four properties were acquired through shell corporations. Not too well hidden, but enough to keep casual inquiries at bay. It could be a fetish ring. They all made purchases at the same auctions, so there'd have been exposure. Cross-contamination. You saw how the buyers were allowed to chat beforehand."

He nodded, his gaze anxious as he studied her face. "Like calls to like. Are you okay, Alace?" He tried to hide checking his phone and she wanted to laugh at his serious intensity. "Is the contraction over?" She nodded. "Okay. Wait, was that okay you're okay, or okay the contraction was over?"

"Both, actually. Even if this is the main event, we've probably got several hours before we have to go to the hospital." Owen's chin dipped to his neck, face twisted into a disbelieving expression. "Yeah, hours. All the books say."

"Books? You did classes, right?" She lost sight of his face when he yanked a sweatshirt on over the tee he wore. "When did you do classes?"

"No classes. No time." She winced. "How long since the last one?"

He glanced at the wall behind the tablet, then back to the camera. "Nearly three minutes. Are you having another one? Already?" She nodded. "Okay, I'll text it to Eric, so he's got it for the record." Eric's phone dinged. "Are you breathing? There's a breathing thing they do, right?" Alace blew out a stream of air, and he nodded. "Damn, yeah, exactly like that. Keep breathing, Alace. You got this."

"Beloved?"

Eric's voice must have been audible on the video, because Owen began shouting again. "She's having contractions. Her water broke. I've been texting like you said." Eric appeared next to the bed and crouched, putting his face close to Alace's. "You left your phone behind, buddy. *Do better.*"

Eric ignored Owen, speaking directly to Alace. "Your water broke? Are you sure?"

"Unless she suddenly developed a watersports fetish, yeah, her water broke." Owen's immediate response stopped dead at a heated glance from Eric, and Owen held up his hand. "Sorry, sorry. It's just exciting."

"Yes, it is," Eric agreed. "Alace, are you having another contraction?" He cradled the top of her belly, which had contorted into a high peak. "Yes, you are. Owen, she'll have to get back to you on everything. I believe she's given you what's needed to start the investigation. Keep us updated on the boy's condition, as well as what you find."

"Yeah, okay." Owen sounded flustered, and Alace spared a glance for the tablet. He was dragging a hand through his hair, raking it roughly away from his face. "You do the same, okay? Let me know how boss lady's doing."

"We will." Eric took the tablet and tapped the disconnect icon. "Let me know when you're ready to move; it can't be comfortable sitting like that." He smiled. "At least we put the mattress protector on last week." The rustling plastic underneath the sheets had been a nightly annoyance to her, but she appreciated his planning now. "I'm going to get towels and a clean nightshirt for you. I'll be right back, beloved. I'm not going far."

"Do you think we should have taken a class?" Alace pulled in a shallow breath and ran her fingers up and down the sides of her belly. "The nursery isn't finished."

"If the class were a must, the doctor would have insisted. He didn't push it when we expressed no interest." Eric came back into the room from the bathroom and dropped a stack of folded towels on the desk. He opened a dresser drawer, dug around and came up with a gray shirt he knew she liked. "As far as the nursery is concerned, the first few weeks she'll be in here with us, and the bassinette is all set up and ready. We've got the basics, and a bit beyond. Everything's washed and ready. Neither of us is experienced at this, but I think we're gonna be fine."

"Okay."

She watched as he picked up the phone, grinning at whatever messages Owen had sent. He noted the times in a small notepad he pulled from his pocket and smiled at her. "Let me know when you're ready to get up. No rush."

The steel bands tightened around her belly and low back again. More fluid gushed out from between her legs, joining the puddle on the floor. She breathed slowly, focused inwards as the pain came towards her in a rush, clawing at her control before it eased. The baby moved in tiny increments, no longer the swooping changes in position she'd become accustomed to. As the contraction eased, Alace took in a deep breath, surprised at how easily it came. *The baby's moving down.* The reality of what was happening hit her like a train, and Alace looked up in time to see Eric stride out of the bathroom. His smile was like a blinding beam of happiness, heating her from the outside in. *The baby's coming.*

"You need to call your mom. I had another contraction. Things feel like they're moving fast, Eric." She swallowed. "Maybe call the doctor, too? See what he thinks we should do about staying here or going to the hospital?"

"I have a call in to his service. They said he was at the hospital already, so we can expect a response quickly. I'll wait to talk to Mom until after, keep the suspense to a minimum." He dropped a towel on the floor and knelt between her feet. "Keep me from having to field her every-five-minutes texts, too."

After the rocky start to their pregnancy, Alace had been wary of letting anyone know about the baby. She had become seriously fond of Eric's mother, and the woman had taken Alace to her heart. That whole relationship wasn't something Alace knew how to navigate, so she'd left most of the talking to Eric. The moment they'd told Phoebe about the pregnancy, she'd flown from Malibu to spend a week in which Alace was forced to idle during the day, making up the work after her mother-in-law had gone to bed. During that week, Phoebe had bought everything needed for the nursery, and Alace had slowly realized her mother-in-law's tastes were in line with her own. One of the purchases was a gorgeous sleigh crib Eric had yet to put together.

"Okay, up you come." Eric's hands under her elbows lifted, and she was on her feet. He'd laid a trail of towels to her work chair, which he'd carefully draped with a double layer of towels. "Off with that." Her wet sleepwear went up and was gone, leaving her chilled, skin pebbling with gooseflesh. Then a nightgown came down, fit over her upraised hands and arms, and arranged until her head poked through the neck hole. "Let's go sit, yeah?" She shuffled with him towards the chair, conscious of the wetness trickling down her legs. At least the gushing waves of fluid had stopped. "And down."

The moment her ass touched the chair, another contraction took control of her body, the cramping sensation more acute than before. She groaned and folded an arm over her belly, fingers spread where the pain was the greatest.

"Another?" Eric's voice held an edge, and she nodded, then realized he'd missed one entirely. The thought was lost in the pain as it crashed against her.

Alace allowed herself to sink inside it again, focusing on the individual areas of her body impacted by the implacable process of bringing a child to air. Her pelvis hurt, aching worse than it had in days. *Moving and spreading to make room for her.* The walls of Alace's uterus were rigid, tightly drawn into a barrel. *This is natural. I just need to work with it.*

"Beloved?"

Needing silence, Alace waved her hand at him, chin buried to her chest as she breathed and breathed, pulse pounding in her throat. She counted each rise and fall of her ribs, the tension in her muscles forcing the pace of steady and slow, Alace going with the dictates of her body. The pain began ebbing, and she blinked as she glanced around, surprised to see nothing had changed in the room. It had felt like she'd been wholly focused on merely breathing for a hundred years. Eric knelt in front of her, palm cupping her cheek.

"The doctor says we should head in now. Something about transition phase." Eric's face was pale. "I'm going to carry you to the car, Alace. We need to go. Now."

"Okay." She scooted forwards in the chair, sodden towels sliding with her. "Oof." She tried to rise and failed, dropping back to the chair, which rolled backwards. "I'm a mess." One hand on her belly, she looked at Eric. "I'm ready, though. I wasn't sure, you know? Before? But I am now. I'm ready."

Eric brushed a kiss across her lips as he gathered her into his arms. "You've always been ready, Alace, my love. You've just given yourself permission now."

CHAPTER FOUR

Owen

The blank surface of the computer monitor mocked him.

Alace is having her baby. Owen scratched at his ear, fingertips finding the tiny ball of gristle and scar tissue in the center of the lobe, the only remnant of the boy he'd once been.

Growing up in the middle of a big family, massive gatherings held every summer meant anyone who held an iota of relationship to the Marcuses, his father's family, or the Thandalls, his mother's family, were invited. It was not unheard of to have more than a hundred people on his parents' farm for the three-day-long reunion. That kind of persistent familial connection was what he'd always seen in the future for himself. Not taking over the land or business, that was for his older siblings, but he'd always expected there would be a place for him, too. The military had never been intended to be a lifelong career. He'd seen it as an opportunity to see the world for a couple of years and earn the chance of having college paid for.

Due to transportation delays, his first leave from basic had been eaten up simply getting to his specialist training docket. Then right after that training ended, a spot opened up unexpectedly for a coveted position. Scheduling for all of that meant the first time he'd gotten to go home after signing up was nearly a year later, when he'd arrived barely in time for the reunion.

He pinched his earlobe, letting the pain zing through him.

His ex-girlfriend had been at the reunion, which didn't make sense. Until she'd turned around with heavily laden arms, and Owen had encountered his own eyes in the face of the prettiest little baby girl he'd ever laid eyes on.

Emma.

Owen abruptly pushed up from the chair and stalked out of his office towards the kitchen. The nightlight was still on in Kelly's room, and he slowed, coming to a stop where he could see the boy.

Curled into a tight ball, Kelly had positioned his hands protectively, one covering his crotch, the other twisted into a fist in front of his throat, holding tightly to nothing. The bath had revealed a lot of what he'd taken to be bruising on the boy's face was a layer of dirt, and with that washed away, Kelly looked much younger than the thirteen he'd claimed. The soil staining the boy's hands and knees hadn't come out no matter the gentle persistence with which Owen had scrubbed. Swallowing hard to drive a swell of nausea back down, he took a cautious step into the room. Listening to Kelly breathe from here wasn't a great diagnostic tool, but the bubbling rasp that had so worried Owen was no longer present. He blinked and caught a shine in Kelly's face, suddenly uncertain the boy was still sleeping. The hair that fell over his forehead shielded his eyes from direct view.

"You up?" Not a whisper, but not a loud voice. If Kelly was indeed asleep, Owen's question was unlikely to wake him.

Moving swiftly, Kelly retreated along the mattress until his back was to the headboard. The move was one Owen had seen many a returning soldier make. *Boy's been to hell and back again*. Making a keening sound, Kelly fumbled frantically at his neck and Owen realized the boy was groping for the wide collar the man who'd owned him had made him wear. Finally reassured it was still gone, Kelly stopped the sound and slumped, shoulders rounding down in exhaustion that had everything to do with the weeks he'd been a prisoner. The way his gaze moved around the room indicated he was immediately alert, but his expression showed no fear. *It was just a reaction to his situation, not me. Nothin' personal.* "You find Shiloh? Anything?"

Owen shook his head. "Not yet. I might have a way to identify the location, though. I wanted to check on you before I got started. You hungry? Need a drink or anything?"

"No." Curling down, Kelly made a nest for himself on the pillows. Feet tucked underneath the shirt Owen had put on him to sleep in, the boy wrapped his arms around his knees and waist. Making himself a small target for any aggression. The position told Owen as much as any story the boy had related so far. His voice held the weight of tears when he reminded Owen, "Just need to find Shiloh."

Owen studied him, nodded briefly, and left the room without responding. Kelly's misery was oppressive, suffocating. It was clear the boy didn't honestly think Owen could find his sister. Not before terrible things could happen to her. Maybe not alive.

Back in the office, he logged into his system and entered the private VPN info Alace had drilled into his head. Once there, he was able to navigate into the folder he needed, finding all the sorted info Alace had promised would be there. She hadn't skimped on anything, and once again, he recognized the enormous benefits of having someone like her on his side.

Alace is having a baby.

He scratched the lobe of his ear, pulling the neck of his shirt up over his mouth. He opened the first folder and dove in, reading through verbose auction notes about the buyers and the lots they'd bid on. Six other male/female sibling pairs had sold on the same night, but it was easy enough to recognize Kelly by the description of him. With the buyer identified, Owen settled into a rhythm of digging through the info Alace had provided to find various tidbits needed to craft inquiries, then circling out to the darknet to chase the info down there. The buyer had a prominent profile on multiple forums, with a high confidence rating, higher even than Alace's alts. *Shit*.

Owen followed the trail, building a portfolio of the man until he stumbled on what he'd hoped for.

A mistake.

This man wasn't one of those Alace had already traced land purchases for, which meant Owen was casting nets in the dark. His net eventually snagged on a detail with the opportunity to give him the break he needed. The man had uploaded images of his constructed cabin and lean-to for his pack. That's what he always called them, the children he bought—and sold. Owen had found him as a source noted by buyers for several single children. After securing himself a pair, at times he'd keep one and dispose of the other. Or perhaps disposed of one as he had Kelly, and then rid himself of the remaining child if they turned out to be suboptimal for his purposes as well.

The mistake he'd made in those images was threefold.

First, he hadn't stripped the metadata from the images, which in this case provided an exact location marker. Within minutes Owen was studying satellite imagery of the site, confirming the existence of both the cabin and outbuilding Kelly'd described. The second mistake was in going back to the same reseller for one of his returns. The boy had talked about a man until the name had made it into a set of business notes about the source. *Earl.* The third mistake was with one of the images where he hadn't bothered to blur out the make and model of his truck shown in the distance. From that, Owen was able to find his license, lock down his name, verify a home address—and the fact he had three biological children. Owen grimaced when he realized they danced around Kelly's age like stair-stepped siblings.

The crux of security was to have something you know, something you have, and something you are.

Earl Warrant wasn't the smartest of perverts.

And Owen now owned him. Earl might not know it yet, but it was true.

Name, social, birth, family info—and tucked into a folder hidden in the man's vulnerable cloud storage—the deed for an isolated cabin near a river in upstate New York. Within three hundred miles of the campground Owen had been in yesterday morning. *Just like the others Alace found. Definitely a fetish ring.*

Owen set aside the personal information he'd uncovered. That would be for Alace to deal with. She did the paperwork, he would handle the wetwork.

A noise behind him had Owen turning around. Kelly stood slumped in the doorway.

"You hungry, kiddo?" He got a nod in response. "Okay. Give me half a minute to shut stuff down." As Owen closed out of connections, he kept an eye on Kelly drifting closer. Minimizing the final window flashed the image of the cabin on the screen.

"That's it." Kelly's shocked voice shouldn't have offended Owen, but it did. *What, does the kid not realize I keep my word, always?* "You found him? That's the place. The cabin. When can we go get Shiloh?"

"*We* aren't going anywhere." Owen began the shutdown routine for the computer and took a breath before spinning slowly to face the boy. Just from the kid's expression, Owen knew he'd be in for a battle. "When I'm ready, I'll go."

"You can't leave me here. I won't stay." Kelly's chin jutted stubbornly. The fire in his eyes was one of the first real signs of the boy's personality Owen had seen. He hated like hell to be the one who'd squash that bit of spirit, but there was no way he could let the boy believe he'd be in on what he'd expect would be the rescue mission. The real mission would be far different, filled with red and pain. And redemption, as Owen would be releasing more children back to their homes.

A memory of a dusty compound from Central America flashed through his mind, the acrid scent of terror filling his nostrils. That had been the first mission after he'd lost Emma, and when he'd seen a tiny girl about her age, dark eyes staring up at her tormenter, it hadn't been a mere decision to alter the trajectory of the mission. It had been a soul-deep imperative.

He shook his head, forcing those thoughts to the back of his mind where they stayed. Never leaving him because it was his fault Emma was dead, and no matter how many kids he saved, he'd still never find redemption. The boxed-up, shoved-down, painful thoughts were his purgatory, the knowledge his crucifix.

Focused glare aimed at Kelly, Owen pulled in a deep breath before laying down the law. "You will if you want to see Shiloh again." The instant those words were out of his mouth, Owen regretted them. Kelly's flinch was huge, as if he'd been surprised by a physical blow. Owen had taken it too far, been too harsh, a needless cruelty used against a boy already brutalized by monsters. *Other monsters.* "I didn't mean it that way, kid. That's not..." Mouth twisting against the emotions swelling inside him, Owen shook his head, not reaching out because he knew Kelly would reject any contact right now. Regret kept his tone quiet, his words simple as he tried to explain. "What I meant to say is I don't work with folks. I do my stuff alone."

"If I promise to stay right here, will you go get her now? I won't be bad. I promise. I'd wait in that bedroom. Wouldn't leave." Kelly's eyes glassed over as he stared into Owen's eyes, growing desperation visible on his features. He tried to strike a bargain. "Now that you know where she is. You can save her. Like you saved me. I won't get in the way. You don't have to worry about me. I know how to behave. I'll be good." As the boy spoke, each word appeared to be another assault against the uncertain control of his emotions, and by the final syllable, his lips were quivering uncontrollably.

Owen's arms were heavy, dragged down with the remembered weight of the boy as he carried him out of the woods, carried him into this house. There was nothing he more wanted to do in this moment than gather Kelly close and promise him everything would be all right. He couldn't do that. He couldn't let this kid get any deeper under his skin than he was already, and promising something like that would be the equivalent of a blood oath for Owen. Instead, he did what he could. He told the truth, trusting Kelly to be able to take it on.

"I have to learn more. I have to know exactly what to expect. I know where the man's real house is now, too, and I've got eyes on it." Owen had sent a signal to the video doorbells of the houses across the street, changing not only their sensitivity but the routing of alerts. When they spotted a vehicle leaving Warrant's house, he'd know. "One day at the most and I'll have what I need." He pressed his palm to his chest, hoping the kid would understand this was a promise he wouldn't break for anything. "One day, one day only, and I promise I'll go get Shiloh."

Kelly's head dipped and shook, more a tremor than a nod, and he took a jerky step towards Owen. Unsure, Owen stretched out a hand, ready to catch the boy if he fell. At his movement, Kelly stumbled into a slumping run, crashing to a halt against Owen's chest. His arms wrapped around the boy instinctively, holding him upright, as Kelly's fingers wound into his shirt. The boy was crying, great whooping sobs of grief and relief, a dam of control that had been under pressure for so long it had finally shattered.

"I got you." Owen spoke the only words he could think of, carefully cradling the boy to him. "I got you." He repeated the words, counting Kelly's breaths, mentally gripping tightly to the single thread of control that was holding him together. "I got you."

"You—" Kelly hauled in a giant breath, his shoulders hitching up and down. "You promise?"

"I promise you. Only hours from now I'll be on my way. I'll be on my way and I'll do my best to bring her back. I'll go and I'll do my best." Owen let his eyes slide closed, darkness swooping in around him, the wetness against his chest proof against the monsters that so often plagued him. "I've got you, and I promise you." He settled back in his chair and let Kelly climb into his lap, curling up against him much as he had the pillows earlier, now with the extra barrier of Owen's arms to hold the world at bay.

As Owen swallowed back his own tears, listening to the boy continuing to weep, his thoughts weren't what he'd expected. Instead of the *I'm so fucked* he might have thought only a day ago, his focus was on helping make everything about Kelly's life better. Starting with bringing his little sister here, dragging her straight out of hell to do it if he had to.

An hour later, he sat opposite the boy at the breakfast bar, having carried him there and placed him carefully on a stool. Owen's sweatshirt was on the boy's frame, plucked from his own body when Kelly had shivered. Scrambled eggs, crispy bacon, and toast with a smear of butter and jam sat on plates in front of each of them.

Kelly was perched on top of his stool, knees drawn up and under the shirt, eating with his hands. Utilizing a fork was beyond him in this frame of mind, and Owen didn't tell him he needed to do otherwise. No need to put more stress on the boy when it simply wasn't necessary.

"Is there anything else about the man you think I should know?" Kelly had expressed a strong interest in doing what he could to help Owen, and while he'd already shared a lot, Owen wondered if there was more the boy might have to say if given the opening. "Do you remember what his normal routine was when he'd arrive at the cabin? Little details can really help me."

Kelly's eyes glittered behind the fall of hair covering part of his face. He studied Owen, paused in the act of taking a bite of toast. "Like what does he do?" Owen nodded, and Kelly sat upright, tossing the hair out of his eyes. With his wrists balanced on his knees, the food dangled, forgotten as he thought hard about Owen's question. "Before he gets there, he checks the batteries. They're in a wooden box outside the wire. He checks those, and if we didn't hear his truck beforehand, we'd hear the hum as he turned up the voltage. The collars let us know." He raised a hand, fingers gliding down his bare neck, a smear of jam left in their wake. "That way, we're waiting at the porch when he drives up, like he likes. Checking his pack, he called it. If one of us was sick and couldn't go to the porch, he'd go looking for us. The shed for the pack is positioned so he can see it from his back porch, but not the front. He didn't like it if he had to go looking for us."

"The batteries keeping the electric fence live are outside the area secured by the wire itself?" That made a brutal kind of sense, actually. If the power source was within the grasp of the older kids, they would have made quick work of disabling it and escaping. "So he stops to do maintenance and then drives into the yard?" Kelly nodded, and Owen let the boy see his pleasure, giving him a quick smile in response. "That's great. Yeah, that's exactly the kind of thing I need to know. What about other visitors? Did he ever bring anyone with him when he came?" This was a fishing expedition to see if any of the same-interest buyers had ever come calling. "Or was it always just Earl, I mean the man?"

"It was just the man. A couple of times he left with one of the pack in the crates in the back of his truck, but while me and Shiloh were there, he never brought anyone in with him. Could hear him talking to people in the cabin, but they weren't actually there. Like a phone call or something." Kelly took a bite of the toast, shifting the bread to one side of his mouth, talking as he chewed. "Both times when he took one of the pack away, it was older kids, ones who'd been there a while." He swallowed, took another bite, and performed the same process of shifting it to one cheek, chipmunk-style. "Hey, Owen, you think he took them to the same place he took me? You think they're out there, waiting for someone to find them?" Kelly's bright eyes dimmed. "You don't think he'd take Shiloh there, do you? She'd be afraid in the woods. She's scared of the dark and being alone."

"No, Kelly. I don't think he's taken Shiloh to the forest. As to whether he's ever taken any of the children to where he dropped you off, I can't say. I didn't see any of them yesterday." He shifted a strip of bacon from his plate to Kelly's, enjoying the boy's appreciative if brief smile. "I did see you. I'm glad I was there when I was. Another thirty minutes and I'd've been walking away, so I'm real glad you woke up when you did."

"So your gatherers are working right now?" That was how he'd explained how he was finding the information needed for him to plan a successful attack on Earl's compound. The description of the scripts set free on the darknet to search and find all of Earl's vulnerabilities had morphed into Owen having helpers. Gatherers, as Kelly had nicknamed them. "When will you know that they're done?"

"I'll get an alert." As he spoke, the phone in his pocket buzzed against his leg, and he held his breath. It had been a simple one-second signal. If it were followed by a more complex signal, it would indicate his searches had been successful. If the one-second pulse continued, Owen would need to return to his computer to see what else needed attention. The device buzzed again, another single-second vibration. *Here we go.* "Hey, bud, you stay there and finish eating, okay? I gotta check on something quick." He shoved his plate towards Kelly. "I'm done, so if you want more bacon, help yourself."

He stood and walked around the breakfast bar, and couldn't stop himself from reaching out to smooth his hand over Kelly's skull, fingers threading through the boy's thick hair. "I'll be back in a minute." Kelly made a sound, his mouth crammed full of toast as his hands stretched towards the food Owen had left on his plate. "Stay here."

In his office, he flipped the monitor on and angled it away from the doorway, just in case Kelly followed him faster than expected. A quick review showed him Earl's vehicle on the move, the man's mass framed in the driver-side window. Owen watched the route taken, keying up a real-time map to track his progress. It was only a couple of minutes later that his destination became clear. The man was headed to the compound.

Shit.

Owen couldn't wait for additional information. Whatever advantage he'd had gained by gathering knowledge had run out. There was no more time. He needed to leave now and drive like hell to beat the man there, sort out what kind of a coup he could stage given the presence of so many children, and locate and rescue Shiloh. The other kids too, of course, but for them, the rescue would entail calling the authorities. Owen intended Kelly and Shiloh to disappear as if they'd never been Earl's victims.

"Think like Alace." He rocked his head back and stared at the ceiling, gaze tracing the faint patterns he could make out in the textured surface. "How can I slow the man's roll?" He could dispatch a fake BOLO easily enough, but he wanted to slow the man, not keep him from showing up entirely. The vehicle's age was working against him, no onboard systems to hijack and foil performance. "Think, man." He could coordinate a blockade that would be looking for a different vehicle, effectively slowing Earl without making him abandon his trip to the remote and isolated cabin. *Hmmmm.*

"Or I can let him make his little trip, and trip-trap him at the actual compound." Owen straightened in the chair and stared at the monitor, a plan starting to take shape. He clicked the mouse and navigated to the imagery of the compound, measuring the distance of the private road to the cabin from the country highway. Earl wouldn't be restricted to the circumference of the entrapping electric fence. If Owen came up on the backside of the cabin and raised the man's interest, he could easily draw the asshole out. "Maybe I'm trying to make this Alace-elegant." He'd never intended Earl to live through the encounter. "Why make it harder than it needs to be?"

"Kelly," he called, pushing away from the computer desk as he leaned over, shutting the system down. "You still want to go with me to save Shiloh?"

***

Alace

Eyes closed, Alace let her chin drop to her chest as she took in a deep breath. They were still waiting on the anesthesiologist to arrive, which meant no epidural yet, and the full fury of each contraction remained her current reality.

She licked her lips. Something cold touched the edge of her mouth and Alace jerked back, her hand coming up defensively. A cup and spoon went flying, ice scattering across the blanket covering her bottom half. Eric stared at her, a growing smirk stretching his lips.

"Shut it." Alace resumed her previous position, keeping her eyes slitted open, this time to watch for another approach. In the three hours they'd been at the hospital so far, Eric had done something similar twice before. If she didn't know better, she'd think he was baiting her somehow. "Let me breathe."

"What can I do, Alace?" The stark helplessness in his voice made her look directly at him. It wasn't often Eric showed any uncertainty, but the smile was erased completely, his brows drawn together in a clump of angst that told her this was perhaps more uncomfortable for him, if for a different reason. "I want to do something."

"There's nothing for either of us to do." The progression of her labor had slowed during the trip to the hospital, something the labor nurse told Eric wasn't surprising. It had given Alace a chance to feel less out of control for a few minutes.

The cycle of contractions had grown familiar at last, and the waves of pain and pressure were predictable. She was currently in the all-too-brief lull between the peaks, her short opportunity to regroup and ready herself. Alace had found the progression oddly comforting, and she'd joked to Eric that it was nice to know her body knew what to do, even if she didn't have a clue. He hadn't found it amusing. She hadn't found his attitude amusing, either, so they were even on that one at least.

"Ah." Alace grabbed the rails on the sides of the bed as a strong contraction stiffened the walls of her uterus. "Oh, man." She pulled in quick breaths through her nose, blowing them out in a controlled fashion. "Oh, Jesus." The muscles in her legs tightened involuntarily, the intense spasm causing her heels to drag up the bed until they were planted on the thin mattress. "God, Eric." Alace dipped her chin towards her neck, gaze fixed on the changing topography of her belly. She grunted and pulled, simultaneously pushing with her feet. "This is different." Each word came out on a bitten-off howl, the pain threatening to break her in half.

"Alace." Eric's voice was thin with concern. "Don't, baby."

"What?" She didn't have time to wonder what he meant, intent on following her body's lead down this rabbit hole of relief-seeking that felt so right.

"I don't think you're supposed to do that." His hand covered hers on the railing. "Let go."

"What?" Nothing he said made sense. His fingers were cold, her body like a furnace in contrast, with sweat beading across her forehead and trailing down her temples.

"Alace, stop it." Eric's other hand landed on her stomach, the bump that was the cause of all this, the temporary prison for their child who was now fighting against her body to make her way into the world.

He can't stop it. The thought burst into her mind fully formed. The course of her labor had changed, and now it felt like being swept along in an avalanche. *She* couldn't stop this now if she wanted.

This is his fault. Men and their penises were the cause of pregnancies all over the world. Sure, she'd talked about a baby in a someday way, but she hadn't meant now. Hadn't meant today.

The contraction slowed, easing slightly, and Alace deliberately turned her head to face Eric, baring her teeth at him. "Fuckin' make me."

The renewed expression of uncertainty on his face would have been comical in any other setting. Right now, Alace failed to find any sliver of humor inside her. She kicked off the blankets and got onto her knees, steadying herself by using the same handrails she'd been yanking on only moments before.

"Alace, what are you doing?" He slipped an arm around her shoulders, and she leaned against him briefly, straightening when another contraction surged over her like a never-ending tide of pain. Eric's grip balanced her, and Alace gave up control to him, trusting him to shore her up without being told or asked. "Baby, should I get the nurse?"

Head swinging back and forth, Alace bent double, groaning deeply, the volume and timbre of the guttural sound shocking as it rolled out of her. She reached between her legs and felt her sex bulging.

"We need some help in here." He didn't move, didn't shift away from where his strength kept her upright, but Eric called out loudly. "We need some help in here, please."

Alace had no attention for anything other than him and her body, and this thing they were going through. She kept her hand between her legs, feeling the ebb and flow of the baby's descent as the contraction grew more intense. The pain was inexorable, all-consuming, so much so that Alace didn't flinch when other hands landed on her body, gloved hands deftly exploring alongside her own. There was a hum of conversation she couldn't be bothered with, dialed in on the changes in the process she'd become so accustomed to.

Demanding touches tugged and pulled, and Alace went with them, the contraction over, for now, her muscles like noodles, bones like jelly. On her back but propped high with pillows and Eric's arm around her shoulders, she stared down her body and into a pair of bright eyes she remembered. The doctor looked at her over the top edge of a mask, the crinkles next to his eyes exposing the smile hidden behind the paper.

"Ready to have this baby, Alace?" He paused and appeared to be sincerely waiting on a response, so Alace nodded once, the movement short and sharp. "Okay, let's do this thing. I'll need your help, Alace. We're going to work together to make it happen." Another pause, ended when she nodded a second time, the same abrupt movement from before. "When I tell you to, I want you to push exactly like you were before. We'll do this together in a little more controlled fashion than you'd worked out yourself."

The monitor next to the bed beeped, and the graph line took on a hockey-stick incline. Alace took in as deep a breath as she could manage, maintaining that eye contact with the doctor the whole time. "Ready."

"Okay then, here we go. I want you to push, Alace. Push hard. Push. Daddy, help Mommy sit up a little more." Eric's arm flexed and lifted her, increasing the angle of her body. She reached out, fingers grasping at nothing as she bore down. "Push, Alace. Push, push, push, push. Perfect. Keep it up, this little one is as eager as you are. Okay, stop pushing, you can stop now. Goodness, if the old wives' tales are true, I bet you've had an upset stomach through the pregnancy, because this little one has a head full of thick hair."

Eric eased her back against the pillows, leaning far over the bed to stay in contact with her. She looked up and saw his gaze was fixed on the doctor, much as hers had been.

It went that way for a few more contractions, until Alace was aware of something shifting inside her. The intense pressure, the brutal pain, the groaning effort of pushing and pushing and *pushing* gave way in an instant to a liquid relief. Her head dipped forwards, and she watched—*oh my God*—as the doctor lifted something—*that's my baby*—and cradled the infant in his arms, head angled down as he deftly manipulated something. Alace experienced a full-body shiver as the room filled with a coo, then a cough, and finally a rising, thin wail.

"It's a girl."

Hands were on Alace, adjusting the front of her gown, snaps pulled apart to bare her chest, and then the baby, still slightly bloody and wet and hiccupping with tiny, beautiful cries, was placed there. Skin to skin, Alace wrapped her arms around her daughter, cradling her close, holding her tenderly, staring down into a tiny face she'd only seen in shades of gray before.

"Oh, Eric." She raised a trembling hand, drawing a single fingertip along the baby's nose, allowing it to gently bump over teeny lips and the curve of a petite chin. "She's…"

Eric's hand covered the baby's back, joining Alace's in holding the child close. He bent and pressed his lips to Alace's temple, then lifted one of the baby's hands, a look of wonder coming over his face when those tiny fingers tightened, wrapping around his.

"Oh, my God. She's perfect." He lifted each of the baby's fingers in turn, dusting a kiss across each. "Ten fingers." Alace improved the baby's position, angling her so she could see the child's entire body.

"Ten toes." Alace lifted her chin, and Eric met her halfway, the kiss they shared chaste, closed-mouthed, but filled with the deepest, most soul-shaking passion she'd ever felt. "She's perfect."

"Lila." He was the first to call their daughter by name, using the one they'd agreed upon days ago. "Lila Sue. Oh, my heart. Welcome to the world. I love you, beloved. Both of you. So much."

"I love you, too, Eric Ward." Alace leaned against Eric's shoulder as he slipped his head in beside hers. Falling silent, they stayed like that until the nurses interrupted to take the baby for measuring and weighing. Alace was struck dumb with emotions flooding through her as they gazed with love at the daughter they held.

Chapter Five

Owen

"We got this, right?" Walking through the parking lot, Owen looked down at Kelly, trotting alongside him in a losing effort to keep up with Owen's long strides. Realizing how fast he was walking, he slowed slightly, giving Kelly a chance to catch up more easily. "You know what to do?"

Kelly smiled up at him, and if he didn't know the boy as well as he already did, Owen wouldn't have seen the shadows in his gaze, wouldn't have seen the tension in his expression. He looked like any boy out early on a Saturday shopping excursion. Then Kelly did something that ripped that illusion like wet tissue paper, rocking Owen to the core.

Fingers fidgeting with the hem of his long-sleeved T-shirt, he quietly agreed, "Yes, Daddy."

Pain exploded behind his eyes as Owen fought the memories attempting to drag him down to hell. Fingers scrubbing across his forehead, he ignored the tear-swollen images of Emma's mother that tried to overwhelm. His head pounded as he stubbornly shoved away memories about the case notes and photographs he should have never had access to, but he'd said "fuck the rules" because he'd needed to know. Couldn't have lived with himself if he hadn't paid tribute to Emma's suffering and death in the only way he'd known.

But within the knowing came the plan, and the plan was the only thing that had saved him through the years. The plan and the missions. Without the missions, he'd have eaten his gun long ago, ending the agony once and for all. But he'd had the missions, had found and worked through the clues, putting puzzles together, saving children and disenfranchised people from slavery and pain. *I did. I've helped set them free.* The missions each had carried a two-fold purpose, and he'd hung tightly to that rope woven not from hope but desperation.

Daddy.

Tugging on his hand brought him back to himself. Kelly's expression was frightened, panicked, his attempts to steer Owen back towards the car laughable. Except that was endearing in its own way, this little weighs-nothing kid, trying to take care of Owen by getting him out of the public eye.

"I'm okay." That was the first direct lie he'd told Kelly, and it burned his throat like fire. He deliberately clipped the tip of his tongue with his teeth, hard enough to beat back the overwhelming emotions threatening to crush him. *A little discomfort is nothing to what this kid's endured.* He couldn't let Kelly down. "Let's go get what we need." Kelly studied him, head tipped to one side, the intensity of his gaze laying Owen bare. It took effort, but he smoothed his expression, deliberately erasing any discomfort or worry from his face. "I'm good, Kelly. It's okay."

He had been tripped up by how far Kelly had been willing to take their little farce. Calling him Daddy hadn't been in the script, but he could see where it made sense and understood why it offered the perfect camouflage. "Seriously, you were perfect. Let's go get Shiloh and the others some clothing." The clothing had been Kelly's first suggestion after Owen had talked to him last night about the plan. Shiloh would be far more comfortable coming with Owen if Kelly were with him to vouch for his integrity, and all the children deserved to immediately start taking back their humanity. "Remember the story we're building."

"I remember. We're a family, a normal family." Kelly's smile wavered, but it was there. "A pretend family."

Fuck, that stings. Owen nodded, responding and rephrasing just enough so the words didn't make him nauseous, "You and me and Shiloh, we're gonna be family. Family sticks together." Owen was getting too deep and knew it, could see it now, how he'd already attached to the boy in unhealthy ways. Unhealthy for him at least. Kelly was getting a little bit of what he needed, probably had always needed, and Owen would turn himself inside out to keep giving it to him, no matter if it would kill him to eventually give the boy and his not-yet-met sister over to the authorities. An act which would only happen once Owen had a chance to run the dirty cop to the ground, the one who had ripped the siblings from their foster home and sold them into torment. Owen had told Kelly his plans, the high-level version of them anyway, and the boy had looked relieved that Owen not only believed him but had planned on making certain the kids would be safe before he threw them back into the system. Right now though, he had to immerse himself in the role of Kelly's not-pretend family to move either mission forwards. "So let's go get your sister that outfit she wants."

Inside the store, Owen was careful to keep his head angled away from the cameras. Not in a way that would trigger any security personnel who might be actively watching the feed, but more like a parent focused on their child, that downward position keeping the cameras from capturing anything other than an oblique profile.

Owen faltered as they reached the little girl section of the clothing options. The leggings and shirt Kelly held up were so small, so tiny, so much like something Emma would have worn—Owen had to take a moment to simply breathe through the pain that was never far away, pretending to study the offerings. Voice unexpectedly gruff, he told Kelly, "Those look good. You think they'll be the right size?" At Kelly's nod, he grabbed a package of underwear and socks to match, then a pair of easy slip-on shoes, holding them up for Kelly's approval. Nearly as an afterthought, he grabbed a booster seat for Shiloh, willfully ignoring the seeming permanence of the item. A single man didn't buy booster seats; that was something a real father would do. *Or a favorite uncle. I can be a favorite uncle.* He breathed in pain, breathed out a forced peace as he told himself a lie. *It's the law, that's all. It's just because it's the law.*

The other children would have less individualized choices for dressing after the mission concluded. Owen selected bulk packages of shirts with muted colors and similar options for some nondescript shorts. They'd be modestly covered, but if curious authorities attempted to look into the origin of the clothing they'd have a hard time pinpointing this specific store, since the same mass-produced articles were sold in literally hundreds of stores within fifty miles.

At the front of the store, Owen was scanning the items through the self-check area when he caught

Kelly staring at the candy display with a longing expression. Leaning down, he put his mouth close to Kelly's ear. "If you and Shiloh have a favorite, grab one, and you can share it afterwards on our way home. Just one, though. Do you remember how your stomach wasn't happy with the food that first day?" Kelly nodded, the scent of shampoo and boy wafting over Owen. "We don't want to make Shiloh sick on her first day out." Kelly's hand hovered over a package of a popular peanut butter candy, and Owen gave him a nudge. "Get it, bud. It'll be your celebration with her." Kelly's grip was so tight, Owen knew the candy was a mushed mess. He didn't scold, didn't offer anything other than grabbing a second bar, double scanning it so both were accounted for in the order total. When Kelly glanced up at him, he shrugged. "I might be hungry later." This way the kids would have one unmangled option.

Walking out to the car, Owen tripped when Kelly grabbed his hand, the boy's grip twining around his index finger. Kelly's head was tucked down, gaze fixed on their feet, and Owen studied him for the space of two strides. Fear rolled off the boy. Not a fear of Owen, but perhaps...a fear of rejection? Without missing a step, he reached down and grabbed the boy under the arms, swinging him up and astride his back. With a tiny cry, Kelly's thin arms wrapped around Owen's throat, latched on tight. Owen balanced the boy and the bags, giving a skipping bump every few steps to jostle Kelly. Finally, right before they arrived at the car, the boy giggled, and Owen's eyes sank closed in a slow blink.

Benediction.

Worth everything.

The trip went quickly, the droning of the tires interspersed by muted melodies from the radio. Kelly was asleep within half an hour of them leaving the store and dozed intermittently through the afternoon and evening. Owen used the time to continue his network searches. He'd thought to bring the subvocal rig with him that he and Alace had grown accustomed to using, and found it worked perfectly for the kind of tasks he had to do. Paired with the glasses, he had a heads-up display of not only what he was seeking, but what the responses were. All without Kelly hearing a thing.

As he zeroed in on the compound location, Owen sent Eric a text. It had been hours since he'd spoken to them last, but his hindbrain reminded him it was common knowledge that first babies took longer.

How goes it?

In response, he got an image that didn't translate through the rig, so he scanned around for the telltale glint of reflections, and not finding any visible police waiting for speeders, went ahead and picked up the phone and thumbed to the text app.

Alace lay on her side in a hospital bed, her body curled around a tiny pink blanket that had the cutest baby face peeking out, button nose framed by chubby cheeks worthy of a dozen gentle kisses. Her entire focus was on the child, and the intent expression of rapt adoration on her face took Owen's breath away.

Lila Sue Ward, 7lb 3oz, 21in – Mom and baby are doing well.

Owen had to swallow back his tears before he could manage a response, starting over twice when the microphone wouldn't pick up everything he wanted to say. Finally he got the message right and sent it.

That's a beautiful family right there. You're a lucky man, Eric Ward. Congratulations.

He rested the phone on his leg, hands back on the steering wheel, and let his gaze fix at the farthest reach of the headlights sweeping through the deepening twilight.

His Emma's middle name had been Sue. *There's no way Alace could know.* No doubt it was Eric's grandmother's name or something along those lines. Owen had worked hard to keep that part of his past private and was confident Alace had never stumbled on those details. His darknet persona that she'd first approached held the event in Central America as his breaking point, which it had been, no doubt.

What wasn't documented for that profile, or any of his others, was the mission before that one.

A sign came into view, and Owen flicked on his turn signal as he glanced in the mirror. Zero traffic on the road around him. *Perfect.* He was within eleven miles of the compound. Time to set the next pieces into motion.

Once off the highway, he identified the private road easily enough, lax chain suspended in a deep swoop across the rough, dirt-rutted lane. It was the work of moments to pick the lock, and he half secured it behind him, slipping the shackle of the padlock through the chain but without snapping the toe into place, making it easier to leave than arrive. Half the distance to the compound by his odometer, Owen found the clearing he'd marked on his map. The area had been exposed to enough sunshine during the day to leave the ground firm and provided ample cover to make hiding the vehicle simple. He backed the car off the lane and in between two trees, pleased with both the positioning and spacing.

Before exiting the car, he opened his laptop and turned on the satellite Wi-Fi device, having to wait only a breath before everything was connected. The imagery he'd requested was ready, and Owen quickly paged through the pictures of the compound. Taken less than half an hour ago, the photos showed the man's truck was parked exactly where expected. From the high-resolution pictures, Owen was able to find the protective enclosure Kelly had talked about, where the power supply for the restrictive electric fence was stored. Owen easily made out the shapes of what looked like a dozen kids sleeping with as many dogs, all scattered in the dirt around the bottom of the front porch.

He stared at the image for so long the tablet dimmed, threatening to go into hibernation mode. Shaking himself, he closed the photo, went to the secure VPN connection, and logged in to access the subnet he used to dig through the Internet's underbelly. Cursing when he saw a note from his service seller, he scowled at the message. One of his orders had been delayed, but he should be assured it was on its way. The guy had upgraded the package, and that had made up some of the lost time, which might mean he shouldn't be running much past his intended timeline after all.

Selecting the icon for his tablet, he began the process of downloading the controllers for the new drone currently headed blindly to a set of coordinates he'd provided the seller. It was a lease only, time purchased on a military-grade eight-prop model that could hover in steady mode nearly forever. That was one critical piece for the mission. The ability to broadcast a prerecorded sound at a specific decibel level was another. Once the software download finished, Owen opened the controller app and found the drone was preauthorized for the tablet's MAC address, exactly as he'd requested. It would mean having to ditch the tablet afterwards, but the security was worth it. No one could hack into the drone while he was controlling it. *Not even Alace.* His grin faded quickly, the memory of that beautiful photo shimmering before his eyes.

Owen hadn't been around when Emma was born. She'd already turned six months old the first time he'd laid eyes on her. But he suspected if someone had recorded the moment he'd seen and recognized his daughter, the expression on his face would have mirrored that on Alace's. The ex-girlfriend hadn't wanted the baby, and Owen knew he'd been lucky she had allowed the pregnancy to go to term. *I might never have had Emma. Would that have been better?* He'd posed the same question to himself innumerable times over the years, always coming down on the side of having her, even if for such a short time.

The device in his hands vibrated, bringing his attention back to the screen. The drone was within range, which meant it was time to start the next phase of the plan. He keyed in a command, waited for the acceptance code, and minimized the controller, locking the tablet. Once out of the car, he opened the trunk and eyed the equipment he'd packed before leaving home. Mental list verified, he began preparing. The tablet was the first item to be secured, fitting into a holder sewn inside his chest protector, accessible via a silent button closure. Other items had hook and loop closures, and he carefully applied them so there'd be no chance of accidental release and subsequent noise.

Once geared up, Owen used his fingerprint to unlock the under-trunk gun safe, retrieving the weaponry he'd previously decided upon. He stared down and hesitated, fingers trailing across a new gun Alace had gifted him with recently. *She's my good luck charm.* If Alace couldn't be in his head for this mission, the gun would still make him feel connected. It was the work of moments to swap out the guns, since they used the same ammunition, and he released a steadying breath once he had the new one settled in the holster.

Only when he was locked, loaded, and ready to go did he return to the passenger cabin of the car. He gazed inside where Kelly lay sleeping on the seat, measuring several of the slow, deep breaths of air the boy was taking. Curled underneath a warm blanket, clean, fed, safe—Kelly appeared to be a far cry away from the condition in which Owen had met him. *I've made a difference.* Squatting down in the space created by the opened door, he refused to follow that train of thought, cutting off any ideas about the future with brutal efficiency.

"Kelly." With that single word, the boy's stillness changed, shifting from easy relaxation to unmoving tension, breaths coming quick and shallow, dark eyes glittering behind that damned fall of hair. "It's time for us to start." With a flurry of abrupt movements, the boy shoved himself up and against the far door, staring across the space at Owen. Kelly scrubbed at his face with both palms as Owen asked, "Do you remember your part?"

Kelly sniffed hard, his mouth twisting. "Yeah. First thing is I hafta wait for twenty minutes." He shoved out an arm, showing Owen the watch that had been one of their purchases. "There's a timer. Then I put on the backpack and follow you down the road." He pointed out the front windshield at the two-rut track Owen had driven into the woods, the one that led to the cabin. "My job is to get Shiloh. I've got a blanket and some clothes for her in the backpack. I'm supposed to bring her here to the car. If no one sees me, it's better, but if she and I need to hide and wait, we will. You won't leave us behind. You'll find us."

Owen nodded slowly. Before the idea of including Kelly in the rescue, the main worry had been how to get Shiloh home to Kelly without further traumatizing the little girl. If it had been a shorter trip, he would have made different plans, but knowing there would be hours before they'd be back at his house, the only real option had been bringing Kelly along for her comfort.

"I'll kill the batteries before I go inside the wire, but none of the kids will know." Owen bared his teeth. That was a critical piece of information it had taken him nearly too long to tease out of Kelly. If the collars carried any kind of alert when the fence went down, the kids would scatter before Owen could control the situation. The risk of any of them being injured by a panicked flight through the dark woods and suffering hypothermia—or worse—simply wouldn't happen with this approach. "That gives you an opportunity to find Shiloh and make a break back to the car before any of them realize what's going on."

"What if he has something inside that tells him something's wrong?" Kelly's deep frown and expression of concentration would have been cute if the situation hadn't been so dire. The boy was trying to think around corners and help concoct a strategy, and Kelly's instinctive involvement in creating a solution made Owen's throat close a little. *Kid just needs a chance at a normal life.* "Won't he know you're coming then?"

"I expect he does. But I've got a device that will keep the monitoring system alive, not showing a fault on the line at all. The dogs won't be barking, either. He won't know I'm coming until I'm inside his cabin." Owen shrugged, the coat he'd put on over his rig settling into place. "If any kids see me coming, they won't sound an alarm, either. Not with what I'll be wearing." He hadn't shown it to Kelly, but after he'd described the mask he'd worn at the warehouse auction takedown a couple of weeks ago, the boy had cringed and nodded, exhibiting well-remembered fear associated with the image. The mask and accompanying bad associations should serve to manage the kids at least long enough to allow Owen entry to the cabin. The drone would control the dogs, emitting a persistent ultrasonic sound that would confuse and distract them. The drone would also provide an infrared view of the cabin and surrounding area, for Owen's review after he had Earl Warrant under control.

Twenty minutes wasn't long, but he had confidence he could both insert himself and gain the upper hand in that time period. Then he'd give Kelly half an hour to retrieve Shiloh and regain the security of the car. Only once he had seen the two kids inside the vehicle again would he deal with Warrant.

Just like not showing Kelly the mask kept Owen from turning into one of the monsters, hiding the truth of his actions from the boy would help preserve a little bit of that faith the kid seemed to have in him. Owen wasn't willing to give it up yet. He needed to know he'd still have Kelly's respect at the end of the day.

"Okay, bud. Sounds like we're ready to roll." He held out a fist and Kelly bumped his knuckles against Owen's. "Set the timer now." As Kelly ducked his head, looking at the watch, Owen extended a hand and tenderly tousled the boy's hair. "See you soon," he promised, then pressed the car door closed quietly, waiting for Kelly to look up, giving the boy's upraised thumb a nod.

Striding up the road, he ran through the plan again in his mind as he slipped gloves on each hand. Given the lane was in regular use by a heavy vehicle, he didn't have to worry about IEDs, allowing him to make good time. He retrieved the tablet and keyed it back up, checking on the drone video stream. The device was now in position over the cabin, and the image showed a tight ring of dark forest surrounding the clearing. Sending the drone higher, he allowed it to hover there until he saw his figure coming into range in the distance. There were no other heat signatures of any note nearby, so he brought the drone back down to the optimal height and studied the forms of the children and dogs.

Owen frowned when he saw three heat signatures inside the cabin. One human form was large, similar in size to Owen's, one form was smaller, most likely a child, and one was clearly a dog. They were all three clustered together in a corner of the cabin, and Owen could only assume it meant they shared a bed.

Well, fuck.

Kelly hadn't mentioned Warrant keeping any of the kids inside as sequestered pets. *That was before he dumped Kelly to die, leaving Shiloh defenseless.* Somehow, Owen knew what he was going to find when he entered that cabin, and the idea made his stomach churn. Even if it wasn't Shiloh, the idea of the man abusing any of the kids in that way promised to earn him a harder death. *Now to sort out what this means to the changed plan.* He picked up speed, traveling at a quick trot to put more distance between him and where Kelly would begin his trek. It might gain him five extra minutes, and he planned on using each of them wisely.

Well before he was ready, Owen could see the forest falling away from the road ahead, thinning and sweeping out to each side in a wide arc, making up the outer circumference of the clearing that held the cabin. Before he got any closer, he set the drone's audio system to broadcast. Immediately, he saw the heat signatures representing the dogs stir and get to their feet, pacing back and forth in short arcs.

Kneeling next to the tiny enclosure that housed the battery array, he yanked the door open, surprised there was no lock or security in place. Of course, the presence of the wire prevented the kids from accessing it, so it made a kind of backwards sense Warrant would see no reason to lock it up. *Not the sharpest crayon in the box.* Owen tapped a fingertip against his chest to activate a dim light bar he'd strapped to the harness. He pulled out his jumper, positioning the alligator clips expertly and pausing only for an instant to verify his accuracy. He attached a small battery pack to one of the clips and used a custom ohm-meter to test the results. Once certain everything was in place, he disconnected the terminals from the industrial batteries one at a time, ensuring the leads were laid to the side without causing a flash or spark, and without interfering with the bypass he'd put into place. He toggled his light off, giving his eyes a chance to adjust to the dark again.

A brief glance at the dimmed tablet screen showed the dogs had done as expected, migrating away from the sound and towards the far outside edge of the fenced-in area. They would have become conditioned exactly like the children, and if anticipating pain from close proximity, probably wouldn't encroach upon a broad swath of ground on the inside of the buried wire. Still, they'd moved towards the back of the house where the lean-to was, which put the house itself between him and them, and gave him even more protective cover against their alerting reaction. The dog's silhouette had disappeared from the cabin, and Owen wondered if there was an access door he didn't know about. *Probably a doggy door.* He dismissed the information, caring only that with the dog gone from inside, it left things wide open for him.

Moving at a crouched run, he darted through the yard and alongside Warrant's truck, bending to pull a wide-bladed knife from a sheath strapped to his calf. Two firm thrusts of the weapon later and the truck listed steeply to one side, the passenger side tires flat and useless. Owen's gaze went between the gray-hued screen on the tablet and the darkness ahead of him, where half a dozen children were curled into individual heaps on the cold ground. He easily identified himself, then mentally mapped his route to the cabin's door. Reaching into the tiny pack strapped to his waist, he brought out the mask matching the one he'd worn while working the warehouse mission and pulled it on, the wide elastic strap secure around the back of his head. He didn't like it, hadn't liked wearing it before, because the eyeholes restricted his field of vision. But the mask had become a critical piece of the plan tonight, which meant he had to simply deal.

Still in a crouch, he took the remembered pattern of strides and sidesteps at half speed, keeping each footfall as silent as possible. On the porch, he froze in place when a board underfoot groaned loudly. One of the dogs reacted, visible via the tablet, but none of the kids even moved. They were either too well-conditioned to remain still, or all truly sleeping through the aches of the cold night.

The door opened easily under his hand, the knob twisting without resistance as Owen let himself inside. *Knock, knock, motherfucker.* The original plan had been to incapacitate Warrant silently, giving Kelly a chance to find and remove Shiloh from the equation. Owen peered through the darkness, seeing the pale circle of a tiny face framed by a mass of tangled hair against the covers. Long tresses didn't mean it was Shiloh for certain, but at this point, Owen didn't hold out hope it would be any other child.

Owen was glad Kelly hadn't expressed any discomfort about the idea of trekking alone through the dark woods, something most kids would balk at. Knowing the boy would be walking on the rough driveway most of the way to the clearing and not through the woods proper, made it a little easier to bear. Now, Owen just had to hope Shiloh was made from the same tough stock, able to follow instructions to get her out of the cabin without losing her shit.

First up was to deal with Warrant.

Owen approached the bed, positively identified his target in the near dark, and leaned in with his hand positioned for a blood choke hold. Fingers digging into the puffy flesh of the man's neck, he compressed the internal and external carotid arteries for a count of thirty, angling for the vagus nerve as well, to slow the man's heartbeat. Owen wasn't concerned with causing brain damage but wanted a minimum two-minute window to restrain and gag the man.

Warrant's arms and legs flopped like an annoying dead weight, making it harder for Owen to wrestle the man into the position he'd planned. With the ankles secured and wrists finally tied behind the back, Owen efficiently threaded the ropes down through the footboard and up through the headboard of the bed. Snagging what looked like a dirty sock from the floor, Owen balled it up and stuffed it into Warrant's mouth. Owen shook a chem light and snapped the plastic tube, mixing the ingredients to emit a steady but dim light. With that illumination, he found the man's shirt hanging from the footboard and cut a strip of fabric, tying it in place around Warrant's lower face. Pre-cut strips of tape finished the layered gag, until Owen was satisfied with his handiwork.

Leaving his mask in place, he made his way around the bed to where the little girl lay on top of the covers. Her hands were knotted together, a strip of leather wrapped tightly around her wrists and secured through a loop in her collar to the leg of the bed. The placement meant she was bent awkwardly, scarcely able to change position at all. He pulled the blade from the sheath and severed the leather strap inches above her wrists. Working quickly, he unwrapped the bindings from around her limbs, carefully chafing the skin to stimulate circulation.

Owen realized Shiloh was awake, her eyes glittering in the low light. Like Kelly, she kept her chin down, masking her awareness. *I don't want her to associate me with this hellish place.* Owen raised his voice an octave, disguising himself as he told her soothingly, "Getting you out of here." She shook her head, gaze cutting over to where Warrant was beginning to stir. Without looking, Owen reached out and reapplied the blood choke hold, stilling the movements within seconds. In no time, Warrant was effectively knocked out with the induced syncope, and Owen had the use of both hands again.

The broad collar was next on his agenda, and Owen felt along the edges of the leather, quickly finding the overlapping area held in place with a tiny lock. The blade would be best for this, but the idea of bringing a blade that close to Shiloh and scaring her any more than she already had to be was abhorrent. Owen cast around quickly, his attention falling on the man's discarded pants. *Surely it can't be that easy.* There was a keyring in one pocket, one for the truck, one he assumed was for the man's home, and a jingling-jangling clump of keys each tiny enough to match the lock. The fourth one he fit to the lock turned easily, and the shackle clicked open.

Sight of the rough, reddened skin underneath the collar turned his stomach, as did the raised burn marks from the electric prods the man had used to keep the girl inside his little torture compound. Shiloh stared at him, at the mask keeping her from seeing him, his big hands cupping each side of her little neck, and she had no fear in her gaze. *Totally like her brother. She's tough as shit.*

Owen swept her up in his arms and walked to the front door, edging it open with his hip. Kelly stood in the yard near the truck, a large boy angled in front of him, fists drawn up to shoulder height. Kelly was talking, explaining the things Owen had authorized when he caught sight of Shiloh. The little girl scrambled, hands shoving at Owen in an effort not to escape, but simply to get on the ground. He set her down feet-first, and the moment she connected with the dirt, the little girl pelted towards Kelly, who was headed her way at a quick trot. Kelly looked at Owen over the girl's head as he wrapped an arm around her shoulders. The stare held for only a breath before Kelly turned her towards the road and the woods beyond.

Standing there watching as the little boy who'd had to be far too grown-up escorted his littler sister to safety, Owen took in a deep breath, the first since walking away from the car. Once beyond the dirt line where the fence was buried, the two kids paused, flashes of light color telling him Kelly was putting the clothing on Shiloh, making the rest of the walk more comfortable at least. Then they were gone, beyond where the scarce light could reach, following the lifeline of the road to the sanctuary of the car, and eventually to the freedom Owen had promised.

The boy who'd been talking to Kelly had turned and was staring at Owen. He took a halting step towards the porch, then teetered to a stop. "You gonna kill him?" Deeper than he'd expected, the voice held an edge of anger, and a hatred Owen experienced a strange kinship with. Owen nodded slowly, glad he'd retained the mask. The boy's chest expanded and held, then he exhaled on a rush. "Good. Kill him slow."

"Kid, what's your name?" Owen studied him, sheer physical size testifying the boy verged on the edge of adolescent, certain in his gut the kid wouldn't have lived another month in Warrant's care.

"Terrence." He backed up a step and his legs folded underneath him, depositing his body into a loose-limbed sitting position. "We aren't supposed to have names, but mine is Terrence."

"Terrence." He gave the boy that affirmation, not missing the downward jerk of his chin that spoke so eloquently of the pain the dehumanization had left behind. "After I leave, the police will come. They'll bring people to take care of you. Of all the kids."

"Not Kelly or Shiloh, though." Owen stared at him, then shook his head side to side in a slow arc. "Good. They deserve better. Far as I'm concerned, they were never here." Standing straight, Owen marveled at this boy's quick grasp of what he'd been asking for. "And neither were you."

A loud thump came from inside the cabin, and Owen was reminded that he was on a time constraint. "Thanks." Terrence slumped to the ground, curling himself into a ball. Owen shucked his jacket and swung the backpack off one shoulder, bringing it around to his chest so he could more easily dig through it. "I've got clothing for you and the other kids. Shirts and shorts, some socks. No shoes, those were too hard to transport." He held the packages out as he made his way down the short steps, crouching down well away from where Terrence lay. "When I'm gone, you and the other kids should stay out of the cabin." He ripped open a pack of shirts and gathered the hem of one in his hands. He leaned far over and tugged it down over Terrence's head, smoothing it into place as the boy struggled to get his arms through the sleeves. "It's not much, but it means you won't face the police naked."

"Kelly and Shiloh are lucky." Owen shook his head, dismissing the statement as he opened the shorts and socks and handed Terrence the additional clothing. "Yeah, they are." Terrence accepted the fabric, cradling it to his chest. "That"—he indicated the mask—"might be scary, but you're a good man underneath."

No, I'm not. Owen couldn't say as much to the boy, couldn't risk any kind of confession, so he chose to say nothing. With the remaining clothing selections piled around Terrence's feet, Owen stood and took a step back, slipping into his jacket. "Don't go into the cabin. Promise me."

"Oh, I can promise that. None of us want to be inside there. Nothing good ever happened there."

Inside the cabin, he found Warrant had worked his way halfway off the bed, arms and legs twisted painfully in their restraints as the knots tying him to the bedframe held tightly. From the position of the ball joint of one shoulder, Owen thought the man had probably dislocated it. The streaming tears and snot-filled nose gave weight to his suspicions. This wasn't just a panic reaction. This was real pain. *About fuckin' time.* He could see it was getting harder for Warrant to breathe, the gag not providing any leeway for acquiring additional air. "You need to control yourself or you're going to die from suffocation." As the tissues in Warrant's nostrils swelled, even less air made its way through, and it was only a couple of minutes before Warrant hung limp in his bonds. "You've effectively choked yourself out." He realized all he had to do was stand there, and Warrant would be dead within minutes. No dramatic speech, no flourish with the blade or gun, nothing to serve as notice that anything of note had happened here. *Maybe that's the better way for this trash.* Without calling attention to himself via the death, this could almost appear to be a gone-wrong death. *Watch and learn, grasshopper.*

Hands clasped behind his back, Owen prepared to stand sentinel on the death of Earl Warrant, witnessing the ignominious snuffing out of a life. It would happen without fanfare, and the moment when the man failed to take in another breath would be nearly anticlimactic.

Warrant's chest lifted with a heave, his body sucking in another lungful of air. Owen glanced at the covers strewn across the bed, gaze catching and holding on the smears of blood marking where Shiloh had lain. He'd ignored that while tending to her and getting her out of the cabin, leaving the challenges of dealing with what was pretty obviously a physical violation of her tiny body for later.

Warrant took in another stuttering breath, shoulders and chest hitching with the effort.

From the corner of Owen's eye, that evidence of Shiloh's abuse glared at him like a neon sign.

Owen could easily wait it out. Death wouldn't be long now.

He narrowed his eyes. Looked at the stain again. Remembered the fearlessness in the girl's face as she let him help her. Saw again the expression Kelly had as he held his sister close.

Looked at the stain again.

Where's the fun in that?

Bending at the waist, he tugged the knife he'd used a couple of times tonight from the sheath, idly flipping it end over end, the handle smacking the center of his palm each time. *He needs to pay. Pain and blood.* It would be the only way Owen would be able to sleep at night.

He stepped forwards, bringing the knife downwards with force, burying it into the man's meaty thigh with a thud. The tiny vibration against his palm stung slightly, and he shook his hand. With the blade safely stowed for transport, Owen lifted the body back to the bed and then removed the gag, staring down as Warrant's skin slowly turned from gray to pink as his lungs and heart worked overtime to save him. *He'll die the same.* Owen shook his head. *But if I can look at Kelly and tell him his little sister's attacker died slowly, it'll mean more if it was at my hands.* For all he'd shied from showing Shiloh that side of him, Owen knew Kelly well understood the monster inside.

When Warrant's eyes blinked open, Owen was there, bent close. One palm caressing the handle of the knife, he wiggled it side to side in a slow dance of steel against bone, the scraping tremors signaling each painful contact. "You're dying today." Warrant stared up past the edge of Owen's hand, clamped tightly over his mouth and nose. "Evil, vile man. Imagine if your own children were in this bed next to you, watchin' daddy suck up his last breaths." The man strained against the bonds holding him to the bed. "It'll be my pleasure to end you. I found you, tracked you, and now I get to deal with you. You and your sick buddies." Warrant's gaze flickered. It was only a millisecond of movement, a sideways tick when Owen mentioned his buddies, but the tell was seen and cataloged. "Gonna fuck you up so bad, your pretty wife won't be able to look at a picture of you without imaging your face like I'll leave it." No reaction. *Interesting.* "Your buddies won't miss you. No more perversion for them." Another tiny jerk towards the side and Owen deliberately turned his head, following the man's line of sight to a picture on the wall.

Shoving the sodden sock back into Warrant's mouth, Owen casually strolled around the bed, ignoring the muffled grunts behind him. He approached the picture, an innocuous pastoral scene completely out of place in the rough cabin, and ran a finger along the frame. The noises increased in volume, and he grinned, seeing only the flat features of the pale mask reflected in the glass covering the picture. A light tug revealed one side of the frame was attached to the wall, and Owen swung the entire unit out, allowing it to pivot on hidden hinges. Recessed shelves appeared, hidden by the picture. On the shelves was a camera with a Wi-Fi connection blinking green.

"You tape that shit you did to that little girl?" A signal booster lay on the shelf next to the camera. Owen examined the back of the picture, finding a hole masked by a see-through screen. "Stream that shit? Broadcast it for your pedo buddies? They pay by the gig?" He glanced back at Warrant, taking in the man's panicked expression. More terrifying than the threat of death, whatever this represented was occupying all of Warrant's mental space right now. "They still watchin'?" He swiveled to face the camera. "You watchin' right now?" He laughed, letting the dark, deep sound roll out of him. "Content warning. This pedo rape porn is about to become a slasher snuff film."

He walked back to the bed and yanked the knife out of Warrant's leg, ignoring the muted scream of pain. Climbing on the bed, he settled one shin over Warrant's legs, his other boot coming to rest alongside the man's side. Leaning forwards, he dragged the tip of the blade up the center of Warrant's chest, leaving a swath of red behind as the steel dug through flesh. "Wonder if you have a heart inside there." Cold fury possessed him, stripping everything away except the pounding need to make this man pay. Skipping the neck, he placed the blade crosswise between Warrant's teeth and pressed down. The tender skin at the corners of the man's mouth split like soft cheese under the pressure, runnels of blood making their way down his cheeks. "Wonder if you understand how your mouth displeases me."

Warrant was heaving side to side, and Owen had to steady himself with a palm on Warrant's neck. He dug under the flopping jaw and closed his thumb and fingers, using a modified version of the blood choke hold for a few seconds until the man stilled. Head tipped to the side, Owen applied the tip of the blade to Warrant's left eye, digging it out of its home until a fragile stalk of flesh was all that held it in place. A twist of the blade severed that, and he plucked it out of the air, holding it in front of Warrant's remaining eye, so it was the first thing the man saw when he came back to consciousness a few moments later. "Here's lookin' at you, you piece of trash."

The man's terror rendered him mindless, bucking hard and fast, twisting to throw Owen's weight off him. The sounds coming from behind the sock stuffed in his mouth weren't words but an eerie, undulating wail. Owen nearly toppled to the side when the man's writhing efforts dislocated his other shoulder, the pitch of the cries increasing at the added pain. Owen rode it out for another few seconds, then shook his head, bringing the blade down to swing in a short, stabbing motion at Warrant's neck, impaling him and angling the blade to sever the outer carotid artery. With the blade still in place, most of the blood poured inwards, following the exposed and penetrated trachea to the lungs. Red liquid frothed out of the wound within seconds, air mixing with the blood to create a fine mist Owen couldn't entirely avoid.

Between the rapid blood loss and the liquid-filled lungs, the end came swiftly for Warrant after all.

Owen swiped at his hands and arms with the edge of a blanket as he verified there wouldn't be any surprises with the body. When he removed the knife from the wound, he found the covers of the bed underneath the man's shoulders were saturated, dark with blood that had escaped while Warrant's heart still beat. Shiloh's blood was separate, and Owen found himself glad the little girl's pain wasn't touched by that of the pervert. He peeled back the man's eyelid, finding the sclera of his remaining eye bloodred with burst veins. The cornea was already growing cloudy, all spark of life and intelligence fled.

Owen brought his head up, twisting to look directly into the camera. "Show's over, folks. If you're watchin', this is me puttin' you on notice." Enunciating carefully, he promised, "You cannot hide from me. I will find you. And when I find you." He glanced down at Warrant. "I'll kill you, too."

Camera off, Owen documented the setup with photos from his phone. There was a tablet on the shelf underneath the filming equipment, and when he touched the screen, it woke with a browser already opened. He recognized the URL as a node on the darknet where one of his personas had spent considerable time, emulating the kind of sick bastard Warrant would be drawn toward.

That would be his target. *That's where I'll find the rest of the like-minded sons of bitches.*

He powered down everything and stowed the pieces in his pockets, not taking the time to make a more permanent home in the backpack he wore underneath the jacket. It was the work of moments to cut away the bloody evidence Shiloh had left behind, and deal with the parts of Warrant that might have touched her. *Too bad I didn't realize I needed to trim the fat until after he was dead.* The heavy copper smell had become insidious, and Owen needed fresh air more than he needed to secure things per protocol. He already knew where he'd be hunting.

Terrence was still where Owen had left him, sitting on the ground, but now with the other children gathered close. Their murmuring voices trailed off as they saw Owen stride out of the cabin, closing the door carefully behind himself. Their hands clutched possessively at the necks and hems of the shirts they now wore. Boys all, the ages ranged from the barely-teen of Terrence to a skinny child who looked no older than six or seven. There were so many of them, it boggled the mind. Owen and Alace hadn't been able to find documentation for all the kids, just the ones acquired through the organization they'd dismantled.

Owen didn't speak but lifted a hand in a wave Terrence returned, the kids swiveling en masse to track Owen's movements through the yard. He stopped at the tree line and used the drone's cameras to study the clump of children, then swept the forest all around the cabin. He turned off the broadcast, and the dogs immediately returned to the front of the clearing, milling through the children.

Owen turned and walked up the road, triggering a single signal from the tablet to the satellite Wi-Fi, and from there to a server in the darknet cloud. Upon receiving the affirmative notification, the man he'd paid extremely well to manage some of the information would begin placing calls. With his voice masked by a variety of technologies, he would emulate a dozen alarmed citizens from several different counties, making it impossible for the authorities to ignore the calls for help.

Within an hour, Owen anticipated the clearing to be awash in lights and people.

Within an hour, each of those kids would be headed to a better situation.

Within an hour, Terrence would stare into the concerned features of a social worker, and he'd tell them everything.

Owen's job was to be anywhere except here by that time.

***

Alace

"Beloved?"

Eric's tone was cautiously questioning. Alace looked up from where she was shoving her feet into her shoes to see him standing, holding Lila.

"We're going home." She waited for an argument, an unexpected tightness in her muscles easing when all Eric did was nod in understanding. "The doctor agreed there's no medical reason to forbid the discharge. We've been here long enough for Lila to have that second blood test they said was required, but beyond that, it's not necessary. She's healthy, and so am I." Alace focused on her shoes, working one heel up and down until the edge of the shoe unfolded, fitting itself more comfortably to her foot. "I wanna go home, Eric. I wanna be home."

He drifted closer, fingers of one hand sliding through her hair in a possessive move that soothed her. Eric leaned down and passed their daughter to her arms, then kissed the side of Alace's face tenderly. No longer questioning, his voice held nothing but support as he said, "Then we go home."

Not for the first time, Alace was bowled over by how well Eric simply *got* her and understood what made her tick. There was limited security at the hospital, mostly focused on preventing a mismatch between mother and baby, or for restricting overeager visitors. It was probably fine for what they were doing. *It is fine,* she reminded herself. But the level of security the hospital might be comfortable with and what would allow Alace to sleep at night—vastly different things.

"Do you have what you need?" He hefted the bag she'd already packed and looked around the room. "Are they bringing a wheelchair?"

"Yes, on the wheelchair. Grundella gnashed her teeth at me to ensure I wouldn't try to walk out under my own power." Alace grinned. Grundella was her name for the troll. The daytime nurse assigned to Alace's room hadn't been impressed by her increasing demands to leave the hospital. She'd muttered and mumbled about new mothers not understanding the demands of infants, and had stalled initiating the call for the promised discharge until Alace had finally used her cell phone to contact the doctor herself. "Also yes on the question about being packed up. What you've got is everything. My go-bag from delivery and the welcome to motherhood gifts from the hospital."

Lila made the tiniest sound, and Alace shifted her gaze down into her daughter's face, feeling a return of the stupefied smile she wore every time she was near the baby. Which was all the time. Eric had taken his opportunities to hold their daughter while Alace had napped, because he'd quickly recognized Alace wasn't easily giving up her girl for anyone, not even her daddy.

"Mother said she'll be here as soon as possible from Malibu."

Alace trailed the back of her finger across Lila's cheek, ignoring the statement for now.

"Mrs. Ward?" The squeaking shuffle of rubber-soled shoes in the doorway signaled the return of Grundella.

Alace looked up and frowned.

"Where's the wheelchair?"

Grundella smiled toothily, red-tinged fleshy lips spreading across her face. "I've requisitioned one, but it could be a bit before it's delivered."

This was nothing less than passive resistance to something the woman didn't like. The nurse could conceivably drag her feet until Lila needed feeding and changing, and then it would be dinnertime, and afterwards there'd be yet another reason for Alace to not leave. Heart pounding at the idea of spending one more night in the hospital, Alace took a calming breath and cleared her throat. "Eric, love, the rules were I can't walk out, correct?"

"Alace, I'm not sure—"

"I am. I can't walk out, not and have the discharge be a normal one." She didn't want any scrutiny applied to her life in any way, and Grundella had made vague threats about calling social services if Alace walked out against medical advice. She didn't know if the woman could actually do such a thing but had decided to adhere to the rule she followed of better-safe-than-sorry. "Wanna run the bag down, and then come back and pick me up?" She angled her head to see Eric's face. He was losing a fight to control his expression, corners of his mouth lifting slightly. "Literally?"

"Whatever my babies need." He stepped to the door and forced Grundella backwards into the hallway. Reaching behind him for the doorknob, he glanced back at Alace and winked. "Back very soon, beloved."

Her attention returned to Lila, Alace smiled as she whispered, "If you ever have a sibling, we're doing a home birth."

She didn't know what Eric might have said to the overbearing nurse, but the door remained closed until he returned, wheelchair in hand.

"You ready to blow this Popsicle stand?" Alace smiled at him, nodding at his question. "Then, milady—" He parked the chair close to where she sat, locking the brakes. "—your humble chariot awaits."

"God, you're so corny." His hand on her elbow steadied her as she stood and turned, backing up a half step to reseat herself in the wheelchair. "All part of your overwhelming charm."

"Good to know you still think I'm charming." Eric bent close and pressed his lips to hers, gazes locked.

He was smiling as he pulled away. "You're so very stuck with me."

"You say that like it's a bad thing." She rebalanced Lila in her arms, bringing the blanket up over the baby, tucking her close. "I happen to like being stuck, but only with you."

"Then that's lucky for me."

Alace glanced around the empty room as they swept through the door and into the hallway. Earlier, she'd requested the nurses rehome the vases of flowers that had crowded her room, gifts from Eric's family, friends, and professional acquaintances. The nursing staff hadn't delayed, placing the arrangements with patients who didn't have any. Sans cards, of course. Those were packed in the bag Eric had already taken to the car.

Grundella stood at the central desk along with a handful of other nurses, hers the only unsmiling face. Eric paused next to them when the woman stepped forwards, and Alace was about to request he continue when she saw the paperwork she held. Grundella—Jessica—crouched next to the chair and extended the folder. "There's a printout for a checklist of things we'd normally go through every few hours, just to make sure the little one's okay. I've put coupons in there for some supports you might find helpful, and at your husband's request, signed you up for diaper delivery. Babies go through a lot of diapers and wipes." Jessica smiled, this expression transforming her face, and Alace watched, fascinated as compassion and encouragement surfaced in place of the disappointed scowl she'd grown accustomed to. Jessica continued, "There's a hotline number you can call with questions, but I've also written down my cell phone number for you. Call me any time, Mrs. Ward. Lila's a gorgeous little girl, and she's lucky to have you for her mother. Be well."

Stunned at the change in the nurse's attitude, Alace accepted the paperwork and settled back into the chair. It took a moment to find her voice, but she eventually murmured a quiet, "Thank you." The other nurses all wore identical expressions of amusement, and slowly suspicion bloomed inside Alace.

The elevator was nearing the main floor when she twisted around in the chair and looked up at Eric. "What did you say to her?"

He threaded his fingers through her hair in that way she loved. "I merely reminded her that you were a best-selling author who may choose to memorialize these moments in one of a couple different ways. Asking if she wanted to be the villain or the hero jarred her loose from that bulldog stance she'd adopted." He shook his head. "Honey versus vinegar, no big deal." The elevator slowed, and he bent to again press his lips to hers, the sway and dip of her belly not entirely due to the mechanical movement. "Let's take our little girl home."

An unfamiliar car purred alongside the curb, engine idling where it was parked in the half-circle drive in front of the hospital entrance. Eric pulled a fob from his pocket, and the locks beeped in a muted and well-mannered tone. Alace stared at the car, then made a show of looking around for the SUV Eric had owned since before she'd met him. Alace had been through a dozen cars in the same time, acquiring and discarding the kind of nondescript junkers she'd needed for her gigs. Eric had held tight to his aging SUV, and she'd often seen him patting the hood affectionately as he approached or left the vehicle. He grinned at her, the slightly embarrassed expression making his already ridiculously handsome face even more so.

"What'd you do?" She remained seated, keeping her gaze on his face as he bent to the side and locked the brakes on the wheelchair, then moved around to crouch in front to flip up the footrests. "Eric?"

He ran a hand through his hair, that damned sheepish grin staying in place on his face. "OJ wasn't a good choice for us anymore."

Alace jerked her head back, the movement startling Lila, who shifted underneath the protective blanket. She soothed the baby absently, her gaze staying on Eric's face. "Your SUV was named OJ? After the most famous slow police chase in the world? Why did I not know this? That's the best kind of fodder for blackmail. I feel like I should have known this, Eric. Kinda betrayed right now, honestly."

"I just—" He swallowed hard, making a thick sound in his throat. "I can't let anything happen to you. You or Lila. This is a super safe car. Todd helped me out with all the research. He got recommendations from all kinds of people."

"Todd." Eric's best friend wasn't Alace's favorite person. "Helped with research?" He tipped his head to the side and nodded again, slower. "In the past twenty-six hours?" Which was how old Lila was. The newborn blood test had to be performed no sooner than twenty-four hours, which was the only reason Alace had agreed to stay at the hospital as long as she had.

Understanding dawned in Eric's eyes, and he huffed a laugh, shaking his head in a definite no. "Not the past day, no." He stood, opened the back door of the sedan, and reached for Lila, gently taking her from Alace's arms. "It's been on order for nearly two weeks and at the dealership for the past three days. I wanted—" He bent far into the car and tucked their daughter into the rear-facing seat in the middle, carefully bringing the straps down over her shoulders to lock them into place. Withdrawing from the car, he left the door open and turned to face Alace. "To surprise you." He threw both hands up to shoulder height and shook them like a cheerleader's pom-poms. "Surprise!"

Alace laughed aloud as she accepted his assistance rising from the chair. Not that it was needed, necessarily, but it felt nice to be cosseted for now, a reaction to Eric's tender care swelling inside like a warm balloon of happiness. "You're such a goofball. Color me surprised, mister. Also, I concur with the selection. This is a great car. Made from metal instead of plastic, it's not quite a tank circa the 80s, but it will definitely hold up in an accident. The safety rating doesn't lie." She settled into the seat beside Lila, lifting her feet into the car. Eric leaned in to buckle her seat belt as she was reaching out to uncover Lila's tiny face. "I would have helped research, you know." She made a face and inched forwards to touch her lips to Eric's nose. "Todd? Really?"

"When are you going to let go of your annoyance with him?" Eric didn't wait for an answer before closing the door. This was a long-standing argument at this point, stemming from Todd's behavior a few months ago after he'd asked for assistance with an issue. His constant calling and requesting reassurance afterwards, pelting her with questions, persistently demanding to understand things she'd made damn sure he'd never truly know about—all of that had been more than enough to sour Alace's attitude towards Todd.

Alace noticed Jessica had followed them down and was standing next to the wheelchair, now speaking earnestly to Eric. He took something from her and shoved it into his jacket pocket, backing away with a brief wave of a hand.

He walked to the driver side and folded himself into the car. Alace let him put it into gear and drive away before she asked, "What'd Grundella want?"

"Jessica"—he drew out the name for emphasis—"reminded me to keep visitors to a minimum for a few days. She said the hospital helps with that, discouraging people from coming in droves, requiring permitted visitors to wash their hands before holding the child, providing sanitizer stations outside the mother's room door. She said it would be on me to corral the masses." He made air quotes with one hand around the word. "I simply thanked her for her advice."

"What was that she handed you?" Alace leaned over to watch Lila sleep, the tiny movements of the baby's lips and nose mesmerizing.

"Hand sanitizer." He chuckled. "I believe she really means well, beloved. You're simply a force of nature she'd never encountered before."

"Okay. Whatever." *What if she's right? What if I've put our daughter at risk because I'm stubborn?* A memory resurfaced, one of Eric carrying her into the ER, blood smeared on the insides of her thighs. She'd nearly lost the pregnancy early on because she'd been too focused on her own wants and needs to be as careful as she should have been. A wave of insecurity broke over Alace, her mouth flooding with acid at the wayward direction of her thoughts. "You don't think this is wrong, do you? Should we have stayed at the hospital?"

"Beloved." Eric's hand appeared between the front seats, reaching blindly back towards Alace. She clasped hold, tight as if she were drowning and he was offering the only hope of rescue. "If the doctor hadn't agreed, the discharge papers would not have been signed. We complied with the only direct request, and if the whole of the nursing staff had tried to discourage us from leaving, I would have probably put my weight behind their requests. It was one woman, and we have no idea the history behind her fixation on the black-and-white rules she'd like to apply to everyone. I don't think it's wrong. I also happen to agree that you and I will both rest more comfortably at home, where we know without a doubt we're secure. The protection of Lila Sue is paramount, and the two of us are definitely focused on that. She's safe with us, sheltered in this ridiculous car I bought just for her, and she'll be far better served by a mother and father who are more relaxed. That's only gonna happen in our home."

Alace squeezed his hand. "I love you, do you know that?" His gaze flicked to the rearview mirror, and she saw the lines crinkling at the corners of his eyes, signaling his response. "You're pretty much my second favorite person right now."

"Second favorite?" He flipped on the turn signal and navigated steering the car around a corner, all without releasing her hand.

She gave his hand another squeeze. "Yeah. These days, you'll be coming in second to little Lila here. She's nudged you out of the top slot."

"A defeat I can well understand and get behind. Not upset in the slightest." He tightened his fingers around hers, then extricated his hand from her grip. "Traffic through downtown will be heavier. I have to take care of my best girls."

"Okay. I'll give you up for now. But once we're home, you're all mine."

"I suspect I'll be sharing you with Lila pretty heavily. And—" His gaze flicked back to the mirror, catching and holding hers for a moment. "—the doctor was particularly adamant about the six-week window before resuming sexual activity."

"Sexy fun times postponed. Got it." Grinning broadly, she stuck her tongue out at him through the reflection, then focused back on Lila's face. "I'm gonna want another one of these, Eric."

His tone was raspy, gruff with emotion when he promised her, "I'm totally on board with the idea. The sooner, the better, so our kids can grow up as friends."

She touched Lila's soft skin with a fingertip, tracing an invisible line across the apple of her daughter's cheek.

"We'll start practicing in five weeks and six days, then."

CHAPTER SIX

Owen

The sun had scarcely begun peeking through the tree canopy as he made his way back to the car. The woods were silent around him, and if he hadn't glanced up occasionally to look at the drone, he would have never known it flew above him, so quiet were its motors and rotors. He pressed the trunk button on the car fob as he approached the vehicle, methodically discarded the equipment he'd put on only a couple of hours ago, stowed his arsenal back into the disguised gun safe, and shoved the remaining items into the duffel bag.

He stripped off his jacket, shirt, and cargo pants, unfastening the ankles to slip over his boots. Those were stuffed into the bag, along with the mask he'd worn and the square of fabric that held Shiloh's blood, and only once he was confident he'd secured everything did he drop the sanitizing pod inside, pulling the tiny plastic trigger as he zipped the bag closed. The contents of the pod would help degrade any of Warrant's DNA that had transferred to the clothing. Warrant's penis and testicles went into a separate container followed by a splash of the solvent over the flesh. Owen took up the package of wipes saturated with the same chemicals and carefully cleaned what skin he'd left exposed during his time inside the cabin. Lastly, he used one of the wipes for the uppers of his boots while standing in a shallow tray retrieved from the trunk and partially filled from a jug of a similar solvent.

Only then did he pull his spare clothing on, stepping carefully into the clean cargo pants, securing the ankle fasteners when he bent over to dump the tray on the ground. The compound would rapidly break down, and within half an hour, the chemicals would be undetectable. Once he was again dressed, Owen closed the trunk gently, leaning on the surface to press firmly until he heard the latch click.

Peering into the back seat, he saw Kelly seated upright, staring out at him. Shiloh was strapped into the booster seat, her head on her brother's shoulder, apparently sleeping. *Probably a good thing.* Ideally, they'd be behind closed doors before she had a meltdown. Owen was surprised she hadn't reacted badly already, with everything that had happened back at the cabin.

A memory of Warrant's ruined face flashed in front of Owen, and he tightened his hands into fists, nails digging into the meat of his palms. Motherfucker had deserved so much worse. The arrogance of that kind of sexual predator made him sick, creating false scenarios where they were the center of attention, their thrill in the high of the moment, meaning the kids earned barely a second thought.

The discovery of the camera setup had been an unwelcome surprise, but one that, in the end, Owen would be able to leverage to his advantage. If he could trace even one more pedophile from the information, it'd be another big chink in the wall of secrecy those sick fucks depended upon to stay in business. From one, he'd dig up another, and then another. He hadn't been kidding when he'd promised to find them. *Won't stop until they're all facedown in the dirt.* He might not be able to fix what had happened to Shiloh, but he would avenge her.

Revenge is mine, saith Saint Owen.

Popping open the driver door, he crawled into the seat, trying not to rock the vehicle too much. Shiloh slept on, her shallow breaths never changing cadence. "She's pretty tired, huh?" Kelly nodded and leaned his head towards the little girl, letting his cheek rest on top of her head. "She was really brave back there."

"She always was." Kelly's voice was rough and aching, older than his years by decades. "He hurt her,

Da—Owen. He hurt her bad." The boy's near-miss on his name had Owen's heart tripping fast in his chest. "I shoulda been here."

"If you were here, it wouldn't have stopped him. He would have killed you, and then still done the same, and where would Shiloh be now?" Owen shook his head and started the car, letting the engine idle. He pulled the tablet out and sent the drone high, scanning the area between where he was parked and the highway. Nothing showed, no incoming cars. He angled the drone back towards the cabin, pleased to see the silhouettes of the dogs and kids remained within the circumference of the fencing. *All clear, and everything according to plan.* "Him dumping you where he did saved both your lives."

"You saved our lives." Owen glanced over his shoulder to see Kelly's gaze boring into him. "If I couldn't kill him, I'm glad it was you."

The bloodthirsty statement didn't bother him, and Owen answered in kind, treating the boy as an equal. *He's earned that, and much more.* "I'm glad it was me, too."

Owen put the car in gear and eased his foot down on the gas pedal, rolling smoothly out of the woods and back onto the private lane. At the highway, he quickly dealt with the chain, leaving it lying across the opening as he drove out and onto the larger road. A few minutes later, they were back on the interstate, free and clear, and rolling south towards home.

Owen turned on the radio and kept the volume low. He selected a local station he knew would interrupt with breaking information and drove, the sun rising to his left, slashing across his face as he wove in and out of traffic. They were an hour away from the compound when the first news briefing hit the airwaves. Owen had already seen a few emergency responder vehicles headed in the other direction, lights on but no sirens.

Any minute now, Terrence would be telling them all about the masked man who'd set the boys free.

Any minute now, law enforcement personnel would storm the cabin, finding only one dead occupant.

Any minute now, the call would go out over the darknet to hunker down, shelter in place, not draw any attention to themselves.

For all of those moments, it was too late.

Terrence could talk about Owen all he wanted; the careful work Owen and Alace had done made damn sure there was nothing to tie his mask-hidden reality to the pedophile ring.

The forensic investigators could take the cabin apart board by board, and they would still only find what Owen wanted them to find. Evidence of the man's depravity, but nothing to point to Kelly or Shiloh ever existing. Even if Shiloh left DNA in the cabin and the authorities managed to find it, he had confidence she wouldn't be in the system. The boys might talk about a little girl, might talk about her being removed tonight, but the state lab couldn't type the entirety of the cabin. It simply wasn't financially feasible.

And for the last tidbit, it was far too late for the sick bastards who had preyed on those children to feel safe. *I'll hunt 'em down one by one. Kill 'em all.* Owen glanced in the mirror, finding Kelly's eyes still directed his way. *Revenge.* That was a currency both Owen and Alace had dealt in for a long time.

He thought about the image Eric had sent him, the contrast between the surreal picture of Alace fully invested in motherhood, and the scene in the seat behind him. "Alace is gonna lose her mind."

"Who's Alace?"

Owen allowed himself a tiny grin at the question. He'd bet even Alace wouldn't be able to fully answer that particular inquiry. "She's a friend. The one I called the other day, and then I talked to her again while you were sleeping. Does the same kind of work as me. She and I work together a lot."

"So she's a good guy, like you?"

The car jerked to the side with his reaction, swaying within the lane, but only barely. "Kelly, I'm not a good guy." Better to burst that bubble right here and now than allow the kid to build him up as some kind of hero. "I'm far from good."

"You saved me and Shiloh." Kelly's shoulders moved up and down in the mirror. "Proof enough for me." Owen opened his mouth, and the boy shook his head fiercely, gaze burning through the reflection. "No, you don't get to say that's not how it is. You think I don't know bad from good? After what I've seen, after what's happened? You said the reason me and Shiloh are alive now is because Earl dumped me in the woods where you were. That means you're the reason we're alive. What if you hadn't been there? What if someone else had been?" Voice shaking, Kelly turned and stared out the window. "It was you. All along what we needed was you."

Lost for words, Owen fixed his own gaze out the front windshield, studiously ignoring the mirror for the remainder of the drive.

After pulling into the garage, he sat in his seat while the overhead door rumbled shut behind the vehicle, listening to tiny stirring sounds from the back seat. The girl's high piping voice murmured something he couldn't make out, answered by Kelly's raspy tone.

Picking up the tablet, Owen woke it with a touch, quickly scanned the view below the still-hovering drone, and grinned. There had to be more than a hundred heat silhouettes in view, with a ratio easily that of four adults for each child. Terrence and the rest of the kids were safe. Owen updated the drone's settings and watched while the scene changed, becoming a racing flow of treetops as the device headed back to home base. *Wherever that is.* Retrieving a USB stick from a recess in the back of the tablet's case, he inserted it and touched the icon that appeared, agreeing to the warning that appeared next. Within seconds, the tablet was not just back to factory settings but had been bricked, requiring a complete software reinstall to become useful again. The device itself would go into the recycle bin at the local electronic store the first chance he got.

He didn't know why he was stalling, not really. But once he carried that little girl into his house, their path would be set. Taking her here instead of a hospital laid the framework for the next few hours at least, and probably the following few weeks. *Still time. I could haul them both to an ER and drop them off. Hospital would call social, and they'd take care of the kids.* He didn't think Kelly would disclose Owen's part in Warrant's death. Doubted if the boy would be able to tell someone how to find Owen. *Take 'em inside, and they're no longer the kids; they're mine.* The thought should have been disturbing, but it wasn't. Mentally acknowledging the connection he'd developed with the two kids settled him, steadying him. *Long as they need me, I'll be here for them. Long as they need me, I'm gonna be right here.*

With a deep breath, he reached for the door handle, stepped out of the car, and turned to see two sets of eyes staring at him from the back seat. Shiloh was definitely wide awake.

Seated side by side as they were, the physical differences were startling. Kelly's paler skin was topped with dark hair, the not-yet-adolescent stretch of his limbs speaking to his eventual size and growth. Shiloh's skin was darker, arms and legs a creamy mocha brown. But the shape of their faces, color of their hair, and the startling clarity of their green eyes were more than enough to brand them at least half-siblings.

"Come on, kiddos. Let's head inside. See what we can do for food and a bath." Owen walked to the door and held still for the facial recognition software, listening to the opening and closing of the car door behind him. He pushed the door open and held it there with a stiffened arm, looking down as Kelly passed through into the house, leading Shiloh by the hand.

Neither child spoke, even as they followed Owen to the bathroom attached to the bedroom Kelly had been in before. Owen started the water running into the bath and turned, staring at Kelly. "I'm going to go grab the rest of the stuff from the car. I'll be right back in to help Shiloh with her bath." The boy's chin dropped, and he developed a pugnacious expression, glaring at Owen. "Exactly as I helped you bathe, Kelly. Mostly by being in here in case she gets lightheaded or doesn't feel well." At least Kelly had recovered from the respiratory illness he'd had that first night, and Shiloh appeared healthy outside of the physical abuse she'd suffered. "Nothing more. She's not sick like you were, so probably won't need anything."

"I can do that." Kelly stood straighter. "She don't need you."

What happened to Owen the savior? "Okay. You stay in here with her and I'll be in there." He pointed through the door to the bedroom. "Close enough to help if needed, but you're right. Her big brother can definitely be her helper instead of me." That let the air out of Kelly, and his body rounded over, shoulders slumping in relief. "Don't let the water get too hot. It'll sting her scrapes. I'm going to get the bags and then make a call. Don't leave her in here alone, okay?"

"Okay." Shiloh leaned into Kelly and whispered something, and the boy nodded in response. "She says thank you."

"You're welcome, sweet girl. I'll be back in a minute." Walking out of that room and leaving the two kids alone was harder even than he'd imagined it would be. His mind was going crazy, running a thousand scenarios where one or the other could be hurt or killed while in the safety of a common bathroom, and Owen had to shake his head forcefully to slow his racing thoughts. Bags of clothing retrieved from the car, he dropped them outside the bedroom and abruptly turned on his heel, striding to the kitchen. He took in a deep breath and then accessed the tablet mounted to the wall.

After needing and not having one when first treating Kelly, Owen had installed a pinhole camera in the bathroom. There was no sound, but it showed Shiloh in the tub, with the overlarge shirt still covering her body. Kelly sat cross-legged on the floor, head resting on his folded arms along the edge of the tub. The boy was turned sideways so he could keep an eye on Shiloh. The physical exhaustion both children exhibited was profound, and seeing it carved a hollow spot in Owen's chest.

He stared at them, then abruptly tapped away from the security camera system, entering a series of passwords to access a secure email server. He pulled up a contact, studied the information briefly, then keyed in a short, cryptic message. The green indicator beside the man's name told Owen his contact was online, so it wasn't a surprise when the response was nearly immediate. The contact had relevant questions, so Owen responded, then confirmed the address and timeframe for the man's arrival, and finished by closing down the connection before turning off the tablet.

Moving to the security system, he tapped a series of icons, then created a temporary access code to match what he'd given the man, who was a doctor at a nearby children's hospital. Owen didn't know him personally, but the other independents who disrupted local trafficking rings had recommended his services as discreet and trustworthy. After bringing Kelly home, Owen had run his own kind of background checks on the man, finding only more of the same. It had bothered Owen to not have reliable medical help for the boy, and when he'd begun entertaining the idea Shiloh would be coming back here, he'd been determined to ensure she had everything she needed to be healthy and whole. The security code would grant the doctor access even if Owen wasn't home, helping make certain her care wouldn't be interrupted for any reason.

Mission accomplished, he retraced his steps up the hallway and gathered up the bags, taking them into the bedroom and placing them on the bed. Without looking through the open doorway, he methodically took the articles of clothing out of the bags, removing tags and folding them, stacking the various types of things together. Still not looking at the kids, he called out to Kelly, "I've got things laid out for Shiloh to sleep in. I'll do a load of laundry tonight, get the dyes washed out of the rest of the stuff." He paused, not surprised when he didn't receive a response. "Is it okay if I come in there now, Kelly?"

"Yeah." The boy's voice was thick with tears. Owen let his head drop backwards between his shoulders and glared up at the ceiling. He could only imagine what was going through the boy's mind.

When he walked in, the dirty water all around Shiloh was still, not even a ripple disturbing the surface. She sat in the center of the tub, legs stretched out in front of her, hands folded in the fabric of the shirt she still wore. Her hair was wet, hanging in strings down her back.

She's stronger than she looks. He reminded himself of the composure she'd shown in the cabin and turned to the cabinet to retrieve a soft washcloth. With a hand on Kelly's shoulder to steady himself, he crouched and then knelt next to the tub, shocked when the boy leaned against his side, still in the exhausted posture he'd seen on the video.

"Let's run some more water." He matched actions to words, turning the faucet and regulating the temperature automatically. Holding the cloth under the stream of water, he dampened the material, wringing it lightly when he pulled back. The bottle of shower gel he'd bought for Kelly stood on one corner of the tub, and he spread a liberal amount on the wet cloth, crushing it in his grip to work up a layer of suds. "Mom always said start at the cleanest part and work your way down." He leaned over and gripped Shiloh's jaw in his hand, turning her face towards him. The unfocused gaze she wore was terrifying, and he had to pause to catch his breath. Clearing his throat, he quietly told her, "So we'll work on your face and hair first." The gel doubled as a tear-free shampoo, so he smoothed the cloth over the top of her hair, working the soap down to her scalp. He applied more gel before moving to clean her face, and then more again to wash her exposed neck and arms, careful of the abrasions her bonds had worked into her skin.

Honoring the barrier she'd set in place, he didn't try to clean her torso, leaving that for much later when she'd be more comfortable. The water level had risen, so he unstopped the tub, allowing a portion of the dirty water to drain away before plugging the drain again. More gel, then an under-the-water washing of her lower legs and feet, again leaving anything covered by the soaked shirt untouched. Owen let the cloth float in the water as he cupped his hands under the running water, bringing it handfuls at a time to rinse her hair. Another round of gel to shampoo her hair was followed by a final rinse, and he sat back on his heels, drying his hands and arms on a towel retrieved from a nearby rack.

Movement in the tub shocked him to stillness. Shiloh had grasped hold of the cloth and was in the process of shoving it underneath the shirt, tears rolling down her face as she scrubbed at flesh he couldn't see, but could well imagine after witnessing the evidence of abuse Warrant had left behind. "Honey, go easy. Careful." She shook her head, shoulders bowing over as her hands worked frantically just out of sight. "Shiloh, stop it. You'll hurt yourself."

It was Kelly who reached in and took the cloth away. He dropped the washcloth back into the water with a pained cry, and Owen stared as red slowly leached out of the cloth. *How the fuck am I supposed to do this?* "Shiloh." She looked up at him, the lost expression gone, replaced by an anguished awareness he found to be far worse. "I've got a doctor coming, honey. A man I trust. He's going to make sure you're okay." The incredulity she felt was clear on her face, and Owen understood the wariness. *Honesty will gain me allies.* "He can't make it okay. What happened to you, to both of you." He put his hand on Kelly's head. "That can't ever be made okay. But he'll make sure that you are going to heal and be well."

"Mm'kay." Soft and toneless, her voice stripped his composure away, and Owen's own tears threatened as her expression began to shut down again.

"Okay," he echoed and then held up the towel he had in his hands. "Let's get you out of the wet and dried off. Kelly, I could use some help, bud."

Kelly flipped the lever to unstop the tub again and climbed to his feet, holding Shiloh's hands as she did the same. Kelly lifted the hem of the shirt, and as it cleared her torso, Owen folded the towel around her, so by the time the shirt hit the floor of the bathroom, she was still covered shoulders to knees.

He lifted her, shocked when her arms went around his neck, head nestling against his shoulder. As he carried her into the bedroom Kelly had been using, he heard a warning ding from the security system announcing the front door had been opened. So it wasn't a surprise when the man he'd messaged showed up in the doorway, his features matching the pictures Owen had paid for.

Following post-residency fellowship studies at a prestigious Boston hospital, Darren Marchant's career path had taken a different direction than expected after he visited a charity hospital in Thailand, only a few years into his practice as a rising star in childhood trauma treatment. According to the information Owen had found about the man, what he'd seen there had changed his life. In that tropical country, the prostitution trade brutalizing children as young as two years old was rampant. Marchant had thrown himself into treating children who were brought to the hospital, but after realizing the worst cases never made it that far, he moved his work out into the community. Seeking justice for the children, he'd battered himself against the government's unflinching walls and barriers, until after only two years he had burned out. The torture of uncovering evidence time and again that Westerners were so often the ones taking advantage of the children, exploiting legal loopholes that allowed them to pursue their abnormal proclivities without fear of legal reprisal, had become too much for his continued sanity. So Marchant had resorted to different tactics.

When the Thai government had censured him a second time for publicizing a US-based businessman's activities, Marchant had found himself socially and professionally ostracized, unable to secure the necessary support to continue his work. That cold-shoulder treatment had followed him back stateside, where he'd had difficulty finding a job in his chosen field. The need was there, but the appetite for a doctor unafraid to call the perpetrators out on their behaviors, regardless of their clout or power—simply not present. Marchant wasn't a good bet anymore and had finally given up on the idea, instead creating his own clinic system, housed in the worst neighborhoods. His professed goal was that any child who needed a protector would find one.

Once in the room, Marchant didn't even look at Owen beyond clearly cataloging his presence. The man's entire focus was on the towel-clad Shiloh, and the tender smile that creased his lips didn't appear forced. He seemed genuinely pleased to see the girl.

"Hey." He came only slightly closer, crouching down, settling back on one heel. "I'm Darren. I'm a doc. I treat kiddos like you." He waved, the movement slow and fluid, clearly designed to not startle the child. "You must be Shiloh, right?"

Shiloh's arms tightened around Owen's neck, and he turned to sit on the edge of the bed. Marchant's gaze flicked to him, and the man patted the floor unobtrusively. *Okay then.* Owen slipped off the bed and settled on the floor, his back supported by the side of the mattress and bed frame. Kelly sat next to him, crowding close.

Marchant didn't let Shiloh's lack of a response bother him, turning his attention to the boy next. "And I bet you're Kelly. Pleased to meet you." The man stuck out a hand, and Kelly turned his face into Owen, hiding as if the attempted contact was a threat. "No worries, no worries. I'm just here to see if I can help. I can't help if you don't trust me, and you don't trust me yet. I know, I know."

Kelly unfolded slightly, head turned to stare at the stranger. "Are you really a doctor?"

Marchant nodded. "I sure am. I'm a children's doctor, specifically."

"Where's your white coat, then?" Disbelief was thick in Kelly's voice, his words clipped after every consonant. "If you're a doctor, shouldn't you have a white coat?"

"I left it at home. Owen here"—Marchant gestured towards Owen—"said things were urgent, so I came straight over. I have a picture of me in the coat, though, and a badge from a hospital that says I'm a doctor. Would you like to see?"

He was impressed by the way Marchant had immediately understood how best to work with Kelly, not talking down to him as if he were a child, but instead treating him as a near equal. He suspected Shiloh would trust once Kelly did, which made Marchant's approach doubly smart.

Kelly's head shifted up and down, and Marchant straightened, reaching into his front pocket. Owen tensed, suddenly conscious that he was supremely vulnerable in this position. His focus had been so entirely on the children, all normal self-protective awareness had fallen by the wayside. The man was in shape, body toned from running or a similar exercise if the fit of his jacket was to be believed. Marchant held no publicly recorded certifications in any self-defense skills, didn't own a gun, and as far as Owen had been able to determine, had never visited a shooting range. He wasn't military with whatever elite training that implied, and sitting across from Owen as he was now, Marchant simply didn't read as a threat. *Nothing but a dude. A guy dude. Not a mark.* Owen shouldn't have to defend the kids against this man but couldn't help his gut reaction at the realization of how vulnerable they all were.

Marchant must have seen the change because he stilled, hand imprisoned within his pocket. "Just getting my wallet. Okay? Gonna bring it out and show Kelly the pictures." Owen nodded, and the man slowly withdrew his hand, square of leather trapped between his fingers. "It's an ID and a couple of pictures." Gaze locked with Owen, he flipped open the wallet and thumbed out a square ID card along with his driver's license. He offered them, and Owen took them, surprised at the steadiness of his hand. With the adrenaline rush still in his system, he'd expected shaking. He held them while the man dug deeper, coming up with a couple of candid photos of him and groups of kids that he also passed over. Owen had seen these images online. They were of the children Marchant had worked with in Thailand, him crouched in front of the mass of petite bodies, one child balanced on his knee and one perched on his shoulders. Owen brought the items closer to his body so Kelly could see. The boy reached out and touched one of the pictures, his finger drawing a line under where Marchant was shown kneeling.

"You're really, *really* a doctor? Did you help all those kids?" Kelly took the hospital identification and held it close to his face, studiously looking at Marchant's information. "What hospital is this?"

Owen studied the boy, surprised. *The info is right there.* Kelly's expression held no recognition. *Transient parents, bounced around the foster system, then the pack...it'd be more shocking if there weren't potential issues.* "It's Sussex County General." He pointed to the top of the plastic square. "This is the name of the hospital." He pointed farther down. "And this says his privileges there are valid through the middle of next year." Kelly touched the dates and looked up at Owen, brows drawn together in a deep frown. "Privileges means he has permission to treat patients at that hospital." With a nod, Kelly returned to staring at the ID. "He's all right, Kelly. I checked him out before we left to get Shiloh. You know what I can do, right?" Kelly nodded without looking up. "He helps people like me. When I find kids that need help, and I don't trust anyone else, he's the kind of guy I'd trust. He's who I was going to have stay here with you, before we changed our plans."

"Okay." Kelly rocked up on his knees and twisted to face Shiloh, turning his back on Marchant, and that physical expression of trust made that hollow space in Owen's chest burn hotter. "Shiloh. The man hurt you bad. The doc is gonna help make it better. If Owen trusts him, I do too. Owen says he's safe. Owen wouldn't lie to us. He's a good guy."

Shiloh stirred in Owen's arms, lifting her head to look around Kelly at Marchant. She'd begun trembling, her tiny body vibrating, and Owen heard her teeth chattering lightly. "Him's a good guy, too?"

"Yeah." Owen answered her, wanting to lend the weight of his approval to Kelly's, not certain he could stand another iteration of the lie Kelly wouldn't let go of. "He's one of the good guys."

"Mm'kay." She twisted around, facing Marchant, and Owen flinched when she let her legs fall open. "Bad man hurt me down in my front butt."

Marchant already knew Shiloh had been attacked. Owen had shared everything he'd believed relevant, including the confinement by shock collar, the bindings he'd cut off the little girl, the malnourished state she was in, and the blood he'd found on the covers where she'd lain. It had felt like an invasion at the time, but he'd answered all the questions the doctor had sent back, and now, seeing the trust the tiny girl had for the man based on his and Kelly's say-so, he was glad for the time spent laying the groundwork, so Marchant didn't have to ask her any painful questions.

The man didn't reach for her but also didn't shy away from what she'd exposed. The pain on his face reflected that of the girl's, and Marchant's voice held an anguished vibrato when he said, "Owie. That looks like it hurts. Did the man hurt you one time or a bunch of times?"

"Jus once." Her tone wasn't as gut-punching flat and affectless as it had been before, but the effects of what she'd been through were present in her voice. Teeth chattering again, the little girl forced out a soft, "Him was a bad man."

Owen's throat closed tight, and he found himself unable to take in even the smallest breath. His mind was awash with images, each more devastating than the last. The little girl shifted around so she could see him, her eyes dark with remembered pain.

"Yes." The word was choked and strained, coming out of Owen's throat rough and filled with gravel. "Yes, he was. He won't hurt you again, sweetie. I promise."

"Because you killed him." She scratched at the side of her nose, then leaned her cheek into her palm, exhaustion marring her features. "The bad man."

"I did." He breathed the words out like an oath, like a vow, like the most solemn statement he could ever give.

"Good." She adjusted again, shifting in his lap until she had nestled her head against his chest. "I'm glad."

The questions from the doctor picked back up, and Owen recognized a similar cadence to what he'd adopted a couple of days ago when initially talking to Kelly. Before laying a hand on the little girl, Marchant was able to develop a good picture of the abuse she'd suffered. When she revealed the man had used his hand on her, not his penis, Owen let out a breath he hadn't been conscious of holding. The disclosure didn't make the abuse any less damaging, but from the look Marchant tossed towards him, it was good news for something at least.

Twenty minutes later, Owen was pulling a fresh shirt over the little girl's arms, drawing the towel out from underneath after she was covered. He helped her stand and step into panties and shorts. Once Shiloh was dressed, he squinted down at Kelly.

The boy had refused to leave, had stayed by Shiloh's side throughout the ordeal of the question and answer with Marchant, and then through the limited physical exam, Marchant pulling gloves and packages of swabs from his pocket. The boy had heard everything and likely drawn his own conclusions. Owen squatted next to him and touched Kelly's shoulder, studying his face when Kelly turned to look at him.

"The man, Earl, he's gone. He can't hurt her, or you, anymore." Kelly nodded before his chin sank back to his chest, gaze steady on his fingers twisted in the hem of his shirt. "I'm going to the kitchen to talk to the doc. Can you stay in here with Shiloh for a minute? I'll tackle getting some food started, so we can get the both of you fed." He bumped the boy's shoulder with his elbow. "I've still got that candy bar for you guys. That'll be dessert tonight, okay?"

Shiloh crowded closer to Kelly. "Cann'y?"

"Yeah, sissy. After supper, okay? Da—Owen has good food." There was that damned slip again, and Owen found himself wishing Kelly had simply gone for it, calling him Daddy as he had in the store. *Was that just yesterday?* It felt forever ago.

He trailed Marchant up the hallway, marking to himself how comfortable he was around the man. It had to be more than the level of care he'd taken with Shiloh, and Owen liked the fact the doctor had dedicated his life to providing services that were complementary to what Owen had been doing. That alone spoke volumes about the character of the man.

"Is she going to be okay?" He opened the refrigerator, staring blankly inside before grabbing two bottles of water. Turning, he held one out for Marchant, who accepted it with muttered thanks.

Setting the other on the countertop, he opened the freezer and took out a lasagna. *Paired with a salad, it'll be enough for dinner tonight.* Oven heating, he removed the packaging and placed the frozen mass of tomato sauce and pasta in a dish, popping it inside without waiting. He was setting the timer when he realized the doc hadn't answered him and turned to see Marchant staring at him. "I didn't read things wrong back there, did I? She is okay, right?"

"Define okay. Physically, she's going to heal. I'd be surprised if he hadn't been at her with something more than digital manipulation. The amount of swelling and abrasions simply doesn't support the lack of implements of some kind. It's likely she didn't see what he used or didn't recognize it. Without the language to describe the abuse, nuance is lost. I didn't observe any fresh blood, and there was no odor that would indicate he'd perforated her vagina or colon. Without running the risk of traumatizing her further, I've conducted the examination my oaths will allow. We'll know more when I get the swabs run, but I truly don't see any major injuries to overcome." Marchant twisted the lid off the bottle and lifted it, draining the water in a series of deep swallows. "Mentally, she's regressed. No surprise there. Her language appears delayed by at least eighteen months, maybe two years. Once she feels safe, you'll likely see that begin to reverse. Expect sleep disruptions, behavioral acting out, overt sexual expression, and depression. Her reactions will depend on not only what she experienced but how stable her future situation will be. Do you know how long he'd owned the kids?"

"Only a few weeks. Before that, they'd been in a holding location, and prior to that had been in a typical foster care situation. Where I took her from—" Owen hesitated, unsure how much to share. "It was intense. Isolated from civilization, the whole scene was dehumanizing in the extreme. She'd lost her protector only a few days ago. Kelly, he's the brother, had been dumped into the Pine Barrens, and I happened to be in the right place at the right time. So she's been dealing with abandonment, too."

Marchant held the empty bottle in his hand, fingers closing around it slowly, the crinkling of the crushed plastic loud in the room. "For clarity's sake, I should tell you that I received a call earlier tonight. Upstate New York has a situation of more than a dozen kidnapped and exploited children held in an isolated location, disciplined with shock collars, malnourished and abused. They were also all clad in brand-new clothing provided by a mysterious benefactor and savior. They want me to come up tomorrow and evaluate the kids."

Well, shit. So much for managing to keep his two kids separate from the rest of the rescued children. He angled his body against the cabinet, freeing the route of access to his holstered weapon. Years of honing his skills allowed him to keep his posture casual, never revealing to the doctor that these might be the last words he said. Masking the importance of the question, Owen asked, "That call you got, it say anything about kids escaping before the cops showed?" Marchant shook his head, the plastic bottle crinkling louder, the walls of the bottle collapsing inwards. "Think hard, man. Did it mention anything else about the guy who called it in?"

"Apparently four different sets of authorities received simultaneous reports from a variety of citizens. So it wasn't a single guy calling it in. I didn't get all the details, but I don't get the feeling the kids are saying anything bad about the guy. Just thought you might want to know."

When the bottle was a crushed ball of plastic, Marchant twirled the cap back into place, locking it into the deformed shape.

Owen stared hard, thinking this could be a metaphor for his life. Damaged beyond recognition, less functional than before, and absolutely, totally stuck in place. Shaking off the unaccustomed melancholy, he gave a heartfelt, "Thanks."

"You don't have anything to worry about from me, Marcus. Whatever you had to do to save that little girl, to save that boy—you've got my full support. Anything I can do, I will. Give me a minute to grab my bag. I dropped it near the door when I came in, thought it would be less frightening if I appeared to be merely a guy. I've got some medicine I want to leave for Shiloh and Kelly. From what I've heard so far about the living conditions for all the kids, I'd be surprised if they didn't have some issues, so we'll get ahead of all that and get them started back towards healthy lives."

Medications retrieved and explained, Marchant left the kids in Owen's hands with a promise to be available for any follow-up questions. He'd been gone for only a few minutes when Owen heard the scuff of a bare foot against the kitchen tile. He glanced up at the screen where he'd been monitoring the kids to see Shiloh on her own, curled up in bed with her arms around the largest of the stuffed animals he'd bought for Kelly. Which meant the footfalls had to be Kelly. "Hey, kiddo. Supper's about ten minutes from ready."

"Is that guy a doctor? For real?" Owen looked over his shoulder and nodded, unsure what to make of the expression on Kelly's face. "And he won't say anything about us being here?"

"No, he won't." Turning to face the boy, Owen gave him the truth. "With him agreeing to treat you guys, we're in a deadlock, but not a bad one. It's more of a moral dilemma for him than anything. By treating you and Shiloh without taking you to a hospital, he's made a stand that he thinks you'll be better off here. But now I know something about him, and he knows something about me, and we'll both keep our mouths shut because the end result is what we both know is right." Owen leaned against the counter. "I'm not comfortable taking you back to foster care until I deal with the bad cop that got you into this mess to begin with."

Something undefinable passed across Kelly's face. "Is that next then?" Owen nodded, noting how the skin of Kelly's face grew taut, impacted by a tension Owen didn't understand. "And afterwards we'll be back with fosters?"

Backs of his eyes stinging, Owen narrowed his lids, trying to maintain a stoic expression. The idea of leaving the kids wasn't something he could contemplate yet, even the thought of the loss enough to knock him off balance. "It's the best place for you, bud." He made a split-second decision to expose his reasoning, so Kelly would understand. "See, I'm not set up for long-term anything. I'm in and out of this place, weeks at a time. Plus, I've been considering relocating out West, so I might not even be in this house long."

"To live near your friend." Kelly took a step backwards. "Without any problems."

"Problems—what do you mean?" Owen cocked his head to the side, studying the boy's face intently. Something was going on here, and he hadn't caught on to what the subtext was.

"Don't matter. Shiloh's safe for now. That's all that matters to me." Kelly shook his head, and that fall of hair slid over his eyes, blocking them from Owen's view. "Can I help with food?"

"No, bud." Speaking slowly, Owen kept trying to read the boy. Something had happened, and he'd missed it. Some crucial clue had passed him by. "I've got it covered."

"Okay." The boy turned on his heel and disappeared up the hallway.

"What the hell?" Owen turned to the screen in time to see Kelly enter the bedroom. He slipped onto the bed next to Shiloh and curled around her protectively. His shoulders moved in a broken rhythm.

Without turning up the sound, Owen couldn't be certain, but it appeared the boy was crying.

Torn whether to go investigate, he let the timer for their food decide, dinging an alert that the meal should be ready to eat. Owen turned his nervous energy to setting the table, waffling with a short-lived internal struggle about cutlery and drink glasses, realizing at the last minute that this dinner was the kind the kids couldn't easily manage with their fingers. He hadn't been thinking when he picked the food, and now cursed himself quietly. Chicken nuggets and fries would have been easier for them than a casserole.

"Nothing for it now. If I can get a few bites into them, it'll be enough." *I'll do better.* These kids had been through so much already; they deserved more responsible care than he could provide. If even simple decisions like appropriate meals were beyond him, the idea of trying to keep the kids on his own was laughable. "Fucking idiot."

He huffed out a sigh and turned to call for the kids to find them already standing in the doorway, Shiloh slightly behind Kelly, probably instinctively placed there by the boy so he could protect her. *He's such a good kid.* Maybe Owen would have a chance to influence the foster care placement, ensuring they'd get a home dedicated to them instead of one with rooms of bunk beds and a rotating door. *I'll make sure they're set before I do anything.* "Food's ready. Come sit, and let's eat. It's been a busy day, and I'm bushed. I bet you guys are, too." He pulled out the two chairs side by side and stepped back to make room. "Sit here, and I'll dish up the food."

Giving them space, he walked to the other side of the table to place hefty servings on their plates. Keeping track of the kids with his peripheral vision, he watched Kelly help Shiloh onto the chair, noting she had to sit on her knees to reach the table. *Dammit, she needs a booster seat, just like the car.* Another strike in the "Owen doesn't know shit" column.

Kelly climbed onto his own chair, perching on it as if it were the barstool, feet on the seat and knees drawn up underneath his shirt. It was startling to see that both kids had made themselves as small as possible. *Less of a target.* Owen dipped a serving of salad onto each plate, then held up the dressing he'd carried to the table earlier. Both kids nodded silently, and he drizzled it over the greens and tiny tomatoes. Standing upright, fists planted on each hip, he considered the table before snapping his fingers. "Drinks. I'll get them. You can go ahead and start if you want." He turned away and grabbed three glasses, filling them with ice and water from the dispenser on the front of the refrigerator. When he returned to the table, neither child had moved, and he frowned as he set the glasses next to the plates. Shiloh was poking at her fork with a finger, studying the implement intently.

"Want me to cut up your lasagna?" She lifted her gaze to him and nodded slowly. "Okay, sweetie. I can do that." Owen went to lean over her and grab his fork and knife, but the moment he did, she cringed away, a tiny sound of distress escaping. Crippling pain ripped through him at the idea of her being afraid of him. "Oh, honey. It's okay. I can go over there and do it." He stepped to the side, but she stayed crunched into a folded-over position, head resting on her knees. "Shiloh, it's okay." He turned to look at Kelly and found himself on the receiving end of a blistering glare. *Can I fuck up more tonight?* "I promise, I will never ever hurt you, sweetheart. Promise, you're safe with me."

He made his way around the table and, from that distance, moved her plate towards him, cutting the food into bite-sized pieces. What had happened to the little girl who trusted him enough to sit in his lap, allowing him to dress her, to take care of her? *She trusted me because Kelly did*. Covertly, he studied the boy who was still glaring daggers at him. *I told him I wouldn't be his forever safe place.* Clearly, that had been enough to shift the boy's attitude, and Shiloh was sensitive enough to pick up on it. The little girl was paying the price of Owen's fears. *Shit.* He knew of only one way he could fix this, but his lifestyle didn't support having children, and he didn't have a network in place to pick up any slack.

Pushing Shiloh's plate back in front of her, he retrieved Kelly's next and began cutting up the boy's food. He held Kelly's gaze as long as he could, trying to read the boy. *Angry and hurt. No, not angry, Kelly's afraid.* He'd basically told the boy that he'd be sending them back into the same system that had betrayed them before. Of course Kelly would be afraid. If it happened once, it could happen again, and Owen swallowed hard at the memory of Shiloh's tiny face staring up at him over her roughly bound wrists.

I don't have anyone to call on here.

Placing Kelly's plate in front of him, Owen went to his chair and sat, then mechanically dished up lasagna for himself.

I do, however, have Alace.

Shiloh unfolded slowly and lifted her head, staring at Owen through tear-clumped lashes. Kelly nudged her with his elbow, and she picked up the fork, struggling to grip it in her hand. Owen watched as she managed to maneuver a bite onto the fork's tines, making a tiny sound as it tipped off and tumbled back to the plate. Owen cleared his throat, ensuring he had both kids' attention before he dropped his fork noisily to the table. The lasagna had held its form fairly well, cut into tidy cubes. It had also cooled sufficiently to be handled comfortably. *Finger foods it is.* He lifted one with his fingers and stuffed it into his mouth, sucking sauce from his thumb.

Kelly dipped his head to hide his expression and nudged Shiloh with his elbow again. A moment later, all three forks were back on the table, and the kids wore matching grins, slight though they were, chewing through their first bite of lasagna.

I can't have any second thoughts. If I'm in this with them, then I'm in it. No takebacks with these two. He'd already seen the results any kind of boomerang could have.

Kelly glanced up, and while he continued chewing, the grin slid from his face, leaving him looking bereft and sad.

Nope, not on my boy's face. That kid deserves only happy.

Owen could put the hunt for the cop on the back burner. *I can even job it out.* The search for the others in the sibling pedophile ring could literally be done from anywhere. *Honestly, Alace has better toys and resources.* The lease on this house was month-to-month, and it would be the work of only a few moments to set about closing down his life here. His electronics and weaponry were the only items he wouldn't want to leave behind. The kids were scarcely settled as it was. *Shit, I could pack 'em up in only a couple of boxes at this point.*

Owen watched Shiloh for the space of a few moments. Marchant had been clear that she'd need assistance, probably long term, and had offered up as much of his time as would be required. *Surely Alace has a doc in Colorado we can shift her care to.* That sucked because Owen wouldn't have minded working with Marchant more. The man was conscientious and didn't appear to balk at the wrong side of legal when kids were the winners in the end.

Am I gonna do this?

He studied the faces of the two kids at his table, happily eating a crappy frozen dinner with a nod towards healthy by an added handful of lettuce. They deserved more. They deserved a family. *I can't give them that, but I can give them me.*

"What do you think about moving to Colorado with me?"

Hope and excitement bloomed in slow motion across Kelly's face, and Owen knew in that moment he'd turn himself inside out to ensure he got to see the expression again and again.

***

Alace

Lila's cry pierced the air, and Alace lifted her head with a groan as she mentally gauged the distance to the bassinette. Moving slowly, she shifted her legs over the edge of the mattress and placed her feet well apart, ensuring she would be steady before she shoved off the bed and to an upright position. She sighed and cupped her belly with one hand, standing in place until the pain subsided.

Two shuffling steps later, she bent over the baby, who was angrily waving her mittened fists in the air, having escaped her swaddling. Again. "Shhhh. I'm here. I've got you." She lifted the infant as Eric rounded the door from the hallway, a panicked expression on his face. "I've got her. She wiggled out of the blanket again." They'd found Lila wouldn't sleep without being swaddled but also hated being swaddled when she woke. There was no win in this situation so far. "She should eat again."

Alace turned in place and backed up to the rocking chair positioned only a couple of feet away, groaning again as she descended faster than intended, her bottom impacting harder than was comfortable. *My body's a mess.* The whole process of giving birth made more sense now, yet it felt like as big a mystery as ever before.

"Every muscle in my body hurts. I moved my ears earlier and found out my scalp is sore." Lila rested in the crook of one arm as Alace maneuvered clothing to expose a breast. "And I guess my milk is starting to come in, because these things are hard as rocks and hurt."

"Should I call Jessica?" Eric gently teased her, coming near enough to capture her lips in a light kiss. He turned and cleared her empty water bottle from the nightstand, plucking a tissue from the box to gather the rest of the trash. "I bet she'd have some advice."

"Oh, sweet holy—" Alace gritted her teeth, holding her breath as the baby latched onto her swollen nipple. "No." The word was hissed more than spoken. "I don't want you calling Grundella. I want you to teleport your mother here. Now."

Eric grinned at her, not steeping in the same irritating feelings towards Alace's former nurse as she was. He was, however, clearly pleased she was looking forward to his mother's visit. "Bebe's flight is in the air as I speak. She'll land in Denver within two hours, and I've got a driver on call to pick her up and bring her here."

Alace let him see her smile, then bent over Lila as he left the room. "Bebe. I think it's freakin' hilarious your grandmother named herself." Now that the baby was nursing strongly, the pain in her breasts was subsiding slightly, changing to a heat and fullness that satisfied in a way she didn't understand. Alace called out, "You didn't want to go pick her up?"

"And leave my babies?" Eric came back into the room with a fresh bottle of water in hand. "Not a chance, Momma." He placed it on the coaster next to the lamp on her nightstand and then surveyed the setup. "You want the pillow thingie to rest her on while she nurses?"

"No, I like holding her." Alace let her head tip backwards against the rocker. "She's so soft and warm."

Crouching at Alace's feet, Eric leaned close and leaned his head against her arm opposite where Lila was, watching their daughter nurse. He stayed in the position until it was time to shift the infant to the other breast, taking the little girl in his arms as Alace adjusted her position and clothing. He placed Lila upright against his shoulder, gently rubbing and patting her back until she emitted the most unladylike burp. Alace stared at him in wonder, her smile matching his as he looked down into Lila's face. "You ready for Momma, little one? I think she's ready for you."

They made the transfer carefully, still learning their way around how these things worked, and Lila promptly screamed and thrashed her arms until Alace got her into the right angle to find the fresh nipple.

Then it was a few minutes of impolite grumbling as she settled back into the rhythm.

"She's so gorgeous, beloved." His gaze stayed focused on Lila, and Alace stifled a sob, tears welling in her eyes as emotions overwhelmed her.

"I didn't expect to love her so much." Her whispered confession made him look at her, soft smile still in place. "Eric, she's so tiny. Anything could hurt her. I won't let it. I won't. I wanna make her safe forever." He leaned in and captured her mouth, one hand slipping alongside her neck to curve around possessively as they kissed deeply, tongues tangling. He ended the kiss with a nip to her bottom lip, then pressed his forehead against hers.

Eyes closed, he gave her what sounded like a promise. "We will keep her safe. We both know the kind of monsters there are out in the world, and between you and me, none of the evil will ever touch her. Ever." He pulled back, hand still on her neck as he lifted his other to palm Lila's head. Their daughter lay between them, protected by their bodies, contentedly nursing. "I've already got a truckload of bubble wrap on order, ready for delivery at the first signs of independence." His teasing declaration made her laugh as he'd clearly intended, her wet sputter gaining her a crooked grin from him. "She's so loved, Alace. By you and me, and Bebe." His mouth pulled to the side wryly. "I love you. Thank you. I don't know what I did to deserve this family, but I'm so blessed and happy."

Blinking fast, Alace complained, "You're gonna make me weepy again."

He leaned in and placed a kiss on each of her eyelids, then settled back.

"I'll kiss away all your tears. You being sentimental doesn't diminish your beauty to me, Alace. I wish I could quiet all your fears." He rolled his eyes. "Hold you close for all the years." Laughing, he pressed his lips to hers. "I simply love you."

When Phoebe "Bebe" Ward arrived a few hours later, Alace was surprised at the greeting she received as the woman walked into the living room where she sat with Lila. Making a beeline straight for the couch, with knees together, Phoebe crouched in front of Alace and leaned close, touching her cheek to Alace's. She whispered, "Oh, my brave girl. You've done so well."

Alace didn't try to hide the tears prompted by the tiny bit of maternal encouragement.

Her own mother was long dead, and Alace had no good memories of her. The worst of the nightmares were behind her at least, sleep no longer broken by memories of waking to strange men in their flophouse hotel room, their brutal use of her mother's body the route chosen to buy the next fix.

When she'd first met Phoebe, Alace had been so fearful she'd been nauseated. Even if the woman hadn't a clue about Alace's role in taking down her ex-husband, she'd expected to face some kind of evil inquisition about her background as it applied to the then-fledging relationship with Eric. Instead, Alace had entered what had seemed like an alternate universe, where Eric's mother adored her and proclaimed her "perfect for my son," encouraging the couple to share a bedroom in her Malibu home. She'd introduced Alace as her daughter to her friends then and there, and Alace had overheard her telling her husband, Eric's stepfather, how much she already loved the woman she hoped would become her daughter-in-law.

It had taken months until Alace believed the first visit wasn't a fluke, brought on by stress over the nationwide coverage surrounding the exposure of Bebe's ex-husband to be the arrogant, abusive bastard he was. From Phoebe's tight-lipped reaction to Ward's press conference announcing his retirement, Alace had known there was more to his mother's story than Eric knew. A dark hatred had swelled in her for a man who could take someone so beautifully giving and make them sit in pained silence. Phoebe had shared later, when Alace had found her sitting on the patio, staring out at the ocean. What she'd learned would earn Ward more pain. *When it's time.*

After Lila's birth, once their family of three had been settled in the hospital room, Alace had immediately voiced her desire for her mother-in-law to visit. She'd done it loudly and intentionally, while Eric was on the phone with Phoebe. His only response had been to pass along the scold from Phoebe to remember to call her Mom, and not by her given name.

Never having a mother worthy of the name, Alace found herself reveling in the idea she'd found one now.

"Phoebe…Mom. I'd like you to meet your granddaughter." Alace shifted and lifted her daughter so Bebe could see her face. "Lila Sue, this is Bebe, the best grandmother in the world."

"Oh, my stars. Could she be any prettier? Oh, Eric, honey, you and Alace made a gorgeous little girl." Phoebe sat on the couch next to Alace and held out her arms. "Come to Bebe, gorgeous."

"Not so fast, Bebe. Wash your hands first." Eric walked towards the stairs, his mother's suitcase in hand. "Hospital rules still apply."

"Of course, of course." Phoebe stood, unbuttoned her coat, and draped it over the back of a nearby chair. "I'm positively excited." She winked at Alace. "Back in a minute, sweet girls of mine."

Overwhelmed, all Alace could do was nod. *How in the hell did I get so lucky?*

Alace didn't know, but she'd do anything to keep this family she'd found safe from any threats.

Anything.

***

Owen

Seated at the desk he'd installed in his bedroom, Owen ran the fingers of one hand through his hair, ruffling the strands. His other hand was being used to tab through information he'd downloaded about the sibling pair pervert group. Mind only half on what he was doing, he glanced at the security video displayed on a nearby tablet. Nothing moved in the room, captured in shades of white and gray, the two blanket-covered lumps that were Kelly and Shiloh lying still and silent in the bed.

Things had gone as well as could have been hoped after dinner, Kelly asking questions with an intensity he'd come to expect from the boy. He'd been upfront with both kids, explaining he didn't yet have answers to most of what they'd want to know but promising to iron out details quickly. Owen wanted to wait until Marchant had at least another chance to look Shiloh over. Before the doctor had left, they'd scheduled a repeat visit for a few days' time, so he had a window of opportunity in which to plan. Shiloh's energy had faded quickly after eating, the little girl growing quieter by the minute until Owen had suggested time for bed.

Movement made the edges of the screen blink red, and he focused on the bed, seeing Shiloh was sitting up. She wiggled to the edge of the bed and got to her feet, then seemed to hesitate, head turning back and forth a few times. The door to the hallway was cracked a few inches, and when she headed that direction, Owen stood and walked to his bedroom door, stepping out into the corridor.

Without the infrared visibility to lend greater clarity, Shiloh came into view gradually, her little girl's nightgown a lighter contrast against the darkness. She stopped and stared up at him, then tucked her chin to her chest.

"Hey, sweetie," Owen greeted, pleased when she looked up at him again. "What woke you up, baby girl?" Her head swung back and forth, hair sweeping across her shoulders. "Bad dreams?" He gently tucked a strand of hair behind her ear as she nodded. "You wanna stay with me for a little while?"

"Pease." Her voice was tiny and quavered, a better reflection of her mental state than the impassive expression she wore.

"Sure thing." He backed up and was turning when she caught at his hand, fingers wrapping around his index finger tightly. "I'm working on something, but I'll be right here, and you can rest on my bed. When you go back to sleep, I'll carry you to where Kelly's sleeping." He led her towards the bed and lifted her to the middle, bringing up a blanket to tuck around her. "You're safe here, sweetheart. Nothing to worry about, I promise you."

Her grip on his finger didn't waver, growing even tighter as he attempted to withdraw.

Owen inched closer instead, and he crouched down to put his head at level with hers, sweeping her hair away from her face. The expression revealed was hesitant, wary. "Shiloh, do you believe you're safe here?"

She studied him closely, the weight of her scrutiny heavier with each passing second; then her bottom lip bowed up and quivered. "No."

Her admission hit him like a fist to the solar plexus, and he struggled to school his reaction. "How can I make it so you trust me? Kelly trusts me. He's been with me longer. Maybe in a few days, we can have this conversation again?"

"I twust you." Shiloh patted his hand consolingly, and at her caring gesture, this sweet baby's attempt to comfort him, Owen lost the fight against the rage flowing through him.

How any human could do anything to hurt an angel like this, he'd never understand. The image of Shiloh waking next to Earl mixed in his mind with the pictures he'd seen of Emma, the things those animals had done to her, and he dropped his face into his hands with a cry. "I'm sorry." He wasn't sure if he was speaking aloud, but Shiloh's hand settled on his head. "I wish I could have been there. I wish I could have saved you." Those words were the same ones he'd spoken over his daughter's grave, on his knees in the snow as the first enormous waves of grief had him in their grip. Numbness had descended into place for so long, Owen didn't know what to do with the emotions battering at him now. "I'm sorry, baby girl. I'm so sorry."

A hand touched his shoulder, and he instinctively knew it was Kelly. The boy leaned against him, resting his head in the crook of Owen's neck. Shiloh crawled across the bed, curling around Owen as best she could, her fingers plucking at his, peeling them away from his face so she could see. He stared at her, eyes hot and stinging with salt. His raw emotions couldn't take much more.

"We know." That was Kelly, his body pressed against Owen's trembling like aspen leaves in a breeze. "It's not your fault." He turned Owen's head, staring into his eyes. "We know."

"I wish…" Owen trailed off, and Kelly broke their stare, twisting to curl an arm around Shiloh's upper body, drawing her closer. "I'm so glad we found each other."

***

Alace

She stared at the computer monitor, working her way through a mass of documents Owen had uploaded. He'd intelligently posed his question in an email, offering her an out if what he'd asked wasn't comfortable. The surprise hadn't lasted long, and she'd quickly found the idea of having him closer wasn't uncomfortable, not at all. It was the opposite. If he were nearby, they could collaborate more effectively and work together to hone the skills they needed to stay sharp.

No matter if she wasn't going to personally work the gigs anymore, she didn't want to lose her edge. Getting stale wasn't an option, not something to consider, even just in her head. Practice—for lack of a better word—had been something she'd carefully organized in the past, setting up sessions with individuals meticulously vetted for what they had to offer. Sometimes it had been a give-and-take process, where Alace would agree to teach something specific and, in turn, learn a different talent from them. Her skills and Owen's were already complementary, so training with him would keep them both in a greater state of readiness.

Owen moving here. With two kids in tow.

That last detail was a bit surreal. Based on his communications, it was clear he was laying plans to keep the two kids he'd rescued—indefinitely. He'd made reference to developing a local support network that would allow him to continue working. Supposedly that was one of the places where she would come in. Alace snorted at the idea of anyone asking her to babysit, even Owen. *Not happening.* They were friends, sure, but babysit?

She stilled as she realized what she'd thought. Not too long ago, she'd been bemoaning the fact she didn't have any friends other than Eric, and now she was making assumptions about Owen, one of her hunters. *He's not only my hunter. I can't deny there's been a shift between us.* Not after the last few gigs they'd worked. The kind of synchronized awareness they'd developed was unfamiliar, but not unwelcome.

Could be he's as lonely as I once was. Before she'd started building her family.

With that thought, Alace toggled the view on the monitor, changing to a map overlay with a single dot in the center of a green rectangle. She zoomed in and saw the park's name matched one Bebe had mentioned before she'd left the house with Lila in her stroller.

"Beloved." That single word—fucking, *fucking* word—rolled over her, and Alace shivered, nipples tingling. *Damn, just his voice does shit to me.* It would be weeks yet before they could attempt intimacy, and she already found herself counting down the days. "Is that my mother and Lila?"

Alace looked over her shoulder, meeting his gaze without shame. "Yes." She glanced back at the screen and clicked an icon, changing the overlay from the static map to the satellite imagery showing greater detail, including the park bench where the dot was positioned. "They're at the park."

"Alace, did you bug my mother?" He sounded bemused, not angry, so she gave him a tiny smirk over her shoulder this time.

"No. I wouldn't do that. Unless you asked me to." She hid the first screen and brought up a portal log-in, entering her complicated pass phrase followed by a security question, which was followed by another pass phrase. Once within the controls, she flicked the display to show the view below the drone she'd had hovering over where her mother-in-law and child sat in the sunshine. "There they are." Zooming in, she smiled at Phoebe's attentive interaction with Lila. "Awww, Bebe looks like she's having a good time."

"Baby." She shivered again, looking up at him as his hands settled on her shoulders. *Damn, he's pulling out the big guns.* "Did you bug our daughter?" She dipped her chin once, slowly. "And you're spying on Bebe's afternoon out?" Alace wrinkled her nose. "Where did you plant the bug?"

"This one is in the stroller." She ducked her head and turned back to the computer, flipping to the overlay with the location indicator. Tapping out a sequence, she pulled up a different control screen, slowly toggling buttons from red to green. As she did each one, a new marker lit up on the screen. "This one is in the diaper bag. This is the pink dinosaur blanket.

This one is the pacifier tether. The bottle holder in the bag. Her dinosaur toy. Her onesie." When she finished, the space around the bench was littered with dots, each a slightly different color. She stared at the screen and took in a deep breath. "It's not what it looks like. It's not that I don't trust your mother. I do. I trust Bebe with my life. With Lila's life."

Eric's lips touched her temple, holding there for a long kiss. "I understand, beloved. Believe me, I truly understand."

"It's too much, isn't it?" Alace dropped her head back and looked up at him again with a groan. "I've officially crossed over into crazyland."

"If it helps keep our daughter safe, then it would never be too much." He bent close and kissed her lips, the upside-down positioning making something so familiar feel different and unique. "And you've been in crazyland a while now, my dear, sweet Alace. I definitely married the Red Queen."

Alace huffed out a laugh, then paused, her gaze tracing how the smile he wore changed his face. *So gorgeous.* "Who's the Red Queen again? Wait, she's the crazy one, isn't she?"

Eric's smile turned sly. "Maybe a little."

Chapter Seven

Owen

Hip angled against the kitchen cabinet, Owen rested his weight in a comfortable stance as he watched the kids through the open archway into the living room. They were positioned in front of the TV, Shiloh sitting on the floor near one end of the sofa, Kelly sprawled out over half the cushioned surface. An animated movie about talking cars was playing, one Kelly had promised Shiloh enjoyed, too. The goal was to keep both kids busy enough to stay there, giving Owen a chance to talk to the guest he'd invited over.

Right on schedule, the tablet screen lit up, the motion-activated security camera showing a car pulling into the driveway. Owen tapped a button on his phone, and the garage door began opening, the SUV pulling inside. He tapped the same button, and the garage door closed, visible on the video as he walked towards the connecting door.

Marchant stood beside his vehicle when Owen opened the door. He was sweeping the space with an attentive glance. On his previous visits, he had entered and exited via the front door, so this was new territory. "Hey," Marchant offered, walking towards Owen with his hand out. "Good to see you again."

"You too, man." Owen gripped and shook, their hands lifting twice before he disconnected. "Come on in. I've got brews or some brew, depending on what you want."

"Brews or brew?" Marchant followed him, and Owen noted once again his danger-radar wasn't pinging at all, no unease at having the man at his back. A mark on the plus side of the column for what he'd planned for tonight. "What's that mean? Hey, Kelly, Shiloh." The kids' heads swiveled towards them, Kelly raising a hesitant hand before looking back at the TV. Shiloh took longer to return to the video, her gaze lingering on Marchant. "They doing well?"

"Yeah, seem to be. Shiloh's healing, and I'm gradually getting them back to fightin' weight. They spook easy, though." He pointed towards the refrigerator. "Brews are in there." Grabbing a mug, he poured himself a cup of the coffee waiting in the carafe. "And brew is here."

"Brew, if you don't mind." Marchant nodded with a smirk. "Clever boy."

"All man, thank you very much." Owen's brain stuttered at the unintentional innuendo of their back-and-forth banter, and he shook his head. "Sugar?"

"Now you're calling me sweet?" Mug in hand, Owen swung around to stare at the man, surprised by the blatant humor on his features. "I'm kidding, Marcus. Black works for me. And it's to be expected the kids will take time to get over the trauma they experienced. It hasn't been long at all. In the grand scheme of things, a couple of weeks isn't enough to lay down enough good memories to block out the bad stuff."

"Are you gay?" The question spilled out before he could stop it, and Owen squeezed his eyes closed, shaking his head back and forth. "Shit. Never mind. I don't care one way or another. That's not why I called you, at all."

"Happily queer, yes. And no, I didn't expect this was a booty call." Fingers plucked the empty mug from his hand, and Owen stepped backwards, lowering his chin to watch as Marchant made himself at home, pouring the mug full of coffee. "I was afraid something was wrong with one of the kids, but you said no medkit needed when I texted back, so that was a fear laid to rest at least."

"Dammit, I'm off on the wrong foot. I've…" Huffing in frustration, he studied Marchant, noting how the man kept his gaze studiously on the steaming mug. Ten feet separated them, and Owen ran a hand through his hair, ruffling and separating the strands as he tried to settle his unexpected case of nerves. *Nothing ventured,* he reminded himself, and pointed at the stools next to the breakfast bar. "Let's sit. Since the couch is occupied by my resident movie-lovers, this'll do."

Wordlessly Marchant followed instructions, quickly relocating to a stool that put his back to the kids. Owen wondered if he'd made the decision intentionally, allowing Owen to have the entire room under his gaze, but shook off the idea.

"Did you have a chance to treat the other kids from that place I never went to or saw?" Owen lifted his mug to hide what he was sure was a strained expression. "And by other kids, I mean those ones who don't have anything to do with mine."

"I know what you mean, and yes, I did. Some of them will be years recovering from what that man did. Every time I see what I think is the worst of humanity, some asshole has to go the extra mile to prove me wrong." Mouth pulled to the side, Marchant allowed his disgust to show on his features. "Half of those kids had been reported dead in foster care, the other half flagged as runaways. They came from all over

America, man. How can there be so many corrupt people within one single system?"

"Money talks, always has. If you're an asshole, have something you don't value much, like someone else's child you're being paid to feed and clothe, and someone comes along and offers enough money—it's not rocket science what happens next." Owen glanced at the kids. *My kids.* "Pair of young children like mine, with a dead mother and father, those parents part of a demographic also viewed as the dregs of society, it's not hard to disappear them. Authorities are jaded, where they aren't outright crooked, so when they're told the worst, they more readily believe it."

"And the kids pay and pay." Marchant blew a stream of air across his coffee and directed his gaze to Owen's face. "Why'd you ask me here?"

Pulling in a long breath, uncaring if it marked what he had to say next as momentous, Owen rested his palms flat on the countertop, steadying himself in that way, too.

"I'm ex-military. My daughter was kidnapped and killed by child traffickers while I was embedded overseas. I came home to a cold granite stone, and damn little in the way of information. Brass shipped me out again right away, well before I was ready. I was…unhinged would probably be the right way to describe my state of mind." He swallowed, fighting against the taste of dust and ash, the scent of smoke thick in his nostrils. He flexed his hands, pressing his fingertips against the cold surface, anchoring himself in the now as best he could. *Now, not then.* It took a few breaths, but gradually, the smell of death faded away. "My mission was to take out a Central American political figure. I was in place, in play, target acquired—and saw a child only two windows down from where my man stood in plain sight. There was a male individual with that child, one I knew was a close confidant of my target. They were amigos, you get me?" Marchant nodded slowly. "So I did what I had to do."

"You killed them?" It was Marchant's turn to swallow hard. "Shot them both?"

"Fuck no. That'd be too fast." Owen straightened his shoulders, echoes of his courts martial proceedings rolling through his head. *I'd do it again, and again, if it meant saving a single child.* "I razed the compound to the ground, walking out of there with all the innocent noncombatants I could. Took me three weeks to return those kids to their parents, scattered around the mountains as they were. Incommunicado the whole time, my bosses were sure I'd lost my hold on reality, and pretty much anyone would agree with them. For sure." He shook his head. "When I finally called for an evac, I spent the entire dust-off with my hands on my head, expecting to catch a bullet the whole time. They tried me, found me wanting, and—since I was back on US soil by then—couldn't do much more than boot me. I'd done what they'd ordered, killed my target. I simply did it by creating a political shitstorm they hadn't expected or wanted. Like I gave a fat fuck about that."

Sipping at his coffee, Marchant betrayed himself, his hand trembling as he held the mug to his lips. "Then what happened?"

"I started hunting for a living. Men like Warrant, mostly. I've got a partner who does the bulk of the investigative work, helps source any assistance or supplies needed, but it's pretty much me on the ground these days." Owen shrugged, cut his glance to where the kids were engrossed in the movie. "I do what you've been doing, but to the extreme."

"I saw the inside of the cabin. I'd say it was pretty extreme."

Owen bristled, back snapping straight. Keeping his voice low, with teeth clenched he hissed, "I walked in there and he had Shiloh tied to his bed—"

Marchant waved a hand, cutting him off. "I didn't mean you. I meant that pedophile piece of shit. I've seen a lot of physical abuse, but breaking those kids down mentally like he did—in a huge group no less. Well, that's nothing I've seen before."

"There're more of them out there. He had a video streaming when I got there." Owen glared at Marchant. "I dismantled it so the authorities wouldn't know. In no way were my actions to keep them safe from the cops or feds."

Marchant opened his mouth, then closed it and took several slow, even breaths before saying, "So *you* can find and deal with them. You think there are others out there doing what he did to those kids?" Marchant's face paled, and his lips pressed into a thin line. "Jesus, Marcus. What can I do?"

Bingo. Here was the reaction he'd been counting on. Now to tease the end game he most wanted.

"Kelly and Shiloh living with me means my actions are going to be limited for a while. They don't know anyone but me, and I wouldn't trust just anyone with them."

"You want me to stay with them while you go out—what was it you called it? Hunting?" Marchant's shoulders straightened, pushing back. "Name the date. I'll make it happen."

"What if the need was for bigger help than merely that? More specifically, what do you have holding you to Jersey?" Having gotten the initial response he'd hoped for, Owen was ready to press his advantage and go for broke. "Family here?" He already knew the answer. Marchant didn't have anyone in the region, he'd stayed in the area for the ease of travel, waiting for his credentials to be restored so he could return to Thailand. Owen knew better than the man did that there was a slim chance his visa would be reinstated, not after how difficult he'd made it for the government there. Marchant was holding out hope, though, and Owen understood how it felt. "Boyfriend?"

"Nothing and no one." Draining his mug, Marchant thumped it on the countertop. "Spit it out, Marcus. I can tell you've got something in mind, and if it helps save even one child, count me in."

"My partner is in Colorado." He let the statement dangle between them for a long breath. "I've got a line on a house not far from where they live."

"I can be packed in a day."

Even though it was the reaction he'd hoped for, Owen felt odd trusting the words. Luck wasn't something he believed in these days. "You sure, man? You might want to hear more details first."

"Kids need help, you help them. Kids need help, I help them. I think we're working both sides of the same street on this one, Marcus. From where I sit, there's no excuse for saying no. Your kids"—damn, it was good to hear his claim so plainly stated—"know and trust me. Between the two of us, we'll provide a continuity of care that'll go a long way to helping them recover and heal. It's a yes from me."

"Well, all righty then. So, here's what I was thinking." Owen leaned forwards and began speaking, Marchant hanging on every word as he spoke for the duration of the movie, during dinner, and well into the night.

***

Owen

Comfortably angled against the doorframe, Owen tipped his head to the side as he stared into the bedroom the kids shared, watching as Kelly eagerly dumped a tangle of the last of his scant articles of clothing into a box. From the moment the decision had become official, things had moved quickly, with Alace helping source a house near—but not too close to—where she lived with Eric. She hadn't immediately taken to the idea of a third on their team—Owen scoffed far back in his throat because that was putting things mildly—but between her own investigation into Marchant and Owen's vouching for the man, he'd finally been able to convince her.

She'd even uncovered parts of the man's past Owen hadn't been privy to, his own digging focused on what had happened in recent years, while hers had been more of a birth-to-grave process. Marchant had been a doctor in Texas and Oklahoma right out of school, working on his residency in emergency medicine. The man had gotten involved in an investigation surrounding a suspected torture serial killer, one who'd preyed on young adult women. The experience had paved the way for his continued focus on trauma, turning his attention to the youngest victims.

Information Alace found indicated the serial killer had never been officially identified and stopped, but word of mouth put his ending at the hands of an organized motorcycle gang. Their motivation had never been clarified, but based on how quickly Marchant had changed locations after the killer dropped off the grid, Alace had shared her suspicions he'd had something to do with whatever had happened.

There'd been a couple of conference calls with the three of them, during which Alace had disguised her voice. The first had her sounding like a gender-neutral, laid-back California beach bum, and the second had given her a male voice with a broad Boston accent. Marchant hadn't been fazed by either, shaking his head in clear amusement once the calls ended. He'd known enough to not say anything denigrating Alace's focus on security, which was good because Owen had seen the nearest tablet wake immediately after the calls terminated. Alace had dropped in to listen to the man's debrief and had admitted to being impressed when she and Owen touched base later. Marchant had been dialed in on the mission, in this case shifting locations to Colorado where they could work out of a better, more consolidated base. The fact he wasn't digging for info on her was a solid indicator of where the man's head was at.

"Last box, buddy?" Kelly looked up and gave him a lifted chin in response, wrestling with the roll of tape to retrieve a long enough piece to secure the top of the box. "Want some help?"

"No." Kelly panted slightly, arms held wide as he pulled the strip of tape free. "I got it."

"Where's Shiloh?" If Kelly hadn't been available to question, Owen would have looked in only a couple of places, expecting to find the girl in one of the two. She preferred her surroundings to be close and dark and often migrated underneath the bed on the end nearest the wall, or inside the closet, sometimes with the laundry basket turned upside down over her. Marchant said it couldn't even be considered acting out, because she wasn't malicious about it. There was no trying to hide or trying to scare Owen; she simply preferred the closeness of those two places. It could be a result of her time in Warrant's compound or a holdover from the foster family situations she and Kelly had been in.

"In the closet." Kelly got one end of the tape tacked down and smoothed the rest in place, sealing the box closed. "Everything's all packed. When are we leaving?"

"Soon as Doc gets here." Owen had settled on the half-title as a moniker for Marchant. It was a nod to his expertise and less intimate than saying his first name. He ignored why it bothered him, since he called Alace Sweets Ward by her first name all the time. *Darren Marchant. See, brain? It ain't that hard.* "We'll load up these last few things, our suitcases, then you and Shiloh, and we'll be ready to go."

Marchant had wanted to keep his vehicle, so they were using it for the drive to Colorado. Owen had made quick work of dealing with the anchors holding him here. He'd sold his junker and booked a moving cube last week, filling it with the household boxes and the furniture he and Doc wanted to take, waving it off on a semi early yesterday. The furniture left in this house would remain, increasing the ability of the landlord to lease the house or give him something to complain about as he tossed it. Owen didn't care either way. The house Alace had found was fully furnished and ready to move in, and what hadn't been now was—up to and including a fully stocked pantry. She hadn't fucked around with anything either, paying cash for the house as well as the empty lots on either side. Owen had been ready to transfer funds to her to cover the cost, but she'd demurred, for now waving him off in a way that made him think she wouldn't be open to having a conversation with him about it at all.

He smiled and watched Kelly wrestle the box to the door. Reaching for the box, he told the boy, "I'll get this, you see if you can coax your sister out." Kelly's lips pursed as he nodded, hefting the box the last couple of inches up into Owen's grasp. "Doc'll be here any minute." He heard the garage door going up and looked over his shoulder towards the kitchen. "That's him now. It's not going to take but a minute to get these few things loaded. I've got your and Shiloh's travel bags packed already. Come on to the garage when you're ready, and we'll get going."

Without waiting to hear Kelly's response, he'd only made it halfway up the hallway before three sharp raps sounded on the connecting door to the garage. It opened, and Marchant strode through, key fob twirling around one finger.

"Is this all of it?"

Owen nodded as he set the box on top of the short stack next to the door. "This, these, and the kids." He pointed towards the three bags on the floor nearby. "I've got snacks and tablets in the kids' bags. Toiletries and a change of clothes just in case we decide to stop at a hotel tonight. We're good to go."

"I'll get the boxes and bags." Marchant lifted two boxes and walked back through the door. "You bring the kiddos."

Owen turned and saw Kelly standing in the hallway, a look of uncertainty on his face. "Does she not wanna come out?" The boy shook his head. "No worries. Help Doc with the bags. I'll go talk to her."

Back in the kids' bedroom, Owen lowered himself until he was sitting on the floor, back against the wall farthest from the door. He rocked his head back and closed his eyes. There was no sound at all from the closet yet. *On to the next maneuver.* Clearing his throat, he began to quietly hum "Three Blind Mice."

The musical round had become his go-to when soothing Shiloh back to sleep after nightmares woke her, and he hoped it would draw her out of her hiding spot without him having to go into the closet. He was on the third rendition of the tune when he heard movement and opened his eyes a slit to see an overturned laundry basket creeping towards him. Shiloh could be seen only in broken images underneath. One eye, a swath of hair, then the tips of her fingers against the floor. With a smile, he closed his eyes again and continued.

Slowly, slowly she neared him, eventually resting half on his legs, her cheek pressed just above his knee. In a broken whisper, she sang along, using the Portuguese lyrics he'd taught her. *"Tres ratos cegos, ver como eles correm."*

He slipped a hand underneath the basket and rested it on her head, fingers stroking across the silken strands of her hair. Everything about her was a far cry from how he'd found her only a few weeks ago. Everything except her fear. "Sweetheart, it's time to go on our trip." Her head rocked against his leg, but uncertain if it was a nod or a shake, he pressed, "We're all packed up except for our Shiloh. Have you seen her?"

Her singing had fallen away, sticking on a soft hum as she kept the music going. Her giggles finally interrupted it entirely, and he smiled at the sound.

"Was that my Shiloh I heard? Is it you under there?" She shifted, and he moved his hand, giving her the freedom to spring to her knees, basket going flying as she held her arms out in a silent "ta-da" of surprise. "It is my Shiloh! I'm so happy to see you. Are you ready to go?"

She sank down, hunching into herself, arms turned from excited streamers into bands of confinement as they wrapped around her body. "Mm'hm." All the enthusiasm had fled her face, leaving only fear and anxiety behind.

"I won't let anything bad happen to you." She angled her head to look into his face, her lips pressed in a bloodless line. "I promise you, Shiloh."

They remained in those positions for a breath. Then she gave a deep sigh, releasing a great breath of air, and crawled into his lap. "Mm'kay." She hummed and he smiled, pressing a kiss to the top of her head. "*Tres ratos cegos, tres ratos cegos, ver como eles correm.*" She broke off and twisted to look up at him. "Sing wit me." Her demand was quiet but firm, and he gritted his teeth to keep from grinning. *My girl's got an attitude on her.* He loved every sign of strength and courage she showed.

Doc and Kelly looked up as Owen walked into the garage carrying Shiloh, still singing that damn song.

Six hours later, both kids were asleep in the back seat, and Owen glanced over at Doc, taking in the man's loosely confident movements as he steered the car. They'd been through all the surface small talk, asking about final details, dropping off keys, running through a drive-thru to pick up a hot snack for the kids versus stopping for a meal—but had carefully edged around the more critical topics so far.

Another quick look over his shoulder reassured Owen the kids were asleep. Shiloh slumped far over in her booster seat while Kelly leaned on the door, forehead pressed against the glass, his mouth dropped open and emitting infrequent snores.

"We'll get there tomorrow, even if we decide to stop for the night." He began by stating something they both knew. It was approximately twenty-six driving hours, barring any traffic delays from construction or accidents. They'd probably drive straight through, but had ample time if they didn't. "There's no strict timeline, though. My partner knows we'll be there this week, but I didn't detail our plans." The "partner" bit was Alace's decision; she hadn't wanted the doctor to know her name until she'd had a chance to meet him. Owen understood and thought Doc probably did, too. *Follow her gut has always been Alace's go-to process.*

"I know." Marchant's nonchalant tone was maddening for reasons Owen couldn't articulate.

"I know you know, I'm just..." His ribs expanded with a deep breath. "They matter to me. My partner does.

They're married. Happily. To a highly intelligent Neanderthal I happen to like, too. So I want you to like them. I want to work with you like we've talked about. If we were still in Jersey, we could do what we want. But in their backyard, they've gotta like you, too." The seat belt rubbed his neck as he shook his head. "I'm rambling."

Looking at his lap, Owen stared at his phone, perplexed. The light next to the camera was blinking. In sequence.

Blink. Blink. Blink. Pause. Four blinks and a pause. Two blinks and a long flash and a pause. A long flash and a pause. A repeat of the two blinks and a long flash, then a pause, and a blink, flash flash, blink.

S H U T U P

In Morse code.

"Are you fuckin' kidding me right now?"

Flash, blink pause, flash flash flash.

N O

Again, in Morse code.

"What?" Marchant's question rode over the information in Owen's brain, but he ignored the man.

"You want me to stop talking. About what? You? Want me to stop talking about you?"

Flash, blink, flash flash. Blink. Blink. Blink. Blink.

YES

"Oh my fucking God."

"What's going on?" The tone of the question caught his attention, and Owen glared at Marchant, who was staring at him as if he'd grown a third head. Which he might as well have done, since there were apparently three adults in the vehicle, albeit one only electronically.

"Nothing." Staring down at the phone, Owen tried to figure out how to tell Alace to stop eavesdropping on the conversation. Squeezing his eyes closed, he wished for the subvocal microphone setup. With the earwig in place, he could have had an entire conversation with Alace without Marchant being any wiser. The phone vibrated, and he looked down to see the light blinking again. She spelled out, "Talk. Just not about me."

Owen lifted his chin and glared at the trees flashing by on the nearby hillside. The phone vibrated again, and he shook his head, denying her request. Another, longer vibration had his chin jerking around and down, turning his irritated glare back on the phone. Blinking, he spelled out his response to her, knowing she'd be able to decipher his intent.

Blink blink close blink. Blink blink close. Close blink close blink. Close, blink, close. Close, blink, close close. Close close close. Blink blink close.

F U C K Y O U

He turned the phone over and removed the back, unseating the battery and putting it into one pocket. A quick nudge with the tool that came with the device slipped the SIM card from its slot, and he lay it loose in the battery compartment, closing the back of the phone. He watched the screen for a few breaths and then looked out the window again.

Why the hell did this whole thing make me so angry? He'd known she had his phones bugged. She'd been upfront with him about it since the beginning of their relationship, and things had gotten even more real after they'd worked on the mission to save her man's best friend. Something buzzed in the back seat, and Owen twisted around to dig through Kelly's bag, honestly not surprised to find the culprit was the boy's tablet.

A video call from Unknown was waiting to be accepted.

"My partner is resourceful." He flashed the screen at Marchant and caught the man's smirk in response. "Why are you grinning?"

"They didn't like it when you killed the phone, huh?" Thumping the back of the tablet with a heavy finger, Marchant laughed quietly. "Better answer the boss."

Pushing out as much irritation as he could alongside a big huff of air, Owen tapped the tablet's screen. It took a moment to connect, and Owen had a second to wonder how it even had a connection, because neither of the tablets had data plans attached to them, dependent on Wi-Fi for access to the Internet. *Alace. It always comes back to Alace.* As the video resolved, he thumbed the volume down a notch, hoping to allow the kids to stay asleep as long as possible.

Finally, the pixilation dissolved, and the whirling circle disappeared, leaving Alace's unsmiling face in its place. He glared at her, noting she'd pulled on her ice queen mask most often used when she felt threatened. *Best to basically jump in with both feet.* "Your control of things is not being usurped. I'm not backing away from our agreement. On missions, I'm still going to want you in my head, want you to be my eyes, need to know you've got my back." Her expression softened slightly, and the tiny microchange told him volumes. *Nail on the head.* That was part of the problem, though. "Me wanting to have a moment where I'm not being listened to isn't me telling you to stop trying to keep me safe. The problem is when your best tool is a hammer, everything starts to look like a nail. There were other ways for you to get what you needed."

He'd kept the tablet angled towards the window, away from Doc's view, hand covering the glass where the reflection would show. *Pay attention, Alace. This is me protecting you as best I can.*

If she didn't speak, Doc wouldn't know for certain even her sex. If she didn't name herself, the man wouldn't have a clue who Owen's partner was. As if she could read his mind, Alace shook her head side to side, once. Left, right, center.

"Darren Marchant, my name is Alace Sweets." Owen cocked an eyebrow at her, and one corner of her lips twitched. She appeared to like knowing she had surprised him. "Turn the tablet, Owen, so he can see the boss." He narrowed his eyes, and she released a tiny huff of air, nostrils flaring slightly. "The digital assistants are always listening. I'm just paying attention to what they're hearing."

Well, one mystery solved. He was surprised she'd given him that much. Alace had always been one to hold tight to her secrets. He twisted the tablet, steadying it on one knee so he could see both Alace and Doc.

Marchant lifted one hand laconically as he gave the digital version of Alace a nod. "Pleased."

"Same. You do good works."

Marchant frowned. "You mean work?"

"No. I say what I mean. Works. The efforts you expended on behalf of those children in Thailand was remarkable. The fact you haven't given up hope of returning shows a dangerous stubborn streak, but the works you've done both in the country here and outside of it all speak to the kind of man you are." Alace's lips closed, touching but not pressing, her unaffected mask in place. Owen could detect no stress points in what he could see, no furrowing of the brows, no tightening of the skin near her eyes or ears; her entire face appeared as relaxed as if she were in the middle of a meditation session. "I'm still unconvinced you can stomach what Owen and I do, but your care for his kids is remarkable. I'm pleased he had you in his pocket to call on when he needed someone to assist."

The pause in conversation next was uncomfortable, and Owen found himself wanting to fill the silence. A miniscule shake of her head held him quiet, waiting. Finally, eventually, Marchant took the bait, responding.

"I'd like to think I'm morally aligned, especially where children are concerned. They are what matters to me, always. I believe I find myself more flexible when it comes to what happens to the ones we're fighting against." Interesting how he'd already settled into the "we" territory. It had taken Owen a lot longer. He and Alace had worked together for months before the Worthington mission when things had come together for them to take the relationship farther and create the true partnership they now had. "I'd like to caution both of you, and Owen's already heard this from me, but I don't think I can take an active part in what he calls the missions. That's not my skill set, and I think I'd be of much better use continuing to employ the talents I do have than trying to develop new ones. I'm an old dog, Alace Sweets. I don't learn new tricks easily."

"But you're saying you can be taught?" Alace's lips pressed together, preventing a moue from developing. Tossup if it was in annoyance or humor. "Regardless of your response, I tend to agree with you. In these things, it is always much simpler to stick to what we do well. In my case, that's morphing from my previous highly active role into a directed focus on a second primary skill, investigation and organization. What happened to your sister?"

Owen blinked. Alace hadn't changed inflection, hadn't indicated she was going to ask a question, and when he glanced at Doc to find him frozen at the wheel, eyes unfocused and staring, he gawped.

"Darren?" Alace's rendering of his name seemed to snap the man out of it, and Owen saw the muscles in his jaw flex and dance under the skin, noticing a tiny triangle of scruff missed in his most recent shave.

"No one knows." Doc cleared his throat roughly, Adam's apple bobbing deep in his throat with a hard swallow. "She disappeared years ago. I was barely out of school, had only recently started my first residency rotation."

"You're pretty sure it was the rodeo serial killer, though, am I right?" Owen split his attention between Doc's evident distress and Alace's impassive interest.

"The authorities never nailed down a strict timeline, but you knew she was attending to watch a friend compete."

"Where's this going? And did you have to do it now? There's a lot of miles yet between us and you, and if we're going to be there anyway, can't this wait?" Doc's hand lifted from the steering wheel, and he dashed his fingers underneath one eye, annoyance clear on his expression. *At least one of my partners is easy to read.*

"I know a guy who knows a guy. I can ask around, see what I can find. Why did you leave the Ark-La-Tex area?"

Doc's head jolted as if he'd taken a hit. Eyes squinting in apparent pain, he didn't answer, that muscle jumping in his jaw again.

"You keep it up and I'll use your middle name." Owen stared at the camera, willing Alace to feel his irritation. "I'll turn off every electronic in the car, and unless you actively bugged the car, you'll be without even a tracking signal to know where we are. We could turn up in your driveway at any moment, and you wouldn't know until I was hammering on your door." A change in her expression gave it away, and he groaned. "Oh, Jesus. You did. You bugged the car." He turned the tablet to face him, lowering his brow and glaring at her. "*Jesus*, Alace."

"Not the way you're thinking. Just something for a location with a mechanical signal. So I'll know if you're broken down or simply stopping for food. Turn it back around, please. I need to apologize."

"Doc, you okay if she apologizes to you right now?" Without shifting the tablet, he looked towards the man in the driver seat, noting the white knuckles and tense line of his shoulders. *She genuinely shook him with those questions.* "Because if you aren't, I'll make her wait and do it in person."

"Yeah. It's fine." His fingers curled around the wheel and tightened, then slipped back and relaxed. Curled around and tightened. "Whatever."

"You get one chance." Owen held up his index finger and pointed it at the camera. "Don't screw this up." Tablet turned, he stared at Alace, watching as she softened her posture, gentling her expression. *A show, or real?* Owen guessed it didn't matter, as long as Doc believed.

"I apologize, Darren—Doc. I was out of line, and you have no reason to trust me yet, so you wouldn't know I'll always have your best interests at heart. Just as I do with Owen. My friends—and I don't have many of them, so they're precious to me—come first. I didn't mind my mouth, and I'm sorry."

"Yeah, okay." Doc didn't turn and look, keeping his gaze aimed out the windshield at the lane ahead of them. "Yes, she disappeared at a rodeo. Yes, I believe that bastard killed my little sister. Believe, but couldn't prove it. I got out of there and headed to Boston, soon as I could. Then Boston wasn't far enough, so I took a mission trip. Thailand happened, and it felt so different to what I'd done before, I stayed. For as long as they'd let me, I stayed. I think she's in the woods somewhere between Tulsa and Siloam Springs. That's where a bunch of the competitors were headed next. I stayed away because I never found her. I stayed away because I couldn't help her. I couldn't save her."

"Few things hurt more than losing those we love." Owen's voice cracked, and he couldn't find it inside himself to be embarrassed. "Makes things heavy. Then places get heavy. Sometimes staying away isn't about feeling like you've failed, but because of self-preservation. If a place, a memory is heavy enough, it can become life-threatening." The memory of cold metal in his mouth, the cool wood of a stock against his bare sole, pressed in, circling around him until all he could feel was the curve of the trigger against the pad of his toe.

"Owen." He opened his eyes and looked at Doc, not surprised to see tears wetting his cheeks. "You're mourning someone very special, and I can only imagine the kind of pain that loss left behind, but you didn't fail them. If I didn't fail my sister, then you can't assign yourself the same kind of guilt you're denying me."

"Heavy." His breaths came short and staccato, building like a steam engine making headway pulling loaded cars. "Shit always gets heavy until it's easy to get lost in the memory, overwhelmed by the might-have-beens."

"Heavy," Doc agreed and reached over to pat Owen's thigh. The light pressure was like a palate cleanser, wiping away the remaining physical reactions to the memories. "Good thing we've got each other."

"Yeah, good thing," he echoed, ignoring the flare of reaction he had to the man's touch. He glanced at the tablet, unsurprised to find Alace's head tilted just the slightest amount, a loud interrogatory from her.

Nope. Not going there.

CHAPTER EIGHT

Alace

She nodded at Owen and disconnected the video call, sitting back in her chair with a sigh of relief. "Oh." She scrubbed a hand across her cheek and jaw, wrapped fingers around the back of her neck, and pulled hard, kneading the muscles there.

"I could have told you he'd be pissed off." At Eric's statement, Alace squeezed her eyes closed tightly, blocking out the light. The sound of the baby fussing had her opening them right back up, turning to look at where he stood in the doorway holding Lila. "Just sayin', Alace. He had a point."

"Did you listen in on the whole conversation?" His lips curled down as he nodded. "Then you heard me apologize."

"I heard you tell the doctor you were sorry for bugging his car. Not tell Owen you were sorry for listening in on his private conversations." With a headshake, he scattered her arguments. "No, Alace, you know I'm right. I suspect you'll have some fence-mending to do with Owen."

Lila fussed again, a noisy mewling cry that had threads of pain lacing through Alace's breasts as her milk drew down. Wordlessly, she held her arms out, and Eric tipped his head to the rocking chair, kept in the bedroom instead of the nursery they still weren't using, Lila sleeping in her bassinette next to the bed each night. Alace glanced at the computer and sighed. The dot representing Owen's phone had reappeared, indicating he'd reassembled the device and turned it on. She grabbed her phone and sent a text, then leaned closer to the desk, reaching for the mouse. A few clicks later, the other location indicators disappeared, and she opened a folder to select a file, using a keystroke combination to do a hard delete.

"What'd you tell him?" Eric bent and placed Lila in her arms as she got comfortable in the rocking chair. Shirt and bra swept to the side, she settled her daughter against her chest, Lila latching on, causing those threads of pain to peak and then dim to a satisfying burn of warmth.

"That I'd stop listening in and would only keep the tracker on in his phone to show me where he is." Eric crouched in front of her and edged closer to press a kiss to Lila's cheek. His close proximity to her, to their daughter, to their child nursing at her breast, caused an unexpected flood of arousal through her, and Alace stroked along his cheek, carding her fingers through his hair. She clenched down and winced, her body reminding her again why the six-week rule was in effect. "I like how much he's invested in those kids. And adding a doctor to our team is smart in a lot of ways."

"You gave him your name. Are you so sure of him?" Eric reached up and trapped her hand against the side of his head, covering and gripping tightly. "Sure enough to risk that?"

"Everything I've found out about him underscores the fact he's a decent guy who doesn't tolerate bad behavior where it impacts kids. After hearing about his little sister, I think I've got a handle on who he honestly is deep down. He might not think he's much like me and Owen, and he'd be right—mostly. But in another way, he unquestionably is. He has channeled his hatred of those who do wrong into helping the survivors. Me and Owen, we're all about the bad guys. Even at the last warehouse gig, neither one of us followed the kids into the system. But we'll gladly track down the bad guys without mercy. That's who we are. He's..." She shook her head, rejecting the term which naturally came to mind, knowing Eric would find the connotation offensive. "Different."

"I'm glad you didn't say what you started to." The scold in Eric's voice steadied her. "I wish you could see what you and Owen do from my perspective."

"Maybe one day." She shrugged and lifted Lila, positioning the little girl against her shoulder as she rubbed and patted her back. "Can you get me a bottle of juice?" He brushed his lips across hers, then kissed the top of Lila's head before he rose and walked out. She listened to his footsteps descending the stairs, and once she knew he was gone, she earned a burp for her efforts before altering their positions to allow Lila access to her other breast. Once the infant had latched on again and was nursing steadily, Alace shook her head.

Crooning lowly, she whispered, "Momma's a good monster, sweet girl." Eyes with startling blue irises flashed open, then closed in contentment. Alace teased Lila's palm with the edge of a nail, smiling softly as delicate fingers wrapped tightly around her finger. Humming, she mouthed the words to a lullaby. "Hush little baby, don't say a word, Momma's gonna buy you a mockingbird. If that mockingbird won't sing, Momma's gonna give you everything. If all those things don't make you smile, Momma's gonna go the extra mile. If that distance doesn't impress, Momma's gonna surprise you with a dress. If that dress it doesn't fit, Momma's gonna learn how to knit. If knit and purl are not her thing, Momma's gonna go with lots more bling. If that bling-bling fails to shine, Momma's gonna find something more divine. If divinity doesn't approach, Momma's gonna dig a hell of a moat. If that moat fails to protect, Momma's gonna explain what she expects. If Momma's expectations are not met, Momma's makin' sure that they'll regret."

"Alace." Eric appeared to materialize in the center of the room, and she jerked, causing Lila to lose her hold on the nipple, startling, hands flying wide as she let out a tiny wail.

"You scared me." Alace adjusted things and winced when Lila's gums clamped hard before creating a seal, the pain easing as the infant started sucking again. Standing motionless, he stared at her, a bottle of juice gripped firmly in one hand. "What?"

"There's a baby monitor in the kitchen." When she lifted one shoulder in response, he pulled in a deep breath, dropped his head forwards, and shook it slowly side to side. "One, I'm glad Bebe is out for coffee with friends. And two, you were not as quiet as you thought you were being."

"It's just a song, Eric." She held her hand out for the juice, Lila's tiny fist grasping the edge of her shirt. "My singing isn't that terrible, is it?" Her attempted joke fell flat as he approached and lowered to one knee next to the rocker. "What's so bad about me singing to Lila?"

"It's not the singing." He cupped her cheek, the chill from the juice bottle transferring to her skin and raising gooseflesh over her body. "If you persist in seeing yourself as a monster, then you'll have to deal with my perception, too."

Carefully controlling her expression and respiration, she stared at him. "What does that mean?"

He leaned forwards, brushing a kiss across her lips once, twice, a third time before he pulled back, still so close each word sent a subtle puff of air across her sensitive skin.

"You'll always be my favorite monster."

***

Owen

Standing at the curb, he surveyed the front of the house, taking in the open space on either side. The lots backed up against an open field, which stretched a couple of acres towards what looked to be dense forest. Movement behind a window captured his attention, and he tipped his head down to hide a smile when he saw Doc staring out at him.

Their arrival in Colorado two days ago had initiated a tension-filled few hours. After they'd swapped off driving right before sunrise, Owen had fallen asleep against the passenger door, expecting to open his eyes at the new house. At some point afterwards, Alace had called and chatted with Doc, changing their plans so when Owen woke, they were already on the final street approach to Alace's house.

"What's goin' on?" He blinked, scrubbing at his face with the edge of a hand, sleep-induced dryness feeling like sawdust against his eyeballs. It only took an instant for his mind to snap alert, recognizing the houses on either side of the street. *"What the hell? This isn't the right neighborhood."*

"Alace called."

Cold water doused Owen's nerves, his breath locking tight in his chest. *"What'd she say?"* Muscles stretched and flexed, his fingers curled into tight balls of flesh. When Doc didn't respond immediately, he whipped his head to the side to see the man observing him quietly. *"What'd she say?"* His strident words echoed within the car and he checked on the kids quickly, relieved to see he hadn't woken them.

"She wants to meet me, officially." Doc shrugged and shifted his gaze back to the street. *"I didn't see any issues with it. It'd give the kids a chance to stretch their legs, too. You want to go to the house instead, I'll turn around. You can remap the nav, and we'll be there within a few minutes."*

Doc made it sound so easy Owen sucked in a silent breath to make sure he still could. Not easily, but still capable.

"Nah. Nah, man. It's cool. If it's her suggestion, then this is actually perfect. You get to meet her, and we can see how the kids respond. Her husband is a softie, so I bet Shiloh will warm up to him fast. Kelly knows about

Alace in theory, and he knows she's part of the reason I wanted to relocate here. He can put a face to a name, and it'll all be good." The longer he talked, the more it made sense in his head. *"It's good. We can get it out of the way, and then afterwards, we can take our time. Settle into the house."* He deliberately eased the tension from his muscles, starting from his feet upwards. Unclench the piggies first, then the ankles. *"Just didn't expect it is all."* He uncapped a bottle of water and upended it, lungs burning for air by the time the bottle emptied down his throat. *"It's cool."*

"Anything I should know before we walk into her house?" Doc's chin lifted, his throat elongating, and Owen watched as his Adam's apple fluidly dipped down towards his collar with a swallow. What a weird thing for me to notice.

"Yeah." He capped the empty bottle and tossed it into the footwell next to his sock-covered feet. Bending forwards, he tugged on first one boot and then the other. *"She's scary as fuck, and it's entirely earned. Don't show fear, don't give her your back, and believe everything she tells you."*

A lawnmower roared somewhere behind him, setting up a homey-feeling echo. It reminded him of growing up in Minnesota, summers filled with lazy days and easy happiness. He swept the neighborhood with a gaze again, tracking everything changed since the last time he'd looked around. A car was backing out of a garage two houses down. Owen lifted a hand,

and the man behind the wheel returned the gesture. Nick Cappiello, mid-thirties, respiratory therapist at the local county hospital, married to Annie, who was an X-ray technician. They had no kids.

Alace had sent a digital folder of information with a dossier on each neighbor in a three-block radius. Owen had built his own investigative research data and then compared the two. Mentally he'd called it an overall tie, because while Alace had dug deeper on a couple of residents based on something indefinable that piqued her interest, Owen had done deeper dives on the same individuals based on his study of details in their surface lives.

Nick and Annie Cappiello were harmless.

He turned and looked in the other direction, focusing on a house three lots down, roof rising over the structures around it as if the large home loomed over them all.

Samuel Donald Ashworth, early sixties, retired, residing with his current wife, Jan Gertrud nee Marlow. She was Ashworth's fourth wife. They'd been married for not quite seven years and were already at the outskirts of the survival range for the man's previous spouses. Owen glanced at the concrete equipment idling at the curb in front of the house, the extended boom pulsing as the pump pushed the mixture through machinery, resembling an articulated spider's leg.

Home improvement projects had coincided with each of his previous wives' deaths. If Owen didn't intervene, Jan was probably scheduled for the end of her spousal run at Samuel's side, a tragic accident in her near future.

I'll get Alace's opinion. Owen tucked his chin to his neck and angled his gaze to the curb running along the edge of the street. Already second nature to consult with his partner on anything and everything. He not only didn't mind the direction his brain had gone but also welcomed the sense of support gained from merely the thought. It wouldn't be awkward at all, since she'd seen the same pattern of behaviors for Ashworth.

Owen swiveled and stared farther down the street at a small, nondescript house poised at a nearby intersection of streets. Aldo Lamar Kuellen lived alone, no relatives nearby. Kuellen had been in the neighborhood for more than twenty years, buying one of the first built-for-speculation homes offered. He was a plain man, living in a plain house, driving a plain car to his plain job.

Alace hadn't been curious about Kuellen, her information thorough but not turning up anything of note. Plain information. Owen had been intrigued, the chameleon aspect of the man's hiding in plain sight enough to make him wonder what was behind the façade. It had taken a little effort, but curiosity drove results as efficiently as suspicion.

Porn. Extreme porn videos on a subscription-based website created specifically for the dangerously violent genres. Owen had surmised the hosting servers were stored within the home, his intuition based on data surfaced regarding long-term electricity use paired with the structure's high-speed fiber connection for the Internet.

Owen had tapped a gig worker for a review of movies he'd extracted from Kuellen's servers. The feds had a program he'd appropriated in the past, and normally Owen would have initiated that, utilizing the software to look for previously tagged and identified porn images, but it hadn't yet been expanded to video. The developer Owen hired had detected multiple movies featuring members of vulnerable communities, including homeless, drug addicts, mentally incompetent individuals, and alcoholics. So many people who could be swayed with a word or a promise, coming out the other end maimed and wounded in unacceptable ways. Or, in several cases, not coming out the other end at all. The apparent snuff films were in the database in limited quantities, but even one was too many.

Need to loop Alace in on this one, too. That would not be an easy conversation. Owen wouldn't downplay his intuitive identification of the pornographer. Alace would find it more offensive than simply laying out the facts. *She'll be all-in on this.* The only real complication was the close proximity to his and Doc's new home.

A glance back at the front of his house showed him Shiloh staring out at him. He waved, grinning broadly when she readily waved back.

Pornographer Kuellen and wife-killing Ashworth aside, this was going to be a great neighborhood in which to raise children. "Just gotta take out the trash," he muttered as he headed up the sidewalk to the front door. "Easy peasy."

***

Alace

"I'm going to invite them over for dinner." Eric's words drifted up the stairs to where Alace sat with Lila in her arms. Head leaned back against the rocking chair, she closed her eyes and waited. "If you're going to be working with this doctor—"

"Doc," she interjected, soothing Lila when the baby startled at her half-shouted word.

"With this Doc," Eric picked up seamlessly, "then I want to know more about him. Not what you can hand me on a piece of paper, but how I feel around him. They weren't here long enough for me to get a good read on the guy."

"He's gay." She pitched her voice differently, pleased when Lila nursed on unconcerned.

"So?" Pans rattled, signaling Eric had started on whatever he was making for supper.

Alace smiled, looked down at Lila, and traced a finger along the curve of the infant's cheek. "Daddy's thickheaded sometimes." Shifting to the same projected voice as before, she called back, "You'll have to keep your shirt on this time. He might be impressed in a different way than Owen was." The computer gave off a soft sound, and an instant later, Lila fussed, fists flailing as she jerked and pulled on Alace's nipple.

"I don't know what you mean." The rattling sound increased, signaling Eric's discomfort with the topic.

Deliberately taking in a deep breath, Alace lowered her shoulders, focusing on her muscles as she relaxed them, Lila's fussing fading away. She'd found the baby was an infallible lie-detector and a stress meter, which was impossible to ignore. The computer made the same sound, but this time Alace successfully masked her response from her daughter.

"I distinctly remember a shirtless you in the kitchen the first time Owen came for dinner."

The computer noises were from a specific communication tool she and Owen used. If he was messaging her via the software and not her phone, it meant the topic was sensitive. Which might mean he'd found the cop who'd taken his kids from their foster home and sold them into the sex slavery ring.

"What do you mean? I'd just showered. I didn't want to be rude and keep him waiting." Eric's voice was louder, accompanied by quiet footfalls coming up the stairs. Alace used a finger to break Lila's hold on her nipple and lifted the girl to her shoulder, using one hand to adjust her clothing. Her soothing pats against Lila's back elicited an overly loud burp as Eric came into the room. "That's my girl." He grinned, beaming proudly, hands out to take their daughter from Alace. "That's my very good girl."

"She's already pretty smelly. Someone made a deposit during dinner." Fingers laced together across her stomach, Alace watched as Eric bobbed and dipped across the room, dancing his way to the changing table that had taken up residence in their bedroom, as had the baby dresser of spare clothing. "We should think about finishing the nursery. Give her some space. Give us some space."

"Or, she could stay in here with Mommy and Daddy for another month." Deftly unsnapping the onesie Lila wore, Eric leaned down and brushed a kiss across her cheek. "Just another month, Mommy."

"Next week." Eric's head tipped to the side as he looked at her, one eyebrow lifted in a question. "Monday, to be exact. She'll be six weeks old." She laughed as understanding dawned across Eric's expression. "Yeah, Daddy. You wanna have to explain to our daughter's future therapist how she was damaged by hearing Mommy and Daddy doing the deed?"

"I doubt she'd be traumatized. She'll be sleeping." One hand on the baby's belly, he held Lila in place while he cleaned her with a wipe, tucking the soiled paper into the set-aside diaper as he grabbed a clean one. He shifted his hold to Lila's ankles, lifting her to push the back band of the fresh diaper under her bottom. "Yeah, she'll probably sleep right through anything." Eric finished and was straightening, a newly diapered Lila held against his chest, as Alace laughed. "What?"

She flicked up one finger. "Sex." A second finger joined the first. "A." The third finger flipped up, and she waggled them back and forth, pretending to fan her face. "Thon."

Eric's laughter was loud and boisterous and set Lila fussing. Alace was mute as she watched Eric soothe their daughter, his capable hands knowing precisely how to stroke and pat to quiet her. *God, I love him.*

"Point taken. What if in addition to dinner, we ask for help setting everything up? That way there's a theme to the evening. It'd have the added benefit in keeping my mother's efforts at assistance corralled." He dipped and twisted, dancing in place with Lila in his arms. A rumble came from him, and Alace realized he was humming to Lila, his comfort of the infant now second nature. She must have been staring too long, because he lifted an eyebrow and without missing a beat asked, "What?"

"When should we try for another one of those?" She tipped her head towards Lila, gaze locked on Eric's face. Heat bloomed between her legs when his eyes darkened, revealing his pent-up desire matching hers. "How long do you want to wait?"

"Let's see what the doctor says next week, but I'm in favor of whatever kind of timeline you want to follow, Alace. You remember how hard it was for you to keep working with the morning sickness, and then later, when you were tired so much of the time. Your work—" He brushed a kiss against Lila's temple, whispering softly to the child. Lila's face relaxed, smoothing out from the wrinkled scowl she had been wearing. "What you and Owen do is important. I don't think you'd be happy without it, and my only hesitation is how you'd feel if you suddenly had two children in diapers and little-to-no time to work on the cases."

"You could quit lawyering and be a stay-at-home dad." Her laughter at what was clearly a ridiculous option was loud in the room. She cut it off immediately, realizing Eric wasn't laughing with her. "I'm kidding, Eric."

"I know." Each dip of his chin brought his lips back to the top of Lila's head—a sequence of soft kisses so sweet to watch it made Alace's heart melt. "To be honest, I have given it some thought. I love our little Lady Lila here, even when she rules our lives with an iron baby fist. When I leave for work, the first thing I think as I'm in the car driving away is 'I wish I were home,' because this is where I want to be." The swaying stilled, his only movement a hand continuing to slide up and down Lila's back. "But I know myself well enough to realize I'd be unhappy if that were the reality. Not because I don't love her, or you, but because I am validated at work. I help people, too. Just in a different way from what you do."

"You think I help people?" The question had flashed through her head a split second before she decided to give it voice, pulling down the curtain of insecurity slightly. Eric knew all her secrets and never flinched from giving her feedback that was real and from the heart. She instinctively knew he'd understand this wasn't a self-serving request from her, wasn't a false cry for reassurance. This was the war she waged inside with every gig she accepted or turned down, balancing the driving need to find vengeance for those who had been denied, doing it against her own feelings of guilt, and the very real fear of getting it wrong.

"I don't have to think it. I know it, Alace. To me, it's an undeniable fact. What you and Owen do isn't legal, and some may consider it immoral, but the justice you deliver is indisputable. Truly." As he resettled their daughter against his chest, she saw Lila's eyes had closed. "And for as long as you find the work fulfilling, as long as the good outweighs the bad in your mind, I will continue to support what you do. If you decided to ever stop and put that part of your life on the shelf, I'd back you a hundred percent. I support you, beloved, and that will never, ever change." He came to her and bent to press his lips to the top of her head, much as he'd done with Lila only moments before. "I don't just love you, beloved. I believe in you, too."

Going with her gut, she put words to the feeling she'd been holding close for a long time, allowing herself to believe a little more. "What did I ever do right in my life to deserve having you?"

Leaning over the bassinette, he darted a glance at her face, mouth wryly twisted to the side. "I'm glad you added the qualifier of 'right' to that statement, or I'd wonder if I was a plague and a trial."

"Never." Alace cleared her throat, salt burning the back of her nose. "Still hormonal here. Might wanna put a throttle on all the sweetness, husband mine."

"The horror. Wouldn't want a rampaging new mother on my hands." She stood as he walked towards her, and they met in the middle, her hands winding up the back of his neck to tangle her fingers in his hair. His arms slipped around her, iron bands holding her tight against his body. "My mother's due to be back in thirty minutes. Wanna make out until she gets home?"

"Defini—" Her murmured response was cut short by his mouth on hers, lips dragging a soft caress side to side. Two backwards steps and her calves pressed against the footboard. Eric's arms shifted and lifted, and she settled in the middle of their bed, his weight pressing her into the mattress. Kisses followed. Long, drawn-out caresses, mouths moving against each other, whimpers and moans swallowed down, heated air expelled on voiceless gasps. She mapped the planes and contours of his back with her palms, fingers slipping down to play along the edge of his waistband. Eric's hands stayed determinedly above the waist, his thumb flicking relentlessly against a nipple until her milk started flowing. Clenching her thighs together, she focused on the points connecting them, dragging her lips along the edge of his jaw to his ear, where she alternated sucking and nibbling on his earlobe, his protests lost in a deep groan of arousal.

The proximity alarm pinged quietly on her desktop, and they parted slightly, gazes locking together. "Bebe." "Mother." Their explanations overlapped, and Alace found herself grinning at Eric's lopsided smile.

"I love you." The damned evocative catch in his breath got to her as it always did, and she arched up to capture his lips in another kiss. "So much, Eric."

"Beloved." That single word wrecked her, tears springing from the corners of her eyes. Head shaking side to side, Eric captured the drops with his fingertips, brushing the tip of his nose against hers. "Mine."

Fucking *fucking* Eric.

God, how I love him.

Chapter Nine

Owen

Headphones on, Owen waited in front of the computer for Alace to initiate a call, glancing at the clock in the corner of the screen. He was a couple of minutes early, but knowing Alace, he was surprised she wasn't already on the line. They'd opted for a video call so he could share the dirt he'd found on his neighbors without sending any files over. Yet. *Discovery phase*, he reminded himself.

Right on cue, the video icon lit up, and he clicked to connect the call. The screen quickly resolved into an image of Alace, wet hair slicked back from a makeupless face, headphones covering her ears much as his did.

"Hey." He lifted his chin as he smothered a smile. She wouldn't have any way to know it wasn't amusement but pleasure, and trying to explain to her would take up time he didn't want to waste. Under the supervision of Doc, Kelly and Shiloh were browsing an online website for backyard playground equipment, and Owen wanted to be there to urge the discussion into realms of absurdity. The kids were so cautious about being a burden, they probably would settle on a kickball or something, when what he truly wanted to see was a castle for Shiloh to rule over from the upper ramparts. *Too long in the system to believe themselves worth the effort.* Narrowing his eyes, he pulled his thoughts away from his kids and back to his partner, noting the dark circles underneath her eyes. "How's the little one?" Now he did smile, because the memory of holding Lila during the short visit to the Wards' house had become a favorite. He'd missed out on Emma's early childhood, meeting his daughter for the first time when she was six months old. "She still smell like baby powder and happiness?"

Alace snorted and rolled her shoulder, eyebrows lifting towards her hairline. "Eric might have mentioned to me how the two of you bonded over the addictive quality of newborn baby smell. It was such a quick visit I didn't get to witness your transformation myself. We'll have to organize another visit again sometime." Her lips quirked. "Soon."

Owen had never met a father prouder than Eric had been of his and Alace's daughter. "He's a great dad."

Studying Alace's expression closely, he noted the tension lines at the corners of her eyes when he spoke, and he tested it by semi-repeating, "Eric's really good with Lila." The momentary stress indicators reappeared as if he'd called them up by magic. "And you're a good mother, Alace. Both of you are great."

"I didn't call so you could tell me how you admire me." The corners of her mouth downturned for a split second, and Owen found his shoulders straightening. "What do you want to do about the pornographer?"

"Let's go back to where I'm talking about your beautiful family and how much I admire what you've built." That statement earned him a tiny smile, quickly smoothed away. "It's a lot of work, and so are newborn babies. This is me asking my friend Alace if she's doin' okay. So what'll it be, Alace? Are you good?"

One edge of her bottom lip disappeared into her mouth, and Owen relaxed slightly. If she allowed herself to be visibly conflicted in her thinking, at least it meant she was considering giving him an honest answer. "I'm tired. She eats every four hours on the dot and poops at least as many times throughout the day. Eric's been back to work as of a month ago, and don't tell him, but having his mother here was a godsend. I don't know what I'd have done without Phoebe. She leaves for Malibu tomorrow, and I don't know how I'll handle being the only one responsible for Lila all day long."

"When you drop Bebe off at the airport, come here instead of going home. We can work on things in person, too, you know. Benefit of proximity. It doesn't always have to be this cloak and dagger with a full twelve degrees of separation. It'll give you a chance to get to know Doc better, and I know Kelly already fell in love with Lila." Owen tipped his grin downwards, shaking his head back and forth in amusement. "Boy's been asking every day when we'd get to go back to Miss Alace's house so he could see Lila."

"Just that easy?" Alace took a deep breath, air rasping audibly in and out. "Don't answer me. I already know what you'll say. I'll be there just after lunch."

"Easy peasy." He pulled in a breath. "I can handle the video guy. There's no clock ticking on that one. I've got a couple of contacts we can turn the info over to whenever we decide." He was careful to keep his language centered on the partnership. If Alace was feeling pressured in her new role, she'd want reassurances on the other side of things, too. "The wife-killer is the one I'd like to have your opinion on first. If my research is right, the current wifey is within days of being his next previous wifey."

"All right. Take me through what you've got." She took in a deeper breath again, blowing it back out slowly. An icon changed on his video chat client, the share button taking on a green hue. "I transferred control to you so you can load up whatever you need."

"That was hard for you, wasn't it?" As he asked the question, Owen was already bringing the various news articles to the front of his screen. Choosing to share the entire screen instead of the single software was deliberate, and something he knew Alace would notice. *Nothing to hide here, boss lady.* "It's okay. We're besties, we should share things. I can't use your makeup or heels, so this is the next best thing."

"You'd look good in heels." Alace's throwaway comment trailed off as she skimmed the first article. "She fell and hit her head. Nothing nefarious there, Owen."

"Right? And if it was a one-and-done scenario, I'd believe it, too. But check this." He brought the second article to the front of the pile and gave her a minute to digest the pertinent details. "And these." Wife number three had earned more than a few news articles, mostly for the sheer unlikelihood of a single man losing so many partners to such random home accidents. "This reporter is one to watch and stay away from. She has a wicked intuition about things. After reading this, I went back and checked on her career. She's made a name for herself by solving the unsolvable cases." He spread the articles across the screen, reserving the one corner where the video window was. "Let me know when you want me to move on."

"The reporter, did you do any kind of a search or trace on her? She looks familiar somehow." Alace's eyebrows knit together in a frown. "I haven't talked to her, I don't think, but does she have family in town?"

"Yeah. Her sister is a nurse at—"

"Grundella." Mouth drawn down into a grimace, Alace nodded slowly. "She's an OB/GYN nurse at the local hospital, isn't she?"

"Yeah, but her name isn't Grundella."

Alace waved a hand as if dispersing an unwelcome smell. "No, her name is Jessica, and she was a pain in my ass. So bad news, I'm already on the radar of the sister of a nosy, intuitive reporter. Said sister only dropped her annoying ways when Eric suggested this author lady he knew might be willing to include someone in a book, and the presentation of personality could go one way or another, no middle ground." Chin lifting, Alace cast her gaze upward, looking away from the screen for the first time. "People are the worst part of anything, you know?"

"Yeah, I so know." Hovering his mouse cursor over the document icon, he found and brought to the front the final article. "Case in point, Ashworth." He allowed his gaze to trail over the first few paragraphs of the article in which a fake-grieving Ashworth was clearly hitting on the reporter. "I know what I'd like to do to this guy, but because it's virtually right here in my backyard, I don't think I'd make an impartial agent, you know?"

"I need a day."

Owen was shaking his head before she finished speaking. "I don't think she's got a day, Alace."

"I need a day. I've already started looking into various aspects of Ashworth, but I need a day to get the information back. I set up a surprise inspection to happen this morning with a follow-up for tomorrow, and all the activity should keep him at bay until we are ready to go." Chin lowering towards her throat, she frowned at the camera again. The defensive posture wasn't like her, and Owen decided to wait for her to finish whatever she was saying, keeping his interrupting questions to himself for now. "The inspector wasn't due for a couple of weeks, but his other projects were shuffled around, and he had a couple of slots open up on his timeline. I didn't call in anything, so he's not going in with any expectations. Ashworth will be cautious simply because of the change in schedule, but there won't be any red flags raised."

Something like that took more than a few hours to set up, and Owen knew it. "Thank you." He flashed a grin at the camera. "That's why you're the boss lady, boss lady."

"Did you see anything to do with prostitutes in what you found about Ashworth?" Expression impassive, she waited, motives shrouded in stillness. "Or anything else in his background?"

"He visits a massage parlor in town known for providing happy endings, but I found no incidents of violence in their records about him as a client. Not even on the shadow server where their real books are." Owen let his head swing side to side once. "In his twenties, he was a fan of drinking and driving, but the threat of a license suspension seemed to push him onto the straight and narrow. There's no contact with kids whatsoever, he doesn't even substitute for his friend's Sunday school class when asked. Found some good-natured back and forth on social media about his well-publicized aversion to kids." Tongue in his cheek, he studied her face, then shook his head again. "What did I miss, boss?"

"You should read the minutes from past neighborhood watch meetings. While the masseuses are entirely female, as have been the women he took to a motel from the various bars he frequented before he got married for the first time, in the weeks immediately preceding the death of the first two wives, he had home visits from known male prostitutes. A neighbor recognized one of the men, claimed he'd seen the man's picture on a police blotter article, but who knows. The neighbor snapped pictures of men he saw parking in front of Ashworth's house. Then, twice he took a picture of Ashworth driving a car that wasn't his away from the house. It never escalated into an official report or anything, mostly because I found a healthy deposit into the investigative neighbor's account after the first real complaint."

"Holy shit. He's bringing male hookers to his house with his wife there?"

"It's unclear if the wife was home at the time. But I can tell you the sex workers I've identified from those pictures have all dropped off the radar completely." She was chewing on her bottom lip, and Owen focused on the tell. "I think he conducted test runs on his 'accident' plans." She lifted one hand and made air quotes around the word. "Whether there's anything else to it, I don't know. The pictures only surrounded the two incidents. But I found community reports of missing male prostitutes, including those, as well as others where the dates line up with the deaths of the rest of Ashworth's wives. Completely ignored by the police, of course." She huffed out a sigh. "Their vehicles were all found abandoned in large parking lots around town, no evidence of foul play in the cars."

"Hold on, are you telling me you think he killed them in the house and disposed of them there?" Owen allowed his eyes to unfocus, staring at a spot on the wall while he worked out the details in his head. "Some kind of a structured rehearsal of the accident, and then he somehow dealt with the bodies at home? Why not put them in the car and leave them to be found or drop the corpses in the woods? We're surrounded by hundreds of acres of forest, which would make an effective dumping site. More than one of the deaths involved blood. If he'd had a successful test run, there'd be proof. Cleaning up the evidence would leave residue and would have shown up on the lab tests."

"Blood markers inconsistent with Ashworth or his wife were found twice. It was noted each time, but effectively dismissed because it was older than the accidental death scene." Alace's eyes were open wide, as if she were asking "Can you believe this shit?" and honestly, he just couldn't.

"How could one ugly old man be this lucky? Why hasn't anyone stumbled on this before?"

"I think the reporter was close, but she was skeeved out by his attitude. While she's got intuition, she seems to lack the dogged dedication of her sister."

"The nurse."

Alace nodded. "Jessica."

"What did she do to piss you off?"

Alace wafted a hand through the air again, and Owen looked past the motion, keying in on her facial expression. Tension around her lips telegraphed disgust.

"Man, she seriously pissed you off. What'd she do?"

"Tried to trap me at the hospital after Lila was born."

"Ohhhhh." Eric had already told Owen about their joint discomfort with the hospital's security, and now Alace's distaste for the nurse who had blocked her efforts at going home made sense. "I hate her too." He thudded a fist against his chest. "I stand with Alace."

"You're ridiculous."

"Yeah, but you don't hate me." He leaned back in his chair, lifting his heels to the edge of the desk as he balanced his chair on two legs. "So I got that goin' for me."

"Ashworth." Alace was trying to bring them back on track, but Owen wasn't done.

"Are you worried about this reporter getting curious because you cockblocked the sister's attempted cockblock of keeping you in the hospital until she said you could leave?"

Alace stared at him for a beat before responding. Mouth pursed, she pushed the single word out so softly the computer mic didn't pick it up; Owen had to read her lips. "Possibly."

"Got it." The unstated truth was while Ashworth might be in Owen's backyard, he wasn't removed far enough from Alace's cover persona to make this a comfortable mission for either of them. "I got a guy."

"I can't run scared."

"We aren't." Admitting to his own potential exposure kept them on an even footing in the decision to farm out the job. "We're conserving our resources to the best advantageous outcome, one that keeps us in the business longest. I want to be able to keep going, Alace. As long as Ashworth is stopped and exposed somehow, I don't mind not being the triggerman on this one."

"Either of them." Her gaze was steady now, unflinching when he scowled into the camera. "It's too risky to both of us, and we've got families to worry about now."

"I can agree Kuellen shouldn't be an up-close and personal thing. I don't like it, simply because of the kind of scum he is, but I can agree with you on that one." Owen allowed his scowl to deepen as he accepted her edict. "But we can't leave him. A lot of his product is run-of-the-mill porn featuring legal-age actors, but the snuff stuff is real, Alace. People killing real people onscreen so others can get their jollies off on it. I hired an analyst who identified no less than ten percent of the sample provided was real violence, not scripted for the camera. And he's preying on not only innocents but people who deserved protection."

"Show me the report."

He hid the articles about Ashworth with a click of the mouse, diving into a different folder on a secure cloud server. "Here." The narrative of the report opened, and he clicked into another folder for the cross-referencing segment of the information. "I've matched four of the women killed to missing person reports in counties in southern Colorado. Of the real videos, fully eighty percent are Indigenous females, Alace. A demographic notorious for a trend in underreporting missing adults. I can show you dozens of reports in the past six months alone about a rash of disappearances in the western United States and Canada. He can't be busted only for porn. Maybe he doesn't get busted at all. Maybe I disappear him and find out his sources."

Alace stared at the camera for so long he could almost think the image was frozen, but he still saw the slight movement of her shirt as she breathed. Deliberately, she cleared her throat, then the share icon dimmed, indicating she'd taken control of the meeting software again.

An instant later, a different report opened on his screen, projected from Alace's computer. A report from a different researcher, based on the name at least, corroborated what Owen had found. With one difference.

Heart in his throat, Owen choked out, "Some of them are kids?"

Her slow nod conveyed a somber tone, backed up by her words. "There was a selection of foster kid runaways in the films my guys looked at. We ran the

FBI's exploitation algorithm against images extracted from the video as stills and matched a bunch of comparative hits. Those hits turned into IDs. Given what happened a few weeks ago, I don't want you anywhere near Kuellen."

Emma's face…concentrate on her face, not what happened. Smoke wreathed the room, the air thick with the stench of bodies burning, human flesh left to smolder in the aftermath of hot flames. He adjusted the backpack strap on his shoulder and studied the ground. Small footprints raced alongside larger ones, two child-sized steps for each stride of the adult. Owen looked around, the image of dust and dark dirt confusingly mixing in with the desk and chairs. He shook his head abruptly, casting the memories away physically, hoping Alace wouldn't have noticed.

"Owen."

Of course she'd noticed. Not for the first time, he found himself annoyed at her perceptiveness. *Get over it,* he scolded himself. *This is Alace, after all.* "I'm good."

"Let's table this until I'm there tomorrow." The document disappeared, Alace's image expanding to fill the screen. "We can go over Ashworth and Kuellen, bring Doc into the conversation if you want."

Dry throat scratchy, Owen swallowed hard. He reminded Alace, "You'll have Lila with you."

"She'll be fine. I'm sure I can offer to pay Kelly to watch her while he and his sister do something on the TV." The skin around Alace's mouth tightened, and she aborted a headshake as she rejected her own idea. Owen wasn't surprised when she followed up with, "Or maybe she can stay with us. It's not like she can understand what we'll be talking about."

"Plus, it can always be a 'do as I say, not as I do' moment between mommy and daughter later." He bit his bottom lip then grinned. "You know, just in case she surfaces the memory later in life."

"Was that everything you had to discuss?"

Owen smiled harder, not trying to hide it. Alace might not often roll her eyes, but she was entirely dismissive in other ways, such as blatantly redirecting conversations.

"I've got a good line on the cop. He retired to an island with the money he got from not only my kids, but several others he'd supplied to the auctions. Given everything going on, I don't think I should take the time to go down and deal with him myself." He stared at the image of Alace, willing her to understand. "I want to. Make no mistake about that. But I think we can farm this one out."

"August would be a good fit. Let me look at his schedule quick." Alace's fingers flew over the keyboard, and a screenshare popped up of a calendar, there and gone before Owen could register more than a few details. "He was due back into the country yesterday, and I expect he'll be ready to get back to work quickly. I'll message him whatever details you can provide, and it'll be taken care of within the week."

"Just like that?" Owen glanced down, fingers resting on his own keyboard. He didn't lift his eyes as he said, "Means a lot, Alace."

"Get me the info. Let me worry about the details. It's what I'm good at." A sound came through the speakers, and Owen looked up to see Alace glancing away from the camera. "I'll see you tomorrow."

"Yeah." He noted Alace's distracted expression, listening closely enough to make out a woman's voice layered over a male murmur. "Have a good evening with the fam."

No goodbye, the video disconnected, and he was left staring at the darkened monitor. It slowly resolved into a picture taken during their road trip to Colorado, Owen in the back seat between his sleeping kids, one leaned into each of his shoulders. His head was thrown back, a serene smile announcing his utter satisfaction at being right there in that moment.

The brief glimpse of the calendar had shown Alace had already planned a mission for her other hunter, the red highlighting indicated it was a high-priority case. She was reorganizing things to take care of a target that likely wasn't going to move, wasn't suspicious or wary, and wasn't urgent in any way.

"Totally besties."

***

Alace

"Oh, I miss you already." Phoebe wrapped her arms around Alace and Lila, pulling them close to her. Cheek to cheek, they stood just outside the security entrance to the passenger concourse at the Denver International Airport. "You take care of yourself, Alace, my sweetheart. Take care of yourself, and the care and love of Lila will be effortless. You have it in you to be a brilliant mother, and I believe in you."

Alace didn't speak; she couldn't, her throat closed off to words. Something about Phoebe's complete acceptance of her as Eric's wife, as Lila's mother, as a person Phoebe deemed worthy of love, stole Alace's ability to communicate.

"I know these things are harder for you, darling. That's okay, truly." Phoebe's grip on her tightened in a reassuring squeeze. "You are a loving, caring mother, and my son thinks you hung the moon. I love you very much."

Teeth clenched, Alace rested her forehead against the side of Phoebe's neck. "I love you, too." Her voice was soft enough she thought Phoebe had missed her words, then the arms around her tightened again.

"I know you do, darling." Lila squeaked and Phoebe laughed, relaxing her hold enough to lean back and look down at the baby in a sling across Alace's chest. "I hear you, too, my sweet baby girl." Her lips brushed Lila's head once, twice, a third time, in an unconscious re-creation of Eric's caresses from every day. "Bring her to Malibu soon, Alace. Come visit me often and stay long." An overhead announcement had them both looking up at the departures board, noting the ever-diminishing time before Phoebe would need to move through security and into the gate area, boarding the plane to take her home. "I've got a suite all set up for you, Eric, and little Lila. Anytime, no advance notice needed."

"You need to go."

Phoebe nodded, then pressed a soft kiss to Alace's cheek. "I do. I'll see you again soon."

Alace stood and watched as her mother-in-law walked through security, jovially chatting with the officers, and then waved at Alace with one hand, using the other to slip her shoes back on her feet. Phoebe blew a kiss off her fingertips, turned, and disappeared from view into the crowds heading into the main concourse.

Lila fussed quietly and Alace soothed her instinctively, palm slipping over the baby's head. She saw movement in her periphery and sidestepped, her arm coming down to strike the would-be thief's hand away from the diaper bag. She twisted her hand and gripped his wrist, turning and yanking with precise pressure, releasing him when he yelped in pain. His arm hung useless at his side, dislocated at the elbow.

"Oww, *bitch*." He leaned back, mouth open as if to shout at her.

"I'd recommend you walk away." Alace stared at him, her palm once again slipping over the curve of Lila's skull in a slow stroke. "Two fingers to your throat and you stop breathing. You don't want that. *I'm not a mark*." She memorized his features, setting them into her memory so she could locate him later, and gave him one sharp headshake. "Walk away."

Five minutes later, she had buckled Lila into the car seat strapped into the back seat and was driving through the self-pay kiosk to exit the parking garage. She activated the secondary security system in the car and initiated a voice call. When Owen answered, she didn't say hello, didn't give him a greeting other than "On my way," and terminated the call before he could respond.

Using her voice, she navigated into a different segment of the car's system and found a pair of responses from August waiting for her. The system read his brief replies aloud, the mechanical voice illustrating they were as short and to the point as hers had been with Owen, consisting of two statements: "Okay" and "Got everything." Which meant he'd received the directive she'd posted to his folder last night and had also retrieved the identification and financial information she'd placed in a secondary location only available if he'd accepted the gig. Which he had. As she'd expected.

Pulling up at the curb in front of Owen's house a few minutes later, she scanned the neighborhood, gaze snagging on Ashworth's house. Easily identified because of the construction debris dumpster in the driveway, it also stood out because of the sheer size of the home itself. Her investigation had revealed there were multiple bedroom suites, four full bathrooms, a den, media room, family room, and living room, along with a variety of other identified spaces in the tax document floorplans.

For one man.

And his wife, she reminded herself. At least for a few more days.

Owen's front door swung wide, and he stood in the opening. An instant later, he was shoved to the side as the boy Kelly darted past, angling across the yard to where Alace had parked. By the time she'd climbed from the vehicle, he was standing next to the back passenger door, one hand yanking on the locked door handle, the other cupped around the side of his face as he peered into the back seat.

"Hey, kid." She clicked the key fob, unlocking the door. "Want to grab the diaper bag?" The irony wasn't lost on her that she was offering up the same piece of gear she'd defiantly protected less than an hour ago. "I'll bring in Lila."

"You can trust me to carry her." Kelly's aggrieved expression made her want to laugh, but she kept the humor in check, giving the boy a testing glare instead. He not only survived, he shot back an answering glare as he said, "I wouldn't drop her. I never dropped Shiloh, and I was lots younger when she was born."

"I'm sure you didn't." Alace opened the door on her side and leaned into the car, unsurprised when Kelly matched her actions on the other side of the car. She flicked the lock securing the car seat carrier into the base strapped into the car and lifted the handle into place.

"You shouldn't take her out on that side. That's the traffic side." Alace looked through the rear and front windshields, then back to the boy's annoyed expression. "Don't matter there's no cars now. You've got to stick to the rules now so you don't forget later."

"You want to carry her inside?" Kelly nodded at Alace, his eyebrows scrunched into a frown. "Okay. If you can get her out of the car without a struggle, I'll let you carry her inside." She lifted the diaper bag and slung the strap over her shoulder. "Wait until I'm over there."

"He's good, Alace." She looked up as she straightened, closing the car door while she took in the incongruous sight of Owen—one of the most competent and ruthless hunters she'd ever known—standing in his doorway with a little girl in his arms. He held Shiloh propped on one hip, her fingers in his hair creating uneven peaks as she combed it into a hairstyle only she understood. "Lila will be fine."

She walked around the back of the car and hesitated when she found Kelly hadn't waited, already lifting the unfastened car seat from the vehicle. He carefully, tenderly rested the seat on the sidewalk, well away from the swing path of the closing door. The boy looked up at her from underneath a heavy fall of hair, but it did nothing to disguise his eagerness. "I swear I won't let her get hurt, Miss Alace. Swear."

On impulse, she held out her hand, little finger extended. "Pinky swear."

The flash of smile was brilliant, blinding, filled with joy and appreciation at her affirmation beaming from the boy. He wrapped his littlest finger around hers and they shook solemnly up and down twice. When he released his grip, he lifted his palm to his face, then graced her with a different smile, more a teasing grin, and she understood in an instant what had made Owen move mountains to ensure Kelly would be safe and protected. *And loved*. "Want to spit on it, too?"

Alace roughly spit into her palm and extended her hand, not hesitating when his saliva-coated hand disappeared into hers. Another two solemn shakes later, and they wiped the excess on the outside of their jeans in unison. "Deal, Kelly. I'm counting on you."

"I'll never let you down." With an ease and confidence she couldn't help but wonder at, he lifted the car seat and held it to the side, so it didn't bang against his legs. Taking the stairs one at a time, he moved past Owen and Shiloh and into the house, disappearing into the dimly lighted interior.

"No," she murmured to herself, heading up the walk to greet Owen, "I don't expect you will." Standing one step down from where Owen stood, she focused on the little girl. "Hello again, Shiloh." Cutting her gaze to Owen's face, she tensed when she saw the amusement on his expression. "Owen."

"You're pretty." Shiloh held out her arms, upper half of her body leaning precipitously towards Alace, who raised her hands in a reflexive action, shocked when Owen readily transferred the little girl to her. "You has pretty eyes." Shiloh was so close their noses nearly touched, the wide eyes of the child staring unblinkingly into hers. "I wike you."

"She likes you, Alace. What do you say?" Owen stepped backwards into the house, creating an open corridor for Alace to enter.

"Thank you?" Alace bent at the waist, intent on placing Shiloh on the floor, but thin arms tightened around her neck. "You're choking me." She straightened, and the girl's grip eased, only to clamp back down in a fierce hold when Alace tried to put her down again. "Look, I can't hold you the whole time I'm here."

"You hair's pretty." Fingers Alace failed to dodge threaded through her hair from the nape of her neck to the crown of her head, tangling in her hair with a rough tug. "I can make it prettier."

"My hair's fine as it is, thank you." Alace tried to grip the girl's wrist to pull her hand away but was unable, the girl evading her attempts while simultaneously managing to repeat the same against-the-grain combing action, hair tangled by the initial pass yanking free. "Please stop."

"It's so pretty." Shiloh appeared enraptured, eyes shining and mouth dropping open to expose tiny white teeth and a pink tongue that curled around the edge of her lips. "So pretty."

Alace shifted the girl so she was in a front piggyback, putting their faces in direct alignment. She loosened her grip enough that Shiloh clutched Alace's shoulders to stay in place. "You're hurting me. Please stop." In front of her eyes, all the shining pleasure fled from the girl's face, replaced by a crumpled pain. Mouth turned down at the corners, Shiloh stared at her and abruptly released her grip, terrifying Alace by flopping bonelessly backwards in her arms. She held on, allowing the girl to suspend upside down, legs still wrapped around Alace's waist. "What are you doing now?"

"I hurted you. I'm hiding." Shiloh gathered her hair in two handfuls pulled across her face, literally hiding behind her hair. "I'm sorry, Miss Alace."

"You're going to injure yourself doing this. I'm okay. Just—" Her sweaty hands slipped slightly, and Alace's stomach flipped over, afraid she would drop the girl. "Get back up here, Shiloh."

Hair released, the little girl latched onto Alace's shirt and yanked herself back upright. Her emotional changes were mercurial, turning on a dime as she reacted to everything in her narrow universe.

"Come here, troublemaker." Owen stepped in behind Shiloh and lifted her, easily taking her back from Alace.

The sudden emptiness of her arms was wrong and disturbing, causing her skin to prickle into gooseflesh. Alace scanned the visible room, relaxing when she saw Kelly seated on the floor next to the car seat where Lila still slept.

"She's been real focused on hair recently. No idea why, except her own is drop-dead gorgeous. Doc and I are learning all about hair care. Who knew there were so many details and options?" Owen kissed Shiloh's cheek, then a brief raspberry blown against her skin had her giggling again. He set her feet on the floor, receiving no resistance from the girl, who immediately abandoned the adults and ran to where Kelly sat. He pulled her to his other side, away from Lila's car seat, and she settled next to him, head leaned against his shoulder. "Watch." He tipped his head towards the kids, and Alace saw what he meant, gaze tracking Shiloh's hand as it rose to wrap fingers in Kelly's hair. "She likes you. That's bigger than you know. She doesn't like or trust most people. Doc said given her age when her folks OD'd, paired with bad foster experiences and then all the shit with Warrant—it shouldn't be a surprise that attachment is hard when Kelly's been the only constant in her life. Her wanting to be friends with you is huge."

Alace transferred her gaze to Owen, staring into his face. He was telling her she mattered here, inside this family he was building from scratch, including her in his hard-won refuge. She let the muscles around her mouth and eyes soften and gave him a single slow blink. "Let's get busy."

"Yah, boss." His chuckle cut through the sting of that title, the humor reminding her he didn't see her in the role as an impediment to his own, but an accoutrement instead.

Her current position wasn't anything she'd ever aimed for, but Alace had fearlessly taken the opportunity when things in her own history went sideways. An image of a smoke column rising in the rearview mirror of a car surfaced and reminded her what not to do. Daily, she touched on the flaws and faults rampant in her previous handler/hunter relationship. Determined not to repeat the past, Alace would push towards a better solution. *Always*.

She looked past him at Kelly, who had an arm around Shiloh's shoulders and a hand on the blanket covering Lila. Two steps later, she quietly dropped the diaper bag to the floor at the end of the couch, then leaned over and touched Kelly's head, slipping her fingers around the base of his neck protectively. "We'll be in the kitchen. Come get me when she wakes up." He looked up and nodded, then returned his attention to the show on the TV. On impulse she bent farther and tucked a strand of Shiloh's hair behind her ear. "Enjoy the cartoons, pretty girl." The bright eyes and quick smile received in return were more than enough payment for her efforts. Alace understood Owen more in that instant, his reasons for keeping the kids brought to life in the flesh and bone beauty before her.

This might be the first time she'd actually been inside this house, but the real estate agent's video tour had been professionally done. So, able to move confidently, she angled towards the back of the house, coming to a stop inside the archway to the kitchen when she saw Doc standing next to the refrigerator, a glass of what looked like lemonade in one hand.

"Hello." She remained in place, allowing Owen to pass her, startled to realize there had been no prickle of unease as a result of having him at her back. Her initial meeting of Darren "Doc" Marchant had gone well, even better than she'd hoped. He'd proven himself nearly immune to unease, not falling into the typical pattern of men in her presence where they took either a tactic of trying to out-intimidate her or were dismissive of her in some way. Doc had ridden a different line, one of comfortable acceptance of everything he'd known about her and the few things she exposed during their conversation. Owen had taken the two older kids into the backyard to run off some energy for a few minutes, giving Alace an opportunity she'd capitalized on to ensure Doc understood his place in the grand scheme of things.

He'd surprised her in a number of ways.

"Few things matter more to me than making a difference in a child's life. I believe you and Owen will provide me with unique opportunities to turn those desires into a tangible reality." Doc popped a freshly washed grape into his mouth, chewed, and swallowed, lips curved into a slight smile as if he had zero cares in the world. *"Without compromising my morals."*

"Care to elaborate on your perception of this opportunity?" Alace tore her gaze from him, glancing to the side to compulsively check the volume on the baby monitor for the third time since Owen had gone outside.

locations. "You have to change anything since you guys moved in?" There was a tiny pinhole camera beside the back door she hadn't installed, and what looked like a laser trip sensor on this side of the archway, set at about knee height. "Was everything like you wanted?"

"We've had these conversations, too, Alace. Why don't you tell me what's going on?" Without breaking their stare, with a bare movement, he flicked a finger at the two locations she'd identified and then pointed out two more. What he didn't do was call them out blatantly to Doc.

Even more interesting.

Either Doc didn't know about any of the security measures Alace had installed—and after the massive argument during the men's drive from New Jersey to Colorado, she didn't believe it would be the case—or Owen hadn't told him about his additional after-market enhancements. Not that she blamed Owen for stepping things up. Frankly, she was embarrassed her research into the neighborhood hadn't uncovered the two festering boils they had to deal with now.

When she'd moved in with Eric, there had been only one individual she'd found who had to be relocated for her peace of mind. He'd been part of an organized crime mail scam, one where they recruited unwitting twentysomethings on the Internet to be so-called quality inspectors. Any blowback from his activity

"As Owen has explained it, you both feel you responsibility lies chiefly in stopping the perpetrators. With my assistance, as a team we can expand to include initial care for the victims. Giving you ample time to deal with your piece of the initiative, without conceding the criticality of rapid triage and first aid." One of the kids shrieked outside, the loud sound filled with trilling laughter, accentuated by the roaring of whatever monster Owen was pretending to be. *"That's a win-win, no matter which way you look at it."*

Doc casually offered the remainder of the drink to Owen, who took it, upending the glass and draining it. Alace blinked, careful to keep her features smooth. Their unconscious interaction wasn't the behavior of two people who scarcely knew each other. The behavior verged on couple territory, something she might do with Eric.

"When did you say you actually met Doc, Owen?" He was standing at the sink to rinse the glass and glanced up at her, then back down as he worked.

"I'd scouted him before I went up to the cabin but placed the first call only after getting home with the kids. He came over right away." Upside-down glass draining in the strainer, he gave her an openly puzzled look. "I told you already. Why are you asking again now?"

"Just curious." She took another step into the room, quickly marking all known camera and security would likely have been restricted to his home, which was half a block down from Eric's, but Alace hadn't wanted to take that chance at all.

So she'd called an acquaintance, who called an acquaintance, who called a family friend—two days later, there'd been a moving van in front of the address. *Having connections is a good thing, regardless of acquisition costs.*

It struck her suddenly that for all she knew, her method of investigating had blind spots. Once upon a time admitting such knowledge would have felt like a weakness, back when she couldn't lean on anyone to get her gigs done. *Except Regg,* her brain was quick to remind her. *Owen isn't Regg.* He'd been nothing but a true partner thus far, bringing her in on everything as soon as circumstances allowed. *Time to return the favor.* "I want you to check out the neighborhood where I live when this is all over." Owen ticked his head to one side at the same instant Doc tocked his head, and she had to stifle a laugh at their unconscious synchronization. "If we're going to be in each other's space, I want you to be comfortable" was the semi-lie she gave them. "With Lila at home, I'd also feel better to have an additional set of eyes on the information." Ending with the full truth felt better, and Alace suppressed the desire to laugh aloud. "And now, about your neighbors."

Wisely, Owen chose to ignore her odd request, unlocked a drawer behind him, and pulled a folder from it. He opened the folder and spread paperwork out over the counter, setting the stage for them to dive directly into the matter at hand.

"Ashworth first." He shuffled papers quietly, surfacing a copy of the inspection report from yesterday. "Not yet stamped and filed, but filled out via their portal, so I've got this. The structural review went fine, with one exception." He pointed at a spot on the form and flipped it to face Alace, who stepped closer to the island countertop. "He found an inconsistency in the previous construction he wants to review, a section of cement that's settled oddly, separating from the base of the wall. Wanna bet if they put radar to it, they'll find the remains of a male prostitute under there?"

"Is Ashworth still in residence, or did he vacate? He's got the money to disappear anywhere if he so desired." She held out a hand. "Give me the tablet you've got in here." Owen opened a different drawer, also locked, and she stifled a chuckle. "You restricting screen time for the kids?" He glared at her as he handed it over. "Doesn't matter, just funny given the amount of time you spend on a computer."

"I work out too." His defensiveness made Doc grin, and Owen turned to face him. "You know I do. I run and hit the gym. Maybe not all the time, but that's because of work." Frowning, he glanced between Doc and Alace, realized they were ribbing him, and he broke into a smile. "Shut up, both of you."

"Neither of us said a word, Owen." Doc pointed out the obvious, and Alace liked that he could spar with Owen fearlessly, showing the friendship the men were building.

Kind of like Owen and me. "Here's what I was looking for." She handed it over. "What he researched online after the inspector left. Check it out."

"Shouldn't he know searches like that leave traces? 'Will organic material buried in cement decay?' Okay, first, shouldn't he know cement is an ingredient of concrete, making the question wrong from the outset? He's supposed to be a smart guy." Owen's scorn had his upper lip lifted, and she saw his hands clenching tightly around the tablet. His anger was out of scope with their investment in this gig, and she watched as Doc lifted a hand to Owen's shoulder, gripping loosely but pressing down, anchoring him physically. "He's been good enough to get away with this for years, Doc. He should be smarter. I shouldn't have been the first person to pay attention."

"You weren't. The reporter was." Alace pulled his attention back to her, and she watched as he visibly relaxed, leaning sideways into Doc's grip. "But we're the ones who are going to put a stop to what he's been doing. I know you offered up a contact for this gig, but I went ahead and re-rerouted August. He should be in town tonight. Gives us enough time by the narrowest of margins. We have to go through what we have and provide him the preferred method so the other deaths are called into question, as well as give investigators something to go on for what we think happened to his test runs." She pointed at the tablet. "Here's one. What else do we have? At least Ashworth isn't looking for island nations that don't extradite." She shrugged. "So we got that goin' for us." Her bad imitation of one of Owen's favorite lines had him smiling, finally. "So to speak."

"So to speak." Doc's echo made her look at him, seeing the somber tone he'd adopted was matched by his expression, vastly different from hers and Owen's. "Will there be a reckoning for all his victims or only those that can be readily identified?"

"As many as we can safely draw attention to." Alace stared at him, not sure what he meant by his question. "I won't have Owen put at risk, and living this close the only thing going for him—and by extension, me—is that your household is new to the neighborhood."

"And the others? They're no more than a footnote to the story? The man is a serial killer, Alace." He swept his hand out over the papers, gaze glancing across the information laid out. "Will they even be a footnote? Or will they be forgotten?" For an instant, she imagined he was talking about her history, something she hadn't fully shared with this new addition to their team. Owen had urged easing the doctor in, and Alace suddenly understood his reasoning. "Will they be like my sister? Never found? Families left mourning without closure?"

His words struck her dumb, and she turned slightly, aiming her gaze out the window into the backyard, still empty of toys or the other trappings of childhood. An unaccustomed heat filled her cheeks, warming her throat and chest.

She'd been standing here making his statements about her, centering herself in his accusations, and he'd not been aiming at her. Not at all. He'd been baring his own pain, and she'd blindly converted it to her version. *Lack of empathy is one of the signs of a sociopath.* Eric had caught her watching a video online, an interview with a psychiatrist who specialized in dangerous sociopaths. He'd been explaining all the things Alace already knew from her own research: psychopaths were a wholly different entity. She hunted psychopaths. She knew intimately what they were like, what they were capable of. She wasn't and had never considered herself a psychopath.

A sociopath, however, hadn't occurred to her until that moment watching a medical pundit whose main focus had been peddling his upcoming book. Eric had shown up beside her chair and leaned over to punch the shutdown button on the computer. He'd cupped her cheeks in his hands and lifted her face so her mouth met his, lips grazing sideways until he had whispered in her ear, "All you are is mine."

"Alace?" Owen's questioning use of her name sounded far away, as if through a tunnel, and Alace fought to bring her attention back to the kitchen. He was leaned against his side of the island, hips pressed tight so he could stretch across, his hand hovering over her arm. She watched it slowly descend, then latch on, fingers curling around and squeezing gently. "Alace, you okay?"

"What's that reporter's name?" She shook off his hand, spinning to look down at the printed reports on the countertop. "How much of this is truly public knowledge? How much did she know back at wife number three, when she first raised suspicions about him?"

"Everything I have is public. You have the report, not yet filed. Whenever it hits the county's website, it'll be public, too." He traced along the edges of his teeth as he studied her. "What are you thinking?"

"She's thinking the author could do an interview with a reporter and mention the prostitute angle, giving enough dates to prod the reporter's brain about her interview with our good neighbor." Doc nodded once, the gratitude on his face enough to express his feelings. "She's going to make sure everyone is found."

"The old blood at the scene of two of the wives' deaths, those would be public too. Maybe not type, but if she pressured the officials, they could make a circumstantial case about that evidence." Owen straightened, standing upright, his shoulders firming into rigid angles. "How can you drag all this information into it? And how can we do this knowing we're on an awfully tight deadline to make sure current wifey doesn't get dead?"

"I can present two distinct potential book outlines. One surrounding the male prostitute disappearances, and one built on anecdotal stories about a local man who's survived multiple wives. I can point to Ashworth without pointing to him, and hopefully she's smart enough to draw all correlations on her own." Alace glanced over her shoulder to where the three children sat in front of the couch. "And I can do it without speaking about the neighborhood or any new residents, so you'll be covered."

"When would you do the interview?"

Alace smiled and brought out her day-to-day phone, the one that had Eric's and his mother's phone numbers, her fake-kind-of-real agent, and a couple of businesses she and Eric frequented. She pressed a button and lifted it to her ear, a moment later hearing the expected "Beloved" greeting.

"Eric, do you still have Grundella's phone number?" Silence followed, and she had to fight to keep her amusement from her voice when she said, "Her sister's a reporter, and I think my next book could use a boost."

"I have Jessica's phone number. In a moment, I'll have her sister's number, too. I'll text both to you."

She listened to him breathe for the span of three inhalations before her phone pinged softly. "What are you doing, Alace?"

"Looking for a little good press."

Eric's soft hum highlighted his unease, but then he gave her everything, as if he knew she needed to hear it. "You'll be brilliant, Alace. You always are."

"I love you." The stutter in his breathing was her reward.

She disconnected and looked at the screen. Eric texted almost immediately, and she tapped the second number he indicated was the sister, not letting herself consider the possible consequences of engaging with the press like this. Willingly. It rang twice, and a woman answered with a brusque, "Hello?"

"You have a sister named Jessica. She was my nurse recently. I'm calling to see if you'd be interested in an interview with me."

Silence stretched for long enough Alace wondered if the call had dropped. A husky chuckle slipped through the speaker, and the reporter showed she was exactly as intelligent and able to connect the dots as Alace had hoped. "Alace Sweets, bestselling murder mystery author. Why are you calling me and not the entertainment coordinator?"

"Knowing Jessica as I do, I hoped I'd have a more personal connection with you." Alace mimed a shrug, sighing in disappointment. "Sorry if I miscalculated."

"Jessica said you were a righteous bitch."

"Yeah, well, so was she."

Laughter flooded the call, and Alace gripped the phone tighter, waiting. "You aren't wrong. How's your baby?"

"My child is doing well." She and Eric hadn't published any announcement about Lila's birth, not allowing the hospital to include Lila's name in their public messaging even anonymously.

"Oh, don't worry, Ms. Sweets. Jessica is a stickler for privacy. She scarcely mentioned you to me, but I know she's an OB/GYN nurse, so it stands to reason you've had a child recently. Girl or boy?"

"We could include the information in the article, if you wanted." Alace bartered, knowing if Eric had a problem with the idea, she'd willingly renege on any verbal agreement surrounding their family.

"At least it would make it more of a human-interest story than simply a promo for your novels." Paper rustled in the background, and Alace imagined her at an enormous desk, paging through a social calendar. "When were you thinking?"

"Now, actually." She put the call on speaker and texted Eric, providing enough details for him to give her approval or not. "I could meet you downtown in twenty minutes." A thumbs-up emoji came through, followed by a more verbose, *I **will** be there*. "My husband will be attending."

The reporter named a coffee shop Alace knew, and the location was quickly agreed upon, the timing shifting to an hour from now to accommodate the need to secure a photographer.

Before hanging up, Alace said, "One more thing, if you don't mind."

"Yes?" The one word was guarded and quiet, as if the woman thought Alace was already having second thoughts.

"What's your name? I can't call you Jessica's little sister in my head as we're talking."

That husky laughter was disarming, and Alace understood it was a triggered thing used to defuse awkward situations. *At least I have one tell to watch for.* "Colleen Houghton. And I'm the older sister by about fifteen minutes."

"I'll see you there, Ms. Houghton." Alace disconnected and keyed in a few final details to Eric, then looked up to find Owen and Doc both staring at her. "What?"

Doc reached out with a shaking hand, silently asking for her to return the gesture. She did, and he clutched at her, weaving their fingers together, his grip painful in its intensity. "Matters more than you know, Alace."

"What?" She eyed Owen, who was staring at their clasped hands, a peculiar expression on his face. "Owen?"

"You're a better person than you'll ever allow yourself to believe, Alace." His gaze lifted to meet hers. "I'm proud to be your friend, you know that?"

"Can we cover Kuellen in twenty minutes?" She untangled her hand from Doc's. But before they fully separated, she gave his fingers a tiny squeeze she hoped told him how much his reaction meant to her. "That's all I have before I need to leave." She looked over her shoulder at the kids again. "I should change Lila before we head out."

"Kelly, is Lila still sleeping?" The boy's head whipped around to look at Owen, and he glanced down, then back up, nodding. "Wake her up sweet and slow for Miss Alace? She needs to change her diaper before they leave."

"Awww. They gotta go already?" His pout was different from the guarded child Owen had described, and even as Alace considered this, it faded, the boy's expression changing to one that was stoic in the extreme. "Yes, sir."

"We'll be back soon, Kelly." Alace caught sight of one disbelieving eye behind the hank of hair that always seemed to be in his face; then he bent over Lila, his soft sing-song voice barely audible. "Kelly?" He looked back up, his finger held tight in Lila's grip as he shook her hand back and forth gently. Alace crooked her pinky finger at him. "I promise." She turned back to Owen, and his broad grin was immediately annoying. "What?"

"Nothin'." He tipped his chin down, and she saw the flash of teeth before he schooled his features. "About Kuellen, he can wait. He's just a distributor, probably one of thousands. Maybe I can find his suppliers if I look that direction. Up to now, I've been focused on the content on his servers. Let me attack it from a different vector for a little bit."

"I'll hold August for a day. We'll see what the reporter gives us. Do you have names and dates I can copy down of the suspected deaths we'll want to put in front of this Colleen?" She huffed out a sigh. "It'll be fun to see how well she can keep up."

"Take care she doesn't lap you, Alace." Doc's cautioning words made her bristle, then she looked at Owen, who appeared even more offended on her behalf. "I'm not saying she's smarter than either of you, but don't discount her acquired skills as an investigative reporter. She will be accustomed to look for the story behind the story. Calling out of the blue will be a flag, and anything you bring up could look suspect. She'll consider everything from a personal vendetta against Ashworth to collaboration, or even whistleblowing if she can draw lines between you and anyone on the force. As someone who has had his fair share of interviews, trust me when I say giving her an hour to prepare means every question has three different outcomes in her mind. How will you broach the topic?"

"Baby talk, introduce Eric, chat about books in general, segue to local history, news articles, allude to confidential interviews with male prostitutes, mention the community complaint without talking about the neighborhood, backed up by a calendar of events I can hand over. Followed by the family photo to accompany the article, a signed copy of my most recent book, and then Lila will need to feed which gives me a chance to bond with her via her sister, when she tells her sister I cut the interview short to tend to my child." Tipping her head to one side, she gave him a real smile, the tiny quirk of her lips few people saw. "My strategy at a glance."

He swore quietly and shook his head. "Owen, you weren't kidding."

"Told you she was scary smart." Owen slapped Doc's shoulder lightly, grinning and nodding like a maniac.

Alace withdrew the smile and instead turned her flat, cold stare on the doctor, pulling on decades of dissociation to generate one of her most useful tools.

"You ain't seen nothing yet."

***

Owen

"Still waiting," Owen called out before Doc rounded the doorframe into the office. Since Alace had left earlier, even knowing it would be hours before they'd hear anything, he and Doc had both been antsy, waiting to hear how it had gone from her perspective.

"I know we are, you ass. I was coming in to ask about dinner." Doc folded his arms across his chest, one shoulder leaned against the doorframe. "Kelly claims he'd like to have hot dogs, again. Wanna guess why?"

"Shiloh asked for hot dogs." Heels against the edge of the desk, Owen rocked his chair back on two legs. "I'm not a fan, personally. What would you prefer?"

"Anything except hot dogs. I've got little in the fridge, though. What would you think about delivery?" Doc's expression didn't give anything away, but Owen knew the man was sensitive to their efforts to stay not just below radar but entirely off the grid. "Or, I could do a pickup instead. Pizza or chicken?"

"I'm glad I don't have a normal office chair." Owen let the front legs drop back to the floor, the thud shaking up through him. "Or I'd have tipped over backwards, no doubt." *Pizza can be delivered*. He liked how Doc had given him options not only for the food but for the acquisition method. "You volunteering to actually leave the house. I'm shocked." Doc seemed to have no desire to learn the city so far. Owen could relate. Beyond the required trips to the grocery store and other places, neither of them had done much exploring. "Chicken."

"You got it." Doc turned to the hallway but paused and turned back, looking at Owen over his shoulder. "I understand it now. I get it."

"You get what?" Hands hovering over the keyboard, he waited patiently for whatever it was Doc felt he had to communicate right now. Doc was like that. A man who could hold his peace for hours and days, but once he'd come to an insight, he'd beat down a door to explain.

"How Alace can be good people, too."

"Alace *is* good people. Never doubt that. It's truth, down to the iron in the earth. It's my true north. I couldn't do what I do without believing in her." He turned his chair, legs catching on the rug he'd placed under the desk. Frustrated, he half stood and lifted the chair, placing it where he'd wanted. His gaze locked onto Doc the instant his ass hit the seat again. "If you believe in me, then you believe in Alace. There's no middle ground, Darren. I thought you had my back already. Was I wrong?"

"No, no. That's not what I meant at all." Doc shook his head rapidly, staring at Owen, his expression filled with consternation. "I do. You're not wrong. I absolutely do. I see my own role supporting everything you do, and nothing's changed. Nothing. I just—" He eased into the room, one hand extended towards Owen. "Conceptually and intellectually I understood everything before I met her. I did. But now, meeting her. Did you see her in the kitchen? Did you see her at all? See how she reacted and instantly had a solution which is genius in design."

"I saw her." Owen rested his elbows on his knees, hands dangling between his thighs. "I know her, inside out."

"She's brilliant." Doc scrubbed along his jaw with the edge of a hand. "Kelly told me how she was outside, too. She balanced her fears and desires for her own daughter's safety and well-being against Kelly and the need she saw in him for affirmation of his caretaker role. She went with the kindhearted response. I think she's empathetic to a fault, and yet clearly believes herself incapable of that same compassion." His mouth twisted to the side. "I get it now, you know?"

"I do know." Owen pushed out a heavy breath. "I do. Thank you. Means a lot, man."

Doc stepped backwards, rapped his knuckles against the doorframe once, and disappeared up the hallway.

Owen twisted to face the computer, elbow hooked over the back of the chair as he awkwardly tried to type on the keyboard. Laughing silently at his own efforts, he shifted the chair around and settled into place. "Time to see if my efforts paid off." Ten minutes later, he heard the car engine rumble from the garage. As it died away, he listened intently for the kids, not hearing anything in the house. A glance at his phone showed a text confirming Doc had taken them with him.

With the promise of complete focus in front of him for the next few minutes, he settled his headphones in place and logged into his secure server, from there to his secure VPN, and finally into an anonymizer system to access his messages from the darknet work boards. "Yaass." He opened an email from one of the operatives he'd tapped to review footage, looking for identifiable individuals. This guy had come through for him in the past, and Owen expected nothing less now.

He skimmed the shared document, hoping to get a sense of scale when it came to the kids. Not that it really mattered. One child on Kuellen's stash was enough to damn him in Owen's eyes, and Alace had already found multiple foster kids. *At least none of those had been—*

Another message flashed into his Inbox from the same guy, with a different attachment. This one came with a narrative: *Repeat actors raised suspicions. Found eight frequent fliers. Cataloged by location if available. Thought you'd want this, too.*

The garage door opening was audible through his headphones, and he glanced at the clock to find he'd been working for not quite an hour. He flicked a look at the doorway, then back to the computer screen. Saving the second document to one of his servers, he then made a copy of the shared document the guy couldn't modify and backed out of his systems.

Running footfalls preceded Shiloh by only seconds, and he turned to face the door, arms stretched wide. She rounded the corner at full speed, her arc bringing her directly to Owen, and he wrapped her in a hug, standing and twisting back and forth so her feet and legs swung wildly.

"Dinner's ready." Doc was grinning at them from the doorway when Owen looked up, Kelly peering around Doc's hip. "Bring the little monster with you when you come."

"She's not a monster," he argued, laughing when Shiloh immediately parroted the words, "I not a monster."

Doc's arms raised zombielike, and he cackled. "You're not the monster..." His stiff-legged walk covered ground, and he was on them before he finished with "I am." Shiloh was sandwiched between them until Doc pretended to try to grip and drag her away from Owen, who dramatically protected and saved the little girl. With Kelly's laughter ringing around them, Shiloh's giggles in his ear, and Doc's amused chuckles, Owen couldn't help but grin at the rightness of the moment.

After the meal and cleaning up the minimal dishes, he sat on one end of the couch while Doc occupied the other, kids sprawled between them. Kelly's head was on Owen's knee and Shiloh slumped against Doc's side, leaving Owen relaxed, gently threading his fingers through Kelly's heavy, thick hair. "Time for bed, kiddos." With no argument from either, they slipped to the floor and headed to their rooms. He looked at Doc. "It isn't supposed to be that easy, right?"

"They'll get there. At some point you'll be silently wishing for the days of easy compliance." Doc's gentle gaze followed the kids to the hallway leading to the bedrooms. "I'll go help them with teeth and jammies. I know you're dying to get back on that computer."

"Hey, it's my work." He didn't argue the desire to get back into the reports he'd received. It'd be a lie Doc would pick up on, and he hated the idea of doing anything stupid that might create friction in their friendship.

"No, it's your calling." Doc was walking along the back of the couch and touched Owen's shoulder. "And it's okay to be passionate about your calling." He disappeared up the hallway, his words floating behind him. "I am."

Owen heaved himself off the couch, stretching as he made his way back to the office. Headphones on, he followed the normal log-in protocol, quickly finding his place in the shared report again, noting the last modified time matched his previous access. He glanced at the page count and sighed. *Only twenty-two to go.* Picking up with the next line of information, he worked his way through the remaining individual segments of the first report, flagging half a dozen for more research. Owen wavered, tempted to call it a night and go back out to see what Doc was doing after putting the kids to bed. The second report appeared to glow in the background, attached to the email, which defined what was likely the sickest of the offenders.

"Fuck it, I have to know what we're up against." Resettling his headphones in place, he queued up a favorite work playlist, one that helped him focus because he knew every word, every riff, and every drum solo.

The researcher had included multiple stills from each video, showing the abused child's face as clearly as possible for identification, then focused on the abuser—many of whom wore masks—and the setting, drilling into the details that could provide clues for the actual site. Electric outlet plugs, lighting styles, knickknacks, even the style of shelves lining the walls were datapoints that would all lead back to a specific location.

As he went through the first several reports, he found the children were all different. Boys and girls, tall and short, thin and chubby. The only constant was they were between five and eleven years old. The abusers ran the same gamut of variance in terms of body type, height and weight, hairy or bald, smooth or bearded. The settings were unique by individual, which meant every scene by the different abusers shared whatever props had been present at one of their previous scenes.

Owen turned the page to the next set of images and froze.

Shiloh's face stared out at him, tears streaking through the dirt on her cheeks.

Shiloh.

Frozen in his chair, he was locked on the picture, seeing her as if for the first time again. Her features too thin, nose beaky in her malnourished state, the collar around her neck resting heavily against her collarbones. Owen realized he could hear himself breathing, the noise rushing through his nose, filling the room. His headphones were on the floor across the room, ripped from the computer.

The memorized weight of a blade rested in his palm, the balance of tang and handle a living force. A metallic scent of hot blood filled his nostrils, and he fought to keep the memory of taking tiny Shiloh through the door to her brother in the front of his mind.

Owen stood, the chair threatening to topple backwards, salvaged by him reaching out quick as a snake to keep it upright. Storming through the doorway, he made a sharp turn up the hall towards where the kids slept, only to come up short at Shiloh's room.

Her pink unicorn nightlight cast enough dim illumination to show the empty bed, and panic clawed up his throat to obliterate his ability to take another breath. He whirled and reached for Kelly's door, always cracked—like Owen's it was never closed all the way in case Shiloh needed him during the night.

A diminutive foot stuck out from underneath Kelly's bed.

Tiny, child-sized, and covered in delicate pink socks.

Pink socks.

Clean pink socks.

The hold on his throat loosened enough to let a sip of air seep through.

Tiny because she was small, not because she was starved. Clean because she had a dresser bursting at the seams with new clothing.

He pulled in another breath, this one deeper, the scents fading away until all he could smell was boy. Healthy, sweaty, safe—Kelly was safe.

Shiloh is safe.

Another inhale, ribs expanding more smoothly, shoulders lifting as muscles relaxed.

My kids are both safe.

Owen looked up the hallway and saw Doc's door standing wide. That was a room normally closed tightly once the man went to bed, not inviting any nocturnal visitors. At the other end of the hallway, a door allowed a broad band of light to shine through, pinpointing Doc's location.

He stalked up the hallway, past his office to arrive in front of the room they'd set up as a home trauma unit, their multi-bedroom house a must to accommodate all they needed. A sturdy, movable table was pushed to one side, the angle of its wheels showing the direction from which it had come. It and the countertops along the walls were covered in containers of various sizes, each filled with medical supplies.

Doc had a label maker in his hands, using his thumbs as if he were texting to input the data for the next identification label. He looked at Owen, offered a nod, then looked back down at the device in his hands. "Hey." Doc's greeting was soft and distracted, and some of the rigid bands around Owen's chest eased a little more.

"The pornographer…the guy I told you about." Owen knew it wasn't a complete sentence, knew it didn't convey anything of the dark, rolling anger still rushing through him, but somehow Doc understood.

"When are you going after him?" He gestured around the room. "I want to be prepared."

Prepared in case Owen needed assistance. There were no children at risk with this mission, not directly. It would be an intelligence-gathering foray, with an eye towards breaking Kuellen to expose his network of like-minded sick fucks. The stills from the abusers his researcher had branded "frequent fliers" made Owen believe they were a pedo ring who taped and broadcast their demented desires. Maybe even the ones who'd been buying sibling pairs. Finding Shiloh in the mix had set the idea in stone. He remembered speaking directly into the camera, talking to whoever had been watching on the other end.

Found one.

"Soon. Very soon. I can't be this close to someone like him and not do something."

"Okay." Doc finished the label he was working on and pulled the paper from the machine, smoothing it on the end of one container. Owen read it. Chest seal. A penetrating upper-torso wound would need that type of treatment.

"You're planning on me getting shot?"

"No." Doc's thumbs worked overtime on the next label. "I'm planning on saving your life if you do get shot." He pulled the paper out and cut his gaze towards Owen as he separated the backing from the sticker. "There's a difference."

"I found Shiloh." Doc froze in place as if Owen's words had the ability to pause time. "I told you about the setup the guy had at the cabin." He needed to share this burden with someone he believed loved his kids as much as he did. "I found her."

Doc swiveled to face him, skin a pasty gray. "Our little girl? Did you watch—"

"No." Owen cut him off. "My guy took stills from the videos of the kids, the men, and the locations. Her image is in those stills, with the inside of the cabin. He's got at least one video of our Shiloh." His cell phone buzzed, and he pulled it from his pocket. *Alace.* "I can't—won't—let anyone else deal with this bastard now."

Doc nodded, then as Owen turned towards the door, phone lifting to his ear, asked a question stopping Owen in his tracks.

"You said there were snuff films, too. Owen, what if he's got a video of you killing the guy?"

"Won't matter." Owen glanced over his shoulder, locking gazes as he gave Doc a promise. "But if he does, I hope it made him piss himself in fear."

***

Alace

"I right now walked in the door, so don't complain I didn't call you earlier." Alace waited for Owen to chide her, surprised when he was silent. "I'd say mission accomplished, but we saw how well that went for folks in the past, so I'll just say mission begun." Still no reaction, and Alace frowned. "No coaching from the sidelines? Color me shocked."

"How did you introduce the idea Ashworth is a wife-killer?" His voice was flat, stripped bare of affect, as if he were reading from a script. Badly.

"My focus was the prostitutes, remember?" Her memories didn't lie; that was the direction they'd discussed earlier. "We talked about this, Owen."

"You're right." The sound of a sigh huffed through the phone. "I've been researching. Give me a minute to put my people hat back on." She could almost imagine the small upturn of his lips now he was more engaged in their conversation. "So she made the leap from already seeing him as a lecherous wife-killer to a prostitute-murderer?"

"She did, actually. I didn't say his name or even mention the neighborhood. I kept it to rumors and talked about the timing and sequence of events as I'd uncovered them in research for a book." Alace unclipped the baby carrier she had strapped to her chest, cradling a sleeping Lila in one arm while balancing the phone on her shoulder. "The woman is exceptionally intelligent and made specific intuitive leaps I didn't necessarily expect." Up the stairs, she set the diaper bag on the bedroom floor and draped the carrier over the top, taking Lila with her to the baby bed. She placed the baby in the bassinette and smiled as Lila groaned and stretched, still sleeping. "It's later than I expected, but I'm home. You can stop worrying."

"Yes, ma'am." His teasing response made her grin, and she knew he'd done it on purpose. "We'll debrief in full tomorrow. Get some rest."

"You, too." She disconnected the call and turned, not surprised to find Eric in the doorway. "Owen's being weird."

"I'm glad you're home." His soft voice was pitched to let Lila sleep. "Did the interview go well after I left?"

She walked towards him, leaning in as his arms spread wide, circling his waist with hers as his wrapped around her tightly. Forehead propped against his chest, she let a measure of her tension seep away. "It was good. Long, but good. I think I got everything I wanted out of the deal, at least. You're lucky you got to bail after the photo session." The photographer had arrived at the same time as Eric, and Houghton hadn't balked at the change in schedule.

"Good." He took a step backwards, then another, leading her into the hallway. "Hungry?"

"Not tonight. I'll double up on a good breakfast tomorrow morning." She yawned and turned her cheek against him, closing her eyes. "You're leading me away from the bed. I'd rather be headed that direction, you know?"

"Oh, I'm aware." He bent slightly and scooped her up in his arms. "I thought we could have some daddy and mommy time for ourselves."

"Did you now?" She leaned backwards to look up into his face. Her exhaustion had disappeared, fading away as if it had never existed. "What exactly did you have in mind?"

"I wanted a chance to kiss my wife." He put actions to the words, effortlessly carrying her downstairs as he touched his lips to hers. "And maybe kiss her again." Another kiss, this one longer, deeper, threaded through with a hunger she found rising in herself to match his.

"And maybe more?" Alace ghosted her fingers up the back of his neck, relishing the crisp thickness of his hair. She gripped gently and tugged, pulling his mouth back down to hers. "More kisses?"

"Definitely," he murmured against her lips as he settled onto the couch. Eric adjusted Alace across his lap, leaning over her as she rested against the arm of the couch. "And then even more."

"Such a rule-breaker, Mr. Ward." She slipped her hands underneath his shirt, tugging until he lifted his arms and allowed her to slide it off him. "We're a full three days early."

"Is this you—" His mouth moved down her neck, teeth gripping and releasing, his tongue trailing a hot path along the side of her throat. "Wanting to wait those extra days?"

"Not at all." Alace arched into him, legs falling wide as he moved to cover her, elbows planted deep in the cushions on either side of her shoulders. She slipped down to lay flat on the couch as he ground their hips together firmly, letting her feel his hardness. Pleasure paired with desire to run hot through her blood, and as always, when she was in his arms, the sense of coming home was overwhelming. "Eric."

"Mmmm?"

"My pants are still on."

"Not for long."

His touch grazed over her body as they kissed, fingertips drawing circles across her belly, knuckles rubbing and chafing her nipples as clothing articles were discarded. Eric settled alongside her, his body pinning hers against the back of the couch as he continued his sensuous assault. Alace's leg bent, heel dragging against the fabric, opening to his touch. She had to stifle a moan when his thumb made a side-to-side sweep across her clit, fingers teasing along her opening.

"Baby." His soft voice penetrated the sexual haze occupying her mind far less potently than his fingers did her body. "Baby." He called again, and she slit one eye open, staring up at him.

"Mmmm?" She borrowed from his wordless reply earlier.

"We want more kids, right?" Surfacing from the fog, she stared and nodded slowly. "You're not worried about it being too soon, if it happens?"

"No. Not at all." She rolled her hips, the movement pushing his fingers inside her farther. "I'd be more upset if you stopped right now." She slipped her hand around his neck, pulling him over her until his cock replaced his fingers. "Love me, please."

He dropped his head, mouth meeting hers as he thrust inside slowly, sliding deep on a single push until he ground his hips against hers.

"I already do."

Hours later, Alace woke from the uneasy sleep her body had claimed after Lila's hungry cries had pulled them both back upstairs for her bedtime nursing. She stared into the darkness, relishing the heat and firmness under her cheek and all along her side. Eric was her pillow, his arm curved around her even in his sleep, their legs tangled together underneath the covers.

Owen was weird.

The thought kept circling through her brain, reasons and justification for his oddness bouncing back and forth. He hadn't been peculiar or different earlier when she was over there. Not even with Doc in the room, a stressor she'd expected them both to react to, but they hadn't.

Something had happened between when she'd left for the interview and when she'd called to tell him the outcome.

Alace glanced over Eric's chest to where his phone was docked, the time writ in large digits on the face.

Too early to call Owen.

Not too early to see what he was looking at.

She eased out of Eric's hold, his arm tightening around her briefly as he fought to keep her close, even in his sleep. His unconscious desire for her was one of her favorite things, reminding her every day that his love wasn't surface and fleeting. Somehow, through their time together, Eric had become her bedrock, the solid land she retreated to at every chance, and the stable foundation her happiness aligned with.

With her desk still in their bedroom, she didn't have far to go, retrieving the laptop from the secure drawer and reassembling it, then able to check on Lila as the computer booted. Headphones in place, she slipped into her seat, hooking her toes around the legs of the caster base.

Months ago, she and Owen had agreed on their version of a dead man's switch. A way for the other to see electronic activity if there were a need, something to protect both of them if there were a disruption in communication for any reason. This wasn't a disruption, not exactly. *But still, a need.*

The digital trail was anonymized, which meant only the person authorized to retrace the online steps of a given account would know whose activity they were reading. She'd spared no expense in the original setup, and both she and Owen had enhanced it as ideas came to them. All this meant was, within moments, she had his entire online history for the previous day in front of her, even the secured elements typically obscured with randomized IP addresses and masked VPN connections.

Their exposure of activity didn't include access to the individual machines or secure email accounts. But seeing he'd received two messages via a work board, it didn't take her long to slip into the account of the sender, finding his deleted messages to Owen and quickly restoring and moving them to an account unique to her.

They'd talked about the research Owen had done into the Kuellen gig, so the shared document she'd saved down wasn't a surprise. It held information validating everything she'd found, providing the same percentage of positive identifications for the kids in the videos.

An icon on her toolbar pulsed red, and Alace switched her view to the local machine, logging into the online dropbox it monitored. August had dropped a note into his folder with information about his arrival in Colorado.

Alace quickly opened the shared document she used with her hunter and found he was still online and waiting. She typed out a second modification in instructions and details, holding back the information about the interview. He didn't need to know the particulars about why the gig was delayed by a couple more days. As long as he trusted her to keep him safe, she'd focus the communications on the active part of the gig.

Her cursor hovered over the disconnect, watching as he typed in an acknowledgment and his on-the-fly change of plans. Normally she'd leave the rudimentary chat without a goodbye, but something Owen had said to her echoed through her head. *"You think people don't care because you don't let them close. If you give others even half of what you've given me, I think they'd surprise you."*

Did you enjoy your time with your daughter?

Kids were probably a safe topic, even if families as a whole might not be. She waited, watching as the cursor indicating August's active presence blinked at the end of his last update to the document. Then it moved down slowly, line by line until he'd created a new paragraph underneath her question.

I did. She loves the ocean. It was nice to be able to give her something she enjoyed.

Alace huffed a frustrated sigh. It was the slightest of openings, not anything with real meat on it for her to leverage into a longer conversation. *Now I'm the one wanting to have a conversation?* Owen would probably say she was adrift in opposite world.

Water seems to be a kid magnet.

That was truth, at least. Lila certainly loved her bath time, nestled safely in the tiny tub of warm, sudsy water. August didn't know about Lila, though, and now she knew a little more about his daughter, which meant it felt like not telling him was edging into territory around untruths.

My daughter—Alace paused there for a long moment, the racing beat of her heart loud in her ears, drowning out the musical white noise she'd been listening to—**loves the bath.**

His cursor moved down faster this time, skipping past her two new lines and planting itself solidly on the next.

I didn't know you had a daughter. What's her name? How old is she?

I did this to myself, she thought, wondering at the tiny pulse of excitement that came with talking about the newest love in her life.

Lila, she's almost six weeks old. Lila Sue.

A bloom of warmth in her chest coincided with typing out her daughter's name, a reaction Alace catalogued for later consideration.

Congratulations, Alace. Babies are the biggest blessing in our lives. I hope you both are doing well. Lila Sue is a great name, very lyrical.

His response was immediate and validating in a way she didn't know she needed. *Lyrical?* Was August into reading, or maybe writing—like her alter ego?

Thank you. I think she's pretty special. I'm sure you feel the same about your daughter.

Alace searched her mind for his daughter's name. She knew it was in his portfolio, but not having it on the tip of her tongue felt like a failure somehow.

For sure, Addison is my heart. Congratulations again, Alace. *Addison, right.* His typing stopped, but the cursor advanced a space, then withdrew, as if he'd begun typing something else and then backspaced before continuing. It advanced again. **I'd be honored if I could give my best wishes in person while in Colo.**

She understood his hesitancy. They'd met once, as she'd done with all her recruits, in a place and time of her choosing. She'd trusted him immediately, something about his personality matching his physical form, solid and sturdy.

I'd like that. We'll set a time. Keep me updated on your location. I should have more info soon about when we move on Ashworth. Might be worth a run by tonight, just to scope the neighborhood.

Just like that, they were back on the information about the gig, and Alace breathed deep, pushing out tension on her exhale. *I can do this.* She'd never be able to tell Owen he was right, though. He'd never let her hear the end of it.

Sounds good. I can do that. See you soon.

Alace exited the document without responding, disconnecting from that server and returning to the other remote session.

She opened the second piece of information the researcher had sent to Owen and skimmed through, freezing about halfway down the document.

The man's face was familiar, immediately recognizable as the mark Owen had eliminated on the East Coast. He was shown in four entries, all kids. Three of them were boys, no older than Kelly, their faces wrecked with maltreatment they'd suffered layered on top of emotional and physical overload. The fourth was a little girl she'd already come to love.

I guess I know what tweaked Owen now.

CHAPTER TEN

Owen

Hands steady, Owen teased at the tumblers with his pick, the steel rod passing tiny vibrations through to his fingers until he knew he could feel all the pins lined up correctly. With a quick twist, he opened the now-unlocked door and stepped soundlessly inside.

His prep had been hurried and rudimentary, not something he would ever have allowed another operative to settle for, but it was only his ass on the line, and he was covered. Enough. *Barely*.

The layout of the structure had been easily memorized. Accounting for the smaller blueprint footprint, as with the house Owen shared with Doc, the entire living space was on the main floor, with a medium-sized basement as a sub-floor. Kitchen and dining room butted up against the living room, with the bedrooms branching off a short hallway that led to and from the door through which Owen had come. The bathroom and laundry area were spaced out along the hallway too, along with a small closet.

There had been no construction permits issued indicating changes to the house since Kuellen had purchased it, and the few things Owen had taken the time to check didn't lead him to any different conclusions. Other than the excessive electricity load and the business-worthy size of the Internet connection, it was just another small house in a tidy subdivision, perched on a corner of intersecting streets. Nothing that stood out against his neighbors.

It could be anyone who lived there.

Evil didn't usually have a calling card.

Owen closed the door behind him, still pausing at the entryway. He listened, but other than a noisy fan on the refrigerator, there were no sounds in the house. If he didn't know the man was home, he'd be questioning his own intelligence gathering skills.

Carefully treading close to the walls, he made his way up the hallway, pausing only for a moment in front of the open bedroom door. Light seeped in around the blinds, not much, but enough to show the empty bed, covers tidily straightened. With the entire house darkened, he knew if Kuellen wasn't in bed, the man had to be downstairs. *In his porn pen.* He scowled as he checked the rest of the house, finding it as empty as he'd expected.

If Kuellen was downstairs, Owen was effectively blind. He'd strapped on the subvocal microphone setup he and Alace had used in the past, more out of habit than any wild expectation that she'd dial in. He cursed at himself. If he wasn't running a cowboy operation, he'd have ample resources at his beck and call.

Suck it up, buttercup.

He crouched in front of the basement door, studying the surface. Knee to the floor, he focused on the hardware, hinges, the space between the door and the floor, the frame—everything he could see, he cataloged. What he found was startling.

The interior door didn't have an evident lock, the paint was chipped along the edge near the doorknob, and it fit badly in the space.

Cheek to the freshly waxed floor, he looked underneath.

"Bingo." His whisper scarcely stirred the air.

Behind the shoddy door was a metal surface, fitting flush against the floor.

Clearly the lack of permits for construction were a red-herring void, because no way was this security door part of the original construction.

Owen gripped the doorknob as he stood, unsurprised when it turned easily in his hand. The door revealed behind was steel and fit into the opening firmly. The edges overlapped the casing and would thwart any attempts to pry it open. The lock was electronic, a digital keypad set flush into the door, making it harder to review the wiring before accessing. He pulled an electronic sensor from the front pocket of his backpack strap, using a smooth movement to run it along the frame and edges of the door. He got a hit near where he'd expect the hinges to be, and the load wasn't excessive enough to be anything other than the connection for the keyboard.

Walking through the house, he'd looked for and failed to find any cameras. Sensor in hand, he walked back through the house and verified what he already knew. Apart from a rudimentary system tied to the outside doors, there was no surveillance inside the house.

How weird would it be if a guy who made his money from pornography was afraid of security cameras?

I've seen weirder.

***

Alace

The green bar on her screen was both infuriating and a relief at once.

It indicated the mic setup she and Owen used so often was currently active.

The red dot to the side, however, was the bastard's phone. Powered down.

The mic needed a connection to work, such as a locally available Wi-Fi or a pairing with a phone to utilize data. The mic and headset alone were useless and had no location tracking available. The system could be on standby in his go-bag for all she knew, the long-lived batteries keeping that ghost signal alive. If that was the case, she could scream into the system from her side, and he'd never hear a thing.

Maybe he took a burner. If he had and paired the mic, then she'd be plugged into his head with the flick of a switch.

She hesitated, finger poised over the mouse, her cursor hovering over the Connect button.

On the nightstand next to the bed, her phone vibrated.

Alace left the chair spinning in her wake as she leaped across the few feet separating her from the device. An unknown number flashed at her, but the timing was too coincidental for her to ignore the incoming call. She hit Accept as she lifted it to her ear.

Silence, then a soft, questioning, "Alace," in a voice that did not belong to Owen.

"Doc, what's going on?"

"Owen is out. On what he called a mission. He found Kuellen has something disturbing on his servers. I asked about involving you, and he claimed the hour too late and your recent pregnancy too fatiguing. I'm a doctor, I knew he was lying about the latter." The information came in short bursts, as if Doc were reciting a patient history at shift changeover. Tersely spoken and concise, but complete and informative.

"Did he say anything about a fallback plan?" Before he'd worked with her, Owen had been an independent contractor, and before that, a military operative. Like Alace, he had connections who specialized in their line of work. He could have called on someone to back him up, and by forcing the mic to a new channel to connect, she could terminate an active link, severing him from his support.

"No. I don't think he's got anyone at his back, Alace. He didn't look scared, though, not nervous."

Doc hesitated, and Alace prompted him with, "What did he look like?"

"Enraged."

Oh yeah, she knew what had tweaked him. She had that same rage in her veins right now. The timestamp on the communications from his researcher meant he hadn't found out about the video from the cabin until after she'd left him earlier today. Between then and when she'd called him upon arrival at home encompassed the full scope of his time to plan.

No backup.

"Doc, I'm going to let you go now. Owen needs me, even if he doesn't realize it yet."

"Thank God." The muttered words of relief were all she heard before she disconnected, carrying the phone back to the desk with her.

"Alace?" Turning, she shaded her eyes as Eric switched on the light on his nightstand. He quickly changed it to the lowest level, and she lowered her hand to look at him. "Anything you need?" He must have heard her side of the conversation and drawn the correct conclusions. She shook her head. "No? You sure?"

"Yeah. I've got to—" She thumbed over her shoulder towards the computer. "Get to it, okay?"

"Yeah, yeah. Go." He shoved up the bed, wedging his back against the headboard, covers falling to his waist, and she had a flash of his body moving above hers only a couple of hours ago.

"I love you." She was back in her chair, headset in her hands, when he laughed quietly.

"I'll never get tired of hearing that from you, beloved."

When she hit the toggle to change the channel on Owen's mic, she was smiling.

Chapter Eleven

Owen

Hunkered down in front of the metal door to the basement, Owen considered the electronic lock. He had a couple of options. He could disconnect the lock, hoping the malfunction would alarm on whatever system Kuellen was working on right now, drawing the man upstairs to check it out. Or he could bypass the lock and open the door—but without knowledge of what the layout looked like downstairs, he had no way of knowing if Kuellen would be positioned where he could see the basement door or the stairs. If armed, the man would have the advantage over Owen, able to react with deadly force before Owen could get even a handful of steps down the stairs.

A barely there buzz in his ear gave him a split second of warning before he heard the voice he'd been praying for. "Do I have eyes and ears?" Without responding, Owen flicked both camera systems on and then twisted the volume control for the normal mic system. "Now, what am I looking at?"

"It is an outswing vault door, looks to be a gun safe modified for residential use. No electronics except the keypad. No optics in the house at all." Out of habit, he used the subvocal mic. "Do you have my location?"

"Copy." Keys tapped in the background, and she sighed. "It's a Hawkish, which is good. There are only six master codes. Bad news is, enter three bad codes, and it'll alarm and lock down."

"Got any more good news?" Owen wanted to relax, step back, and let Alace do the driving for the mission, but that didn't feel right. *Shiloh's my little girl. It's up to me to exact vengeance.* "I could use some after what I saw."

"I saw it too, Owen. I'm here because I'm a hundred percent behind you. Now." Her keyboard sounded off again, furious racketing noises from her typing coming through the headset. "Give me a half a minute, because I have an idea."

"Roger."

She grunted, and there were tones indicating a phone call. She next spoke in a dual presentation of her voice, female in his ear, and male for whoever was on the other end of the call she'd made.

"Yeah, this is Aldo Kuellen, and my phone said to call you for help. I've got a new one, just bought it, and I'm trying to get it set up." She provided details confirming Kuellen's identity, and less than three minutes later, she'd disconnected with the service provider customer service, the active device profile moved as she'd asked.

Back to a single voice, she said, "Code incoming in a minute."

"You take control of his SIM card?" An affirmative sound was all he got. "What will that do for us?"

"Password resets. I've seized his email and triggered a reset for the vault door. It's coming as an email, so I'm ready to go as soon as it comes in." Her voice took on a musing quality. "Nope, you don't need to know passwords were updated, so we'll delete that email, and that one, and boom, gone forever." Becoming brusque again, she told him, "Got it. Six digits, I'll reset using four, five, six, one, two, three. Watch the keypad for the confirmation pulse from the vendor. Should flash the lights."

The lights on the keypad changed from green to red, then to amber, and finally back to green. "Got it in one. Entering code now." When he touched the screen prompt, the keys rapidly scrambled and turned green as they settled into place. "Four, five, six, one, two, three." The keypad pulsed green twice and the door unlatched with a solid metallic sound, bounding away from the doorframe a couple of inches.

"We're in." More keystrokes in his ear and Owen waited for instructions, muscles straining for action. "I pulled some old images of the basement he has on his phone. Pushing those to you now." There was a soft ping in the background, and Alace cursed. "What number are you using? Your phone's off?"

"New Jersey burner." Faster than giving her the number, and he pulled the phone out just in time to see the text message notification. "What do we have?"

"Stairs go down to an alcove, tucked behind a room he's built in the basement. His servers are across the north wall, directly underneath the living room, where the Internet connection comes into the home. He's got a workstation in the middle of the room, but it's facing west. The way the stairs are placed, you'll be at his back."

"So I will be exposed while on the stairs, and if he turns around, he has me." He stared at the images. "What is in that room?"

"No clue, there aren't images of the space. What's your plan when you have him in hand, Owen?"

"Honestly, other than subdue and interrogate, I have not thought that far ahead." Silence, something he wasn't accustomed to from Alace, shook him. "I was going to wing it, boss lady."

"Well, I guess we'll have to wing it. I'm scrambling August to your location. He's already in the area." That was it, he realized, the sum total of her reaction. She wouldn't ride him about his decisions, good or bad, but would go with the flow to provide a positive outcome for the mission. "Should he enter or wait outside?"

"Back door is unlocked, no surveillance anywhere in the house. Our main electrical signal is the basement, and this lock is the only nod to security I have seen anywhere." Thinking fast, he came up with a solution for the lack of eyes into the basement. "I have a telescoping rod and tape, let me secure my phone to the rod and I can extend it into the space, see what we can see. If you are not tapped into it yet, do so now."

"Roger." Alace's way of agreeing with his on-the-fly planning. Owen smiled as he separated strands of tape to bind the phone to the rod without obscuring the camera. The screen of his phone flashed, and he grinned down at the camera.

"Hey, boss lady. I am glad to see you." He could imagine Alace shaking her head at his tension-cutting antics. Just because she didn't do them herself didn't mean she couldn't appreciate them. "ETA on August?"

"Outside right now."

Owen's head lifted, and he cringed as the realization sank in that he'd derailed their op on Ashworth. "Sorry, boss."

"De nada." Alace's indrawn breath rushed through his ear, and he could practically visualize the way she'd settle her shoulders, squaring up and ready for anything. "Let's get this show on the road. Is your telescope articulated, or a straight shot?"

"It is bendy bendy, gets through cracks that way." Without touching the door, he placed himself beside the two-inch gap between the flange and wall and inserted the phone. Clicking the rod, he bent the first joint to a ninety-degree angle, then advanced it until he met resistance, adjusting things so the first joint changed back to straight, and the second adopted the angle. He advanced the rod that way until the joint directly above his handle was bent. "What do you see?"

"Rotate a hundred and eighty." He manipulated the rod to change the direction the phone sat. "Clear visual of the workstation. Empty." Owen's brain did a rapid replay of the intelligence he'd gathered before entering the home. Garage held the car, there were no cab runs or ride-share calls to the house, nothing to indicate the solitary guy who lived here would be anywhere except *here*. "Rotate ninety to your left." The rod disagreed with the movement, and Owen had to withdraw it by one shaft length to get the angle Alace needed. "The room boxing off part of the basement has a solid door. There's light coming from underneath it. You're clear to enter."

"Where's August?"

"Where do you want him?" That was Alace's nod to Owen's headspace. He hadn't met August, only heard about him from Alace, and she knew he'd be buggy if she shoved an unknown into the mission with him. At least without his input.

He made a flash decision, jaw clenching as he gave up the rest of his autonomy to her. "You decide. You want him in here, I can be cool with that. Does he have comms?"

"He does. I can patch him in now." She hesitated, such a change from her normal take-charge attitude it had Owen paying close attention. "I wanna make sure you're safe and walk away from this with what keeps you healthy. I *need* you to be okay, Owen."

"I am okay, Alace. You have my back, always. I know that."

"Okay." Right back into the swing of things, her tone adopted the brusque manner of speaking that epitomized Alace in the middle of a mission. "August, can you hear us?"

"Five by five." The military response eased even more of Owen's nerves. "How do you read me?"

"Loud and clear." Owen chimed in on the channel. "I am inside in the hallway, crouched beside a door." He began retrieving the rod, still without touching the door. "Our entrance is secured, and the subject is secluded without eyes. We are a go." Owen's nerves prickled immediately, and he turned his head to find a hulking mass in the process of crouching down next to him. He kept his hands working steadily and nodded, then gave a greeting, out of habit activating the nonverbal mic. "Welcome, partner."

"The fuck?" August's rumbled response was quieter than a whisper but clearly audible to Owen, enunciation slurring the words into a southern slang of surprise, *dafug*.

Alace actually laughed, the sound bright and cheery, at odds with what they were doing and where they were. "Owen's got a throat mic, heard but not heard. He's got a normal mic on his tech harness, so you'll hear anything he hears. You ready, boys?"

"Yes, ma'am." Owen pushed her button just a tiny bit, glad she wasn't holding a grudge about him going off on his own with this one. "Summarize August's brief for me." Not knowing what August had been told would have Owen working in the dark as to what kind of reactions to expect from the guy. He'd rather know upfront if they were on the same page. "Did you read him in already?"

"When I redirected him, yes. He knows this target is part of a circle we're looking to crack and track, and that some of the content of his video library is personal to us."

Us. That was the clearest validation of their friendship she'd given him to date. Aligning herself on his side where it came to his kids was important. He'd think it was more than she knew, but Alace was smart enough to understand the instincts he worked with to protect his kids. She'd do the same for Lila, and so would he.

"Roger." Back to work mode, he swung to look into August's eyes. Dark hair, full trimmed beard, and warm brown eyes behind his heads-up display visor. "Stairs are unknown construction and age. Servers and workstation come after we secure the subject, who appears to be inside a room constructed downstairs. Unknown activities." August nodded, but Owen wanted a verbal confirmation. "Target is the subject. We cannot allow him to trigger any kind of server wipe before we gain control of his servers. We clear?"

"Roger that. Understood."

Owen shifted out of the space needed to swing the door open and held in place as August did the same, positioning himself at Owen's back. He took a moment to realize his instincts weren't screaming, reveled in the fact he'd found another person he apparently intuitively trusted, and then gripped the edge of the door, swinging it wide.

Going down the stairs quickly but quietly, he and August kept to the wall-side of the treads, ensuring there'd be little pull on the nails or screws securing the steps into place. Feet on the sealed concrete of the basement floor, he moved to the wall blocking off a section of the basement. The persistent hum from the servers and HVAC keeping the room at a constant low temperature blocked the noise from inside the room at first. Only when August cursed lowly did Owen focus on the music and sounds coming underneath the door.

Music to writhe to would be his title for this song. The slapping sound of flesh meeting flesh, he'd call it something else.

"Look at how it's set back into the wall. This has been soundproofed, except for the door itself." August settled a hand on Owen's shoulder as he adjusted their position, moving them both to the knob side of the door. He reached past Owen and gripped the simple knob, installed so the deadbolt control was on this side of the door.

"It is a cage, Alace. A containment facility." Owen shook himself, rattling the memories of another basement, a warehouse, a cabin—everywhere he'd seen people dehumanized and kept for pleasure—back to the recesses of his mind.

The doorknob turned effortlessly under August's manipulation, and the door slipped open—Owen grasped August's hand, holding the door in place. He pulled out his phone and turned on the camera. "Be our eyes." Holding the phone carefully between fingers and thumb, he eased it into the gap and angled it with a movement that should provide a clear view, sweeping from left to right.

"Kuellen is present. A young male, too. Owen, he's got the boy on a bed in the far-left corner of the room." Owen moved the phone, stopping when Alace broke in with, "Wait. There's something else. Go back to your right a little." He did and held the phone still. "There's a video recording setup in the corner of the separating wall. It's active, it looks like he's recording right now. I'll find out if he's streaming it live." Owen pulled the phone back, and August soundlessly closed the door.

Owen turned to meet August's gaze, finding a dark scowl had settled on the man's features. "I have a bandana. You?"

"Same. All I got, though. Wasn't expecting to have to mask up on the op I was on."

Both men repositioned packs to retrieve the articles they could use as face coverings. Whether Kuellen was live-streaming or not, neither of them wanted to be on video that would then have to be managed. There'd always be a tiny fear something would surface, sometime or somewhere. Owen had to thread the ends of the folded bandana under and around his headset, watching August do the same. Both were already wearing thin gloves, so with only their eyes visible, and those partially blocked by their visors, they would be unrecognizable on tape.

"Owen." He dropped his head, focusing on Alace's voice. "He's streaming. It looks like—I think he's part of the ring. The ones we identified with like-minded perversions. That's why he had not only the one video of our girl but others from the same sick bastard. Do you remember what you did there? What you said?"

"I do. Oh, how I remember." He'd looked straight into the camera after killing Warrant and promised everyone watching he'd come for them, too. "Looks like I am making good on my promises." He pushed out a slow breath. "Age on the boy?" Knowing up front would stop any mental stuttering upon seeing; at least he hoped it would.

"Teens. Mid-teens. Fifteen maybe."

"Okay." Not the worst. Not the best, of course, no age was right to have your personal dignity taken from you. No age the right one for sexual violence to be perpetrated upon a child. "Okay. We are going to do this thing. Leave the recording going, do not kill it yet, Alace. I have a message to deliver once August has Kuellen secured."

"Terminal force or containment only?" Owen appreciated August's question; one he'd have asked himself if he'd been brought into a mission late.

"Containment if possible. He has a lot of videos not from this circle jerk of perverts, and I would like to be able to sabotage many of those."

"Roger." August shifted behind him, rising on the balls of his feet before settling back. "Green here."

"Green. Roger." This time it was his hand that reached for the doorknob. As he opened the door, the sounds he'd been suppressing flooded back full force, the music pounding throughout the room. Kuellen wouldn't be able to hear them, or see them, he realized. Both the man and boy's faces turned towards the back wall of the room, away from the door.

"Open yourself." Kuellen held a bag aloft, something Owen didn't recognize. Too large to be a bag of IV fluids, the tubing attached was larger, thicker. The boy's hands drifted along his sides as he lay on his stomach, naked ass in the air, cheeks reddened from what must have been a spanking. *Prelude to the main event.* The boy's hands gripped his own cheeks, pulling, and Owen realized he was presenting himself, the order Kuellen'd given a known and expected piece of instruction.

It took only seconds for Owen and August to dart across the room. Kuellen's reactions were slow, delayed so much he wasn't even looking at them yet when August gripped his arm, a twist causing the bag to fall. It splatted on the floor, tubing breaking free and sudsy liquid spewing across the concrete. *An enema.*

Owen had the boy in his arms, putting his body between where the cameras were and the child, trusting August to contain Kuellen. He grabbed the thin blanket rucked up at the foot of the bed and draped it around the boy, who was staring up at him with wide eyes. Blood rimmed the boy's mouth, the bright color mixing with an old scum. "I've got you," Owen said aloud. "You're safe now."

The boy's lips opened, and a toneless screech came from him. Owen could see the boy's tongue had been split, severed about halfway back, so he had two fleshy stubs inside his mouth. *Oh my God.*

"You're safe. Safe." Changing to the throat mic, he instructed Alace. "He needs medical. Call Doc and tell him there will be an incoming patient that is not me." Speaking aloud to the boy, he attempted to reassure him. "I'm going to take care of you."

The boy screeched again. His eyes rolled up and back into his head, and he went limp in Owen's arms. *Fainted. He didn't die. He's still breathing. He fainted is all.*

"I'm locking the vault door." Alace's voice was steady, calm, and so in control, Owen knew there'd be no way she'd let anything go sideways. "He won't get out without you, Owen." The pressure around them changed, pressing in on his skin, and he realized how lucky it had been that Kuellen was preoccupied when the door had opened earlier.

Owen muscled the boy through the door and into the basement proper, seeing the bars stretching the width of the server section, noting for the first time the temperature difference between the jail room and the server space. He bundled the boy into the blanket and settled him at the foot of the stairs, out of the way, and without a direct line of sight into the jail.

"Set your phone up to watch him. I'll keep an eye out." Owen nodded, knowing she'd see the movement. "I've got you, Owen. Go back in and deal with Kuellen."

"Yeah, boss." Camera activated, he leaned the phone against a nearby post. "Good visual?"

"The best. Go do your job."

He walked inside to find August had Kuellen on his stomach on the floor, arms already angled behind him, zip-tied in place. August's boot was against Kuellen's upper back, pushing the man's face against the floor. Kuellen's bare feet were scrabbling against the concrete, finding no purchase to execute an escape.

"What are you doing? You can't do this."

Owen ignored him and pulled two zip ties from his backpack, then secured the man's ankles together, running one through the other as he latched it. The roll of tape was next, and unlike earlier when he had to be quiet ripping a strip off, Owen made certain the sound was clearly audible to the man on the floor.

"Stop it. You can't do this to me." Kuellen's voice had gained a higher pitch in the extremity of his fear, the sound bouncing around the small room, overpowering the music. Owen taped Kuellen's calves together first, then his thighs, before moving to run a final strip of tape around the man's upper arms, inches above the elbow. "Please."

Bitter bile rose in Owen's throat, and he stifled his body's automatic reaction, his implacable gaze trained on the man's face.

"He's a log." Owen pushed up from the floor as August flipped their captive over. He placed his boot over Kuellen's groin this time and shifted forwards, pressing hard enough the man groaned and whipped his head side to side, the only movement Owen had allowed him to retain.

"The boy?"

"Safe." Owen looked around August's back, directly into the camera. "Y'all watching? Y'all see this? Ain't the first time we've met, motherfuckers." He stepped towards the equipment in the corner, the light on the camera blinking as it streamed live. "I made you all a promise last time, and this is me making good on that. Gonna find you and kill you all." He snapped his mouth closed, switched to the throat mic, and asked, "Alace, can you see who is watching this shit?"

"Already on it. I've dialed in on Georgia, Texas, Montana, and three back in Jersey. Counting Warrant and Kuellen, that's eight total, which is what we thought based on their attendance at the auctions. None of them have disconnected. I'll track them all down, Owen. You do what you need to do."

"I'm coming for you." He returned to normal speech for the sake of the camera, staring down what he hoped was a pipeline of terror connected directly to the screens these perverts sat in front of.

"You think you're so smart, all scattered like you are in different states."

He wouldn't say where they were, because the omission would leave them believing they were still safe. If one member of the ring got spooked and moved, it was likely the rest would remain in their bunkers, feeling protected until he came and busted down their door.

"I'm the big bad wolf, and you're all just little piggies. Gonna blind you now, little piggies."

He ripped off another piece of tape, leaning close as he secured it lightly to the camera lens. He wanted light and shadow to still enter, knowing the play of bright and dark would be more terrible than severing their visual channel altogether.

Closer yet, he breathed on the microphone attached to the setup, then hoarsely whispered, "Gonna let you hear everything, though. I want you to imagine this is you, helpless on the floor. Got you under my thumb, subject to anything I decide to do. Listen to it. Listen, and think about what's gonna happen to you when I find you. Gonna blow you all down in the end."

"Jesus, Owen. You're scary." Alace chuckled darkly in his ear. "Gave me goose bumps."

"Yeah, well, they made me angry." He turned back, seeing August's cheeks had risen behind the mask, indicating approval of Owen's tactics. Still using the throat mic, he said, "Need to hook all your guys up with the same gear, boss lady. Would make this mission a tad bit easier."

"Is this the point where I get to remind you that you went rogue on me, striking off on your own and scaring Doc half to death?" Her mention of Doc gave him pause, wondering what she meant. "He called me, you know? That's why you've got the help you do have. So one, don't bite the hand that feeds you, and two, don't ditch the partnership again." *Welp, that explains everything.* "Do you think Kuellen knows anything that doesn't also exist in his data?"

"Doubtful. He is an angry intellectual, but obsessive. Have you seen the organization of his porn videos? Each is categorized in multiple ways, from sex acts to age of participants, even type of vocalizations. I have no doubt his network of perverts exists inside his computers." The man had continued to sputter, trailing off into more groans as August leaned more weight into the leg pinning him to the floor. "I think I go for dramatic effect, then we toast him and dispose."

"Owen." Alace's voice was lower, quiet, as if she was guarding her words, and it brought him back to full alert. "He's got the video of you and Warrant. It's titled *End of a Friend* and is filed under remarkable deaths. He's got you on video. It's been downloaded—" She sucked in a gasp. "Nearly two thousand times." He flinched at the knowledge. "Let's finish this. I want to take it down, and then track each of those downloads."

"Can you do that?" Owen flinched again, this time at his verbalization of doubt in Alace's abilities. "Strike that, of course you can." Straightening his shoulders, he locked gazes with August and held until the big man nodded, taking a big step backwards, ceding the scene to Owen.

Kuellen's face was pale. He was sweating profusely as Owen knelt and put one knee directly in the center of Kuellen's chest. Leaning forwards, Owen pressed hard to rob him of air. Aloud, he said, "You're dying today. Any last words from the pervert in the room?"

"I can pay you."

"Oh, I'm sure you can. What you don't realize is I'm not interested in a payout." Owen shifted more weight to his knee. "Payback, now that's another thing." He feigned surprise. "Hey, you know how focused I am on an eye for an eye." Owen shook his head back and forth, tracking the size of Kuellen's pupils as they widened, darkness engulfing his eyes. "You gotta know I saw what you did to that boy's mouth." Thumb flicking the safety strap away, Owen tugged his knife free of the sheath. "Hold his head." When August moved, Owen shifted so the toe of his boot dug into Kuellen's dick. "Gonna get messy. Real messy." A pair of pliers appeared in front of him, and Owen took them with a silent thanks. He gripped the tip of Kuellen's tongue and pulled hard, earning a muffled scream from the man. It was loud enough for the livestream listeners to hear. He did it again, harder, eliciting a louder scream. "Equal force effects equal resistance. Now let's see how well I can do with my carving technique. Thanksgiving was never my favorite holiday."

Selecting a point on the surface of the extended tongue just behind the teeth, Owen sliced decisively through the muscle. Blood pooled around the blade immediately, swelling as he neared the tip. By the time he was finished cutting through the organ, blood was filling Kuellen's mouth, choking off his inhalation and cutting off his screams.

It didn't take long. Between Owen's weight controlling his breath and the suffocating blood, Kuellen was dead within minutes.

Owen stood and walked back to the video station, got near the microphone again, and whispered, "That'll be you, sooner or later. That's gonna be you." Using the throat mic, he told Alace, "Cut it. Shut it all down."

"Done." Her response came at the same instant the red light died, and he smiled behind the bandana. She'd waited for him, for his request, giving him control for this. "The boy's stirring."

Looking down, Owen saw less blood on his torso than he'd expected, Kuellen's inability to take a real breath having restricted the amount of blowback he'd coughed onto Owen's clothes. "On my way." He tossed the tape to August. "Close him up." Binding his mouth closed would help keep from leaving a massive trail of DNA wherever they wound up taking the dead pervert. "I'm checking on the kid."

Back out in the main room, he realized the noise from the servers had changed, lessening until the only sounds he could identify were the whistling of the HVAC exchange vents. Angling to where he'd left the boy, Owen found him awake, blanket strategically wrapped around him to allow freedom of movement. Subvocally, he asked Alace, "Can you make it warmer in here?" To the boy, he said, "I'm not going to hurt you. No one here can hurt you, ever again." He couldn't promise the boy wouldn't ever be hurt, because he didn't plan on being around the kid that long. From the boy's skeptical expression, Owen knew the kid didn't think he'd keep even that tiny promise. "The man who was keeping you—" Owen hesitated over which word to use, and the boy filled in the blank.

"Prisoner. I'm a prisoner." Soft consonants ran together, giving little distinction between phrases. Without the ability to use his tongue to shape the words, they were slurred and scarcely intelligible.

"Yeah, he was keeping you a prisoner. He's a bad guy. You're a good guy. I get it." Owen wanted to reach out and physically reassure the boy but remembered how long it had taken his kids to accept that overtures from Owen were always going to be positive ones. He didn't want to scare this boy, not when the kid wasn't afraid of him. Not yet, anyway. "What's your name?" He briefly considered giving the boy his in advance but wanted to wait. *There's more than me at stake now.*

"Wobme. I'm Wobme."

It took an instant and another repetition of the set of sounds, but Owen finally recognized what the boy was saying. "Your name is Rodney." The boy—Rodney—nodded frantically, eyes widening at hearing his name spoken aloud. "Rodney, you're safe now. I have a friend who's a doctor. I want to take you to see him, and then we'll get you to the authorities."

Taking the kid to the cops would be a huge gamble. Owen could take measures to restrict the boy's knowledge of his location. Assuming Kuellen had brought him in unconscious or incapacitated, Owen's house, even just a few doors down, would be safe. If he could get Doc to wear a mask, even a surgical one, and use nitrile gloves, there'd be nothing tying them to the boy. "Can I do that? Take you to my friend?"

"He won't hurt me?" This came through clearer, and Owen wondered if he was already developing an ear for the boy's vocalization efforts.

"No, Rodney." Owen considered how Warrant had stripped Kelly and Shiloh's individual personalities away, and wanted to start the process back to normalcy for Rodney now by reaffirming his name every chance he got. "My friend's a good guy, like you."

The boy's jaw worked as he tried to frame a response, the stump of his tongue retracting towards the back of his throat, the movement so alien Owen had a hard time not flinching.

"Owen, August needs you back in the room. Keep the kid outside." Alace's voice was as calm and composed as she always was, and Owen appreciated it a lot in this moment. When nothing else around him was normal, Alace remained dependable.

"I have to go back into the room, Rodney. I have a friend with me here, a different friend but still a good guy. He's going to help me get you out of here." Better to position their mission around the boy in his mind, give Rodney a little faith maybe someone had missed him and sent rescuers. Rodney's fingers dug deep furrows in the blanket, pulling and twisting the fabric in his agitation as he tried to speak. Owen pushed, "Rodney, can you stay out here for me? Right here by the stairs. Those lead up to the rest of the house. In a few minutes, we'll go up them and through the door. I'll unlock it, and we'll go out, and then we'll get you to my doctor friend." Emphasizing the rescue aspect, he struggled to find a tone that would reassure the boy—Rodney's attempts at talking grew more difficult to watch as he became agitated.

Reaching a breaking point, the boy threw his head back and screamed, the same keening shriek from before. Head still angled backwards, he said in a slurred rush, "Aldo will hurt you. I'm scared. Aldo will kill you." The sounds of tape ripping came from the room behind him, and Owen ignored whatever August was doing, remaining focused on the boy.

"No, Rodney." Owen took a chance and rested a hand on the boy's shoulder, bringing his arched frame upright so he could lock their gazes. "Aldo won't hurt anyone else, ever again. I promise you that."

Fear fought with another emotion across Rodney's face, finally settling into something Owen recognized as relief. "He's dead. He's dead, isn't he? He's real dead." Owen didn't respond, didn't react, but kept his gaze steady on Rodney's face as the boy crumpled into tears. "Thank God. Thank God. I prayed he'd die." He lifted his hand, showing Owen a stump where his little finger had been. "I've been here three years. I prayed. I prayed." Rodney shoved at the blanket to free his lower extremities and pointed to his feet in succession, indicating the missing little toe on each. He held up his other hand, all five digits. "Tomorrow. Tomorrow was four years."

"He's never hurting you, or anyone, ever again."

"Okay. Okay. Never again. I prayed for you." Rodney nodded as he sat up, shifting so his back leaned against the wall. "I'll wait here." Fingers fussily plucking at the blanket, he arranged it around him. "Right here."

"Owen." Alace's tone warned him, and he stiffened his spine as he waited for her to finish her thought. "I found him. Rodney Faust, age fourteen. He's been missing for seven years. Against all odds, his parents are still looking for him. Oldest of three kids, he was taken from a birthday party at a park in Georgia. Seven years, Owen. He's special needs, but there's no real detail, the file simply says cognitive delays."

"Perfect, Rodney. Thank you, buddy. Stay right here." Owen scooched back before rising to his feet, not wanting to loom over the boy. "I'll be back before you know it."

Owen couldn't let himself focus on the nightmare Rodney's parents had been living. *Are still living.* Seven *years. God.* Dialing in on the little he knew, he recited the pertinent details to Alace. "No ligature marks on wrists or ankles, he has been restrained differently, probably in cages or locked rooms, like here. Is he on our list from the auctions?" Owen stepped through the doorway, noting the wedge August had placed on the hinge side, keeping the door from shutting completely, protecting them from being locked inside. Continuing with the subvocal, he nodded at August. "I know you are keeping your voice from being heard. Smart. Show me what you need."

August's cheeks lifted again, revealing he was evidently a smiley type of fellow, and he pointed at Kuellen, now unnaturally bent double at the waist, broken in half with his legs already bound to his torso. August mimed lifting something heavy and pointed to Owen, then upstairs.

"You need me to go upstairs and find a bag?" August shook his head, tipping his chin towards the outside of the house. "You have one in your vehicle?" That earned him a nod, and he grinned, hoping August could see it in his eyes. "How about if I get the kid out of here, and you deal with our friend?" August gave a decisive nod. "Okay. We can meet up later to debrief." August blanked him on that, neither giving affirmative or negative reactions. "No, for real. We should meet later to discuss." August looked straight at him for a long beat, then slowly dipped his chin. "Deal. Alace has my address if you don't already have it. Literally a block and a half from here."

August pointed at the door and made a shooing motion.

"Yeah, yeah. I am going." He turned, then looked back. "Appreciate this. Gratitude, man." Back in the main room, he saw Rodney hadn't moved. Audibly, he said, "You ready to go, Rodney?"

"Doc is primed, Owen. How will you keep him from knowing where you live?"

Switching to subaudible, he told her, "I will tell him to get in back and lie down, then I will drive around for half an hour."

"Copy that, relaying the delay to Doc."

"Rodney, let's go upstairs and see if we can find a pair of shorts for you to wear, then we'll go to my friend's house." He walked past where Rodney sat, then turned and bent, offering a hand to help the boy rise to his feet, blanket clutched around his body, held in place with bone-thin fingers.

"Door at the top is unlocked."

"Thanks." He masked his unthinking audible response with a cough. "Nearly there, Rodney. You're doin' great." At the top, he swung the door wide, glancing back to see Rodney's eyes wide, as if he were taking in the house for the first time. *Probably is.* Owen aimed them towards Kuellen's bedroom, sickened by the idea of the boy wearing clothing belonging to his tormentor but more motivated by the idea of giving the boy back some of his dignity. Social mores required clothing, and Kuellen had taken that from Rodney. Owen would give it back, much as he'd done with the kids in the compound around Warrant's cabin. "Here we go."

Once in the darkened room, Owen saw a dresser along the inside wall. In the top drawer, he found a pair of briefs, and in the bottom, both a T-shirt and a pair of drawstring sweatpants. Handing them to Rodney, he went to the doorway and stood with his back to the boy, giving him privacy to dress.

Sounds of hopping, then the soft shurring of fabric being pulled into place were the only noises Owen could hear. "Help me?" The boy's slurred request for assistance made him look over his shoulder. Rodney was fumbling with the string of the pants. "I can't." In his mind, he saw Doc with Shiloh, patiently showing her the bunny ears process of tying her own shoes.

"Sure you can, buddy." He moved slowly, pleased when Rodney didn't flinch away. "Over, under first. Then make two bunny ears with the string, and loop one over, bring it through the bunny hole." *Seven years in this hell. My God. He was only seven when he was taken.* "Easy peasy, buddy." He pulled the loops tight and stepped back. "There you go." He held out his hand, pleased when Rodney took it right away.

"Where's your car, Owen?"

He stutter-stepped at Alace's question, then started walking again. Using the subaudible mic, he asked, "Can you have Doc move the car to the curb?"

Alace laughed and sighed. "Only for you, Owen. Only for you." He heard her shuffling something around; then she said, "He's on his way to you, but he needs the car parked on the curb. He probably doesn't have keys, either, so if you could leave them on top of the front tire on the driver side, that would be appreciated."

"Almost there." Rodney was stumbling in his exhaustion, no doubt malnutrition exacerbated by the attack he'd been withstanding from Kuellen combined with the unexpected activity of passing out, climbing the stairs, and getting dressed for the first time in who knew how long. "We'll go as slow as you need. The car's right up the street."

Rodney's grip dragged on his hand and halted their forward progress. Owen turned to find him slumped against the hallway wall, head hanging loosely from his bowed neck. "I'm tired."

"I can carry you if that's okay." Rodney nodded, his head wobbling with the movement. "Okay, then. I've got you." Owen repeated what he'd first told the boy. "I've got you. You're safe now." Scooping the thin child into his arms, he winced as the boy's hips and elbows dug sharply into him. "Just about there."

Owen navigated their way out of the house and to the quiet street, passing a darkened car parked halfway between Ashworth's house and his own. *Probably August's ride.* Another minute slipped by, and he stopped next to the car Doc had backed out of the garage. He looked down and realized Rodney had passed out, either overcome as he had been earlier or simply asleep. Either way, what he'd hoped to accomplish was effectively done, because the boy would never know if they'd driven away or not.

Using the throat mic, he told Alace, "Tell Doc I am walking up the sidewalk. Meet me at the front door. I am afraid the garage opener would wake the boy." Within seconds, the front door swept wide, the room behind Doc darkened so he didn't stand out as a target silhouette. Doc moved back as Owen approached, closed the door behind him, and led the way to the treatment room. Faint light coming from the kitchen illuminated enough to see Doc had on a medical mask, as requested.

"Owen, I'm switching you to a different channel. I can focus on August better that way." His earpiece buzzed, then she said, "Clear your throat if you can hear me." Doc cleared his throat in sync with Owen, who stared at the man's back.

Subaudibly, he asked, "Can Doc hear me?"

Doc nodded, cleared his throat, then nodded again, the uncertain movements telegraphing his nerves.

"Got it. Here is what I know. Rodney Faust, fourteen years old. Probably repeatedly sodomized. Had fingers and a toe amputated, those wounds are long healed, the newest about a year old. His tongue has been split and amputated about halfway back. The tongue is healed but looks irritated and was bleeding recently. Exhausted, underweight, I estimate he is about ninety pounds, probably should be one fifty given bone structure. Taken from family in Georgia seven years ago." Doc made a choked sound as he turned into the treatment room. He stood to one side as Owen walked past, closing the door behind him.

"He's lucid?" As he'd done when first meeting their kids, Doc crouched several feet away, putting himself in a lower position than Rodney would be when he awoke.

"Lucid and aware." Owen paused, knowing this next bit would be telling. "Compliant, not complaining, even when he was too exhausted to take another step. He has been pleasing people for a long time, Doc."

"I hate that for him. You said his name is Rodney? Did he tell you that?"

"Yes. His speech is impacted by the mutilation, but he is not unintelligent."

Alace broke in. "The file said he was cognitively delayed."

"Does not mean he is stupid." Taking a seat on the treatment table, Owen wrestled with his growing anger, knowing the emotion was without a target. *Kuellen is already dead. That's a goddamned fact.* Audibly, he whispered, "Rodney. Time to wake up, buddy. My friend is here. The doctor, I told you about him." Owen adjusted the boy across his lap, setting him up straighter. "Rodney? Time to wake up. You slept the whole way. What a good boy. I've got you, remember? You're safe."

Confused brown eyes blinked up at him, taking a couple of deep, even breaths before Owen saw recognition set in.

"There you are. Did you have a good sleep?"

The boy's mouth opened, jaw waggling side to side as his tongue worked at the back of his mouth. Almost as if it too were waking.

"Yes." His slur was pronounced, the single word emerging as yaff. "Are…" His lips lifted and spread, as if he were stretching them in an effort to better pronounce the words. "Are." More movement, like a physical and vocal tic. "Are you okay?"

"Yeah, I'm okay, Rodney." He was touched by the boy's remembered fear that Kuellen would somehow rise from the dead and hurt Owen. "This is my friend, Doc. Will you let us help you?"

Rodney's head swung so he could look Doc's direction, his mouth closing with a wet snap.

"Hey, Rodney." Doc waved, hand low to the ground, as far from threatening as he could get. "How are you feeling?"

The two of them went on with their greeting, Owen gradually easing Rodney off his lap and onto the table. He stood, stretching, and activated the throat mic.

"Alace?"

"Yes?" Her response was immediate. Either she was closely listening to both communication channels as she'd promised, or August was in a quiet period so she could focus on Owen and Doc.

"Thank you for coming to my rescue tonight. We make good partners."

"Thank your other partner. He's the one who made the call." Owen glanced down to see Doc's gaze trained on him. "Also, what the actual fuck, Owen? You didn't have an entry strategy, much less a planned exit."

"He had video of Shiloh. I could not fail her. I was not there when it happened, and that has been killing me." Time to open the door to his past a little, something Alace had no idea about. "I had a daughter, Emma. She was taken, like Rodney. They kept her alive for months. I was deployed, deep enough there were no messages in or out. I came back to find her dead and buried, the bastards who did it in the wind. My bosses did not give a shit. It was a turn and burn home leave, no exceptions made."

Alace's sigh held empathetic pain. "They redeployed you before you had a chance to come to grips with what happened." It could have been a statement, but he answered as if it were a question.

"Yes. Sent me down to Central America, where I proceeded to lose my mind."

"That's the reason you went rogue on 'em. Your daughter, Emma, she's not part of any official history for you." He wished he could see Alace's face, know if she were angry he'd never shared, hadn't trusted her with this personal part of himself. *If wishes were horses.* The tone was plaintive when she asked, "Why, Owen?"

"Her mom put unknown on the birth certificate. I did not love the girl, and that lack was a two-way street. I loved my Emma, though. So, so much, Alace. From the moment I saw her, six months old and laughing, I loved her."

"Did you find the guys who took and killed her?"

"Some, yes. But not all of them, no. I do not think so."

"Sounds like we've got a joint mission. Let's plan on talking this through after you and I debrief August. Can he stay with you tonight? Guest room or couch, he said he's not particular."

"Sure. Put him in channel when he is ready to head this way."

As he and Alace had talked, Doc had made Rodney more comfortable with a clean blanket and bottle of water.

"My friend and I will be just a moment, Rodney. Can you stay here, please?" Rodney was again showing signs of exhaustion, his head wobbling as he nodded slowly, lifting the bottle of water to study the label. "It's only water, promise. See how it's sealed?" Doc pointed to the lid. "I haven't opened it. It's safe, Rodney." He stood and motioned to Owen. "We'll be right down the hall if you need us."

In the kitchen, Doc leaned against the cabinet, his shoulders slumping as if he shared Rodney's exhaustion. A glance at the clock on the microwave said he probably did, and had guilt stealing over Owen.

"He's malnourished but is otherwise surprisingly healthy. Alace said he'd been kept in an enclosed small space, so little to no exercise, which, if he was regularly going without food, is probably a good thing. The amputations to his small toes and finger healed cleanly, and he remembers bandaging. They appear to have been cauterized, so I'm glad he doesn't remember that part of the procedure. The tongue is more problematic. The split extends back into the root and severed the bundle of muscles underneath the tongue, but because the amputation was about half an inch forward of that, he has better speech than I'd expect. The continued irritation and subsequent bleeding is because the split was not stitched, and so hasn't healed completely. He doesn't know how old he was, but it was before Aldo, whatever that means."

"Aldo Kuellen, the guy we dealt with tonight."

"Did you know he had a prisoner when you went down there?" Doc scrubbed across his forehead with one hand, fingers repeatedly shoving through his hair. "No, don't answer that. I'm sure you didn't because you didn't take the time to do your homework."

"Doc's not wrong," Alace said in his ear, and Owen tipped his head back, gritting his teeth together. "Not part of this conversation, though. Doc, is he okay to transport? I hope he is. I've got someone on the way. ETA less than five minutes. Can you prep him to move?"

"Yes, and yes." Doc leveled a finger at Owen. "I know you can see me, Alace. We're not done with this topic. You and I have to work together on this one."

"I hear you loud and clear." Owen wished he could see Alace. "The lady's name is Astrid, and she's driving a gray sedan. She'll take Rodney to the children's hospital in Aurora." Owen waited, knowing the pause meant Alace was about to disclose something either he or Doc wouldn't like. *Learnin' the boss lady's tells. Go me.* "Doc, he needs to be asleep."

"He is." Doc stated it so baldly, Owen nearly missed the significance of the phrase.

"He is? How do you know? We're in here."

"The water was drugged. Little technique I learned in Thailand. Run the cap under hot water for thirty seconds, and it pulls straight off, but without breaking the seal ring. Insert the drugs and heat the cap again to get it back on." Doc shrugged. "I have a few tricks up my sleeve."

Ten minutes later, they watched through the open garage door as the woman backed out of the driveway. It had been fortuitous Owen's car was parked on the curb after all.

"Guys? I'm adding August to the channel now."

A rumbling filled Owen's ear, and he jerked, seeing Doc similarly startled.

"You there?" The same southern accent he'd heard earlier dripped from those two words, and Owen grinned.

"Yeah, we're here." Owen stepped backwards and turned, headed towards the interior door. "You comin' back, or what?"

"Or what, asshole. How big is your garage?" This came out as "gayrodge" and Owen stopped, staring at

Doc. *Is this guy kidding? What a fucking asshole.* "Got room for a bike?"

"Our garage? It's a two-and-a-half car. Yes, we have room for a bicycle, or two." Shaking his head, Owen stepped through into the kitchen. "We'll leave the door open for you."

"Not a bicycle, what the hell? A motorcycle. I ditched the car and picked up my ride." This was pronounced like motorsickle, and fully cemented Owen's understanding of the man's origins. The assumed slur was nothing more than his accent, because August was southern, through and through. The rumbling grew louder, echoing through the garage and into the house.

Standing shoulder to shoulder, he and Doc watched August ride a motorcycle right into the garage, as promised. One quick three-point turnaround later, August dropped the kickstand and killed the engine, the ringing silence somehow more startling than the overwhelming noise had been.

Owen glanced back at the tablet on the wall, but nothing indicated either of the kids had woken from the unexpected noise. He turned around just as August stood up off the bike and took a step forwards, hand out. "Doc, right? I'm August."

Doc showed the depths of his composure by grasping the man's hand and pumping it up and down firmly. "I'm Doc, that's right. Good to meet you,

August. Alace has good things to say about you." Doc released the handshake and dug into his ear, pulling out an earwig. "She doesn't need me now. I'll go put this by your computer, Owen, and then I'm going to straighten up my room."

"Is he for real right now? He can't do that. Owen." Owen lifted his gaze and met August's amused one as they listened to Alace's increasing annoyance. "Stop him. The two of you are having a moment, I get it, but stop him."

"Doc, Alace isn't done with you. She politely requests you resecure your comms, please. She said please like five times. It's amazing really. She sounds honestly distraught. I've never heard anything like it. Can you get back on comms?" August's lips spread in a smile as Doc slowly turned and stared at Owen as if he'd lost his mind. "Pretty please?" Doc fumbled the device, placing it back inside his ear.

"Jesus, Owen. Remember me telling you I sometimes didn't hate you anymore? Remember? This is not one of those times." Alace sounded annoyed, but Owen knew it was a front.

"Doc's back on comms, Alace. Feel free to thank me later."

"Time to debrief, boys. Let's get into the house. Get that garage closed, too. Just leave the car outside for now. Owen, set up in your office. We can use the camera on your laptop so you can get out of the gear."

Alace's take-charge attitude would always be welcome, Owen realized. "I've got about thirty minutes before Lila wakes up, so let's make it count. Call me in three minutes. Your time starts now."

The disconnect severed the channel between all of them, and he laughed softly at Doc's stunned expression.

"She's always like that." Owen turned and pointed at the tablet mounted to the wall as he took off his glasses and peeled the throat mic from his skin. "And she's almost always present. Let's get started."

The actual debrief didn't take long, less than the twenty-seven minutes Alace had allotted. August had aborted his walk-through of the planned mission to assist Owen with his, so Ashworth remained to be dealt with. They wound up in the kitchen afterwards, unanimously gravitating towards the empty coffeemaker. Five minutes of small talk from Doc filled the time until they all held mugs of hot coffee, Owen and August adding only stilted responses when pressed.

Owen hated it.

He and Doc had fallen into an easy friendship so quickly, and even Alace was more comfortable around him than this man. He decided to attack the issue directly, get whatever it was out in the open.

"What bugs you about me?" Owen lifted his mug and sipped noisily. "There's something off, and we both know it, so spit it out." The man's eyes flitted toward the mounted screen, and realization flooded through Owen. It wasn't him the man had a problem with; August was censoring his speech with the expectation Alace was listening.

Owen pulled out his phone and tapped into the security system. He walked over and showed the screen to August, the data indicating he was the only connection at the moment. "Don't mean she won't dial back in, but she's good about announcing it when she does. We have an"—he grinned at Doc, remembering the hard-earned truce between Doc and Alace—"agreement."

"You have an agreement. With Alace Sweets." August shook his head, glanced at the phone screen again, and lifted his mug to hide a disbelieving grin. "You think she abides by your agreement?"

"Yeah, I do. The woman is intelligent, and sure, she's hyper-inquisitive; that's what makes her so good at the research and investigation part of any mission. That and her tenacity. She'll follow a thread for longer than most, but she also finds much more than anyone else." He gave a slow side-to-side shake of his head, emphasizing his belief in his own words. "What she isn't is disloyal. She says something, you can believe it. She's not going to fuck her people over." Owen realized he must hold more knowledge of Alace's background than she'd given August. *Some of it isn't mine to tell.* If she hadn't trusted the man with the info, he didn't even want to allude to it. "She and I have worked together in the field." Yeah, he could stick to what he'd witnessed and still make the same impact. "She had more than one chance to angle things her way, but we were in lockstep all the way. Loyal to a fault. So when she tells me she won't intentionally eavesdrop on our conversations here, I believe her."

"I second that, actually." Doc nodded towards Owen. "I haven't known her as long as either of you, but when I called her tonight, she not only picked up, she immediately switched into work mode without a word of annoyance. She was soothing me, handling a dozen things at once, and still asked permission to tap into the system here so she could talk to me easily."

"Consider me enlightened." August's southern accent stretched the letters out long, his tone still disbelieving.

"No, man. I get it. Alace Sweets is a force of nature, someone who feels unfuckable with. But Alace, the Alace I know? She's my friend. At the end of the day, not only are we partners and equals when it comes to the missions we choose, but she's my friend, and I have to trust she's always got my best interests at heart." He drained his mug and set it on the counter, grinning when Doc brought the coffee carafe over, refilling it. "She's scary as hell, but she's my Alace."

"You met the husband?" August's expression held a transitory touch of distaste, and Owen wondered if he imagined it. "Thinkin' to poach, might want to think again. He's a good dude."

"Yeah, Eric and I are acquainted." Owen remembered their first conversations over the comm system, Eric often siding with Owen when it came to thoughts on how to keep a pregnant Alace safe. "Our first encounter couldn't have gone better." Jealous Eric would always be Owen's favorite, because it meant the man was still as deeply in love with Alace as he'd ever been. "But if anyone deserves a happy ending, it's Alace Sweets."

***

Alace

Head in her hands, she massaged her scalp with stiffened fingertips, running the sequence of events back through her mind.

"Alace, it's done now. Do you want to go downstairs or come to bed?" Even without turning around, she could picture Eric's expression. Supportive concern and his love for her was a rock she'd break against if she were too near him right now.

She started the process of securing her workstation, first checking the entire video collection had uploaded to a cloud server, then verifying her address seeker was working on hits to the previous location. She'd written a quick script that would attach to every individual trying to gain access and snake back to their location. IP addresses weren't as anonymous as most folks thought, and even the ones who'd used an anonymizer weren't immune to the script. If it encountered a secure VPN connection, the script would write a sequence of malware bytes to the computer, inserting in the registry of the computer to make them harder to eradicate. That malware would then replicate itself, turning on various functions until it was a working keylogger that would dial home upon demand.

With the battery removed and laptop stored, she locked the drawer and stood, still facing away from Eric. "Shower first, then bed. I'll be back in a couple of minutes."

"Alace." She hadn't taken a single step yet, and Eric was already on to her. The mattress moved, covers rustling, and then his warmth enveloped her. Even before his arms encircled her, before his feet braced hers on either side, before his lips pressed to her temple—she felt owned and possessed, supported in ways she'd never be able to put words to. "Beloved, it's okay to be upset."

"I'm not angry." He scoffed gently, mouth against the side of her throat. "I'm not, not really. I could have been, had already decided to be pissed as hell that Owen would put me in the position he did, risk the team by going off on his own and being a hero. I was talking to Doc and redirecting August, and all the time I was writing my speech in my head, calling him reckless and careless, angry he didn't care about what we've been building."

"What happened? If you aren't angry now, what is it? What are you feeling?"

"I'm not sure. It's a lot less familiar than anger. When Doc told me where Owen'd gone, it was like something broke loose inside me. He said Owen was upset, something I'd already discerned from my own read of his behaviors earlier in the evening. By that point, by the time Doc called, I had already seen the videos." She twisted around, peering up at Eric's face. His arms tightened around her, holding tight.

"His little girl. The girl he rescued only weeks ago. Eric, one of the videos was of her. It had been taken only hours before he got to the compound, and I know Owen had already been beating himself up that she suffered the assault *after* he knew the location. He'd known where Kelly's little sister was for a day or more but held off until he could get things sorted. And then the video happened." She shook her head, staring at Eric.

"As soon as I realized he knew about the video, I understood he wouldn't wait for long, but I didn't expect him to go off on his own like that. He didn't have a strategy at all, exit or otherwise." Alace fought for control of her face, hating how her chin trembled.

"He didn't call me. Not first, not before, not even last. Why didn't he call me, Eric?"

"I don't know, Alace." He bent to press his cheek to hers. "And you won't know until you ask him."

"I should have asked tonight. Just now, I could have asked."

"It's harder when you can't see him, read him. Not only his face with the video but everything. You're a master at interpreting someone's body language, and if you'd asked tonight, you'd be cutting off that avenue of information." Eric swayed back and forth, moving them in a slow rhythm. "I bet when you do talk to him, though, you're going to find there's nothing malicious in his reasons. That it wasn't a lack of trust in you and your partnership. He values you and your opinion, Alace. But more than that, he likes you."

"I thought we were friends." She hated how her voice shook.

"You are friends. I consider him a friend, and I don't have the same kind of relationship you do. He and I aren't close, but we're friends." Mouth next to her ear, he reassured her, his certainty a force to be reckoned with. "If he knew how he hurt you tonight, Owen would be devastated. He will be once he sees. Trust me, once he realizes what he almost threw away by not thinking, he's going to be pissed at himself."

"This all feels so stupid."

"Feelings are harder than facts. Feelings are messy, unpredictable, and sometimes uncomfortable." Eric leaned back, his expression soft and sweet as he stared at her. "And they don't come with instructions. It's okay to be angry. It's okay to be scared. It's not stupid, not at all." Brushing the tip of his nose against hers, he smiled. "It's human, Alace. It's human."

"Yeah?"

"Yeah." The single word—that fucking, *fucking* word—held enough confidence and assurance much of the tension in her muscles melted away. "And it needs to be said. Alace, it's okay to be human." He gave her a squeeze and touched her lips with his. "We're all human. Now, go get your shower, and if we're lucky we'll have a nap before the lovely Lila decides it's time to eat."

It's human to feel these things. Something she knew intellectually but always felt on a plane above. "What you said helped. I just—I don't want to lose him, Eric. I told him, I told him when we set out that he couldn't start down this path with me and then change course."

"Then remind him of what you both will lose." He gave her a nudge. "But do it tomorrow after sleeping."

"Yeah." She straightened. "The important thing is he's home safely."

"And Shiloh is safe. Among the most important things are the facts Shiloh and Kelly are safe and experiencing the true love of a family for the first time ever." Eric glanced towards the bassinette and back to Alace. "It's never too late to love."

Shiloh. She remembered the little girl dangling from her arms upside down, trusting Alace wouldn't drop her, would hold her tight, keep her safe. Everything in that child's life had been topsy-turvy for so long, like that nerve-jangling dangle, and things were barely beginning to right themselves around her. "I get why Owen would have reacted the way he did. He was protecting his family. Instinct, to take on the largest and closest perceived threat." She turned to look at Lila, sleeping with arms thrown over her head, open and vulnerable.

"We do everything we can to defend those we love."

Eric dipped close, his mouth capturing hers, lips softly caressing. When he pulled back, his eyes were dark and hooded, face taut with desire.

She leaned into him, chin tipped up for more as she murmured, "Shower later. Love me now."

"Always."

One word.

Fucking, *fucking* Eric.

Chapter Twelve

Owen

Two weeks after Kuellen had been disappeared, Owen sat in the kitchen eating cereal and watching an early morning news app on his phone. He had the sound turned down to keep from disturbing the kids, only loud enough to hear as the reporter read from her prompter.

"Today the county prosecutor suggested a high level of confidence Ashworth will plead guilty to one count of manslaughter at his arraignment tomorrow. However, a confidential source indicates more charges are pending, which means a guilty plea for Miles Garcia's death will not necessarily stop the judicial clock. There has been some discussion Ashworth will enter an Alford plea, implying innocence while still pleading guilty, but the defense counsel would be well advised to consider Colorado's statutes surrounding victim restitution. With so many potential victims, it's unlikely Ashworth would be able to secure a cash bond to escape pretrial detention."

He tuned her out until the piece was nearly over, looking up to watch closely as the camera zoomed in on her face. Alace had texted him earlier that Colleen Houghton was supposed to end her segment with a shout-out.

"Finally, before we sign off for the morning, I wanted to give my personal book club recommendation for a local best-selling author. Alace Sweets has written several criminal thriller novels and has a healthy fan base, not just here in Colorado, but around the world. My great-aunt, who grew up in Northern California, has proclaimed them riveting. Of course, my great-aunt also refers to her old Berkeley professor as 'that nice Mr. Kaczynski,' so you might not want to follow her lead." Houghton smiled at the camera, the edges of her mouth curling up so gradually it happened in slow motion. "Take it from me, these books are to die for."

"What's wrong?" Owen looked up to see Doc standing in the doorway and realized he was standing, the half-full bowl of cereal and milk splattered across the floor. Kelly peered around Doc, curious eyes scanning Owen up and down before landing on the phone still in his hand.

"Dropped the bowl." Owen closed the app then locked the phone's screen, laying it facedown on the countertop. "I'm a klutz today, apparently." He grabbed a handful of paper towels and stooped to gather the bowl and spoon, swiping the puffs of cereal off the floor. "At least the bowl didn't break." He looked up as Doc drifted closer, his gaze now tracking between the phone and Owen. "Did I wake you? Is Shiloh still sleeping?"

He hoped she was...that he hadn't woken her. The nightmares had returned with a vengeance a few nights ago, sending her screaming to hide underneath Kelly's bed multiple times per night. The timing was interesting, because while August stayed with them, taking the guest bedroom as his own, Shiloh's dreams had pretty much ceased, disappearing quickly. She'd been intrigued by the giant of a man, preferring his company over even Kelly's. Owen had talked to Alace last night, hoping for an update on when they could expect him back.

Weird how he fit into the household as easily as he did. Owen recognized it was odd, but anything that made his kids happier or healthier was way up on his list of good things. August, with his rough country speech and loud laughter, had found a fan in the tiny little girl, and Owen wanted to give her anything she desired. *I'll call Alace in a bit, check again if she's got an update for me.*

"What were you watching on the phone?" Doc knelt next to him, more paper towels added to the mess soaking up the spilled milk. "You looked like you'd seen a ghost when I walked in."

Owen checked the room, verifying Kelly had retreated back up the hallway towards the bedrooms, then still kept his voice low as he explained, "The reporter said something that caught me off guard is all. The way she said it made me wonder if she knew something." He shrugged as he stood, tossing the saturated paper towels away. "Just my imagination."

"That's Colleen Houghton, right? The reporter Alace met?" Doc handed him the rest of the trash for disposal. He turned on the water at the sink, rinsing his hands and leaving the water running for Owen. "I'll catch the piece online, see if I see anything."

"Good idea. Two sets of eyes and all that." Owen turned off the water and accepted the kitchen towel from Doc to dry his hands. "It struck me odd. Off, you know?"

"Yeah."

Doc's hand settled on his shoulder, and Owen caught himself before he leaned into the man. *Get a grip, Marcus.*

"Dad?" Owen was running up the hallway before Kelly's shout had a chance to die away. He loved that title, being verbally acknowledged for the position he found he wanted more than anything. Both Kelly and Shiloh had readopted it when August was here, the man's not-too-subtle encouragement all the motivation the kids needed. Him referring to Owen as "your dad" carried more weight than Owen's repeated "my kids," and it had become another reason they'd enjoyed having August with them.

"What's wrong?" Owen swung through the open doorway into Kelly's room, his ears telling him both children were present, his eyes confirming Kelly held Shiloh in his lap, the kids seated in one corner of the room.

He didn't need Kelly's response to tell him what had caused the kid to call out.

The window above the bed was closed, intact, not even a crack. But on the outside looking in were two large eyes, luminous pupils glinting in the dark. They were too far apart to be human eyes, too tall to be a dog. He cautiously approached the window, and they pulled back, then rose higher. He was close enough now to see more details, the dark fur and snout definite clues.

"It's a goddamn bear." Owen lifted his arms as he waved and shouted, "Yeah, bear. Ware, bear. Go on now."

The bear fell back to all fours, turned away, and began to trundle off through the backyard.

"Life is always interesting with you, Owen." He turned to see Doc crouched next to the kids. "Being a natural bear repellant one of your many specialties?"

"Yeah, they take one whiff of my pits, and it's game over for them." He settled on the floor next to Doc and held his arms out for Shiloh. "Come here, pretty girl. Were you scared?"

Shiloh settled into his lap, her cheek pressed to his chest, face turned away from the window. She nodded and mumbled, a muffled "Uh-huh," coming from the vicinity of her mouth.

"Most bears are more scared of you than you are them." Doc made a sound of disbelief as he leaned against the wall, Kelly curled up in his lap. "No, really, they are. There are exceptions, of course. Apex predators like a grizzly fear little, and bears that have been acclimated to human contact won't be afraid either. Those are what the DNR calls nuisance bears, because they've been taught to depend on people for their food. Most of the time, an encounter outside of the woods will be something like this, where a bear wandered out and something smelled good, so they got curious."

"And in the woods? What happens then?" Kelly shifted so he could see Owen, apparently unwilling to move from Doc's embrace.

"In the woods, you'll often catch only a glimpse of them as they move away from you. That's what I mean by they're more scared than you. Wild bears prefer not to be around people. We smell, we're noisy, and we disrupt the natural order of things. If a bear approaches in the woods, either they're sick and confused, they have a baby nearby and are protecting their cub, or you've not been practicing good craftsmanship and you smell like food." He rumpled Shiloh's hair, then smoothed it out, fingers threading through her locks to straighten them. "Avoiding the encounter is best, by backing away, or you can make yourself big like I just did, so you look like more of a threat. Running is never a good idea."

"What about a grizzly? Wouldn't you want to get away from them as fast as you can?" Doc's grin said he already knew the answer to his own questions but wanted to hear Owen's version anyway.

"Well, grizzlies can outpace a human running. They're a lot faster in a short distance sprint than we are, so running isn't really an option." He made a face and looked down at Shiloh, rewarded by her soft giggle. "One accepted way to deal with a grizzly is to play possum until they lose interest. I don't have any grizzly stories, but I've seen plenty of black bears. It's all about respecting the animal and their space and letting them be wild—which means the person gives way."

"What are you gonna do about the backyard bear, Daddy?" Shiloh's soft voice made Owen smile. Complete sentences were always good to hear, meaning more forward progress for her. A journey straight to mental health after all the suffering she'd endured.

He hadn't watched the video of her in the cabin. Owen knew he couldn't, not and keep his own sanity. Doc had observed the activity captured on the film, but muted, so they couldn't hear Shiloh crying. It was in moments like that Owen wished he'd killed Kuellen and Warrant slower, more viciously, taking the eye-for-an-eye to greater heights. With the video in their possession, it had been easier to locate other copies of the film online and eradicate them, marking each server for later destruction. Owen had vowed to get to them all.

"Our little ole backyard bear might be a nuisance bear. I'll call the local ranger station and ask about it, see if they've got any tagged bears in the neighborhood." He gave her a squeeze, laughing when she pretended to squeak from the force of his hug. "I'll clean the grill, make sure we're not enticing Mr. Bear close to the house, and I'll put in some motion-triggered lights farther away from the house. We're safe here, Shiloh. You don't have to be afraid of bears. Just remember the rules."

"Okay, Daddy."

Owen's eyes dipped closed, and he soaked in the power of the emotions rolling through him.

Something he'd believed taken from him forever, in the most dire of ways, and yet here he was, sitting in a house surrounded by people he cared about. Filling a paternal role for two kids he loved more than life. Not more than Emma, never that, but in opening himself to these kids, he'd found his capacity for love was so much more than he'd ever believed.

"Shiloh, I love you, you know that, right?" Owen blinked, clumped lashes making it hard to see at first. "Kelly, I love you, too. Do you guys know how much I love you?"

Kelly shifted around on Doc's lap, sharing a long look with Shiloh before turning his gaze on Owen. "Do you love Doc, too?"

Startled, Owen lifted his eyes to find a similar amount of surprise in Doc's expression. The man's features were asking a question Owen didn't understand. Maybe a version of, *You gonna answer that, buddy?* "Yeah," he told Kelly slowly. "I love Doc, too."

Shiloh giggled and turned to face Owen, cupping his cheeks with her hands. "We lub you too." She giggled again, the sound light and airy and full of happiness. "It's like we have two daddies."

Owen's gaze locked with Doc again. The man smiled slowly, then broke their shared stare as he shook Kelly lightly before setting him on his feet to one side. "It's a love fest, for sure. All that love still won't fill our bellies, though. I think it's past time for me to see what I can make for breakfast. Half a bowl of cold cereal isn't enough fuel for the day." He climbed to his feet with a groan, then laughed. "Gettin' too old to hang out on the floor like that." Doc glanced at the window, empty now of the early morning visitor who had kicked off their gathering. "I need some helpers for the kitchen. Daddy Owen needs to get some work done, which means you two little monsters are with me."

"Yay." Shiloh's arms pushed straight up into the air, her clenched fist nearly clipping Owen's jaw. "I a monster hepper now." He lifted her, and she giggled at him, determinedly raising and folding her legs in a crisscross, so she dangled above the floor. "Carry me, Daddy Owen." Resting her hands on his forearms, she nodded twice, her expression solemn. "Daddy Doc needs hepp."

"That's gonna stick, huh?" He pulled her close, propping her on his hip as he rose from the floor. "I don't hate it."

"Hate's wrong." Her chin bounced twice, tears threatening. "Hate's mean."

"Then it's a good thing I don't, huh?" Gathering her hair loosely in one hand, he swept it over her shoulders, setting it loose in a stream down her back. "How do you feel about being a monster?"

They exited the room, following Doc and Kelly up the hallway towards the kitchen.

Shiloh's face scrunched as she thought seriously about his question. "Kelly says if I do somethin', I needs to own it." Leaning against Owen's shoulder, her voice got small when she asked, "Is bein' a monster bad?"

"Not at all." Owen stopped as Doc turned, addressing both of them. He locked gazes with the man again, reading only sincerity and support, and his shoulders lowered a couple of inches as he accepted the meaning behind Doc's words. "In this house, there are only good monsters."

Leaving the kitchen and breakfast in Doc's hands, Owen made his way to his office, closing and locking the door behind him. Doc had a key and permission to enter at will, but securing the door was about protecting the kids from the kind of images Owen would be looking at.

He'd gotten a message from one of his darknet researchers earlier, the notice waking him in time to catch the live version of that reporter's segment. The notification, ignored until now, indicated a potential connection had been identified. Taking out two of the pedo ring members had only built a more ferocious fire in Owen's chest to find and deal with the rest of them. These deviants who believed buying and owning people—stealing children from their families and homes, and delivering them into hell—was their right. They would find out just how wrong they were.

Logging into Alace's secure network, he opened their shared document, the same one they'd been using for months. Owen didn't care; it made for a nice consistent method of communication. Alace was pragmatic, too, but also a little superstitious. The document had kept them in touch even under dire circumstances, and continuing to use it was an extension of the same luck they'd enjoyed then.

He was surprised to see Alace's icon was active, pulsing with color instead of being grayed-out as it would have been if she weren't logged into the system.

"She's either asleep at the computer, or already up." Owen slapped his forehead, uttering a muffled, "Duh." The reporter. Of course, Alace was up and watching, analyzing, and no doubt dissecting every word.

Words appeared on the document, the letters flowing from nothing into coherent thoughts in front of his eyes. *Magic.*

That segue about the Unabomber was a bit much, I thought.

Owen grinned as he typed in his reply.

Did her great-aunt even go to Berkeley? And that smirk at the end, like she was playing a cat n mouse game? Someone should tell her to keep her best cards closer to the vest.

Alace's cursor jumped down and then sat on a new line, blinking monotonously, unmoving. After a moment, he filled the void, wondering what Alace was thinking.

Her info on Ashworth was good to hear. I worried when they just charged him with the one m. I know you said not to sweat it, but he needs to pay for everyone he killed like that.

The investigation into Ashworth had shifted from their brand of justice to what the rest of the nation expected. August had tipped off the cops about what he'd found in the house before Alace had pulled him out to help Owen. August had taken a thermal imaging infrared camera with him, one that plugs into a phone for the display, allowing for easy video recording of what was seen. Using the device, it had been easy to spot one male prostitute's body in the basement wall, the location for the construction project that had been used to kill Ashworth's second wife.

August had pretended to be with the contractor actively working on the new project, explaining his presence in the house and lending validity to his claims with one fell swoop.

The cops had gone in with guns drawn, hustling Ashworth out of the house and into the back seat of a cop car, complete with light bar blazing blue and red. Twenty minutes after the forensic team had entered, they'd escorted the current Mrs. Ashworth outside, taping off the whole house as an investigation scene. The first body had been one Miles Garcia, a local boy known to the police as a male prostitute.

Confirmed, her great-aunt did attend Berkeley during the period Theodore Kaczynski was on staff. Odd she'd pick that killer to use to build a connection with. We don't deal in innocents.

Owen's laughter spilled out and he shook his head.

Not like there's much out there similar to us. We're one of a kind, and I'm sticking to my story on that.

He imagined Alace fighting not to roll her eyes.

It's early. What do you need?

True to form, she put the unknowns and unknowable behind them, deciding to focus instead on the reason he'd approached her this morning.

In a split-second decision, Owen launched the encrypted video chat software they used, grabbed his identifier from this session, and pasted it into the document, knowing she'd understand what he wanted. Sure enough, within seconds, his video window lit up with an incoming call. Owen picked up the headphones as he clicked Accept, settling them into place before the image fully resolved.

"I've got a lead. I need your input on my plan, and if you're willing, we can work the mission as a team."

"Yes. Whatever you need." Alace answered without hesitation, her gaze drilling through the screen and into him, her annoyance that he'd suggest she might respond differently scarcely hidden. "We are a team, Owen. We have to be transparent, or all this, everything we've built will, at best, fall apart." Her mouth twisted, and he stayed silent, waiting for whatever it was that pained her. "I don't want it to fall apart. This, and yes, by extension you, matter to me. Don't push me away again."

"I'll hold so tightly you won't see a separation between us, Alace. That was—extenuating circumstances sounds like a cop-out, I know. But it involved my kids, and all I could see or hear was red."

"Then you need to get a grip, because we know there are at least six other copies of those videos out in the wild. None have appeared on any darknet nodes, yet. That tells me the ring kept certain things private, reserving them for those most trusted members. Probably through some semblance of self-preservation, they knew their personal enacting of scenes shouldn't be for public consumption." The muscles next to her eyes tightened, lids lowering a fraction of an inch. "You can't go rogue on me every time we uncover a new repository."

"I won't." He hesitated, then decided to share a truth with her. "I scared myself, Alace. I was all emotion and no coherent thought, and I could have fucked things up badly. That would have only hurt my kids more. I won't do that. I'm not going to promise, but you'll know I'm for real by what I do over the next months. I won't go off like that again."

Alace was still, unmoving. He couldn't even see her chest rise or fall with breath. He knew this wasn't a stalled video connection. No, this was Alace thinking, weighing options, and making a decision.

"Tell me what you've got." Her words came slowly, deliberately, as if she were evaluating each as they flowed from her lips.

Owen breathed deep, his jaw thrusting forward as he gritted his teeth tightly. The level of anger took him by surprise, and he forced it back, shoving it down until it wasn't an immediate concern. *Need to do my job.* Blowing the air out, he reminded himself, *Alace is waiting.* Through the video, she offered a tiny nod, an acknowledgment of how hard this was, and why. "Donald MacLeod. He's in Jersey, down near Philly."

Her fingers worked the keyboard out of sight of the camera, and he did the same, pulling up his folder of information and clicking the button to share his screen. "My guy got into his financials and ran dates to ground. Around the time of the auction Shiloh and Kelly were in, he's got some major outlay that doesn't line up with anything going on in his life. Transfers narrowly underneath the federal alert level, but multiple." Owen tore his gaze away from the photos of bank transactions to lock eyes with Alace. "More than enough to buy a couple of kids."

"Any priors, official or not?" She blinked and angled her head away as if she already knew the answer to her own question.

"You know this already." Owen's laughter morphed into a sigh. "No official priors, not even any looks from law enforcement. But those in the know, they know him for sure. He's got his fancy house in the suburbs, then owns a multi-building compound in upstate Pennsylvania. Plenty big enough for parties. Funny thing is, his wife and family never travel with him. I can't even find information that the wife knows about the second property."

"She probably does. Women hide information absolutely as well as men." Alace gestured towards the camera in a way he took to mean she wanted control, so Owen unshared his screen. A moment later, Alace's computer popped up on his monitor, and he moved it out of the way so he could keep the video in view. "The wife isn't pristine." A series of photos flashed across the screen, children in various private moments, each image shot from high above in an angle that looked like a stationary camera. "She's got this on her computer." Alace's lips twitched. "My guy," she deliberately used Owen's language, "couldn't get her financials, but he did drop a USB in their driveway she picked up."

"I want them both." Teeth worrying his lip, he studied the image of the wife Alace had parked in one corner of the screen. "They have kids, Alace."

"Okay. So here's what I'm thinking."

Forty-five minutes later, they had a solid plan, just the two of them, how they preferred things to be. With a couple of helpers.

Knuckles rapping at the door behind him startled Owen, and he snapped upright, out of the deep slouch he'd adopted while he and Alace went through the ideas and concrete details for the next couple of days.

"Owen, breakfast is ready."

Now Alace smiled, white teeth glinting briefly between broadly stretched lips. "Sounds like you need to go, Owen."

"Be right there, Doc." Owen had called over his shoulder and turned back to face Alace fully. A nagging sense of guilt and anger at himself simmered in his blood, acid burning his stomach. "I didn't mean to put you in a bad spot, Alace." He gave her a headshake, the movement sharp, jerky with tense muscles. "I wouldn't do that."

"Partners." By not acknowledging his apology, she was telling him it truly was in the past, and clearly communicating she didn't want to talk about it again.

Message received. "BFFs," he agreed and sat there, watching as she disconnected without another word. "She's my best frand." He spoke truth to the still air within the office. The sense of unease that had been hovering over him throughout their conversation slowly bled away. "She don't even know we're besties."

Computer shut down, he exited the office and turned into the kitchen in time to see Doc shooting a burst of canned whipped cream directly into Kelly's mouth. "Me too," Shiloh shouted, clapping, then stood with her mouth open like a baby bird. Doc obliged and looked up at Owen.

"Want some?" The innocent words were delivered with a salacious wink, wickedness personified that stroked along Owen's skin, standing his hair on end.

What the hell. Wordlessly Owen stalked across the width of the room, coming to a halt right in front of Doc. Then, gazes locked, enjoying seeing how Doc's eyes widened, Owen opened his mouth and wagged his tongue. Doc lifted the can, Kelly and Shiloh clapping wildly, and shot a burst of gas-driven sweetness into Owen's mouth.

"Mmmmm." He made a show of licking his lips. "Good stuff, Doc."

***

Alace

Owen's voice sounded in her headphones, as clear as if he were next to her in the room. "In place. Where's our guy?"

He was out in public, casually patrolling a section of street near Ramblewood, off the New Jersey Turnpike. His circuit consisted of a not-yet-open pizza place, a gas station, and a gym where he'd already complained the guys lifting inside were staring at him funny. And a bank, which was their actual target.

"Incoming. Three blocks. Get close enough so the reader can—"

"Yeah, I know my part, Ward." He'd planted a minimal skimmer on the ATM at the bank, one designed for only close-range live transmission of data. "He's the Jag, right?"

Owen knew the make of the car, so the unnecessary question was nothing but his nerves showing. Alace played along, responding with an affirmative sound.

The dot representing Owen was close to merging with the one indicating the man they were hunting. Donald MacLeod had been a bit of a conundrum as they'd investigated him more aggressively. Not a man of influence or great wealth, he owned a chain of heating and air conditioning sales and repair stores—an impressive accomplishment for someone who'd come up from the streets like MacLeod had. In fact, his profile closely matched not only Warrant and Kuellen, but three of the other ring members she and Owen had identified.

The software on Owen's phone activated, and she saw the chip transaction information show on the screen, followed by the key sequence of the man's PIN. Embedded within the microchip of the card were additional details, all the info they needed to turn this man's life inside out.

"Got it. Everything we need." She saved the information to their shared secure server, then replicated it to another similar secure location. "Belts and suspenders. You're good. Head back to the RV." They'd purchased an old run-down recreational vehicle for this gig, and it was currently parked in a nearby shopping plaza. "Time to work our magic on things."

"What if he's heading there right now?" Owen's dot hadn't moved, was poised next to the bank's exit driveway, exactly where he should be if their intentions today were to intercept the man. They weren't.

"He's not." She spoke with confidence, pushing the surety Owen needed to hear into her voice. "He's going to his Marlton store. There's a breakfast meeting with his store manager. We saw the appointment on both of their calendars, so it's not merely a placeholder. Go to the RV, Owen." The software shut down, indicating the card had been withdrawn from the ATM. MacLeod would be leaving the bank at any moment. "Owen—"

"Yeah. Headed out." His tracker moved, angling across the four-lane street towards the shopping plaza. MacLeod's dot arrived where Owen had been standing, then turned in the opposite direction, towards Marlton. Alace let a pent-up breath seep out silently, not wanting to call Owen's attention to her anxiety. "Keep his tracker turned on. Make sure we know where he goes." Owen's dot moved faster, and his breath was loud, rough and ragged as he ran headlong through the city streets. "It's just—" He rounded a corner, only yards from where the RV was parked. "If he does have kids at the compound, and he'd gone up there? I can't. It'd be like Shiloh all over again, Alace."

"I know. But he's not. You are, remember?" That was their plan. She'd needed Owen to assist with the skimmer, so he'd diverted to town for the day. "You've got the invitation and are going to show up a day early, see if you can gain access. You're the one with a reason to be there. Any guards will err on the side of keeping MacLeod's friends happy."

That was going to be the hardest part of the gig, hands down. Sending Owen in without backup felt wrong, but it had been hard enough to acquire an invitation for one semi-unknown to a party MacLeod had scheduled for the weekend. Using Owen's established darknet persona had earned them an open door, but it would have been impossible to gain access for two. August was in the vicinity, and once Owen had the RV inside the perimeter of the compound, August would slip inside and set up in the vehicle. He simply wouldn't be inside the buildings until the end.

"Now to see where the money, in fact, takes us." The material her researchers and Owen's had uncovered was good, but it only showed part of the picture. With the new intelligence gleaned from his credit card, she'd be able to obtain even more of his information. She already had access to his home network, but it was mostly cluttered with data from his kids. They'd drawn a blank from the wife, which had Alace's instinctive alarm ringing loudly. "You good to drive up?"

"Yeah." Nothing remained of the joking and jovial Owen in that single word. His voice had turned hard and determined, and Alace understood the need to divorce himself from the gig, but it was foreign. Now that she'd gotten to know the real Owen, she hated any incursion back into stoic Owen's more limited interactions.

On a whim, she pulled up a web browser and typed in a quick inquiry. The results made her roll her eyes, but she decided to plow through and see if she could bring him back to himself, even by a little bit. "Hey,

Owen, what do you call a person who runs behind a car?"

She sat through a beat of silence, then Owen asked, "What? I'm in the RV, heading out in five minutes." A door slammed, and she heard a rustling sound, then he said, "I don't get it."

"He's behind a car, so he's exhausted. From the car's exhaust. You know, it loses a lot when I have to explain things to you."

"Oh, hardy har har." The RV's engine rumbled to life. "Funny one, Alace."

"What do you call a person who runs in front of a car?" His dot was on the move again, as was the tracker she'd had him install in the RV. When he didn't answer her, she supplied the punchline. "Tired."

"Heh." He clipped the sound off short, then snorted. "That one wasn't half bad."

"One more, and then I've got things to do."

"Don't hurt yourself, Alace. Humor's not a native language for you. I know it, and it's okay. I *can* get by without jokes, you know."

"I know, but this one is pretty good."

"Sock it to me, momma." True humor threaded through his voice, and Alace found herself smiling. "Gimme."

"How do crazy runners get through a forest?"

"I'll play along." His chuckle was music to her ears, and he sounded much more relaxed, ready to work. Able to bend without breaking. "How does a crazy runner get through a forest?"

"They take the psycho path." His groaning complaint made her laugh. "I'll check back in soon. Ping me if you need me."

"Take the psycho path she says," he grumbled. "I'm headed to the woods right now, you realize that, right? I'll take the psycho path all right. I'll take it all day long."

"Drive safely." She disconnected, leaving his humored words behind.

She checked in with August and found he was ahead of schedule, having completed tasks assigned to him with time to spare. His vehicle sat a couple of miles away from the compound's entrance, parked on an unused logging road, camouflaged against casual discovery with branches and foliage. He sent her a picture of the inside of his backpack, and she counted the items in view carefully.

One expensive bottle of cognac, the container shaped so uniquely it had been easy to devise a bug and adhere it within one of the folds of glass.

Six small, discreet cameras capable of transmitting on a shielded frequency for up to twelve hours on the internal batteries. They'd continue to record for longer than that, and footage could be retrieved later.

Two portable parabolic microphones for long-distance listening. While less convenient than a handheld device, these would be easy to place and hard to spot, and would give August insight into what was happening inside the compound.

Armed with recent satellite imagery, Alace and Owen had pored over the compound setup. Drawing conclusions based on expected floorplans lifted from the files of the construction contractor, they'd decided to focus on the two main structures. Isolated cabins were used to house party guests, and while they might bring in their own entertainment, the plan was to stay on point with first rescuing anyone being held captive by MacLeod. Their layouts were simple, so if a rescue was needed it wouldn't be hard to fold into the overall plan. One of the target structures was a sprawling house with multiple wings joined in the middle by a main hub. That hub was two stories high with a basement, and the open room on the upper floor was a likely candidate for where party activities would be conducted. The second building looked more like a livestock barn on the architect's drawings, but Alace and Owen both knew it was unlikely the occupants of the individual holding areas were animals.

August would place the listening devices as close as he could safely do so, adjacent to those two buildings.

She saw four incendiary devices, ones guaranteed to burn hot enough to catch nearly anything on fire. At the end of things, they'd burn it to the ground. Knowing Owen's aversion to open flames, Alace had initially shied away from the idea, but he'd circled back to it again and again. "Scouring the earth," he'd called it. She didn't disagree. Those would be planted at opposite corners of the two main structures after they were certain all innocents had been removed from harm's way.

"Miss Alace?" The questioning call broke her concentration, and she glanced towards the closed bedroom door.

"Looks good, August. Carry on." After issuing the assurance and order, she terminated the connection and locked her computer. A quick look at the bassinette showed Lila still sleeping, sprawled on her back, arms carelessly tossed over her head. Alace reached the door and thumbed the simple doorknob lock she'd engaged before starting work. Opening it, she looked down at Kelly, standing hand in hand with his little sister. "Yeah?" She squatted, bringing herself down so she could look him in the eyes. "Whacha need?"

"Is it okay if we go outside and play?"

Alace mentally calculated the amount of time she needed to kick off the research on the data they'd acquired from MacLeod's card, added in some necessary analysis cycles, and decided she had ample time to spend an hour outside with Owen's kids.

"You bet. Let me just get Lila, and I'll come with you." She smiled, knowing it looked forced but hoping the kids wouldn't notice. Babysitting wasn't an inherent talent, and she still wasn't sure why she'd allowed Eric to go into the office today. "Be right there." She stood and took a sideways step towards the bassinette, not giving the kids her back. *Okay, I'm being ridiculous.* "Go ahead. I'm literally ten seconds behind you. But don't run in the house." *Don't run in the house?* "I mean, be careful if you do run."

Another sideways step had her next to where Lila slept, and she bent to gather her daughter into her arms, startling into stillness when Kelly appeared next to her. He stooped and grabbed the diaper bag, slinging the strap over his shoulder. "Thanks," she called after him as he disappeared into the hallway.

Knowing there would be kids who might need immediate medical attention, Doc had flown to Philadelphia hours after Owen landed, his tickets requiring a quick turnaround on manufactured identification, a need Alace hadn't anticipated. He was parked at a motel close to the compound under the same false name, rental car completing the look of a vacationing out-of-towner. Once everything was under control at the compound, he would head in, prepared to treat patients in the RV, which would also be used to transport any kids they found. Alace would activate a local asset to pick up the rental and return it on time to the agency, completing the image of the tourist.

But that meant Doc's planned role in Owen's life was disrupted.

Hence, the appearance of Owen's kids at her bedroom door.

Lila squirmed against Alace's shoulder, rubbing her face across the fabric and snuffling. Alace cradled her close, humming softly as she descended the stairs. The rear sliding glass door was open, the screen thoughtfully closed to keep bugs at bay. Seeing the two kids running wide circles through the backyard, Alace detoured into the kitchen briefly, grabbing a couple of juice boxes, a container of donut holes, and the divided plate from the refrigerator that held Lila's lunch.

After making her way outside, Alace settled into a lounger, lifting her legs and crossing them at the ankles, presenting a façade of relaxation to anyone watching. *No one is watching.* She reached into the diaper bag Kelly had left near the chair and retrieved a lightweight blanket to protect Lila from the sunshine beaming down from the sky. Alace leaned her head back and closed her eyes, soaking in the warmth.

"Miss Alace?"

She opened her eyes to find Kelly next to her. Looking past him, she saw Shiloh was still running drunken circles, giggling when she staggered sideways as she spiraled in a tighter circuit.

"Yeah, Kelly?" Underneath the blanket, Lila shifted, snuffling again as she moved. Alace moderated her voice. "You need a drink?"

"That boy, the one who came to the house a few weeks ago. Is he gonna be okay?" Alace froze, concentrating on Kelly, his breathing, his face, the tiny muscles twitching his expression into one of concern. "Don't be mad. I didn't mean to see. Promise. I woke up and thought maybe I'd heard Shiloh, so I checked on her and saw the light on in Doc's workroom. It's been bugging me, but I didn't want to worry Owen." His forehead crinkled, brows drawing together. "I figured I could ask you."

"What do you know about him?" No use denying Rodney had been in their house, not if Kelly had actually seen him. Better to mitigate any possible fear or concern and play off the occurrence as something normal. "What did you hear that makes you worried for him?"

"Well, he was there to see Doc." Kelly shrugged in that effortless way little kids always had, like their bones were fluid. "And he sounded like someone had hurt him bad. I just wanted to make sure he's gonna be okay." He glanced around at his sister, who had fallen to the ground on her back, arms and legs sprawled akimbo, her laughter floating towards the sky. "Like me and Shiloh are."

In her mind, Alace reviewed a video she'd been sent of Rodney's homecoming.

Once Rodney underwent initial treatment at the Aurora Children's Hospital, things moved fast. Too fast to transport his parents to Colorado, not with Alace expediting everything from behind the scenes. The children's hospital in Atlanta was prepared to receive him, but Alace diverted the ambulance to his parents' house along the way from the airport. The driver had recorded the encounter, from moments before the door burst open until the back of the ambulance closed, Rodney's mother seated on the gurney with her son in her arms.

The glimpse into the woman's life had ripped at Alace, building an inferno where a flame had barely kindled before. In the room behind her had stood an unseasonable Christmas tree, seven years of unopened presents piled underneath. On the mantel were montage photo frames declaring things like "Happy 10th Birthday," two of the available slots filled with photos of Rodney's siblings, one rectangle standing empty. When the woman leaped toward the ambulance, Alace had noticed a tattoo on her arm. A quick online search surfaced not only the tattoo but the meaning. A tree, the main branches made from renditions of her children's signatures, one space starkly blank. *Waiting*. Everything was about waiting for Rodney, even as her other children had forced time to keep moving forwards.

Rodney had already endured one reconstructive surgery, with two more planned as soon as his wounds healed enough. For a certain sum of money, that same ambulance driver had happily transferred to a hospital staff position and was feeding Alace more videos as things changed. Even swaddled with bandages, tongue stitched and swollen, Rodney had talked about his savior. "The man with kind eyes," he'd called Owen. "My hero," his mother declared.

Yeah, Rodney was going to be absolutely fine.

"He's with his mother and father again." Kelly tilted his head to one side, considering her response. "I get regular updates on him. Do you want to know he's okay going forwards?"

"Yeah." Kelly's smile was without subterfuge, bright and loving. "That'd be great, Miss Alace." He held out his hands. "Want me to take Lila for a little bit?"

Lila's movements hadn't ceased this time, and Alace looked down to see her daughter's face peeking out from underneath the blanket. Her toothless grin was as brilliantly innocent as Kelly's smile. Alace drew her closer to plant a kiss on her forehead. "Wanna go with Kelly, baby girl?" The grin widened, Lila's approval of the offer clear. "Here you go, kid. Bring her back when she gets heavy."

She handed Lila over, watching as the little girl gripped tight to Kelly's shirt, holding herself close so she could wobble forward and plant an open-mouthed kiss against the boy's cheek. True to form, Kelly held her securely, one hand splayed across Lila's upper back. When Lila pulled away, her mouth was shiny, wet with saliva. Kelly grinned at her and swiped his face against his shoulder. "Hey, kiddo."

Alace kept an eye on them as Kelly wandered into the yard, both of his arms wrapped around Lila. Alace pulled her phone from a pocket, unlocked it, and launched her text string with Eric. Snapping a photo, she uploaded it there, and then after a moment's thought, sent the same picture to Owen and then Doc. Kelly was half-turned away, staring into Lila's face, both children in profile while behind them Shiloh was falling out of an attempted handstand, hair in a tumbled halo as her legs came down.

Sunshine AND outdoors with children. It's like I don't even know you.

That text was from Owen, of course. In between his words, she read gratefulness for how she was taking time for his kids and had sent him a reminder of why they did the work.

Sunscreen is your friend.

That text came in from a different contact, quickly followed by a second.

Looks like fun. Tell them I love them.

Both were from Doc, unsurprisingly. He was the most open of any of them with his affection, and she enjoyed that about him.

My heart.

Eric.

You've convinced me. On my way home.

Alace blinked back tears.

These three men were such unexpected gifts, filling places in her life she hadn't known were empty.

Eric, her heart, forcing her to explore emotions for the first time.

Owen, her head, bulldozing past fear of motivation and forcing her to develop an unexpected trust and friendship.

Doc, everyone's careful balance, his healing the yin to the yang of their violent retribution.

"Lila." She called across the yard, loving how her daughter's attention zeroed in on her mother. Kelly watched them both, standing where he could see Shiloh, also. *He's definitely a caregiver kid.* She'd seen evidence of his nature time and again and treasured this side of the boy. "Daddy's coming home. Are you excited?"

Lila released her grip on Kelly but never wavered, his hold on her secure. She clapped her tiny hands together and squealed loudly, joined by Kelly's echo of Alace's words. "Daddy's coming home."

Shiloh lifted her head and looked excited. "Daddy?"

"No, Shiloh. Not our dads, Lila's daddy." Kelly jumped in place, his movements cautious and slow. "Lila's daddy, Lila's daddy, Lila's daddy." Shiloh surged to her feet and joined in, her leaps much more enthusiastic. "Lila's daddy, Lila's daddy, Lila's daddy."

"I've got juice boxes for when you're thirsty." Alace found herself smiling, this one not forced or manufactured, but a pure reflection of the joy on the children's faces. "Crazy kids."

When Eric arrived, he and Kelly conferred for a brief span of time, then set to work rearranging the patio furniture, carrying various pieces into the yard and placing them at angles from each other. Alace couldn't figure out the intent until Eric passed by on another trip from the house to the yard with an armful of blankets. Impromptu tent erected, he took Lila from Alace and shooed her inside.

She paused in the doorway and turned back to watch. Eric settled Lila onto a blanket in the shade between two loungers and crowed, "Who needs sunscreen?"

Shaking her head, Alace went upstairs to her computer, surprised at the reluctance she felt. This had nothing to do with worry about Lila. Eric would care for her in all the ways Alace would. No, this was more an unwillingness to miss out on something, anything, to do with the kids.

Job to do, she reminded herself, locking the door and unlocking the computer.

She brought the tracking software to the front of the screen and checked on everyone's location. All as expected.

Fifteen minutes later, work-board posts complete, Alace was digging into Donald MacLeod in earnest.

She was still working away when her computer dinged, the sound loud through the headphones she wore. Taking them off, she realized she could hear rumbling chatter from downstairs, Eric and the kids apparently back in from the yard. Glancing at the clock in the corner of the screen, she realized nearly three hours had slipped past.

I've got them, though. The time spent had been worth it. She had identities on virtually all expected participants for MacLeod's party this weekend. As fit the profile so far, none were uber rich or highly connected. It was almost as if they'd been recruited for the ring because of their ordinariness. *And shared perversions.*

Alace set the files to upload into the folder shared with Owen and then navigated to the other window with the darknet request. She'd hit paydirt there, too, her researcher finding six accounts for MacLeod that weren't in his official portfolio. She downloaded the data, immediately queuing an upload to the shared folder before opening the file.

As that all worked in the background, Alace shifted to the tracker software. MacLeod was back at home for the day, August still in position, Doc waiting at the motel, and Owen was a scarce hour out from his destination. So many moving pieces to their plan, and while she'd built in room for error, most things had to fall into place for them to find success in the end.

She keyed into a texting application on the computer, entering the number for the burner phone Owen was using.

Stop for food and supplies at the next town.

There hadn't been enough time to stock up the RV before he had to be in place for the bank skim, and while Doc had shopped at several stores for the over-the-counter medical supplies they might need, she hadn't thought to ask him to grab things like water or snacks.

Doc's got food covered. The bubbles appeared that said he was sending another message, so she waited before responding. **It was nice to send him that picture too. Thanks.**

Her stomach gave a slow roll.

Alace chewed on the corner of her bottom lip, trying to find the source of her instant unease. It wasn't that she didn't want them talking. She expected a certain amount of interaction between her guys. All three had burners, all three phones had three numbers in them, each of the other two guys, and one for her.

Pristine numbers, not supposed to lead any investigator anywhere. Certainly not bring them back to her doorstep.

The picture.

Her blood ran cold, then hot, heating her chest from the inside out as a flush rose up her neck.

Oh my God.

She hadn't thought twice about sending the picture to the devices, which was a serious breach of protocol. It hadn't sunk in until she realized Doc had used the same phone to send it on to Owen.

Shit.

She'd been so caught up in the normalcy of the moment, she'd forgotten who she was.

Forgot what I am.

"Alace?" Eric's voice shook her free from stasis, breaking the pall of disbelief and disappointment. The doorknob rattled, his words coming from just outside the door. "Beloved, the kids and I have food ready. Do you want to take a break and eat a bite?" *Eric, kids, Lila—I'm not what I once was.* She didn't know how to classify herself in this changed circumstance, but it felt oddly healthy.

She looked up to see several unanswered texts from Owen, the last few sent with greater urgency in the messaging. The final simply said, **Goddammit Alace**, a clue that her silence had frustrated him.

"Alace, honey?"

She shook her head, not a denial of response, but an awakening. "I'll be down in a minute."

"Everything okay?"

She rested her fingers on the keyboard, attempting to compose a reply to Owen. "Yeah, it's all good. Everyone's good." **Husbutt and kids made dinner. AFK for 15.** "I'm right behind you."

She stood, and before she could step away, she saw another text from Owen flash into view.

My kids feeding my friend. Sounds about right. Talk soon.

A tap of her fingers locked the screen, pictures of Lila slowly fading in and out. More evidence of how her priorities had changed.

Life is never boring.

***

Owen

"I'm not going to be able to stomach these guys."

He was back in the RV following the initial meet and greet with the other attendees, and had found having to shake MacLeod's hand the final straw breaking his limited patience. Pleading exhaustion and implying a base desire to rest up before tonight's main event, Owen had escaped back to the RV.

August looked up from where he sat next to Doc, both heads bent over a map. Without raising his head, Doc asked, "What's plan B this time?"

"Plan B." Owen stalked past them to where a tablet was mounted on the wall. "I'll show you plan B." He tapped the surface to wake it, snarling, "Alace, we need a solution now. I can't go through with the original op." Turning around to face Doc, he lifted his chin. "Alace is plan A, B, C, and D, all rolled into one." He twisted back to the tablet, the surface now showing an empty chair. "Where the hell is she?"

"She is right here." A shadow moved across the far wall in the video, and Alace stepped into frame, perching on the edge of the chair. "If we don't wait for the event to begin, we won't have viable evidence for the cops."

"I'm past wanting the cops in on this one. He's got six kids, Alace. Six little girls. Other than being scared and a little shook up from the rough handling, they're not hurt. Not yet." His head moved back and forth in an uncontrollable rejection of their original plans. "I can't do it."

She looked past him, and Owen turned as August stood tall. "I vote plan B." The man's rumbling agreement settled Owen, helping him dial back the disgust and revulsion that had been flooding through him. "Kids are already separated from the guests; it won't take much to bring the little ones back to the RV. Doc can tend to them while Owen and I wipe a little bit more of the earth clean from the pollution of these bastards."

Alace's bottom lip disappeared into her mouth, and she stared at them, her gaze flicking from one to the other, then slicing towards Doc. "Doc? What say you?"

"You don't even have to ask, Alace. I will always side with the kids."

"Okay." Her chin dipped, and she glared at Owen from underneath her brows. "Most of the guards are in their barracks right now, only one guy on the gate, and two in the barn. I can cut the phones between the main house, the barn, and their housing, then terminate the outside lines. Cell phones are a problem."

"I have a jammer. It's channel specific, and I've already enabled the one our phones will be on, so we won't be impacted." Owen brought his duffle from the floor and placed it on the cabinet next to where he stood. "Two, actually, so we can plant one on either side of the residences for overlapped coverage. Drop them next to the ears August placed yesterday." He lifted his head, relieved beyond belief that Alace was rolling with the change in plans. *I can't have another Shiloh. I can't.* "You're already in their security system, should be able to lock the pervs in their rooms at the same time. They've got electronic locks on nearly everything." He glanced at August. "I'm all about the scorched earth policy, too, man."

"We're in agreement, then." August was taking a variety of items out of his backpack, and Owen immediately identified several as a type of incendiary device he'd used in Central America. "This was always plan B."

"Owen, can you put the drone out?"

He nodded at the tablet and grabbed a box from a nearby cabinet. The device inside was preassembled and already programmed for the frequency Alace would use. As he watched the tablet, the screen split so half showed Alace's face and half had a view of the countertop under the drone. He caught a glimpse of the tiny camera underneath moving, and the image changed to show the three men. Owen put a boot on the bench, then his other on top of the table, reaching overhead to fit his fingers to the sliding locks alongside the light fixture. He pushed and pinched, then twisted, and the entire light assembly dropped down a couple of inches before sliding to the side on a hidden track. August handed the drone up to Owen, who set it on top of the RV's roof. He descended from the tabletop to the floor, leaving the hatch open.

The image changed again, the bright white of the RV roof shifting to browns and greens of foliage and yard.

"Kids are in their cells?"

As they'd suspected from the fruits of their research, the barn wasn't truly a barn, but a holding arrangement for children brought to the compound.

"Yeah." Owen cleared his throat, remembering for an instant two brave boys who'd confronted him from their own cells, what seemed a lifetime ago. "Nate, Walt, Tony, and Natalie—you ever find out what happened to them?"

Alace's answer was immediate, the information as close to the tip of her tongue as if she'd anticipated his question. "Both sibling pairs were returned to family members. They'd been removed from the parental homes before being kidnapped, but after they were rescued, grandparents stepped up for the kids in both families." Alace laughed softly. "Turns out the grandmothers had been friends in childhood but had lost track of the other. Now they've moved so they live side by side, and with the virtual merger of households, the kids have strong, extended family support." Owen looked up at the tablet to find her staring at him. "We did a good thing then, Owen."

"And we're doing a good thing now." He gave her a short, decisive nod as he transferred items from the duffle to his smaller, more portable backpack. "I'm ready whenever you are."

"Doc?"

"I'm good to go. My supplies are easy to unpack as needed." Doc's gaze moved between Alace and Owen. His pause was brief but deliberate, and Owen experienced the emotion behind each word as he continued, "If you want me to take a more active role, I'm willing." The reversal from his previous stance said volumes about the investment level with this mission.

"No need, Doc." Alace's voice was distant, dreamy as she focused on flying the drone. "I'm parking our bird here, so you can keep watch on the compound. I've already killed the phones both internal and external, and I've posted a notice on that company's social media that there's a known outage in the area. Owen, by the time you and August get the jammers deployed, I'll be ready to rock and roll with locking the guests and guards inside."

"Just like that?" Doc looked a little shellshocked, shaky in his disbelief.

Owen walked to him and rested a hand on his shoulder, gripping firmly. "Yeah, just like that. We've got the high ground here, Doc. Our job is to make sure the kids get out alive and unharmed. Anything past that is fate."

"Fate?"

"Yeah, fate."

"Fate, and a plan B." Alace's tone was strict, brutal in its firmness. "Ensuring all the kids and all my guys come home safely."

"Yes, ma'am." He didn't have to wait for it, Alace gave him the eye roll right away, caught herself midroll and glared at him as if it was his fault for her physical reaction. Owen didn't say anything else, merely grinned as he lifted the backpack and slung it over his shoulder.

CHAPTER THIRTEEN

Owen

Steering the RV down the winding Pennsylvania highway, Owen glanced in the side mirror, the surface reflecting nothing but open road behind them.

The ease with which they'd separated the guard staff from the guests had been a little surreal. Even the guard on the gate had been a simple shot, one made mentally easier to take once Owen had seen the kind of magazine the man had been flipping through. Foreign language, southeast Asian most likely, the images made up entirely of underage children.

Once into the compound's systems, Alace had surfaced more information around MacLeod's staff. Each guard was a released pedophile with violent crimes in their past, and remembering the men's fevered enthusiasm earlier in the day, Owen hadn't suffered any qualms about their plan.

August had joined him at the barn, and together they'd dealt with the two guards in place there. Quiet and efficient, August was as skilled as Owen, moving with a sense of confidence Owen had appreciated.

Once those guards were dead, they'd moved to the enclosures where the kids were being kept. Scared and embarrassed by their nudity, the rescued kids had been quick to don the clothing Owen found in a locked cupboard inside the building. There were more kids than had been exhibited earlier in the day, and August had been in charge of counting heads, ensuring none of the kids slipped off. The big man had wound up carrying the youngest among them, leading the way to the RV as if he were the pied piper, even without his wooden flute.

As soon as Doc indicated he had the situation in the RV under control, August and Owen had moved on to the next phase of the mission: neutralizing the remainder of the guards. The thuggish men had cowered before August's and Owen's size and displayed firepower, and meekly lined up on their knees. There were no messages to send here, no statements to make, and efficiency had ruled the day. Starting at either end of the row, the men hadn't time to react as each received their single tap to the back of the head like a benediction. Owen had left the bodies where they'd fallen, stepping over the blood to reach the door closest to the main building.

The guests had proven to be a different, more difficult breed.

Entitled white men, aggressively argumentative, shouting insults and wild threats until Owen pulled one out of the mass and dealt with him right there, letting the body drop to the floor without a word. Silence had fallen like a shroud until MacLeod stepped forwards and to the side, separating himself from the rest of the men.

On the off chance there was security Alace hadn't located, they'd decided to go the safer route. Which meant Owen had worn a ski mask, same as August. Staring out through the eyeholes, he'd longed to tear it off to show his face.

Locking gazes with MacLeod, Owen had delivered justice as effectively as possible. "Norton, Tambor, Barnes, Riss, and Burton." MacLeod's eyes had widened at the carefully enunciated names of the five remaining members of the ring he was so deeply embedded with, and Owen dipped his chin in a slow nod. "I told you I'd come for you. I told you, and I showed you. Eye for an eye, tongue for a tongue, and life for a life." Without more discussion, Owen had lifted the handgun he held and shot MacLeod in the forehead, the bullet exiting the back of his skull in a messy shockwave of blood, bone, and brain matter.

Shouting men had jostled backwards, angling to get behind something, someone—anything, as long as it was away. As if they'd practiced the maneuver before, Owen and August had taken their shots, working similar to how they'd handled the guards, from the edges of the shifting crowd into the middle. Owen dropped their final target, the dead man falling gracelessly amidst the tangle of limbs and shocked expressions.

He shook himself as the RV rumbled, tires drifting onto the warning strips ground into the surface of the road. Drawing the vehicle safely back into his lane, he glanced over his shoulder at the scene still unfolding in the back of the RV.

August was seated at the table, one little girl collapsed against his side, his arm curved around her shoulders. Another child, this one probably the boy they'd found in the mix of kids—it was hard to tell for certain from this distance—was in his lap, held there securely by August's other arm.

Doc was farther back in the living area with a child who was slightly older than the others, urging her to drink from a bottle of water. With several sleeping children scattered across the fold-down bed, she was the lone holdout, the only one still awake, and as Doc spoke soothingly to her, she lifted the bottle to her lips.

Good.

The plan was to deliver the children to a physician Doc knew from his time in New Jersey. He trusted this man to ensure the kids got the help they needed without drawing attention to their trio of vigilantes. They'd offload the kids into an unused weekend camp close to Philly, wait for the physician to arrive on site, then make like a tree and leave.

His phone buzzed and vibrated from its current position in a tray on the console, the sound loud. Owen wore a headset paired to the phone and tapped the earpiece to answer the call. Given there was only one person other than the two behind him who had the number, he smiled as he asked, "Can't get enough of me, huh?" He and Alace had hung up only a few miles back, after she'd relayed the updated information about their transfer location.

"Oh, I'd say I've seen more than enough of you."

Owen's muscles locked into place. His ears buzzed, and his throat pounded with each beat of his heart. The male voice was unknown, the tone deep and casual, as if the speaker had all the time in the world.

"Who is this?" Owen deliberately pitched his voice loud enough to capture August's attention, and a quick glance around saw the man on alert. Owen motioned towards his ear and the phone, then raised his hand to his ear with the thumb and little finger extended, a military hand signal to call the radiotelephone operator. Facing front again, Owen heard movement behind him and then August's voice, hoping it was him calling Alace. "Who are you? How'd you get this number?"

"Funny thing, that. When cell signals are jammed in a particular area, it makes the ones which are able to connect a lot easier to find." The man chuckled, a dry and dusty sound as if he were on the verge of coughing. "You basically handed me the information."

Not only was this a clear threat, the man had identified himself as being associated with the ring of pedophiles. The only other answer could be a similar agenda to their group, which Owen knew was unlikely. As he'd told Alace recently, there weren't many out there like they were. Good news was, if the caller was one of the remaining ring members, there was a limited roster to review and identify.

"What do you want?" The sound of the call changed, echoing thinly. Owen glanced at the GPS map to see relatively smooth terrain all around them. The change wasn't due to environmental interference, which hopefully meant Alace had tapped into the call. "Who'd you say you are?"

"I didn't, actually. I won't, honestly. Why would I give you an inch of advantage when you've already proven so adept at mitigating sophisticated countermeasures?" Another bout of laughter that sounded more like an asthma attack, the rattling of air in the man's throat painful to hear. "I'm not stupid...Schmitz."

August fell into the other captain's chair at the front of the RV, phone sealed tight to his head. Owen struggled to pull in a breath. This was as direct a threat as he'd ever encountered out in the bush. More terrifying than facing down more than a dozen men earlier tonight. Schmitz was his alias for this mission, his cover identity for travel and identification.

"Shocked you silent, hmmm?" Oily and grating at the same time, the man's voice ripped along Owen's nervous system, causing his fingers to clench hard on the steering wheel. "You have taken a lot of my property. I hope it's not simply shock that's stolen your voice. Ideally there'd be a tiny bit of fear there, too."

"Norton—"

"Don't be ignorant. Norton, Tambor, Barnes, Riss, and Burton are pawns in my game. They're oblivious to the lines of stress surrounding them. Little men with little desires, content with the smallest of scraps." Anger bled through now, and Owen focused on stoking that emotion, hoping to force a mistake.

"Weak men lean on little men. Weak men give their possessions away, unable to protect what they hoped to keep."

"I'm not weak. Don't equate my courtesy reaching out this one time to warn you with any level of weakness. You and your companions are targets for more than myself. Swooping in and ruining individual scrimmages, disrupting the order of things. I'm not the only one looking for you."

"You want to find me?" Owen kept his response just shy of a bellow with effort, the rage in him surging forward. August motioned, and Owen looked over in time to see August draw the edge of his right hand, palm down, across his neck in a throat-cutting motion from left to right, signaling "danger area." *No shit, Sherlock.* "Maybe I'll find you first."

"I'd love that, actually. Should I issue an invitation for yourself and the two men with you?"

Yeah, keep talking. So far the man didn't indicate he knew anything other than what they'd potentially exposed on this mission. Keeping the man in the dark about Alace and her capabilities gave them a significant edge in any game he could devise.

"You do that, asshole. You just do that. I've got kids to save." He waited, but nothing else came through the headset, and August relaxed in his seat, phone still pressed to his ear, but his alert posture lessening. "Is he gone?"

August nodded as Alace spoke to Owen, her voice a balm after the past few minutes of tension. "Yeah, he's gone. I got within two miles of his location, and he shut down his transmitter and repeater. I got the MAC address of both, so if they come back online as a pair anywhere, I'll know. Unfortunately, with the transmitter or repeater alone, they'll pick up new virtual addresses."

"Who is he?"

"I missed the first part of the conversation. Clue me in?"

Owen repeated the back and forth, noting how Alace allowed him to continue to the end, either in an attempt to ensure he remembered everything, or so she could experience the continuity of communication in case of a latent clue.

"Ideas?"

"I don't like that he picked up your alias." Alace's grumble was barely audible.

"Yeah? Me either. Who is he?" The GPS beeped, and he glanced down to see a turn coming up. "Should we continue with the plan for tonight? Are these phones compromised?"

"Nothing is attached to your signal or August's. I packed a scanner in your duffle. Once you stop, you should run it over the RV, but my guess is it's going to come back clean. His point is well taken about how isolating your devices at the compound would have made them stand out like a beacon if he were already watching. If he had video and got the RV's plates, he could have tracked back to when you got gas or anything where you used the card I gave you and picked up your name there. I don't think he got beyond that. From his manner, he clearly thought he could ruffle you, but you bested him in that arena." Alace's even tone went a long way to settling him, her calm assertions of minimal exposure helping bring things into perspective. "He didn't have August's or Doc's names, and I think both of them parking outside the compound are the reason why. We're good as we can be, Owen. If he had ongoing surveillance, you'd have seen something by now. He doesn't know where you are but took a chance you were still in the area. He's hoping we'll make a mistake."

"We won't." Owen braked and turned the wheel, guiding the RV onto a smaller road that would lead directly to the mothballed camp that was their destination. "Not with your hand at the helm. It's straight sailing."

"You give me too much credit."

"Nope." Owen let the corners of his mouth creep up, his face still so tense it felt as if it would crack in half. "You don't give yourself enough."

Chapter Fourteen

Alace

Shifting Lila from her shoulder to a breast to begin the post-burp second half of her feeding, Alace found herself concentrating on the scene outside Owen's living room windows instead of the miracle in her arms.

Eric stood in full sunlight next to Owen, August, and Doc, the men engaged in building a massive piece of playground equipment Owen had determined needed to live in their backyard. The large structure was going up about as quickly as the nursery furniture had last weekend, and with the four of them working in tandem, it looked as if they'd have it completed in no time.

Off to one side, a barefoot Kelly and Shiloh rested, their shoes lined up neatly next to the quilt. Spread on the grass in the shade of a canopy, that tiny oasis would be Alace's destination as soon as Lila was done nursing.

She glanced down and teased the edge of Lila's hand with a finger, smiling as the baby captured the annoying digit, holding on tightly.

This moment wasn't one she had ever believed possible, and at times Alace still wondered if it was a dream from which she'd wake.

"I love you so much. I'll never let anything hurt you." Her whispered promise didn't disturb Lila, those long curving lashes that were so adorable on a baby scarcely fluttering on cheeks so soft they demanded only the tenderest of caresses.

The screen of her phone lit up with an incoming call. Alace shifted only enough to see the name on the display, and then eagerly grabbed the phone with her free hand. "Bebe," she greeted with a smile. "Your granddaughter is eating dinner right now."

"Oh my darling girl, sketch in the scene for me, make me believe I'm there."

Alace loved Eric from the top of her head to the depths of her soul. She loved Lila entirely, every ounce of emotion coming from every cell of her body.

But she adored her mother-in-law, the feeling so effortless and light it made her giddy. Phoebe had declared them best friends during her monthlong visit right after Lila was born, and Alace had preened to know the affection she felt was returned.

"We're over at Owen's so the men can build this huge fantasy castle for the kids. Everyone else is outside, but Lila and I are in this Victorian armchair Doc found at some auction. It's covered in hideous brown velvet but is the most comfortable chair I've ever sat in, outside of my rocker. We're positioned so we can see outside and listen to their laughter and chatter as it drifts in through the open windows."

"Secluded, not isolated." Phoebe summed it up effortlessly. "Sheltered but included."

"Yeah. They all made sure we'd come back out soon. Even the kids. Oh, you'd love Kelly and Shiloh. Especially Kelly." Alace liked both kids, but the way Kelly was with Lila set her heart soaring. "I know you got to meet them, but if you had a chance to be around them more, you'd fall in love."

"Good kids are like that. They collect the adoration of adults because in them, we see the best possibilities we'd wished for ourselves." Phoebe made a soft, wistful sound. "You must come to Malibu and bring everyone with you. Must, not should. Make it happen, Alace."

"I will." A promise she could gladly make.

"Give that darling child a kiss from her Bebe."

Another promise easy to keep. "I surely will. I love you." Alace didn't hesitate to give her mother-in-law affirmation of something she already knew. "I'll remind Eric to call you later."

"I'd love that."

The call ended without goodbyes, Phoebe having learned long ago it was Alace's preference, and even if it wasn't her own, she adopted it when speaking to Alace because that was the kind of supportive person she was. Without being asked, she found her place beside those she cared for and lifted them up in a thousand tiny ways. Together her actions amounted to a tsunami of love Alace was still becoming accustomed to.

When she looked outside again, Owen had separated from the group, head bent over his phone as he stood to one side. He straightened and turned to stare at the house, face set in an easy smile, and she knew exactly what he'd been watching.

She'd received another video from the hospital source in Georgia this morning, had watched it, and uploaded the file to Owen's folder.

Rodney's parents had been interviewed by a local news outlet. His mother had spoken eloquently of the anguish from Rodney's kidnapping that had never faded, of being swept hither and yon in the waves of hope and despair as months and years passed without news of her child. In a scene set inside their house, she'd shared the couch with her husband, the couple somehow beating the odds and remaining a source of strength for each other. The background of the room had changed from the first video Alace had seen, detritus of Rodney's absence scoured from existence. The doorframe leading from the living room to the kitchen held a mark for his current height right alongside his siblings. The photos on the mantel filled, no more holes to remind the viewer this couple had more children than could be seen and held.

Then the interview jumped, and suddenly, Rodney sat next to his mother, his shy smile filling the screen. He'd talked, the words coming slowly, his enunciation careful. The surgeries were working magic for him, removing the impediment he'd suffered through since being so brutally mutilated by a hateful man.

The reporter had touched on the anonymous rescue, Astrid having done her job of ensuring the child arrived safely at the hospital in Aurora without giving anything away.

When asked about who rescued him, Rodney's answer hadn't changed from the beginning. "An angel," he'd said repeatedly. "My guardian angel."

At the end of the interview, the reporter asked what Rodney would say to his angel if he had the chance.

The boy had stared straight into the camera as instructed and then laid it out for everyone to hear.

"I'd say I'm glad Aldo didn't hurt you. I'm glad you found me. You saved me." His voice thickened, and he paused, the video capturing each expression change from pain to fear, to gratefulness. "Thank you for saving me."

Validation for the lives they chose to lead couldn't be more profound and powerful than that single statement.

Thank you for saving me.

If able, she imagined each of the children they'd set free from the hell of captivity would echo the sentiment. A chorus of unneeded gratitude, but it truly amplified her desire to keep going.

She remembered the way Rodney's mother's arm had curved around him, pulling him close. He was her child, born from her body as Lila had been Alace's. His mother accepted him, no matter what had happened. She'd counted herself blessed to have him back and loved him wholly.

"No matter what, I'll always love you." Lila had gone to sleep, a trail of milk on her cheek. Alace resettled her own clothing and grabbed a cloth to gently wipe her daughter's face. "To the moon and back isn't enough. I'll love you forever and ever."

"Need some help, beloved?" Alace smiled as she looked up at Eric. "My mother texted, said perhaps it was time for you to rejoin our party."

That's the kind of love I want to give back. All-consuming, never-ending, fully supporting, enduring, and stalwart.

"Want to carry our daughter?" She lifted Lila slightly, and Eric's arm slipped underneath, raising Lila to his chest. He reached out with his other hand, palm up in an offer she didn't need but would take. He pulled her to her feet and then tugged so she fell against his side, his arm firm around her waist.

"I'd love to," he responded belatedly and smiled down at her.

"I love you." She watched for the reaction and wasn't disappointed. His cheeks lifted, corners of his eyes crinkling, and his mouth spread wider. She loved how he easily accepted her words as truth but never took her love for granted.

"Alace." That use of her name carried so much emotion, two syllables fraught with fear and love and hope and belief, Alace found herself blinking hard as her eyes welled.

Fucking, fucking Eric.

Chapter Fifteen

Kelly

Owen sat close to Alace, but Eric was closer, his arm around her shoulders an ownership statement Kelly still found amusing. They were quietly chatting as they watched where he sat across the room. Shiloh was perched on the floor at his feet, head down, hair hanging on either side of her face, the shining sheets of hair a shielding curtain from the world as she flipped through the picture book in her lap. Kelly was scooted far back in Doc's favorite chair, Lila Sue on his lap, his arms around her holding carefully, feeling as comfortable as if he'd done this a thousand times.

He ended the soft song he'd been humming for the baby, then lost sight of the adults as he bent to press a tiny kiss to the little girl's head. It was calm in the room, the adults seemingly happy to watch him and Shiloh.

Kelly kissed Lila again, then quietly whispered, "I won't let anything happen to you, ever. I'll protect you from the bad monsters. Promise." He lifted his head and stared across the room at Owen and Doc, the men he'd slowly become comfortable calling Dad. They both made it easy to hope this thing that felt like family was sturdy and wouldn't go away.

Built from broken pieces, they were so much stronger together. No addiction would come along to whisk away the love he believed they had for him and Shiloh.

The muscles in his face relaxed, shifting from a scowl into something far lighter, trusting the peace they'd given him was secure. He knew Lila had the same from her parents, a never-ending source of love the little girl would not once have to question. Still, he reassured her, "There are no bad monsters here."

Spoken over the baby's head, directed at where Owen sat with Alace, he hoped his intent was clear.

Kelly understood they were monsters, but he was placing his faith in them. Owen and Alace might feel underneath everything that they had become like the monsters they hunted, but he wanted them to know the people who loved them could learn to live with it.

There were good monsters, too.

Epilogue

Bend, Oregon

She cowered against the wall just inside the swinging doors where the ambulance driver had told her to wait. Outside in the hallway, she heard a voice, deep and thundering, asking where his wife was. She knew that voice. Intimately.

The crowd of medical professionals surrounding the gurney in the center of the ER treatment room parted, and for the briefest of moments, she could see the face of the woman on the table. Lips tinged a dark and terrible blue, but apart from that, they could have been twins. Shining gold hair on the woman's head echoed on that of her own, and the child nestled on her hip.

He was not quite three years old, head pillowed against her shoulder, asleep despite the bustle and noise surrounding them. Voices called out incomprehensible numbers and acronyms, things she could only imagine the meaning of as alarms sounded from multiple pieces of equipment.

The thundering voice drew closer, and she tightened her arms around the boy.

One man, a doctor based on the deferential way the other medical staff treated him, looked up at a clock mounted high on a wall.

No. The thought echoed through her head. She'd watched enough daytime TV to know what came next, and her knees threatened to buckle.

An arm, rigid as a band of steel, circled her waist, holding her upright. Heat pressed against her back, and a muttered, "There you are," resonated through her. Butterflies in her chest took flight, breaths coming fast and hard at his proximity.

"Time of death…"

She blocked out the rest of what the doctor said, his red hands taking up most of her attention. With a towel handed off by one of the others, he wiped the color away as he walked towards them. His gaze fastened on her face, and she imagined he could see something was amiss. Something more than the death of the only person who'd ever loved her. The only person in her life she could trust. The man behind her shifted, and that look fled, a solemn mask settling into place instead. "We did everything we could."

"We know you tried your best." The blades of his words scraped at her control, leaving bloody furrows behind. "Death comes for us all."

She must have made a sound, because his arm tightened around her with a warning pressure. He shook her once, rattling the boy awake, his cries joining hers.

"No, please, no."

The man at her back gripped her hip tightly, bruisingly, nails sharp enough to be felt through her home-sewn dress. Her father let loose a sigh, shaking her again, less forcefully this time. "Her mother and I don't blame you. We thank you for your kindness in our time of loss."

She stared at her dead mother, wishing there'd been enough pills for them both, for the three of them. Wished with all her might to be away, to be gone from the pain that would inevitably follow. When he laid claim to her arm and pulled, she turned and followed. It would be futile to fight him.

And that's how she became her mother, wife to her father, and mother to her brother.

~

THANK YOU SO MUCH FOR READING
An Embarrassment of Monsters!

This story is the third in what's been a fun-to-write series. I'm so pleased you've taken this journey with me and my dark characters, and I hope you enjoyed and rooted for Alace and Owen as much as I did.

ABOUT THE AUTHOR

Raised in the south, *Wall Street Journal* & *USA TODAY* bestselling author MariaLisa learned about the magic of books at an early age. Every summer, she would spend hours in the local library, devouring books of every genre. Self-described as a book-a-holic, she says "I've always loved to read, but then I discovered writing, and found I adored that, too. For reading...if nothing else is available, I've been known to read the back of the cereal box."

Want sneak peeks into what she's working on, or to chat with other readers about her books? Join the Facebook group! **bit.ly/deMora-FB-group**

deMora's got a spam-free newsletter list she'd love to have you join, too: **bit.ly/mldemora-newsletter**

~~~~~

Also by MariaLisa deMora

Please note that books in a series frequently feature characters from additional books within that series. If series books are read out of order, readers will twig to spoilers for the other books, so going back to read the skipped titles won't have the same angsty reveals.

Rebel Wayfarers MC series:

> *Mica*, #1
> *A Sweet & Merry Christmas*, #1.5
> *Slate*, #2
> *Bear*, #3
> *Jase*, #4
> *Gunny*, #5
> *Mason*, #6
> *Hoss*, #7
> *Harddrive Holidays*, #7.5
> *Duck*, #8
> *Biker Chick Campout*, #8.5
> *Watcher*, #9
> *A Kiss to Keep You*, #9.25
> *Gun Totin' Annie*, #9.5
> *Secret Santa*, #9.75
> *Bones*, #10
> *Gunny's Pups*, #10.25
> *Never Settle*, #10.5
> *Not Even A Mouse*, #10.75
> *Fury*, #11
> *Christmas Doings*, #11.25
> *Gypsy's Lady*, #11.5

Cassie, #12
Road Runner's Ride, #12.5

Occupy Yourself band series:

Born Into Trouble, #1
Grace In Motion, #2 (TBD)
What They Say, #3 (TBD)

Neither This, Nor That MC series:

This Is the Route Of Twisted Pain, #1
Treading the Traitor's Path: Out Bad, #2
Shelter My Heart, #3
Trapped by Fate on Reckless Roads, #4
Thunderstruck, #5

Rebel Wayfarers & Incoherent MC (NTNT) crossover stories:

Going Down Easy
No Man's Land

Mayhan Bucklers MC series:

Most Rikki-Tik, #1
Mad Minute, #2
Pucker Factor, #3
Boocoo Dinky Dau, #4 (TBD)

Borderline Freaks MC series:

Service and Sacrifice, #1
More Than Enough, #2
Lack of In-between, #3
See You in Valhalla, #4

If You Could Change One Thing: Tangled Fates Stories

There Are Limits, #1
Rules Are Rules, #2
The Gray Zone, #3

With My Whole Heart series

With My Whole Heart, #1
Bet On Us, #2

Alace Sweets series

Alace Sweets, #1
Seeking Worthy Pursuits, #2
An Embarrassment of Monsters, #3

Other Books:

Hard Focus
Dirty Bitches MC: Season 3

More information available at **mldemora.com**.

CPSIA information can be obtained
at www.ICGtesting.com
Printed in the USA
LVHW022117300720
661978LV00015B/1511